Drugs and Theater
in Early Modern England

Drugs and Theater in Early Modern England

TANYA POLLARD

OXFORD
UNIVERSITY PRESS

OXFORD
UNIVERSITY PRESS

Great Clarendon Street, Oxford OX2 6DP

Oxford University Press is a department of the University of Oxford.
It furthers the University's objective of excellence in research, scholarship,
and education by publishing worldwide in

Oxford New York

Auckland Cape Town Dar es Salaam Hong Kong Karachi
Kuala Lumpur Madrid Melbourne Mexico City Nairobi
New Delhi Shanghai Taipei Toronto

With offices in

Argentina Austria Brazil Chile Czech Republic France Greece
Guatemala Hungary Italy Japan South Korea Poland Portugal
Singapore Switzerland Thailand Turkey Ukraine Vietnam

Published in the United States
by Oxford University Press Inc., New York

British Library Cataloguing in Publication Data
Data available

Library of Congress Cataloging in Publication Data
Data available

ISBN 0–19–927083–x

1 3 5 7 9 10 8 6 4 2

Typeset by Regent Typesetting, London
Printed in Great Britain
on acid-free paper by
Biddles Ltd,
King's Lynn, Norfolk

Acknowledgments

In the process of writing this book, I have received help from many sources, and have accumulated countless debts. The project began as a doctoral thesis under the supervision of David Quint, who patiently read countless drafts of dubious quality; I have benefited immensely from his judicious criticism, healthy skepticism, and wry sense of humor. The late Thomas Greene was an unofficial second advisor who listened, read, discussed, guided, and encouraged throughout. At a later stage, the manuscript benefited greatly from the advice of Katharine Eisaman Maus, who read the entire thing and offered valuable advice on how to turn it into a book. Many others have read, listened, and responded to significant chunks of it. I am especially grateful for thoughtful advice and information at points along the way from Gina Bloom, Baris Dawes, Jim Dawes, Heather Dubrow, Lynn Enterline, Raphael Falco, Jonathan Gil Harris, Natsu Hattori, Heather James, Yu Jin Ko, Jennifer Lewin, Pericles Lewis, Lawrence Manley, Gail Kern Paster, Annabel Patterson, Joseph Roach, David Wilson-Okamura, Susan Zimmerman, and, since moving to New York, my writing group here: Pamela Brown, Bianca Calabresi, Julie Crawford, Sasha Roberts, Nancy Selleck, and Cristine Varholy. Lucy Munro has been strikingly, and characteristically, generous with her vast knowledge of plays and theater history. Two friends, in particular, heroically took on the mammoth task of not only reading and responding in detail to the entire book, but rereading sections as they evolved, sometimes multiple versions. Katharine Craik read, advised, brainstormed, and inspired persistently during a happy summer of long lunches at the British Library, and has continued ever since; Matthew Greenfield listened and guided from the beginning of the project, and especially in the final stages of revision was unfailingly available to read, critique, reread, and, crucially, reassure. For their generosity, insights, and friendship, I am deeply grateful.

Institutions, as well as individuals, have been generous in their support. I would like to thank the Warburg Institute for a Frances

Yates Fellowship, during which substantial chunks of this project were researched and written. I am also very grateful for the support of the Wellcome Centre for Medical History at University College, London, where I have regularly been adopted as a Research Associate; Sally Bragg has been invaluable at sorting out practical support, and I am grateful to Vivian Nutton, Andrew Wear, and the late Roy Porter for conversations and advice. I would also like to thank the Folger Institute for a grant allowing me to participate in Susan Zimmerman's 1996–7 colloquium on Subjectivity, Sexuality, and Representation, in which Susan and my co-participants offered not only advice, but a wonderful model of intellectual community. A Whiting fellowship made much important early research possible; later, Macalester College was generous in supporting research, especially in the form of three Wallace Faculty grants and one Keck grant. The knowledgeable staff at various libraries but especially the British Library, the Folger Shakespeare Library, the Wellcome Library, the Warburg Library, and the Bodleian Library, have been tremendously helpful. Last, but certainly not least, at Oxford University Press, Andrew McNeillie, Sophie Goldsworthy, other editors, and the press's anonymous readers have crucially helped to turn this project into a book.

Parts of this book have been previously published in other venues; I am grateful to their original publishers for permission to reprint them here. An earlier version of part of Chapter 1 was published as " 'No Faith in Physic': Masquerades of Medicine Onstage and Off," in *Disease, Diagnosis and Cure on the Early Modern Stage: Praxis and Performance*, ed. Stephanie Moss and Kaara Peterson (Aldershot: Ashgate Press, 2004); copyright 2004 Stephanie Moss and Kaara Peterson. An earlier version of Chapter 2 was published as "A Thing Like Death: Poisons and Sleeping Potions in *Romeo and Juliet* and *Antony and Cleopatra*," in *Renaissance Drama* 32 (2003); and earlier versions of Chapter 3 were published as "Beauty's Poisonous Properties" in *Shakespeare Studies* 27 (1999), and "Les dangers de la beauté: Maquillage et théâtre au dix-septième siècle en Angleterre," in *La Beauté et ses monstres*, ed. Line Cottegnies, Tony Gheeraert and Gisèle Venet (Paris: Presses de la Nouvelle Sorbonne, 2002).

The least tangible contributions to this book's development are the most important. My interest in the relationship between minds and bodies comes especially from my mother, Vicki Pollard. She and the rest of my family have contributed in countless ways to my thinking, much of which is reflected in this book. Most of all, I am grateful to my husband, Will Stenhouse, both for all the practical and intellectual ways that he has helped me with my research and writing, and, especially, for all the other immeasurable ways that he contributes to my happiness.

Contents

Introduction: Dangerous Remedies   1

1 "Unnatural and Horrid Physic": Pharmaceutical
Theater in Jonson and Webster   23

2 "A Thing Like Death": Shakespeare's Narcotic
Theater   55

3 "Polluted with Counterfeit Colours": Cosmetic
Theater   81

4 Poisoned Kisses: Theater of Seduction   101

5 Vulnerable Ears: *Hamlet* and Poisonous Theater   123

Epilogue: Theater's Antidotes   144

Notes   149

Bibliography   187

Index   205

Introduction:
Dangerous Remedies

In the second act of *A Midsummer Night's Dream*, Oberon, frustrated by Titania's refusal to give him her Indian boy, tells Puck of another powerful male figure thwarted in his attempt to control the opposite sex. Cupid, he explains, once hurled one of his golden arrows towards the earth in an attempt to hit a beautiful virgin, but instead hit a flower, now called love-in-idleness. "Fetch me that flower," he commands;

> the herb I showed thee once.
> The juice of it on sleeping eyelids laid
> Will make or man or woman madly dote
> Upon the next live creature that it sees.
> (II.i.169–72)[1]

The magical herb that results from Cupid's failure offers Oberon a remedy for the problem of Titania's insubordination: drugged with its juice, she will lose control over her affections, humiliate herself thoroughly, and surrender to his will. This solution, however, ultimately causes as many problems as it solves. Oberon's control over love-in-idleness proves as tenuous as his control over Titania: between its application to the Athenian lovers, and Puck's problematic role as proxy, the drug leads to unexpected crises and chaos. Like Cupid, Oberon brings about a transformation, but not exactly—or only—the one he had in mind.

With the upheaval that it inspires, and the links that it forges between the play's three worlds of Athenians, fairies, and mechanicals, love-in-idleness proves central to the play's comedy, but its role goes far beyond that of a plot device. Oberon's description of the drug's operations emphasizes its power over eyes and vision. Its juice must be laid "on sleeping eyelids," and its recipient will fall in love with "the next live creature that it sees."[2] Imagining Titania asleep among the wild thyme, oxlips, violet, luscious woodbine, sweet musk-roses, and eglantine, "lulled in these flowers with dances and delight," he plans "with the juice of this [to] streak her eyes, | And make her full of hateful fantasies" (II.i.249, 257–8). Disarmed by the pleasures of sleep, performances, and her luxurious herbal bed, Titania will be at her most unguarded and vulnerable, unable to resist the drug that will imprint her eyes and imagination with new, and potentially alarming, desires. As a tool for altering the vision of pleasurably distracted sleepers, the drug forcefully links its onstage recipients to the play's external audience. "If we shadows have offended," Puck tells the audience,

> Think but this, and all is mended:
> That you have but slumbered here,
> While these visions did appear;
> And this weak and idle theme,
> No more yielding but a dream.
> (Epilogue, 1–6)

Shakespeare has already implicitly identified the audience with the Athenians by making the latter onstage spectators at the mechanicals' play-within-the-play; here Puck self-consciously expands and intensifies this identification. By depicting the play's external spectators as sleepers waking from a dream, Puck aligns them with Titania and the lovers, all of whom wake from their drugged sleeps to imagine that the strange events they have undergone must have been dreams. Given the suffering that the lovers undergo as a result of love-in-idleness, this alignment raises troubling implications for the experiences and transformations of those watching the play.

Oberon's love-in-idleness, like the other drugs that this book examines, is an image not only *in* the theater, but *of* the theater. Applied to the eyes of passive recipients lulled into an unguarded state by visual and verbal pleasures, it alters them both affectively and physically: not only do they feel new emotions, but their eyes operate in strange and different ways. If the experience of the play's drugged lovers is meant as a model, moreover, the transformations it effects have an ambivalent status. It is not clear whether the play will bring spectators back to earlier versions of themselves, as Demetrius claims has happened to him in rediscovering his love for Helena, or, as with Lysander and Titania, create in them new and troublesome desires. Either way, the play joins Bottom in offering a warning—

"let the audience look to their eyes" (I.ii.22)—that critics have not yet taken with the literal, physical force it demands.

Although *A Midsummer Night's Dream* is one of the best-known plays of its time to focus on the intriguing and alarming consequences of a strange and exotic drug, it is hardly the only one. The theater of the early modern period is awash with dangerous remedies: chemical interventions that complicate or intensify the problems they were intended to solve. In a wide range of plays, drugs, including medicines, sleeping potions, face-paints, and poisons, are deployed as cures, solutions, or improvements, but end up backfiring. As in *A Midsummer Night's Dream*, moreover, these substances repeatedly take on functions linked with those of the theater itself. In Jonson's *Volpone*, a charlatan mountebank sells both miraculous elixirs and engaging theatrical performances, blurring the lines between drugs and plays. In *Antony and Cleopatra*, the soporific drinks associated with Cleopatra and Egypt mirror the narcotic power of Cleopatra's own seductive spectacles. In *The Revenger's Tragedy*, Middleton identifies poisonous face-paints with disguise, role-play, and ultimately a murderous masque. In *Hamlet*, Shakespeare parallels Claudius's poisoning of his brother's ears with acts of verbal violence and manipulation, culminating in Hamlet's staging of *The Mousetrap*. In play after play, dramatists repeatedly link ambivalent, invasive, and transformative drugs with different aspects of the theater itself.

This book argues that the medical, bodily, and pharmacy-steeped vocabulary of early modern plays and contemporary writings about the theater not only demand our attention, but point to a crucial, and previously ignored, context for understanding the intense controversies surrounding the theater in early modern England, controversies in which playwrights' own complex and ambivalent conceptions of their medium play a significant role. Calling attention to the inseparability of body and mind in early modern thought, this language attributes to the theater the power to harm, heal, and otherwise transform spectators in immediate, forceful, and physical ways. Variously associated with the palpable effects of medical power, political manipulation, and erotic allure, pharmacy suggested a wide range of models for theatrical efficacy. Drugs, with their ambivalent tension between curative promise and uncertain threat, offered a powerful vocabulary through which to imagine the effects of theatrical performance on spectators.[3]

DANGEROUS PHARMACIES

With their potentially threatening ambiguity, drugs offer intrigue in all periods, but writings from the late sixteenth and early seventeenth centuries show a conspicuous preoccupation with the uncertain effects of herbal and chemical substances.[4] Not only were the plays of the time permeated with risky potions, but contemporary medical and political writings highlighted similar concerns about the dangerous consequences of drugs turned bad. With their powerful capacity for transformation, drugs suggest both cure and its opposite, harm. Then, as now, even primarily beneficial drugs and remedies could bring about serious, even lethal, damage, while the most toxic substances could, paradoxically, have medicinal value. Etymologically, the idea of pharmacy is intrinsically linked with ambiguity. The word itself stems from the Greek *pharmakon*, meaning poison, remedy, and love potion; both poison and potion come from the Latin *potio*, or drink; venom, Venus, and venereal all stem from the Latin *venenum*; and even medicine itself can mean its opposite.[5] These linguistic overlays point to the inextricability of remedies from both pleasure and danger, an idea that continues to live on in debates about not only the side effects of new drugs, but also the medical, ethical, and legal status of drugs taken for pleasure.

The ambiguity of medical remedies was particularly unsettling in the rapidly changing and controversy-ridden world of early modern pharmacy.[6] Medical ingredients, preparations, and uses expanded quickly and spectacularly in the late sixteenth century. Explorers to the new world brought back new diseases, such as syphilis, and new medicinal herbs, such as tobacco, opium, and guiacum, a tropical plant used to treat syphilis. Recurring epidemics of plague, meanwhile, raised fears about vulnerability to diseases, but there was little consensus regarding the correct contents, preparation, and dosage of remedies.[7] New translations of classical medical writings threatened the stability of medical knowledge, and the increasing availability of medical books contributed to a rapid expansion of the medical marketplace, making it hard to tell who had reliable expertise.[8] Most significantly, the widespread influence of the Swiss physician Paracelsus (1493–1541) led to the rapid growth of the controversial medical theory and practice he espoused.[9] While the traditional medical system, inherited from the Greek physician Galen, sought to balance bodily humors by treating an ailment with its opposite,

Paracelsus built on a homeopathic doctrine from folk medicine of treating like with like, or poisons with poisons. "Poison is in everything," he noted, "and no thing is without poison. The dosage makes it either a poison or a remedy."[10] Under this rubric, he brought highly toxic chemicals such as mercury and arsenic into popular use, sparking a wave of anxieties about the effects of new, mysterious, and powerful substances.

Chemical medicine had immediate roots in alchemical experimentation. The word "chemical"—from the Greek word for juice, or infusion—entered the English language in the late sixteenth century as a variant of "alchemical" and then came to refer to Paracelsian medicine, with its processes of distillation and sublimation. Defenders of chemical treatments argued that these operations purified even the most dangerous ingredients, and intensified their medicinal powers. In response to concerns "that Chymicall Medicines being subtill and pure, can more easily disturbe nature, and moue the body more sodainely then other Medicines do," Angelus Sala held that the "sharpe and piercing" nature of some chemical medicines "be very requisite and necessary . . . very beneficiall and wholesome."[11] In fact, he insisted, "Chymicall Medicines of a vehement nature . . . are more gentle then any violent vomitiue Medicine which our Ancients prescribed, yea farre more safe then any vomitorie under *Hellebore* or any aboue named," and "euery Medicine in generall bereaued of its earthiness and feculencie, and made pure cleane and well digested by fire must of consequence be lesse hurtfull, lesse dangerous, and lesse offensiue, and is also farre more apt to worke."[12] With their complex processes of refinement and concoction, chemical medicines were to simple herbal medicines as art to nature. Accordingly, they sparked both admiration and anxiety.

Unsurprisingly, chemical medicines met with a significant amount of hostility. The physician Thomas Herring, for instance, voiced suspicion about the possibility of poisonous materials ever being put to medicinal use:

That the corroding Qualitie of Arsenicke, may be cleane taken away, you shall pardon me if I beleeue not your Chymists, if they doe (as you say) affirme it neuer so confidently. We haue an homely and true saying, The Diuell will be the Diuell whether you bake roste, seeth, or broile him, or howsoeuer you handle him. *Naturam expellas &c*: So Arsenicke so long as he remaineth Arsenicke . . . will vndoubedly shew of what house he commeth by corrodings and corrupting.[13]

Skeptical of the transformative and purifying processes of the chemical art (which he likens to homely forms of cookery), Herring describes arsenic as having an intrinsic and unchangeable identity: that of an active and determined evildoer. Like the devil, arsenic may be able to hide its identity temporarily through protean disguises, but inevitably reveals its dangerous nature through its effects.

Although chemical remedies were newer, more powerful, and more controversial than traditional remedies, they were by no means the only ones viewed as dangerous. Tobacco, an herbal drug brought in from the new world in the late sixteenth century, was both touted as a panacea and condemned as poisonous.[14] Plant-based narcotics such as opium and mandragora were similarly controversial.[15] As many doctors noted, even standard and typically gentle herbal treatments from the Galenic medical tradition could and did go wrong.[16] The physician John Cotta argued that even the mildest remedies could be harmful in certain circumstances:

Cassia is esteemd for a delicate, wholesome and harmelesse lenitiue vnto old men, children, babes, women with child, and the weakest amongst the sicke; yet the learned know it in some cases not onely vnprofitable, but of maine mischiefe. Rhabarb is said to be the life of the liuer, yet in some conditions thereof it is an enemie; And for the generall remedies . . . they are variabile, sometime necessary, sometimes profitable not necessary, sometimes neither profitable nor necessary, but accursed.[17]

Cotta's account of the hazards of cassia, rhubarb, and other "generall remedies" points to the difficulty, if not impossibility, of identifying any treatment as reliably safe. Writing about tobacco, no less an authority than James I noted that "Medicine hath that vertue, that it neuer leaues a man in that state wherein it finds him."[18] Any transformation was unpredictable, and inevitably risky.

As drugs like tobacco and opium began to cross the line between medicine and pleasure, medical writers began to worry not only about the uncertainty of drugs' effects, but also about their irresistible power over consumers. To some, drugs' ability to seduce people into accepting something dangerous was their most disturbing aspect. Using the example of tobacco, Cotta argued that transformative substances—particularly those that were new and exotic —woo their susceptible consumers with the promise of pleasure and the masquerade of health, until it was too late. Tobacco, he claims, lulls its consumers into a pleasing narcotic oblivion:

And men haply led by some present bewitching feeling of ease, or momentarie imagined release from paine at some time, hereby vnaduisedly with such meanes of their ease, drinke into some weake parts, such seede of future poison, as hauing giuen them for a time supposed pleasing ease, doth for time to come secretly and vnfelt settle into their bones and solid parts, a neuer dying disease (while they liue).[19]

Powerful medicines, according to Cotta, tease the imagination into a temporary—and illusory—sense of ease and security. Under the influence of this power, which Cotta likens to witchcraft, patients are not victims passively receiving this poisonous medicine: they actively choose it, "drinke [it] into some weake parts." Rather than just medicating or transforming, then, drugs complicate questions of agency by seducing consumers into medicating themselves, raising the troubling specter of addiction.[20]

FATAL POISONS

Cotta's fears about the poisonous properties of apparently medicinal drugs were echoed and intensified in the case of literal, fatal poisons: drugs that were unambiguously toxic, and intended to harm. As concerns about drugs rose in the sixteenth century, cultural and political preoccupations with poison intensified as well. In the wake of a 1530 poisoning case, a Royal Act distinguished poisoners from other criminals by condemning them to be boiled alive, marking the crime as more terrible than others.[21] By later in the century, this sense of alarm had exploded into a spate of fears and notorious accusations of poisonings. Amid political fears about conspiracies on Elizabeth's life, stories of poisoning attempts—real or apocryphal—flourished. Roderigo Lopez, a Spanish Jew who was physician to the queen, was convicted in 1594 of attempting to poison her medicines, and Edward Squire was charged in 1598 of poisoning the pommel of her saddle, reputedly at the behest of Jesuits.[22] The Earl of Leicester was rumored to have poisoned the Earl of Essex, the Lord Sheffield, and his own wife; during the Jacobean period, meanwhile, Buckingham was suspected of trying to poison King James, and James himself of trying to poison Prince Henry.[23] The most famous case was that of Sir Thomas Overbury, whose gradual poisoning while imprisoned in the Tower of London in 1613 became the center of a large-scale scandal involving adultery and conspiracy among powerful figures at court.[24]

With many of these affairs rooted in nothing more substantive than rumor, it is far from clear just how prevalent actual poisoning attempts were in the period. Death by poisoning was difficult, if not impossible, to distinguish from death by disease, and accusations of attempted but failed poisonings were even harder to prove—or disprove. In practice, available poisons seem to have been relatively rare, and remarkably inefficient. Overbury ate arsenic-laced food parcels for months before finally expiring, and almost none of the other fabled poisonings actually resulted in death. Yet the sheer quantity of these and other stories, combined with the fantastical poisoning narratives on the contemporary stage, show that dangerous drugs held a privileged place in the popular imagination, entirely disproportionate to their actual threat. Contemporary complaints about poison's unique evil reinforce the sense of the crime's distinctive status. In 1621, George Eglisham, one of King James's physicians, asserted that "of all murthers, the poysoning . . . is the most heynous."[25] "[A]mong all the deuises of murderers, which are many," the moralist Thomas Tuke wrote in 1616, "these Italian deuises by poisoning are most vile and diuelish."[26] Anatomizing crimes in 1602, the Lord Chief Justice Sir Edward Coke similarly held that "poison . . . is, as hath been said, the most horrible, and fearfull to the nature of man, and of all others can be least prevented, either by manhood or by providence."[27]

Coke's emphasis on the impossibility of prevention struck a recurring note in arguments for the exceptional status of poison, as well as for concerns about drugs more broadly. With their threat of invisible and stealthy infiltration, drugs challenge not only the integrity of boundaries—those of individual bodies as well as larger units, such as houses, cities, and states—but also notions of agency. Poison, like other drugs, cannot be actively outwitted or outfought. In fact, as so often happens in the plays of this period, it may deceive people into actively embracing it, forcing them to become, albeit unintentionally, their own murderers, and/or the murderers of their most beloved intimates. Drugs and poisons also pose epistemological challenges. In the absence of clear signs of a pending threat, there can be no defenses; all points of entry are left open and vulnerable. Their invisibility and protean powers of disguise translate a failure of knowledge into a matter of physical and immediate danger.

Commentators' emphasis on the impossibility of prevention points also to the problem of invisible, or at least inconspicuous, perpetrators: because administering drugs does not require strength, or even presence, the evildoers could be figures not traditionally viewed as physically threatening, such as women—typically entrusted with food preparation—as well as outsiders associated with intelligence and subtlety, such as Jews, Catholics, and especially Italians.[28]

PLAYS AS DRUGS: THE DEBATES

The striking changes in medicine, and the popular debates and anxieties they sparked, laid a crucial foundation for playwrights' interest in drugs by emphasizing the twofold capacity of transformative substances for both cure and danger.[29] Yet, as noted earlier, theatrical representations of drugs not only reflect cultural concerns about drugs and poisons, but also repeatedly identify drugs with the workings of theatrical performances. Playwrights' preoccupation with drugs, then, must be seen not only in the context of contemporary concerns about pharmacy, but also in the light of contemporary preoccupations with the theater. A chorus of voices—from both attackers and defenders of the theater, as well as from playwrights themselves—saw the theater not only as a vehicle for representing drugs and poisons, but as a kind of drug or poison itself.

The identification of theater with pharmacy derived from a broader classical idea of literature as having a druglike power over its consumers. In his *Moralia*, widely read and translated in the Renaissance, Plutarch explicitly likened literary writings to drugs of uncertain nature:

> For verie well and fitly it may be said . . . of Poetrie:
> *Mixed drugs plentie, as well good as bad,*
> *Med'cines and poisons are there to be had,*
> which it bringeth foorth and yeeldeth to as many as converse therein.[30]

Plutarch quotes here from the fourth book of *The Odyssey*, when Helen eases Telemachus's weeping and lulls him to sleep with a potion—a *pharmakon*—that soothes men's souls. The original quotation has no direct reference to poetry, but Plutarch's allusion to this moment, in the context of a discussion of poetry, implicitly yokes together the epic's many scenes of mesmerizing songs and poems with the seductive charm of Helen: a charm responsible not only for the fall of Troy, but for the troubles of Odysseus and Ithaca that constitute the epic. Although he ultimately counsels that poetry's risks can be offset by being joined with the stabilizing forces of philosophy, Plutarch's discussion makes clear that poetry's pharmaceutical functions are deeply suspect, and potentially dangerous.

Plutarch's vocabulary of drugs and poisons echoes throughout commentaries on the theater in early modern England. As many critics and scholars have pointed out, the commercial theater—an extremely new institution—enjoyed tremendous popularity and financial success in the late sixteenth and early seventeenth centuries.[31] Alongside this success and the attention it generated, however, the theater also incurred savage attacks, as Jonas Barish and other critics have noted.[32] In the wake of these controversies, antitheatricalists found in drugs a concise way to articulate the dangers of plays. Disapproving moralists referred to plays as "charmed drinkes, & amorous potions,"[33] "vigorous venome," and "Souledevouring poyson."[34] "I must confesse that Poets are the whetstones of wit," the antitheatrical critic Stephen Gosson wrote in *The School of Abuse* (1579), "notwithstanding that wit is dearly bought: where hony and gall are mixed, it will be hard to seuer the one from the other. The deceitfull Phisition giueth sweete Syrropes to make his poyson goe down the smoother . . ."[35] Gosson describes poetic wit as a liquid potion, with an immediate effect on corporeal sensations: the sweetness of honey temporarily cloaks the underlying, and presumably more potent, bitterness of gall. Juxtaposing this image with one offering more frightening consequences, he implicitly likens the poet to a malevolent doctor, a figure expected to provide remedies but instead concocting the exact opposite: a deadly poison made appealing through the disguise of seductive pleasure. In case his readers should miss the endpoint of his metaphors, Gosson goes on to state his case in even plainer terms: "playes are venemous arrowes to the minde" and "ranke poyson."[36]

There are, of course, many varieties of risky drugs, and critics emphasized different effects in different contexts. Some writers described plays as aphrodisiacs. Describing the wantonness of contemporary comedies, Anglo-phile Eutheo (generally believed to be Anthony Munday) asked in 1580, "Do wee not vse in these discourses to counterfet witchcraft, charmed drinkes, & amorous potions, thereby to drawe the affections of men, & to stir them vp vnto lust . . .?"[37] John Downame similarly argued in 1613 that plays "poyson the mind with effeminate lust."[38] Others, though, referred more generally to plays as physically and spiritually toxic. William Rankins harangued in 1587 against "these Plaiers, . . . whose pleasure as poison spreddeth it selfe into the vaines of their beholders,"[39] and in 1615 the author I. G. (conventionally referred to as "John Greene") claimed that plays were "as bad Poyson to the Minde, as the byting of a Viper to the Flesh."[40] In 1633 William Prynne, the most prolific and rabid critic of the theater, obsessively likened plays to "vigorous venome," "grosse corruption," "Rats-bane," "fatall plagues," "Soule-devouring poyson," and "sugered poysoned potions of the Divell, by which he cunningly endeavours your destruction when as you least suspect it."[41]

Curiously, rather than shying away from the risky chemical metaphor, supporters of the theater actively turned to this same vocabulary to combat antitheatrical attacks. In a 1579 direct response to Gosson's accusations that poetry's lies were poisonous, Thomas Lodge wrote of poets' reliance on metaphors and myths that "they like good Phisitions: should so frame their potions" as to be palatable to their audiences' stomachs.[42] In an intriguing reformulation of the medical model, Lodge and other defenders of the theater also argued that the audience ultimately determined the nature of the play's effects. "[T]hose of judgement," Lodge wrote, "can from the same flower suck honey with the bee, from whence the spyder (I mean the ignorant) take their poison. Men that haue knowledge what Comedies and Tragedies be, wil comend them."[43] Lodge draws on a commonplace image here in order to suggest that the transformative effects of theater are elicited and activated by their consumers, who seek out particular elements of the plays they watch.[44] While shifting the source of potential harm from plays' contents to their spectators, this equivocal defense nonetheless portrays the theater as the font of ambiguous potions, equally capable of producing danger and pleasure.

PLAYS AS REMEDIES: PLAYWRIGHTS AND THE
THERAPEUTIC TRADITION

Critics and defenders, meanwhile, were not the only voices attempting to characterize plays. Playwrights themselves took an active part
in debates about the theater, within their plays as well as in other
writings, and their contributions both echo and complicate claims
made by other commentators. In the explicitly metatheatrical
Induction to *The Taming of the Shrew*, Shakespeare suggests that
plays were commonly understood as having medicinal properties.
Having sunk into a drunken sleep, Christopher Sly wakes up to find
himself encased in the habits of a lord and the imaginative fantasies
of a play. "Your honour's players," a messenger tells him,

> hearing your amendment,
> Are come to play a pleasant comedy,
> For so your doctors hold it very meet,
> Seeing too much sadness hath congealed your blood,
> And melancholy is the nurse of frenzy.
> Therefore they thought it good you hear a play
> And frame your mind to mirth and merriment,
> Which bars a thousand harms, and lengthens life.
> (Induction 2.126–33)

Theater, according to Sly's messenger, operates as a medicine prescribed by doctors towards therapeutic ends.[45] Within the humoral
system of Galenic medicine, the "mirth and merriment" of the theater are presented as a remedy to counteract the chill and congealed
blood of melancholy, "the nurse of frenzy."[46] The messenger's playfully alliterative clusters of words—play and pleasant; seeing
sadness; mind, mirth and merriment; lengthens life—suggest the
whimsically pleasing rhythms and repetitions which will dispel ill
humors and restore health. The messenger's speech is directed
specifically at Sly, but it speaks also to the other, external, audience
members who watch the play along with Sly. The play implicitly
alerts its spectators that it is at some level casting them all in the roles
of patients, who will be medicined—for better or for worse—by the
spectacles that follow.

The messenger's claims for the theater in this scene are echoed by
similar uses of theatrical spectacles in other plays. In Webster's
Duchess of Malfi (1612), Ferdinand arranges to have his sister re-
galed with a theater of madmen as a purported medical treatment.

"Your brother hath intended you some sport," a servant tells the Duchess;

> A great physician when the Pope was sick
> Of a deep melancholy, presented him
> With several sorts of madmen, which wild object,
> Being full of change and sport, forc'd him to laugh,
> And so th'imposthume broke: the selfsame cure
> The Duke intends on you.
>
> (IV.ii.39–45)[47]

In this scene, however, as in *The Taming of the Shrew*, the idealizing rhetoric of curative theater masks other underlying intentions and effects. The apparent remaking of Sly, not unlike the "taming" he witnesses, is as much an act of mockery as generosity—he accuses the feigning servants of trying to drive him mad with their deceit—and the primary change it brings about in him is eagerness to undress the boy-actor who masquerades as his wife.[48] More violently, despite citations of apparently successful theatrical cures, Ferdinand's masque of madmen is designed to undo rather than to heal.[49] Through its means, the Duchess will be taunted and tortured, although ironically—despite his intent—she not only responds with dignity, but ultimately finds respite in this diversion from her own sorrows. The gaps between rhetorical claims, actual intentions, and practical effects show that while a medical vocabulary offered an important way of imagining the theater's effects on both minds and bodies, the analogy was far from a straightforwardly positive one, even for playwrights themselves.

As these scenes suggest, defenses of literature have historically relied heavily on a therapeutic analogy. Like medicine, which aspires to bring comfort and improvement to the body, literature has traditionally been valued for its ability to bring pleasure and improvement to the mind and soul. Antitheatricalists' reflections on this analogy, however, confirm Derrida's observation that "there is no such thing as a harmless remedy."[50] Historically, the relationship of literature to medicine has been a contentious one. At least since Plato and Aristotle, debates have raged as to whether poetry's effects are remedial or poisonous. In his notorious attack on poetry in *The Republic*, Plato refers to the falsehood of literature as a *pharmakon*—an ambiguous blend of poison and remedy—which only the rulers of the city can be trusted to know and administer.[51] Similarly, he describes false and immoral stories as "symbols of evil, or a garden of poisonous herbs [*kakē botanē*]."[52] Aristotle departed radically from his teacher in his famous claim that "through pity and fear, tragedy effects the catharsis of such emotions," using a technical medical term to describe a model of art in which the act of representation has the power to avert the danger represented.[53] Both Plato's contagious theory of poetry and Aristotle's apotropaic model rest on the idea that words and symbols have in and of themselves the power to alter reality—to exert an impact on the soul, and even the body—an idea that held considerable sway in early modern medical and literary theory.[54]

In an early modern context, these debates are intensified by the perceived tenuousness of the separation between mind and body. While it may be unsurprising to us that Sly's messenger and Ferdinand speak of the theater as having an *affective* impact on its audience—the ability to drive away sadness—their explicitly physiological references, to melancholy congealing blood and to an impostume breaking, remind us, as does the work of critics like Gail Kern Paster and Michael Schoenfeldt, that the humoral discourses so dominant in early modern medicine refused to draw boundaries between the mental and the corporeal.[55] According to Galenic doctrine, a change in emotion brings about a corresponding change in the body, and vice versa; in treating one, the theater treats both.

One particularly crucial link between the mind and the body in this period is the imagination, understood to be a part of the body and capable of exerting a material impact on it.[56] The physician Thomas Fienus, among others, described the power of the imagination as capable, through its effect on the emotions, of bringing about physical changes in the body:

> The imagination is fitted by nature to move the appetite and excite the emotions, as is obvious, since by thinking happy things we rejoice, by thinking of sad things we fear and are sad, and all emotions follow previous thought. But the emotions are greatly alterative with respect to the body. Therefore, through them the imagination is able to transform the body.[57]

If the imagination can alter the body through the emotions, then the theater can be understood to alter not only the imagination and the emotions, but, through them, the body as well. This idea, crucial to understanding the controversies surrounding the early modern theater, lies at the root of the many contemporary descriptions of theater as either medicinal or poisonous.

Plays were not the only literary genre to be identified with medical treatments. In his *Defense of Poesy* (1595), Philip Sidney described poetry as "a medicine of cherries," more effective than other remedies because sensually appealing to consumers.[58] George Puttenham, similarly, claimed in *The Arte of English Poesie* (1589) that the poet had "to play also the Phisitian, and not onely by applying a medicine to the ordinary sicknes of mankind, but by making the very greef it selfe (in part) cure of the disease."[59] Puttenham's striking formulation echoes Aristotle's conception of catharsis: pity and fear are the best treatment for pity and fear. It also evokes the logic behind Paracelsian medicine: treating an ailment not through its opposite, but through more of the same, or fighting poisons with poisons.[60]

Although arguments about medicinal value were applied to literature in general, the theater, as the period's most visible, powerful, and economically successful literary institution, became a particular magnet for these debates. Perhaps even more pertinently, moreover, theater is the literary genre most intimately dependent on actual bodies, those of both performers and audiences. In early modern London, the physicality of the theater was one of its most controversial features, in more ways than one. As places where large groups of people gathered and crowded together, the theater sparked threats of both violence and the spread of contagious diseases such as plague; during virulent epidemics, theaters were closed down.[61] The theater's appeal to the senses also raised both physical and spiritual concerns. The visual nature of plays sparked debates about idolatry and erotic desire, while their engagement with other senses (most notably sound, but also smell and touch) expanded and intensified these concerns.[62]

If its physicality made theater a particular target for attacks on literature, then, it also singled it out as a uniquely powerful form of remedy. Robert Burton, in *Anatomy of Melancholy*, urged sufferers to "Use . . . scenical shews, plays, [and] games" to drive away ill humors.[63] The playwright Thomas Heywood similarly argued for the capacity of plays

to recreate such as of themselues are wholly deuoted to Melancholly, which corrupts the bloud: or to refresh such weary spirits as are tired with labour, or study, to moderate the cares and heauinesse of the minde, that they may returne to their trades and faculties with more zeale and earnestnesse, after some small soft and pleasant retirement.[64]

Heywood's account of the theater envisions it as treating not only the mind, but blood, and spirits. His utopian vision abounds in references to bringing spectators *back* to an imagined earlier idyllic state: recreating, refreshing, returning, retiring. The idea of a play as a new version of something else—a reproduction, re-enactment, or representation—here carries over to its relationship to its audiences, whom it builds anew.

Heywood and other writers demonstrate that plays were seen as unusually effective vehicles through which the emotions could act on and alter bodies, an idea with significant implications for our understanding of early modern thought about both literature and physiology. Ultimately, these early modern commentators on the medicinal uses of theater show not only that the *mind* was understood to exert a power over the body, but that *language* and *images*—in particular, the privileged language and images of the theater—could do the same. Literary language, especially when spoken aloud, was understood to be directly linked with the imagination and to have special rhetorical properties, taking on a synesthetic power to transform the body at a physiological level.

This perceived power, I argue, lies at the heart not only of the early modern theater's preoccupation with drugs and poisons, but also, more broadly, of the heated debates surrounding the theater's status in London. The vivid physicality of writings by both antitheatricalists and defenders of the theater has generally been either ignored, or understood merely as a metaphor addressing other problems; even more strikingly, the anxieties about the theater expressed by plays themselves, and the powerful physicality of their consequences, have been largely overlooked or explained away. The interest of playwrights and their defenders in exploring and exploiting the pharmaceutical analogy in the wake of these debates shows that it is precisely because of, rather than despite, its ambivalent associations, that the analogy is so compelling. The identification of the theater's impact on its audiences with the effect of drugs on consumers offers a striking model for theatrical power, one in which the words and images of the theater bring about a potent, and often dangerous, transformation in the minds and bodies of their audiences.

Like drugs, plays were understood as offering a remedy, seducing consumers with promises of pleasure, escapism, and at times improvement; also like their chemical counterparts, they were seen as having volatile, unpredictable, and dangerous side effects. The language of pharmacy facilitated and authorized a model of the theater as exerting a powerful impact on its audiences, fusing together mental and corporeal effects. Just as drugs enter the body, through orifices or skin, with consequences for both physical and psychological well-being, plays were conceived of as invasive forces that not only crossed the boundaries of the self, but raised questions about the nature and viability of such borders. The extent to which the vocabulary of drugs informed and constituted discussions of the theater points to the inseparability of body and mind in early modern thought, offering a striking, and at times threatening, model for theatrical power.

Upheavals in early modern pharmacy, combined with the controversies surrounding the new commercial theaters, long-standing ideas about the therapeutic nature of literature, and medical beliefs about the physiological impact of the imagination, offer a powerful explanatory framework for the theater's preoccupation with ambivalent transformative drugs. The sharply specific time-frame of this phenomenon, however, points to another important factor in the pervasiveness of this motif. Although plays begin to dramatize drugs as a metaphor for their own effects in the last decades of the sixteenth century, not long after the opening of the commercial theaters, and continue until the closing of those theaters in 1642, it is striking that the plays that embody this metatheatrical dynamic with the most richness, complexity, and self-consciousness date from the first decade of the seventeenth century: *Hamlet* (1600–1), for instance, *Volpone* (1605), *Antony and Cleopatra* (1606–7), and *The Revenger's Tragedy* (1607). The intensity of this cluster raises provocative questions about the relationship between this theatrical preoccupation with ambivalent transformations and the particular ambivalent transformation overtaking England (and especially London) at this time: the replacement of a long-ruling and near-mythic queen with a new (and only recently identified) male successor.[65] James I's well-attested fascinations both with theater (as both spectator and actor) and with drugs (he wrote lengthy treatises on both tobacco and witchcraft) suggest that playwrights' fixation on this particular theatrical trope at this time is heavily overdetermined.[66]

In yoking together pharmacy and theater, this book seeks to open a conversation between two important but separate areas of early modern studies: inquiries into the status of the theater, and critical

work on medicine and the body. New historicist critics have demonstrated the pervasiveness of theatricality as a metaphor and discourse
in early modern England, and its uses in the construction and main-
tenance of power.[67] Yet although studies of attitudes to the theater
have often been concerned with the malleability of the self, they have
yet to overlap significantly with the insights of recent work on the
body.[68] Similarly, although early modern physiology held that the
imagination was part of the body, and exerted a physical impact on
it, scholars of medicine and the body have not explored the implications of their findings for our understanding of early modern ideas
about literature, in general, and the stage in particular. This book
builds on the insights of these two branches of study, yet departs
from them by insisting on their crucial interdependence: the body is
constructed by the imaginative fantasies it consumes, and the theater
defines itself, in large part, by its power over spectators' bodies and
minds.

As noted earlier, the model of pharmacy necessarily implies danger as well as beneficial powers, and one of the ways this book
departs from other critical accounts is in its insistence that we take
seriously dramatists' ambivalence about their own medium.[69] In her
compelling study of antitheatricality and effeminacy, for instance,
Laura Levine engages with similar questions about the effects of
plays, but comes to very different conclusions in her conception
of playwrights' intentions and motives. Asking "why a playwright
would rehearse and even heighten or embody the arguments of his
attackers," Levine argues that early modern playwrights "are both
contaminated by the anxieties of the attacks they defend against and
obsessively bent on coming to terms with them."[70] Where Levine
suggests that dramatists explore antitheatrical fantasies in order to
refute them, this book argues that the shared vocabularies and arguments reflect genuine commonalities between the two groups.[71]
Playwrights and their critics draw on the same cultural assumptions
about literature and the body, and, accordingly, arrive at related
claims about the effects of the theater: that it is powerfully transformative, that it affects both mind and body, and that its consequences
are ambivalent in nature. Not only did playwrights seem to revel in
the power this model attributed to the theater, but, for a variety of
reasons, including (but not limited to) the financial imperative to
cater to the tastes of mass audiences, playwrights themselves were
often deeply suspicious towards the theater.[72] What distinguishes

playwrights' contributions to these debates from those of their critics, I argue, is not that one attacks and the other defends, but that where their commentators want to reduce and simplify theater's pharmaceutical effects—usually to erotically inflammatory, and/or poisonous potions—playwrights instead complicate and multiply the possibilities, offering a more variable, eclectic, and surprising array of models for theatrical efficacy. Theater, in the plays this book examines, can be curative, soporific, poisonous, narcotic, addictive, aphrodisiac, soothing, intoxicating; it can alter its spectators, its actors, even its directors and writers. Like Cleopatra's infinite variety, the expansiveness of the pharmaceutical model offers playwrights a compelling image of the theater's elastic nature.

In exploring concerns about theater's effects, this book also intervenes in a larger conversation about spectatorship, gender, and power. Contemporary criticism, influenced strongly by models such as Foucault's analysis of Jeremy Bentham's Panopticon, has assumed that power lies primarily in the eyes of the viewer, while persons or objects viewed must be in a passive, and powerless position.[73] In the wake of Laura Mulvey's compelling argument about the objectifying power of the male gaze, moreover, the spectator has become conventionally identified as not only controlling, but male, while the role of spectacle has been widely conceived as not only passive and objectified, but intrinsically female.[74] Writings on Renaissance staging have often emphasized similar claims, both about the power of the spectator and about the powerlessness of female objects of the gaze.[75] Renaissance playwrights and antitheatricalists, however, repeatedly demonstrate both fears and convictions that the opposite is true. The seductive beauty of the female spectacle—such as Juliet, Cleopatra, Vittoria of *The White Devil*, or even the dead Gloriana of *The Revenger's Tragedy*—repeatedly intoxicates, undoes, and potentially annihilates its male spectators. Plays, however, are not only composed of spectacles: they are also built of words. Although their visual images tend to be associated with women, many of the most rhetorically manipulative figures in these plays are male, such as Volpone, Sejanus, Vindice, and Hamlet, and many of their most susceptible audiences are female.[76] This book also argues, then, that while the theater is widely presented as exerting formidable power over its consumers, the gendering of these power relations is complex and variable, and accords much more agency to women than is commonly held.

CHAPTER SUMMARIES

The chapters that follow trace the dramatic treatment of a series of dangerous remedies. Rather than moving in chronological order, they begin with literal medicinal drugs, and progress to increasingly abstract notions of remedy, exploring substances associated with oblivion, pleasure, beauty, erotic desire, and revenge. The chapters argue that their subjects—medicines, sleeping potions, face-paints, kisses, and words—are all in some way understood as remedies, yet are all depicted as capable of achieving the exact opposite of their intended effects. They also argue that these subjects are each identified, in different ways, with the seductive and potentially restorative powers of the theater, and accordingly that each illuminates a different aspect of contemporary concerns about the theater.

The first two chapters explore comparisons between the theater and actual medicinal drugs. Chapter 1 examines depictions of dangerous doctors and medicines in Jonson's *Sejanus* and *Volpone*, and Webster's *The White Devil*. This chapter examines the dangerous theatrical powers attributed to doctors in each of the three plays, with particular attention to the risks of purgative drugs and poisons, including antimony, aconite, mummia, and mercury. After exploring the way medical uses of dangerous drugs parallel political and theatrical manipulation in *Sejanus* and *The White Devil*, the chapter examines the more complex and variable model of theater's physiological effects depicted in *Volpone*. Chapter 2 continues the first chapter's examination of literal, medical drugs, with a focus on the dangers of sleeping potions. The chapter considers the juxtaposition of sleeping potions and poisons, and their parallels with the uneasy relationship between comedy and tragedy, in Shakespeare's *Romeo and Juliet* and *Antony and Cleopatra*. In the context of complaints from antitheatrical tracts about the theater's capacity to lull spectators into sleepy oblivion, the chapter argues that Shakespeare identifies the effects of the theater—at first tentatively, in *Romeo and Juliet*, and then forcefully in *Antony and Cleopatra*—with the ambiguous soporific pleasures of controversial narcotics such as opium and mandragora.

The third and fourth chapters move from medicinal drugs and potions towards a more abstract notion of remedy, identifying the visual spectacle of the theater with the chemicals used in face-paints, and the allure of beauty, femininity, and erotic desire. As a form of physical self-improvement, cosmetics—or "face-physicks," as one English book on beauty described them—were widely understood as a subset of medicine, yet like other medicines they were suspected of both chemical and spiritual hazards.[77] Taking as its starting point a fatal face-painting scene in *The Devil's Charter* by Barnabe Barnes, Chapter 3 explores representations of face-paints as poisonous in plays, anti-cosmetic treatises, medical writings, and antitheatrical diatribes; it goes on to demonstrate how this association worked to identify the theater as a seductive poison. The chapter argues that depictions of women suffering from poisonous face-paint offer a disturbingly literal image of the vulnerability of the body to the invasive force of spectacle.

Chapter 4 extends this topic by examining the threat that female beauty posed for men. A surprising number of plays from this period dramatize the motif of death by poisoned kiss. The chapter focuses on three plays—Middleton's *The Second Maiden's Tragedy*, Massinger's *The Duke of Milan*, and *The Revenger's Tragedy*—in which men die from necrophilic embraces with female corpses painted with poisons. The chapter argues that these plays identify sexuality, and particularly the desirable female body, with both remedy and poison. Furthermore, these plays identify an idolatrous attraction to painted corpses with the risks of being seduced by the artificial world of the theater. Where Chapter 3 emphasizes the women who absorb paint directly, this chapter studies the male admirers who absorb its effects indirectly, and examines the grotesquely material consequences attributed to spectatorship.

Chapter 5 draws together the book's concerns with the effects of the theater and the vulnerability of the body in an examination of the vulnerability of the ear and the power of language in *Hamlet*. With its strikingly self-conscious attention both to the workings of the theater and to the effects of dangerous drugs, *Hamlet* embodies this book's themes with particular forcefulness. The chapter considers the play's preoccupation with the vulnerability of the ear in relation to the parallels it suggests between words and dangerous drugs. It draws on early modern anatomical studies of ears, as well as early modern debates about the material impact of words, to argue that Shakespeare offers a model of corrosive theatrical power with both affective and material consequences.

The book's epilogue revisits the play with which the book opens in order to explore the idea of the antidote. *A Midsummer Night's*

Dream features not one, but two drugs: love-in-idleness and the unnamed herb that undoes its effects. By examining the antidote and what it reflects about the effects of the original drug, the epilogue imagines what antidotes might be required to undo the effects of the book's other plays, and what it would mean for the theater to be its own antidote.

In all the plays this book considers, as in other plays and writings of the period, drugs and poisons conflate concerns about unreliable appearances and material danger, evoking fascination and fear by identifying a convergence point between the imagination and the body, the literary and the scientific, the magical and the rational. This book explores that same convergence point, and considers its implications for the study of the early modern theater. By examining the interpenetration of medical and theatrical discourses in this period, this book seeks to demonstrate how these discourses work together to dramatize beliefs about the power of theatrical spectacles, and anxieties about the vulnerability—both mental and bodily—of their consumers.

"Unnatural and Horrid Physic": Pharmaceutical Theater in Jonson and Webster

Towards the beginning of Ben Jonson's *Volpone* (1605), Corbaccio —waiting expectantly on Volpone's apparently imminent death— advises Mosca that Volpone "should take some counsel of physicians." "I have brought him | An opiate here," he adds, "from mine own doctor." In defending his refusal to administer this so-called medicine to Volpone, Mosca claims that his patron is deeply suspicious of doctors. "He will not hear of drugs," Mosca tells Corbaccio; "He has no faith in physic: he does think | Most of your doctors are the greater danger, | And worse disease t'escape."[1] Corbaccio's stratagem, and Mosca's consequent anti-medical polemic, appear at first glance to be little more than a humorous aside, a mocking illustration of Corbaccio's avarice and ineptitude as a would-be poisoner. The possibility that this episode articulates, however— that drugs and doctors are not what they seem, and may in fact be their own fatal opposites—adds a physical charge to the play's representation of the dangerous consequences of dissimulation. In general, the devious charades of Volpone and his gulls highlight moral and epistemological concerns. In the case of counterfeit medicine, however, they threaten immediate death.

Volpone's purported skepticism towards doctors offers a concise summary of contemporary complaints against the dangers of medicine. Yet the real threat to which Mosca responds in this scene is not medicine, but Corbaccio's duplicity. Corbaccio plays the role of a solicitous friend and mourner, but he is in fact eagerly awaiting a financial windfall from Volpone's anticipated death. His apparently curative drug, similarly, masks a mortal poison designed to hasten that death. In a play preoccupied with the twin themes of pretense and bodily vulnerability, this scene suggests a causal relation between the two: lies, or misrepresentations, bring about material, physical consequences. As elsewhere in Jonson, moreover, duplicity is intimately linked to theatricality. Corbaccio's mercenary scheme mirrors those of Mosca and Volpone, who revel in staged entertainments, and turn to costumes, props, and play-acting in order to lure and manipulate their gulls. Ultimately, Mosca's and Volpone's plots fail, just as Corbaccio's does: all the players are exposed as immoral, and punished, by the end of the play. Just as false medicine, then— even if it stems from error rather than malice—can lead to danger or even death rather than increased health, Jonson implicitly suggests that play-acting is a volatile drug, which, if administered incorrectly, may result in spiritual and physical harm, rather than the comfort and improvement to which it should aspire.

Jonson's ambivalence towards the theater and his condemnations of contemporary playwrights are legendary, but he was far from the only dramatist to identify the theater with dangerous doctors and medicines. In the context of the long-running association between theater and medicine, and the recent outbreak of cultural fears about pharmacy, playwrights who were skeptical about the dramatic medium found in powerful and uncertain medicines a vehicle for exploring the ambivalent effects of plays on their audiences. Like Jonson in *Volpone* and also *Sejanus*, John Webster, another learned and cynical writer, depicted dangerous drugs and doctors in *The White Devil* in order to confront the consequences of ambiguous remedies in general, and the nature of the theater in particular. This chapter begins by examining how *Sejanus* (1603) uses drugs and poisons as analogies for dangerous forms of political and theatrical manipulation, and moves on to consider how Webster imitates and alters this play's medical symbolism in his similarly drug-drenched revenge drama, *The White Devil* (1612). It ends by moving back, chronologically, to *Volpone* (1605) in order to examine its more complex and variable model of theater's physiological effects.

ACTING AND DRUGGING IN *SEJANUS*

Written two years before *Volpone*, Jonson's *Sejanus* also attributes powerful and dangerous physical consequences to theatrical duplicity. In his depiction of the rise and fall of a wily, conspiring political figure in imperial Rome, Jonson draws on a vocabulary of drugs, medicine, and bodily violence to portray the palpable consequences of words and schemes. The play repeatedly describes the way lies, rumors, and flattery alter both individual bodies and the body politic. The skeptical observer Silius notes that Sejanus's parasites can "cut I Men's throats with whisp'rings" (I.30–1).[2] In response to unctuous praise, the Emperor Tiberius warns himself to "make up our ears 'gainst these assaults I Of charming tongues" (I.389–90), and Silius echoes that he must "shun I The strokes and stripes of flatterers" (I.413–14). Through his power over the art of verbal influence and persuasion, Sejanus has transformed himself from an apparently passive and manipulated body—"the noted pathic of the time" (I.216)—to "the now court-god" (I.203), a powerful manipulator of bodies and minds alike.

Although Sejanus does not directly handle drugs or medicines in the play, he carries out his most significant political accomplishments, wooing the princess Livia, and murdering her powerful husband Drusus, through the services of a doctor. The physician Eudemus is not a central character in *Sejanus*—he appears only in the first two acts—but he serves as a key double for Sejanus in embodying the play's central focus on duplicitous intrigue and plotting. With his intimate access to the princess Livia and other important women in Rome, Eudemus is aptly seen by Sejanus as a crucial gateway to power. "You're a subtle nation, you physicians!," Sejanus notes, "And grown the only cabinets, in court, I To ladies' privacies" (I.299–301). Upon Eudemus's agreement to secure a private meeting with Livia, and essentially to act as bawd, Sejanus exults:

> Let me adore my Aesculapius!
> Why this indeed is physic! And outspeaks
> The knowledge of cheap drugs or any use
> Can be made out of it! More comforting
> Than all your opiates, juleps, apozems,
> Magistral syrups . . .
>
> (I.355–60)

What Sejanus identifies as physic is precisely the access, the intimacy and trust, which the physician can secure. The influence that Eudemus exerts because of his position is both more potent and more consoling than any "cheap drugs . . . opiates, juleps, apozems, | Magistral syrups." These concoctions and infusions, all identified with cooling, soothing, and narcotic effects, evoke the drowsy inert state that Sejanus himself tries to induce in those around him, the better to control them. The medicine of Eudemus's influence, then, proves comparable not only to these pharmaceutical elixirs, but also to Sejanus's own political powers; it will also prove at least as dangerous.

At Sejanus's well-paid bidding, Eudemus agrees to use his skill in physic to poison Drusus, Livia's husband. They plot an assault that will be intimate and invisible, and will come from apparently trustworthy sources: drugs not only prepared by a doctor, but served in wine presented by Drusus's trusted cup-bearer. "And, wise physician," Sejanus bids him, "so prepare the poison | As you may lay the subtle operation | Upon some natural disease of him" (II.107–10). Through his skill and subtlety, Jonson suggests, the physician can not only prepare and administer poisons, but can also mask their artificial effects, making them look like natural perturbations of the body. Not only does Eudemus dissemble, concealing poisonous intents under the guise of a bringer of health, but his poison itself becomes theatrical, capable of deceiving both its victim and those who will later examine his death.

Eudemus's murderous dissimulations evoke commonly voiced anxieties about doctors in early modern medical writings. With their arcane knowledge, access to transformative potions, and power over those who came to see them, doctors were widely feared as duplicitous, unreadable, and protean figures, with the dangerous capacity to poison rather than heal.[3] As the physician John Cotta explained, "wholesome medicines by the hands of the iudicious dispenser, are as Angels of God sent for the good of men; but in the hands of the vnlearned, are messengers of death vnto their farther euill."[4] Cotta attributes medical poisonings primarily to ineptitude based on improper training, but others envisioned more malevolent motives.[5] The doctor Thomas Herring, in his translation of the German physician Johann Oberndoerffer, worried that, given the untrustworthiness of doctors, "neither the Patient, nor his Friends, shal be able to know whether in stead of a Soueraigne Medicine, far set, and deare bought, they receiue rank poyson, or at least some vncouth, vnfitting, or counterfeit Dregge, or Drugge."[6] Echoing him, the physician John Securis took the point one step further by metonymically equating false doctors themselves with unseen poisons: "I would to god that al men wold beware of such felowes, & remember the proverbe that saith: *Dulci sub melle saepe venena latent.* Under swete meats is many times a poyson hidde."[7]

Intriguingly, in the context of plays' interest in medical poisoners, writers concerned about the proliferation of unreliable or inauthentic doctors routinely drew on the traditional *theatrum mundi* metaphor—the notion of the world as a theater—to describe the unreliability of the self-claimed physician.[8] Cotta complained of "many wicked practises, iuglings, cousinages & impostures, which maske vnespied vnder the colour and pretence of medicining."[9] More explicitly, Primerose cited Hippocrates on medical duplicity: "Touching Physitians he saith that many of them are like to dissembling Stage-Players, who represent the person, which notwithstanding they doe not sustaine: so as indeed there are many Physicians in name, but in performance very few, which as in Hippocrates his dayes, so also in our age experience shewes to bee most true."[10] Equating actors with a Protean instability, Oberndoerffer similarly wrote that the quack doctor, "being himselfe more variable then the Polyp . . . is in twentie seuerall Mindes in an houre, turning and winding, too and fro, like a Tragedians Buskin, and vttering quite Contraryes."[11] He continued the metaphor to complain about false or unlearned doctors,

Thus these two Veterators, or Couzening Copsemates [accomplices], act their Parts, as it were on a Stage, circumuenting and insnaring simple Men and Women, altogether vnacquainted with these quaint Deuises, laughing them to scorne behind their backes, ryding them for Asses, boasting of their slye and cunning conueyance of their matters, and each of them vaunting that he played his Part best.[12]

Oberndoerffer's actors revel in ensnaring their victims for sheer sport and entertainment, taking pride and pleasure in their successful performance. The theatrical metaphor lends connotations of deception and conspiracy to doctors' already threatening specialized knowledge. False doctors parallel stage players in their dangerous capacity for dissembling, for representing something that they are not, taking up a part that they can not sustain. While critics of the stage argued that the lies of the theater could threaten one's immortal soul, the lies, or even unwitting errors, of a doctor could be clearly seen to threaten the immediate security of the body.

   This threat is demonstrated by Eudemus, whose skill in dissimulation, under Sejanus's guidance, leads to the play's first murder. Eudemus's intimate access and artful duplicity emerge most forcefully in his longest scene, in which he applies cosmetic remedies to Livia while advising her on Sejanus's merits, and discussing his poison for Drusus. Medicines and poisons, in this scene, directly engage with the false faces that emblematize both Eudemus's work and Sejanus's conspiracy. Poisons, paints, and cures collide uncomfortably: in answer to Eudemus's question "When will you take some physic, lady?," Livia replies "When I I shall, Eudemus: but let Drusus's drug I Be first prepared" (II.121–3). "I have it ready," he responds;

> And tomorrow morning,
> I'll send you a perfume, first to resolve,
> And procure sweat, and then prepare a bath
> To cleanse and clear the cutis; against when,
> I'll have an excellent new fucus made.
>   (II.124–8)

The apparent non-sequiturs of this curious exchange point to the intimate relationships between the various drugs of this sequence. Livia's medical treatment collides first with Drusus's poisons and then with the perfume and bath that will purify her skin, and the fucus, or paint, that will adorn it. These cosmetics, her enticements for Sejanus, are linguistically interwoven with both the medicine she will take and the drug that will kill her husband. As a standard theatrical prop, as well as a symbol of the disguised and protean identities central to the theater, face-paints here link Sejanus's duplicitous treachery, and the poisoning of Drusus under the cover of innocent drink, with the deceptions of theatrical performance.[13] Eudemus, quietly at the hub of all of these operations, becomes a pivotal symbol for the power and danger of theatrical duplicity, a shadowy double for Sejanus himself.

   Eudemus's poison is successful, and Drusus, the only figure who has actively threatened to check Sejanus's political ambitions, is quickly pronounced dead from natural causes. Having employed a literal doctor and literal drugs to advance his schemes, Sejanus turns to figurative drugs as he prepares for the next step in his plans, his larger, bolder plot to bring down Tiberius and install himself in his place:

> Well, read my charms,
> And may they lay that hold upon thy senses,
> As thou hadst snuffed up hemlock, or ta'en down
> The juice of poppy and of mandrakes. Sleep,
> Voluptuous Caesar, and security
> Seize on thy stupid powers, and leave them dead . . .
>   (III.595–600)

Echoing his earlier evocation of opiates, juleps, and apozems, Sejanus's catalogue of pleasurable but perilous soporific drugs suggests that he sees his political manipulation of Tiberius as a malevolent form of physic: like Eudemus, he will use dissembling stratagems that seem to medicate, while eradicating suspicion and even consciousness, and ultimately killing. With his famous hedonism and lechery, Tiberius seems easily susceptible to the luxurious appeal of this drug-induced, trance-like oblivion. After the success of Eudemus's artful poisoning, Sejanus imagines continuing his rise by emulating and appropriating this pharmaceutical authority himself.

Sejanus's conception of Tiberius as slumbering peacefully while being practiced upon, however, proves a fatal error. Despite his apparent easy acquiescence towards Sejanus, Tiberius is in fact an even more sophisticated and calculating actor than his protégé. After watching a particularly persuasive piece of dissimulation in the senate, Arruntius, the play's most reliable spokesman, muses on "the space | Between the breast and lips—Tiberius' heart | Lies a thought farther than another man's" (III.96–8); later he wryly notes "Well acted, Caesar" (III.105). Like Eudemus, moreover, Tiberius knows how to conceal a marred face with medicines: Latiaris refers to him as hiding "his ulcerous and anointed face" (IV.174), deftly conflating his status as anointed ruler with his application of remedial ointments. Tiberius casts himself in the role of physician in more substantive ways as well. Mulling over the troubling ambition apparent in Sejanus's bid for Livia's hand, he decides to send for Macro, another ambitious and manipulative sycophant, to be the instrument of Sejanus's demise:

> I'have heard that aconite,
> Being timely taken, hath a healing might

> Against the scorpion's stroke. The proof we'll give—
> That, while two poisons wrestle, we may live.
>
> (III.651–4)

Like Sejanus, Tiberius draws on a vocabulary of drugs to plot his political strategy. Rather than trying Sejanus's diversionary tactic of administering soothing but incapacitating narcotic potions, however, he turns directly to forceful and fatal poisons, drawing on the classically Paracelsian idea of using poison to expel poison.[14] Aconite held a distinctive place in early modern pharmacology. Not only was it viewed as an exceptionally powerful poison—Holland's translation of Pliny noted that "we know there is no poison in the world so quicke in operation as it"— but it was identified with the horrors of hell, reputed to "be ingendered first, of the fome that the dog *Cerberus* let fall vpon the ground, frothing so as he did at the mouth for anger when *Hercules* pluckt him out of hell."[15] Despite, or rather because of, this malicious force, its identification as a cure for scorpion venom was a commonplace. Pliny wrote: "howbeit, as deadly a bane as it is, our forefathers haue deuised means to vse it for good, and euen to saue the life of man: found they haue by experience, that being giuen in hot wine, it is a counterpoison against the sting of scorpions,"[16] and noted that "scorpions if they be but touched with Aconite, presently become pale, benummed, astonied, and bound, confessing (as it were) themselues to be vanquished and prisoners."[17] Macro, in Tiberius's model, will serve as aconite, leaving the scorpion, Sejanus, "benummed, astonied, and . . . vanquished." While Sejanus imagines Tiberius as drugged into a narcotic trance and plots his demise, then, it is in fact Sejanus who is oblivious; Tiberius is wide awake, and carefully calculating his survival by setting his detractors' poisons against each other.

Despite imagining himself in the powerful roles of actor and doctor, Sejanus is not subtle enough to resist the false rumors and flatterers that turn him into a susceptible audience, manipulated by someone else's performance. After a series of attacks on the statue that symbolically represents him in the theater of Pompey, Sejanus meets his downfall at a trial of sorts. Giddy with anticipation that he is about to receive the tribunicial power at a senatorial gathering, he is instead accosted by a damning letter from Tiberius and sent offstage, where he is quickly condemned "by the Senate, | To lose his head" (V.815–16).

Orchestrated by Macro, the public reading of Tiberius's letter, and the so-called trial that follows it, enact Tiberius's remedy for the problem of Sejanus's wiles: poison will purge poison, aconite will purge scorpion, and one dangerously duplicitous politician will purge another. Macro demonstrates this idea most explicitly in his brutal treatment of Sejanus's body after the reading of Tiberius's letter. He will, he tells Sejanus,

> Kick up thy heels in air, tear off thy robe,
> Play with thy beard, and nostrils—thus 'tis fit
>
> .   .   .   .
>
> To use th'ingrateful viper, tread his brains
> Into the earth.
>
> (V.685–9)

Almost as if he had overheard Tiberius's thoughts on aconite and scorpions, Macro justifies his physical abuse of Sejanus by describing him as a viper that must be killed for the safety of the empire. His assault both foreshadows and encourages the even more savage attacks on Sejanus's body that follow. Describing the events that take place offstage, Terentius reports on the

> Sentence, by the Senate,
> To lose his head—which was no sooner off,
> But that and th'unfortunate trunk were seized
> By the rude multitude; who, not content
> With what the forward justice of the state
> Officiously had done, with violent rage
> Have rent it limb from limb.
>
> (V.815–21)

The dismemberment of Sejanus, like Macro's original attack on him, reflects Tiberius's maxim that while "two poisons wrestle, we may live" (III.654). Through the violent wrestling of the mob with Sejanus's body, both Tiberius and Rome's body politic are purged of his poisonous influence.[18]

If the dramatic conception of the trial originally invites the audience to join Tiberius, as well as Jonson, in passing judgment on Sejanus, it quickly complicates that process by not only mimicking, but intensifying, the corruption and brutality it ostensibly sets out to purge. By the same token, its effects are ambivalent. Although Tiberius succeeds in ridding Rome of a danger, the success of his remedy hinges on the question of whether Rome will be better off as a result. Sejanus himself, with his lies, flattery, and conspiracies, will be gone, but the play suggests that Macro will be his mirror-image replacement, leaving Rome subjected to more of the same dangerous whispers, cajolings, and insinuating verbal venoms.

More troublingly, the play suggests a threatening model for the impact of theatrical performances on their consumers. If Sejanus and Tiberius are the play's two primary examples of dissembling actors, they generate two different kinds of pharmaceutical effects, both dangerous. Audiences to the manipulative lies, rumors, whisperings and flatteries of Sejanus find themselves unconscious, drugged into a narcotic oblivion that incapacitates them; the victims of Tiberius's schemes, meanwhile, find themselves scourged and purged with brutal, poisonous expulsives. The incommensurability of their positions, moreover, points to variations within the theatrical model. Tiberius, strikingly, is physically absent from the scene of Sejanus's accusation, trial, and dismemberment; he shapes the outcome from afar, through both his ventriloquized letter and his instructions to Macro. If Sejanus is an actor, then, Tiberius occupies a more powerful position in relation to theatrical performance: he is both scriptwriter and director, manipulating the actors from behind the scenes. Participating in the spectacle, this play suggests, by no means guarantees immunity from its effects. Actors, in fact, may be even more vulnerable than their audiences to the dangerous effects of dissimulation.

If Jonson intended *Sejanus* to teach its audiences a lesson, it was not well taken. The play's fate, at the hands of spectators, critics, and censors, was notoriously dismal. In his Folio edition, Jonson noted to his dedicatee, Esmé Stuart Seigneur d'Aubigné, that the play "suffered no less violence from our people here than the subject of it did from the rage of the people of Rome" (Dedication, 9–10). Rather than apologizing or altering *Sejanus*, however, Jonson defended it fiercely, and continued to insist on following his own artistic principles rather than bending to popular tastes. The popular response to the play, as his striking analogy for it suggests, confirmed and intensified his dim view of the public theater as catering to an ignorant and vulgar mob, who needed to be corrected and educated, even if against their will.[19] Jonson, in fact, used the metaphor of harsh medicines to describe a playwright's moral obligation to improve his audiences, even if it meant inflicting pain on them.[20] "If men may by no meanes write freely, or speake truth, but when it offends not," he

asked, "why doe *Physicians* cure with sharpe medicines, or corro-
sives? Is not the same equally lawfull in the cure of the minde, that
is in the cure of the body?"[21] In describing Jonson's response to the
hostile reception of *Sejanus*, Jonas Barish seems instinctively to have
echoed this idea, noting that "when Jonson sat down to write a
second tragedy for the same troupe a few years later, far from con-
ceding anything to the preferences of his audiences he defiantly administered a double dose of what they had already once spat out, as
though to coerce them into swallowing his medicine even if they
found it unpalatable, on the presumption that he knew better than
they what was good for them."[22] Jonson's conception of using sharp
medicines to cure the mind, and Barish's characterization of the play
as a bitter purgative medicine, both call to mind Tiberius's aconite,
and suggest implicit support for the notion of using poison to drive
out poison. Though the consequences were uncertain, and frequently unpopular, Jonson insisted on taking forceful, even painful,
measures in his commitment to improve audiences' moral and intellectual health.

POISONOUS REMEDIES IN *THE WHITE DEVIL*

Although Webster is not often likened to Jonson, the two playwrights show striking parallels both in their shared skepticism, even
hostility, towards the public theater, and in their detailed explor-
ations of duplicitous doctors and ambivalent, dangerous drugs.[23] In
particular, *The White Devil* shares the dark cynicism of *Sejanus*,
with its revenge plot of duplicitous conspirators scheming to destroy
each other through artfully administered drugs. Webster's play portrays the adulterous affair between the Duke of Brachiano and
Vittoria Corombona, which results in multiple vindictive murders,
including those of their spouses, and, ultimately their own. The play
not only draws on an extensive vocabulary of medicines, but point-
edly emphasizes remedies that are risky, if not out-and-out poisonous, drawn from the controversial repertoire of Paracelsus.[24] As in
Sejanus, one evil drives out another: Flamineo, Vittoria's scheming
brother, claims that "Physicians, that cure poisons, still do work
| With counter-poisons" (III.iii.62–3).[25] The idea of the counter-
poison, echoing Tiberius's aconite, creates a powerful focus for the
play. Dangerous medicines offer Webster a vocabulary with which

to articulate the seductive but ultimately fatal threats that permeate
the play, threats that ultimately reflect on the potential dangers of the
theater itself. Where Jonson's most theatrically compelling figures
are male, though, and their persuasive power comes largely from
words, the figure most centrally identified with theatricality in
Webster's play is female, and her power is defined more in terms of
visual, and erotic, spectacle. The effects the play attributes to the
theater, accordingly, are more explicitly feminine and seductive than
in Jonson's plays. The fact that Vittoria's opponents are tainted by
misogyny, moreover, complicates the legitimacy of their claims and
the question of her status in the play. In general, where Jonson indicts
and punishes his villains, the moral status of Webster's characters is
complex and ambiguous, and their changeable fortunes seem more
arbitrary than earned. While the power struggles of *Sejanus*, moreover, are worldly and political in accordance with their setting in
ancient Rome, Renaissance Italy, with its cast of corrupt cardinals
and an eventual pope, imbues *The White Devil*'s politicking with
weighty concerns about religion and sin. Most distinctively, whereas
Jonson's plays aspire to improve their audiences, even if doing so
requires inflicting pain, *The White Devil* is more interested in the
possibilities of drugs for torture than for cure.

　　The White Devil opens with a metaphor of poisonous medicines.
In the first scene, Gasparo tells the newly exiled Count Lodovico,

> 　　　　　　　　　　　Your followers
> Have swallowed you up like mummia, and being sick
> With such unnatural and horrid physic
> Vomit you up i'th'kennel.

> 　　　　　　　　　　　　　　　(I.i.15–18)

An extraordinary medicine made of powdered dead human flesh,
mummia would have evoked Paracelsian medicine at its most
morbidly magical extreme.[26] Paracelsus held an exalted view of
mummia's medicinal powers, which he extolled in a treatise, *De
Mumia Libellus* (1526), and abstracted into one of his four
principles of the wisdom of the body.[27] Though made from a dead
body, the powder was meant to contain a life force: the best mummia
was supposed to come from the flesh of a saint, or at least a healthy
young person recently killed by unexpected violence, so that the flesh
would be still strong, vigorous, and radiant with life.[28] Mummia's
privileged place in the Paracelsian canon points to his attraction to

an array of magically vested folk remedies from among the so-called "dirt pharmacy," including exotica such as unicorn horn, ostrich feathers, egg shells, toadstools, and vipers' blood.[29] Understandably, mummia was one of Paracelsus's more controversial remedies; adherents to the established Galenic doctrine, such as the conservative academic Thomas Erastus, attacked it as a prime example of Paracelsus's close affiliation with witchcraft, black magic, and the devil.[30]

Gasparo's choice of mummia as metaphor for Lodovico, the disgruntled evicted count who becomes the play's primary instrument of revenge, has a number of literary implications. Most immediately, it becomes a point of identification between Lodovico and Vittoria Corombona. Responding to her husband's adulterous love for Vittoria in a quasi-staged outburst of hysteria, Brachiano's spurned wife Isabella threatens

> To dig the strumpet's eyes out, let her lie
> Some twenty months a-dying, to cut off
> Her nose and lips, pull out her rotten teeth,
> Preserve her flesh like mummia, for trophies
> Of my just anger!
>
> (II.i.245–9)

Vittoria and Lodovico stand in direct opposition to each other in the play's dichotomy of conspiracy and counter-conspiracy. Lodovico is a banished count whose own unrequited desire for Isabella, Brachiano's divorced and eventually murdered wife, places his sympathies firmly against the adulterous and murderous lovers; Vittoria is a one-time courtesan whose beauty and Machiavellian wiles raise her to the status of duchess. Yoking them together under the rhetorical rubric of mummia, Webster links both figures with the idea of violent victimization at the hands of angry aggressors: Lodovico is swallowed and vomited forth by the body politic, while Vittoria is envisioned as being murdered and dismembered by her resentful rival.

While Gasparo describes Lodovico as an already regurgitated dose of mummia, however, Isabella imagines Vittoria's future mummification, suggesting that Lodovico's violent rejection from court at the start of the play foreshadows Vittoria's imminent fall from the more comfortable heights of Fortune's wheel. Webster calls attention to the curious double chiasmus of their fortunes: at the start of the play Lodovico has just fallen as Vittoria is beginning her rise, and towards the end Vittoria has been not only publicly shamed, but murdered by poison, while Lodovico has apparently secured the good graces of Francisco, the Duke of Florence, and Monticelso, the Cardinal-turned-Pope. Lodovico's seizure under arrest as the play closes, however, suggests that the turnabout is cyclical rather than final; ultimately, the shared dependence of Lodovico and Vittoria on brutal higher-ups renders their fates more similar than different.

By linking Lodovico with Vittoria, the figure of mummia charts complementary tragic trajectories in the play, pointing to the underlying instability of all its characters' positions. Yet the medicine simultaneously reflects on the nature of Lodovico and Vittoria themselves. Portrayed as an "unnatural and horrid physic" which, when ingested, sickens rather than cures, mummia identifies the two figures with an ability to insinuate themselves intimately into people's lives and affections, promising pleasure only to wreak havoc within. Paradoxically, the identification of Lodovico and Vittoria with mummia both palliates and intensifies their guilt: the image emphasizes their helpless dependence on figures more powerful than themselves, but also identifies them with a seductive and invasive threat that sickens once accepted into inward parts.

While mummia is the only poison or medicine to which Lodovico is compared, the term's application to Vittoria evokes a wide range of related references. The poisons that pervade the play find an apparent convergence point in Vittoria: "You, gentlewoman," Monticelso accuses her in her trial scene, "Take from all beasts, and from all minerals | Their deadly poison" (III.ii.103–5). While Vittoria is consistently represented through imagery of poison, however, the ambiguous potential of these poisons for medicinal purposes, as well as the uneasy equivalence between her poisons and the counter-poisons identified with her enemies, serve to complicate rather than clarify her moral status in the play.[31]

At the opening of the play, in encouraging Brachiano to act on his adulterous love for Vittoria, Flamineo brushes away a query about "her jealous husband" with the disclaimer, "Hang him, a gilder that hath his brains perished with quicksilver is not more cold in the liver" (I.ii.26–8). By presenting Camillo as a passionless, even impotent, victim of mercury poisoning, Flamineo apparently intends to facilitate Brachiano's pursuit of Vittoria, but his metaphor ironically suggests the possibility that Camillo is a victim to a dangerous medical substance associated with Vittoria herself.[32] Jests about

Vittoria's possible cuckoldry elicit Camillo's sour response, "This does not physic me" (I.ii.97), and Brachiano later explicitly identifies Vittoria with mercury, snapping at her "Thy loose thoughts | Scatter like quicksilver" (IV.ii.98–9).

Mercury, or quicksilver, was at this time the toxic medicine with perhaps the strongest hold on the popular imagination. Despite its well-known dangers, it was becoming an increasingly popular medicinal remedy: in the wake of catastrophic syphilis epidemics, its success in treating the disease's most recalcitrant symptoms played a significant role in upholding the new iatrochemical medicine, and undermining faith in traditional Galenic remedies, which proved powerless before the new disease.[33] Paracelsus was one of the leading exponents of the metal's medicinal powers.[34] Like mummia, mercury played a central and magical role in Paracelsian doctrine. The term came to refer not only to the metal but to an alchemical principle, representing fluidity, the intellect, and mathematics.[35] Again like mummia, mercury became one of Paracelsus's more controversial medicines. William Bullein voiced the ambivalence of many doctors in noting that "Marueylous thinges be done by meanes of Quicksiluer as the Chimistes doth know," while also cautioning that "it hath vertue to consume, and it is perillous to be vsed in oyntments to kill scabbes with all, for it is percing, and subtill, that at length it wil come into the inwarde partes, where as finally it will mortify and kill."[36]

Like the mercury and mummia with which she is associated, Vittoria is presented as a powerful but volatile medicine, intimately invasive, with dangerous side-effects. As Camillo's metaphoric suffering from mercury poisoning suggests, Vittoria's sexual power is identified as toxic. Upon discovering Vittoria in Brachiano's embrace, Cornelia, her horrified mother, describes Vittoria's apparent adultery as worse than venom:

> O that this fair garden
> Had with all poisoned herbs of Thessaly
> At first been planted, made a nursery
> For witchcraft, rather than a burial plot
> For both your honours.
>
> (I.ii.272–6)

At Vittoria's trial, Monticelso similarly identifies sexuality—hers, implicitly—with poison. "Shall I expound whore to you?," he asks.

"Sure I shall; | I'll give their perfect character. They are first | Sweetmeats which rot the eater: in man's nostril | Poisoned perfumes" (III.ii.79–82).

Isabella also associates Vittoria's and Brachiano's adultery with poison. Discussing with Monticelso and Francisco her plans for winning her husband back from Vittoria's snares, she says

> I do not doubt
> As men to try the precious unicorn's horn
> Make of the powder a preservative circle
> And in it put a spider, so these arms
> Shall charm his poison, force it to obeying
> And keep him chaste from an infected straying.
>
> (II.i.13–18)

The unicorn's horn, another item of the "dirt pharmacy" associated with Paracelsus and the new magic medicine, was meant to be so powerful an antidote to poison that the venomous spider would be repelled by, and find itself unable to cross, the boundary of a circle made from its powder.[37] Isabella's simile, in this context, is curious: the "infected straying" to which she refers seems to associate the feared poison with an external contaminant, presumably Vittoria, yet the venomous spider seems to be Brachiano himself. Isabella seems more concerned with containing Brachiano's poison inside her circle than with keeping out that of Vittoria.

If Vittoria is presented as a drug, albeit of dubious effects, she is also portrayed as a doctor in her own right. In the first scene of courtship between Vittoria and Brachiano, the metaphor of physic becomes an explicit part of the lovers' banter. In response to Brachiano's declaration of distress, Vittoria declares courteously, "Sir in the way of pity I wish you heart-whole." When Brachiano responds, "You are a sweet physician," Vittoria continues, "Sure sir a loathed cruelty in ladies | Is as to doctors many funerals: | It takes away their credit" (I.ii.207–10). This brief flirtatious exchange both attributes to Vittoria a kind of medical authority, and complicates the play's association of her adulterous sexuality with poison, suggesting that for her to be cruel, or sexually reticent, would be a failure of responsibility akin to doctors killing their patients.

Vittoria's identification with medicine is problematized by the play's images of physicians. Throughout the play, doctors, like medicine, are a source of anxiety; when physicians visit the dying

Brachiano, Flamineo curses them: "a plague upon you; I We have too much of your cunning here already" (V.iii.11). The play's demonization of doctors reaches a peak in the parodic villain Doctor Julio. A caricature of negative medical stereotyping, Dr. Julio is introduced as "A poor quack-salving knave, . . . one that should have been lashed for's lechery, but that he confessed a judgement, had an execution laid upon him, and so put the whip to a *non plus*" (II.i.292–5).[38] He is from the outset associated with dissimulation, not only in his capacity as a pseudo-doctor, but in his witty escape from punishment for lechery by confessing to the crime of debt.

If Dr Julio's deceptive wiles are both comic and disturbing, his homicidal enthusiasm is more so. Flamineo tells Brachiano,

> He will shoot pills into a man's guts, shall make them have more ventages than a cornet or a lamprey; he will poison a kiss, and was once minded, for his masterpiece, because Ireland breeds no poison, to have prepared a deadly vapour in a Spaniard's fart that should have poisoned all Dublin. (II.i.298–303)

Dr Julio's various scatological feats are witty, and farcical to the point of absurdity, but their humor is black. His plots highlight a sense of bodily invasion and infiltration: the physician's uneasy access to the body allows him to rupture the integrity of bodily boundaries, penetrating them with weapons and pills. This power of invasion is identified with the power of poison: Dr Julio ingeniously devises a way to contaminate Ireland, and "will poison a kiss," echoing the play's imagery of toxic sexuality.

As Dr Julio's plan to poison a kiss suggests, mouths and kisses are depicted throughout the play as both contaminated and contaminating, literalizing the dangerous power of eros.[39] When accosted by Francisco that Vittoria "is your strumpet," Brachiano angrily responds, "Uncivil sir there's hemlock in thy breath" (II.i.58–9). Later, Brachiano shuns Isabella's kiss with a dangerously topical reference to epidemic disease, crying "O your breath! I Out upon sweet meats, and continued physic! I The plague is in them" (II.i.163–5).[40] Ironically, still later, after having been poisoned himself, Brachiano will have to acknowledge his own kiss as fatal, warning Vittoria, "Do not kiss me, for I shall poison thee" (V.iii.27).

Framed within the play's many references to poison in lips, the poisoned kiss that Dr Julio designs to kill Isabella provides the most morbid association between medicine, poison, and sexuality in the play. Strikingly, it also links dangerous drugs forcefully with the effects of the theater itself. The murder is presented in an elaborate series of frames within frames: a conjuror steps in and reveals to Brachiano a dumb show in which Doctor Julio and Christophero annoint his portrait with poisoned fumes. Isabella's death follows what is apparently her nightly ritual: *"she kneels down as to prayers, then draws the curtain of the picture, does three reverences to it, and kisses it thrice. She faints and will not suffer them to come near it; dies"* (s.d., II.ii.23).

The fatal kiss dramatized by the dumb show directly implicates medicine. Commenting on Isabella's nightly rites at Brachiano's portrait, the conjuror explains that "Doctor Julio | Observing this infects it with an oil | and other poisoned stuff, which presently | Did suffocate her spirits" (II.ii.28–31). The kiss that kills Isabella has been brought about by medical technology and ingenuity, suggesting a parallel between its intimate, contaminating power and that of the doctor himself. The doctor and conjuror are portrayed as conjoined halves, who respectively perform and present murder by disguising poison as an apparent object of desire.

As a metatheatrical framing device, the dumb show also aligns Dr. Julio's invasive poisons and, correspondingly, Brachiano's murderous schemes, with the contaminating power of the theater.[41] The implicit identification of the dramatic medium with the murder itself is intensified by the explicit linking of the poison to the aesthetic spectacle of a "fum'd picture" (II.ii.25).[42] Webster's choice of a work of art as the site of literal poisons calls attention to the figurative poisons of the play's various deceptive and duplicitous artifices. It also implicitly links the scene of the murder with the play's central character, Vittoria—who, like Sejanus, Eudemus, and Tiberius in the prior play, is associated not only with medicines and poisons, but with theatrical performance as well.[43]

Vittoria's first scene is carefully staged by an array of managers, commentators, and audiences. Flamineo arranges her interview with Brachiano, prepares him (as well as the audience) for Vittoria's entrance by detailing her merits, and goes on to serve as commentator to their encounter, both distancing the audience and drawing us into the action. Brachiano admires Vittoria's beauty, anxiously awaits her with Flamineo, and goes on to woo and win her. Camillo, Vittoria's hapless husband, worries about her disinterest and possible cuckoldry. Zanche, Vittoria's maid, sets the scene for her encounter with Brachiano by spreading out a carpet and two cushions at the site of their conversation. Finally, Cornelia, Vittoria's mother, enters unseen to spy and eavesdrop on the encounter. As onstage spectators who witness and assess Vittoria's performance, each of these figures imitates and complicates the audience's relationship to the scene.[44] Seen from the vantage points of these various figures, Vittoria is alternately romantic heroine, suspect wife, or whore: medicine, uncertain drug, or poison. To all of them, however, she is the focal point of attention, the play's central spectacle.

Framed among so many attentive spectators, Vittoria establishes herself as both artful and duplicitous, the white devil of the play's title.[45] She communicates her interest and availability to Brachiano through demurely flirtatious banter, and goes on to convey a carefully coded message about how he can secure her affections over the threats of their angry spouses. "Excellent devil," Flamineo notes from the sidelines; "She hath taught him in a dream | To make away his Duchess and her husband" (I.ii.254–6). Vittoria's subtle leap from adulterous flirtation to intimations of murder shows both the power and danger of her allure to her audiences: a tension implicit in the medical metaphors (mercury, aphrodisiacs, sweet physician, and poisoned herbs) that describe her throughout the scene.

Vittoria's theatrical power is even more evident in her most striking scene, that of her trial. As in *Sejanus*, the trial scene implicitly both invites the audience to join the judges in casting moral judgment, and offers a remedy for the play's disasters. In *Sejanus*, however, although the trial itself is hardly a model of justice, the correct moral judgment is clear—the audience know that Sejanus is guilty of lies and murders—and it seems to be the case that expelling him from the body politic will be beneficial for Tiberius and for Rome, even if his replacement, Macro, threatens to be much the same. Vittoria's culpability, however, is less clear-cut, and her intelligence and verbal skill complicate the question of her guilt. Her defenses show impeccable logic: faced with Monticelso's accusations that she has not only murdered her husband but has been irreverent in not wearing mourning, she exposes the contradiction in his claim: "Had I foreknown his death as you suggest, | I would have bespoke my mourning" (III.ii.123–4). Similarly, she is clearly correct when she refutes the limits of their evidence of her affair with Brachiano, his passionate letter: "You read his hot love to me, but you want | My frosty answer" (III.ii.201–2). She has not, in fact, carried out the murder of either Isabella or Camillo, nor do the judges have evidence to convict her, and their eagerness to do so is clearly rooted in misogyny, as well as a grudge against Brachiano.[46]

Despite her virtuoso performance, the illegitimacy of the evidence, and her unmasking of the judges' vested motives, however, Vittoria is not innocent either. The audience knows what the judges do not: that she suggested the murders to Brachiano, and that she is, in fact, carrying on the passionate affair that they suspect. Where Jonson demonstrates clear villainy and challenges audiences to join him in punishing it, despite the unfitness of the instruments of justice, Webster shows us a world with less moral clarity, and challenges us to find a defensible position within it. Although the play does not celebrate Vittoria, and her eventual suffering and death suggest that she is punished for her sins, it ultimately leaves a question hovering over her moral status. Similarly, the ambiguous medicines with which she is associated, and the deceptive theatricality which she embodies, remain suspect but ultimately unjudgeable within the frame of the play.

Webster was not nearly as prolific an author as Jonson, and he wrote little in the way of critical reflections on the theater. *The White Devil* and his other plays show, however, that he had much in common with Jonson's cynicism and elitism. When performances of *The White Devil* failed at the Red Bull Theater in 1612, Webster blamed its undiscerning audience; in the letter with which he opened the play's quarto edition, he lamented that the play "wanted (that which is the only grace and setting out of a tragedy) a full and understanding auditory" ("To the Reader," 5–6). More generally, he complained that "most of the people that come to that playhouse, resemble those ignorant asses (who visiting stationers' shops, their use is not to enquire for good books, but new books)" ("To the Reader," 8–11). Not only did Webster's tone closely echo that of Jonson, but he explicitly referred to him in the same dedicatory letter, noting "the laboured and understanding works of Master Jonson" as a model for his own works.[47] If Jonson saw his plays as bitter medicines for his audiences, painful remedies to set them on the right moral course, Webster's emulation suggests even harsher tonics, with an emphasis more on punishment than cure.

PERFORMING MEDICINE IN *VOLPONE*

Although *Sejanus* offers a compelling model for the physical effects of theatrical duplicity, and one which seems to have been popular in the revenge tragedy model exemplified by *The White Devil*, Jonson explored his ideas about the medical effects of theater in more complex ways in the genre for which he is best known, comedy. Jonson revisited his disturbing study of wiles and dissimulation in *Sejanus* two years later in his farcical, if dark, portrait of the same phenomenon in *Volpone*.[48] Like Sejanus, Volpone turns to plotting, counterfeiting, and dangerous drugs to achieve his goals of manipulating gulls for pleasure and profit. The play is a long way, however, from the political machinations of imperial Rome and the dark forebodings of tragedy, in which medical wiles and theatrical deceit lead to both literal poisons and multiple deaths. Within the protected arena of comedy and the carnivalesque display of Volpone's Venice, threatening drugs exist but are never actually consumed; the consequences of Volpone's deceptions, similarly, are limited to humiliation, discomfort, and loss of property. Like *Sejanus*, *Volpone* both dramatizes and enacts the workings of risky substances, but its drugs, like its performances, exert different, and more variable, physical effects.

Perhaps most acutely of all Jonson's plays, *Volpone* is preoccupied with the competing attractions and dangers of theatrical pretense.[49] With the play's central deceit based on the fiction of Volpone's pending death, moreover, its feigning is framed within the arena of drugs and medicine.[50] While theatrical stratagems and games provide Volpone with the restorative pleasures of wealth and entertainment, and seem to promise riches for his gulls, their effects backfire to produce not only humiliation, but also physical pain. Throughout the play, Jonson's emphasis on drugs and bodies insistently equates moral dangers with material consequences. Theatrical dissimulation promises to translate into physical pleasures, but instead ultimately turns into the literal dangers of poisonous threats and corporeal punishment.

The episode from *Volpone* with which this chapter opened offers a caricature of theatrical depictions of doctors as untrustworthy to the point of murderous. When Corbaccio's gift of an opiate is refused, he protests indignantly:

> Why? I myself
> Stood by, while 't was made; saw all th' ingredients;

> And know, it cannot but most gently work.
> My life for his, 'tis but to make him sleep.
>
> (I.iv.14–17)

"Ay," Volpone responds in an aside, "his last sleep, if he would take it" (I.iv.18). While Corbaccio's feigning is no match for the quicker wits of Volpone and Mosca, his unsuccessful attempt to play at deceit establishes medicine as the most dangerous arena for the theatrical games the play explores. To Mosca and Volpone, play-acting is a remedy for ennui, bringing both the pleasure of outwitting their gulls and the "great *elixir*" of gold: "true physic, this your sacred medicine" (I.iv.71, 70). While other dissembling tricks in the play rob their victims of money or pride, however, those of medicine threaten to kill, a possibility that edges the play's comic farce uncomfortably towards the domain of tragedy.

Mosca's diatribe against doctors, while spoken largely in jest to justify the refusal of a clear poison, identifies the medical profession explicitly with murder, evoking the complaints against doctors cited earlier in this chapter. "[H]e [Volpone] says, they flay a man | Before they kill him," Mosca tells Corbaccio, implicitly identifying financial extortion with the cutting open of bodies;

> And then, they do it by experiment;
> For which the law not only doth absolve 'em,
> But gives them great reward: and he is loath
> To hire his death, so.
>
> (I.iv.27–32)

"It is true, they kill," Corbaccio agrees, "With as much license as a judge." "Nay," Mosca rebuts, "more; | For he but kills, sir, where the law condemns, | And these can kill him, too" (I.iv.32–35). Mosca portrays doctors as wielding an omnipotent power over all men by virtue of their license to experiment and their privileged knowledge, which no one else is qualified to question. Clever, unhampered by accountability, and revelling in the cruelty from which they profit, they sound in fact remarkably like Mosca and Volpone themselves as they enrich their pleasure and wealth by toying with the susceptibility of their gulls. Whereas Mosca's imagined doctors revel in killing their patients, however, Mosca and Volpone engage in a milder cruelty. In keeping with their Venetian world's emphasis on wealth, display, and idle recreation, they are satisfied with the entertainment of humiliating their gulls, as well as collecting money and lavish gifts from them.

Volpone's overpowering delight at a successful performance manifests itself in physical sensation: his body cannot contain his glee and laughter. "O I shall burst," he tells Mosca after their persuasive counterfeiting in front of Corbaccio; "Let out my sides, let out my sides" (I.iv.132–3). The scene's wit exerts a purgative effect on him, leading to the forceful and uncontrollable expulsion of his humors. In response to Mosca's stern "Contain | Your flux of laughter, sir" (I.iv.133–4), he continues unabated, incapable of reining himself in: "O, but thy working, and thy placing it! I cannot hold; good rascal, let me kiss thee: | I never knew thee, in so rare a humor" (I.iv.136–8). Although Volpone prides himself on being part of the performance, he has been a silent and supporting actor at best, and his pleasure here is primarily that of a knowing spectator responding to Mosca's theatrical skill. Mosca, maintaining control, downplays his accomplishment, but similarly phrases it in physiological terms: "I but do, as I am taught; | Follow your grave instructions; give 'em words; | Pour oil into their ears; and send them hence" (I.iv.139–41). Mosca's pragmatic account, rooted in a proverbial expression for deception, identifies theatrical efficacy as a kind of drugging, in which words are the oils, unguents, and elixirs that will intoxicate and incapacitate one's audiences. Although Mosca's "them" technically refers here to the duo's gulls, Volpone, in his intoxicated state, seems to be the exemplary consumer of Mosca's medicating words.

Volpone puts Mosca's model of performance into action, and underlines implicit parallels between the roles of actors and doctors, when he sets aside his primary role of a deathbed invalid to play a doctor himself in order to catch a glimpse of the beautiful Celia. As a word-swirling mountebank, Volpone revels in enacting, with parodic hyperbole, precisely the traits of which Mosca accused doctors in his earlier speech, fused with the playful theatricality that is his own hallmark. This scene, in which Volpone is finally allowed to regale an audience with the full force of his virtuoso verbal skills, offers the play's most explicit reflections on the pleasures and perils of the theater. In locating Volpone's medical parody on a stage, with a large public audience, Jonson identifies the dangers of medical charlatanism with the pleasures and perils of the theater itself.[51]

In his performance as Scoto of Mantua, Volpone purports to sell a miraculous medicine, his "blessed unguento" (II.ii.98), yet his marketing address immediately, and explicitly, evokes the specter of poisoning. "Let me tell you," he vaunts,

I am not, as your Lombard proverb saith, cold on my feet, or content to part with my commodities at a cheaper rate, than I accustomed: look not for it. Nor, that the calumnious reports of that impudent detractor, and shame to our profession—Alessandro Buttone, I mean—who gave out, in public, I was condemned *a sforzato* to the galleys, for poisoning the Cardinal Bembo's—cook, hath at all attached, much less dejected me. (II.ii.40–7)

Volpone's Scoto begins his marketing, ironically, by calling attention to the two most common complaints against mountebanks: their mercenary motives, shown in extortionate pricing, and their propensity for poisoning. By pointing to an accusation of poisoning, even to deny it, Volpone flaunts his vulnerability to suspicion. Wittily parodying the genre he enacts, he virtually invites taunts from the audience, as if testing them—as he routinely does with his gulls—to see how far he can push the limits of their gullibility.

Volpone goes on to escalate the riskiness of his performance. He follows his denial of poisoning by making precisely the same accusation of his rival mountebanks:

These turdy-facy-nasty-paty-lousy-fartical rogues, with one poor groat's-worth of unprepared antimony, finely wrapped up in several *scartoccios*, are able, very well, to kill their twenty a week, and play; yet, these meagre starved spirits, who have half stopped the organs of their minds with earthy oppilations, want not their favourers among your shrivelled, salad-eating artisans: who are overjoyed, that they may have their half-pe'rth of physic, though it purge 'em into another world, 't makes no matter. (II.ii.59–67)

Ironically, when Volpone echoes Mosca's earlier attack on doctors, it is in the guise of a doctor himself. His offhand reference to his rivals' ability "to kill their twenty a week" plays with a standard jest at murderous doctors; in Webster's *The Devil's Law Case*, Romelio similarly boasts of his medical expertise, "Why look you, I can kill my twenty a month | And work but i'th'forenoons."[52] Despite his apparent effort to distinguish himself from the rascals he describes, however, these accusations, fast on the heels of his refutations of similar accusations about himself, serve to underline the unreliability of his own position. This becomes clearer on examining the specific medical practices that Volpone discusses in this passage. Drawing on one of the central features of Galenic medicine, Volpone identifies these dubious medicines as purgatives.[53] Seizing the opportunity to identify his rivals firmly with excrement, he describes them as "turdy-facy" and "fartical" rogues, refers to their "earthy oppilations," or obstructions, and derides their medicines by claiming that they will "purge [their patients] into another world." In particular, he refers to the use of antimony, a popular purgative drug widely noted to be dangerous. Writing of the "*Operation* of *Purging Medicines*, and the *Causes* thereof," Francis Bacon attributed their efficacy to different qualities, one of which, "*secret Malignity*, and disagreement towards *Mans Bodie*" was exemplified "in *Scammony, Mechoacham, Antimony,* &c."[54] Although Bacon counted antimony as a viable medicine despite its disturbing secret malignity, he used this example to point to the tenuous boundary between purgatives and poisons, cautioning that "if there be any *Medicine*, that *Purgeth*, and hath neither of the first two *Manifest Qualities*; it is to be held suspected, as a kinde of *Poysons*; For that it worketh either by *Corrosion*; or by a *secret Malignitie* and Enmitie to *Nature*: And therfore such *Medicines* are warily to be prepared, and vsed."[55] Not only does the odd repetition of "*secret Malignitie*" serve to identify these corrosive and poisonous purgatives with his description of antimony, but Bacon further noted that this drug could bring about particularly dangerous effects: referring to a biting, burning, or prickling sensation, he claimed that "if this *Mordication* be in an ouer-high Degree, it is little better than the *Corrosion* of *Poyson*; And it commeth to passe sometimes in *Antimony*; Especially if it be giuen, to Bodies not repleat with Humors."[56] The drug that Volpone singles out to characterize his rivals' medicine, then, offers a complex and ambivalent set of associations not only with purgation and danger, but with secrecy, malignancy, and poisonous corrosion.

Volpone's attention to the dangers of purgation takes on an added significance, however, in light of the fact that his performance as Scoto closely imitates the medical model that he discusses. Not only does he hawk his own version of a purgative medicine—a "blessed *unguento* . . . that hath only power to disperse all malignant humours" (II.ii.94–5)—but, at another level, he uses his elaborately rhetorical performance to purge his listeners both of their skepticism and of their money. This performance, then, has much in common with the scenes Volpone stages with Mosca, which, as noted earlier, have their own purgative functions: not only do they succeed in ridding gulls of their money, but their entertainment forces Volpone to burst his sides, unable to contain his "flux of laughter" (I.iv.134). In broader terms, moreover, the play's comic wit could be seen as exerting both of these effects on its audience members, who not only pay for their tickets but are also moved to laughter by the play. Although Volpone purports to be selling medicines, his performances themselves can be seen to function as the drugs he is marketing. They are the exotic wares with which he not only dazzles and seduces his audience, but purges them of their skepticism, their laughter, their humors, and their money. In the context of the play's own model for its theatrical workings, Volpone's attention to purgative drugs that gain their efficacy from a secret malignity, bordering on corrosive poison, suggests a warning to the audience.

Despite, or perhaps because of, Volpone's attention to the dangers of the mountebank's trade, his performance wins the admiration of his spectators. Not only does he ultimately achieve his desired effect of luring Celia to her window to purchase his wares, but he quickly earns the approval of the ever-impressionable Sir Politic Would-Be. Just as medical writers worried about the susceptibility of patients to medical fraud, the play mocks the naive gulls who are taken in by Volpone's performance. In reply to Peregrine's casual condemnation of mountebanks as "quacksalvers, | Fellows that live by venting oils and drugs" (II.ii.5–6), Sir Politic Would-Be defensively offers a proud panegyric to their medical knowledge:

> They are the only knowing men of Europe!
> Great general scholars, excellent physicians,
> Most admired statesmen, professed favourites,
> And cabinet counsellors, to the greatest princes!
> The only languaged men, of all the world!
>
> (II.ii.9–13)

Sir Politic's words are characteristically ironic, revealing his inept analysis of what he sees. He is also, however, unwittingly apt. His language offers an intriguing echo of Sejanus's praise of Eudemus: "You're a subtle nation, you physicians!, | And grown the only cabinets, in court, | To ladies' privacies" (I.299–301). Although Volpone has no real medical training, and lacks the political power attributed to medical knowledge, he is knowing: not only in his performance as Scoto, but throughout most (though not all) of the play. Similarly, "languaged" may be the single best description of what is distinctive and alluring about him. "Excellent!," Sir Politic exclaims after listening to Volpone's colorful tirade against rival mountebanks; "Ha' you heard better language, sir?" (II.ii.68). "Is not his language rare?," he interjects again later (II.ii.117). As a comic parody of the susceptible consumer, and the vulnerable audience, Sir Politic points to the hypnotic effects of language as the source of medical and theatrical power.

If Volpone's impersonation of Scoto offers a parody of medical charlatans, it also offers a parody of the theater.[57] Volpone's medical performance portrays the popular stage as a commerce of pleasing lies aimed at naive consumers. As a representative victim of Volpone's medical performance, Sir Politic survives the play with injuries only to his dignity. Celia, whose susceptibility to Volpone's words and wares propels her to a rare moment of self-display during the mountebank scene, ultimately suffers more serious harm. Volpone casts his performances of seduction, both as Scoto and as a Marlovian poet, as offering remedies for both health and beauty: along with "*oglio del Scoto*," his "blessed *unguento*," he offers "the poulder that made Venus a goddess . . . that kept her perpetually young, cleared her wrinkles, firmed her gums, filled her skin, coloured her hair" (II.ii.94,134–5, 236–9). After this alluring display of medicines, ointments, and powders succeeds in the public sphere of the mountebank, however, in the intimate setting of his own house Volpone offers a bolder and more figurative remedy—erotic freedom and pleasure—as a cure for what he sees as Celia's real ailment, confinement by an old and jealous husband. "Why should we defer our joys?," he asks her; "Thou hast in place of a base husband found | A worthy lover . . . See, behold | What thou art queen of" (III.vii.174, 185–8). To Celia, however, his lascivious apparent remedy is worse than poisons or disease: "flay my face," she urges him, "Or poison it with ointments for seducing | Your blood to this rebellion" (III.vii.251–3). As her plea for flaying or poison suggests, Volpone's apparent chivalry quickly reveals itself as the violence it actually is: in the face of this horrified refusal, he resorts to insisting "Yield, or I'll force thee" (III.vii.265). His romanticized idea that he is offering a solution to Celia's problems is turned inside out: the cure is more dangerous than the disease. Like antimony with its secret malignancy, the alluring "unguento" of Volpone's mountebank performance proves a risky drug. While it may not be literally poisonous, the exposure, abduction, and near-rape which it produces suggests that it is not only spiritually toxic, but physically dangerous as well.

Although Celia is the most obvious victim of Volpone's performance, the consequences of this scene may ultimately fall hardest on

Volpone himself. The loss of control that leads him, uncharacter-istically, to misread his audience and overreach himself, sets into motion the events that lead to his trial and eventual punishment. Crucially, like Sejanus, Volpone is revealed to be not only an actor, but also a vulnerable audience, even while performing. After looking upon Celia at her window, he borrows a typically Petrarchan vocabulary to profess himself "wounded": "angry Cupid, bolting from her eyes, | Hath shot himself into me, like a flame" (II.iv.1, 3–4). As in his earlier responses to Mosca's performances, Volpone per-ceives the impact of this spectacle in starkly physical, sensual terms: "My liver melts, and I, without the hope | Of some soft air, from her refreshing breath, | Am but a heap of cinders" (II.iv.9–11). This sen-sation of overwhelming heat represents a very different physiological response from the laughter provoked by Mosca's performance, and one which, though pleasurable in itself, requires an antidote, of more of the same. When Mosca persuades Celia's husband to bring her to Volpone's sickbed, it is under guise of medical benefit: "the college of physicians," he explains, have insisted that "some young woman must be straight sought out, | Lusty, and full of juice, to sleep by him" (II.vi.27, 34–5). Volpone, the would-be actor and doctor, turns out to be both audience and patient. Although as Scoto he offers alluring displays and medicines for the delight of his audiences, Celia, his apparent audience, has herself unwittingly become the alluring dis-play and medicine for his delight.

Volpone's susceptibility to Celia's beauty, and the recklessly staged assault to which it leads him, ultimately brings him to trial for judgment by the magistrates of Venice. If the trial is meant to be a remedy against injustice, however, it fails; Volpone continues to masquerade successfully as an impotent old man, supported by the perjured testimony of his greedy gulls. Yet the strain of this public performance diminishes his control and strength, converting his feigned ailments into real ones. "I ne'er was in dislike with my dis-guise," he soliloquizes,

> Till this fled moment; here, 'twas good, in private,
> But, in your public—*Cavé*, whilst I breathe.
> 'Fore God, my left leg 'gan to have the cramp
> And I apprehended, straight, some power had struck me
> With a dead palsy.
>
> (V.i.2–7)

Much like Jonson himself, who preferred small, intimate audiences of educated people, and complained at the indignities of having to expose his plays to the poor judgment of the masses at public theaters, Volpone is undone by the expanded scale of his performance.[58] Both weakened by his success and intoxicated by the "bowl of lusty wine" that he drinks "to fright I This humor from [his] heart" (V.i.11–12), he becomes bolder in his theatrical addiction and aspirations: "Any device, now, of rare, ingenious knavery, I That would possess me with a violent laughter, I Would make me up, again!" (V.i.14–16). Driven by a desperate need to regain the triumphant thrill of his earlier theatrical successes, he ultimately takes on the one role—death—that he cannot cast off without turning himself back over to the magistrates.

The play finally produces a legal remedy with the last and unobstructed trial, when the magistrates and the play cast their judgment on Volpone's play-acting and bring all involved to justice. His gulls, implicated by greed and perjury, are subjected to punishment: Voltore is dispossessed and confined to a monastery to die, and Corvino is condemned to be displayed as a spectacle of humiliation, with his eyes "beat out with stinking fish" (V.xii.140). In a curious turnabout from the usual triumphs of Jonson's witty pranksters, though, Volpone's and Mosca's dissembling exploits harm themselves more seriously than anyone else: Mosca is whipped and jailed, and Volpone is ordered "to lie in prison, cramped with irons, I Till thou be'st sick, and lame indeed" (V.xii.123–4).[59] Theatrical performance, conceived by Volpone as a restorative bringing new life and vivacity to his mundane existence, instead brings pain, in both body and mind, to its actors and audiences alike. From another perspective, though, these punishments recall the play's interest in purgative medicines: with Mosca and Volpone expunged from the social body of Venice, the city can now return to health.

The play's ending raises the larger question of how Volpone's performance has affected the play's audiences. Speaking the epilogue, Volpone tells us

> The seasoning of a play is the applause.
> Now, though the Fox be punished by the laws,
> He, yet, doth hope there is no suffering due
> For any fact, which he hath done 'gainst you.

If there be, censure him: here he, doubtful, stands.
If not, fare jovially, and clap your hands.

(V.xii.152–7)

By asking his audience to season the play, Jonson employs a culinary metaphor to present its performance as a commodity to be eaten, or preserved for later. Linking the play's interests in consumable commodities to its trial scene, he then turns to a legal vocabulary as an alternative means of conceptualizing remedies for damage. Although the epilogue is in many ways conventional in inviting the audience to vote on the play's success, it is striking that what is in question is not whether they like the play, but whether Volpone has harmed them in the performing of it.[60] The ambiguous "if there be [suffering]," and the implicit comparison with the harm Volpone has done against others, hint at the possibility that the spectators, along with the play's internal audiences, will not emerge unscathed. Alternatively, however, if the audience offers their applause, they are both preserving the play's ingredients and in effect acquitting Volpone of his criminal convictions: reversing, that is, the judgment of the magistrates, and affirming the play's mischievous play-acting.[61] By putting Volpone on trial yet again, Jonson casts the play's spectators as the ultimate judges of the ambivalent theatricality that the play explores. In so doing, however, he is implicitly putting them on trial as well, testing their moral judgment. Will they censure or clap, and which is the correct response? Can their seasoning, for that matter, temper and cure the play's contents? The ambiguous ending leaves these questions uncertain, and the audience uncomfortable.

While the cruelty of the play's ending may come as an implicit rebuke to spectators, who are encouraged by much of the play's structure to identify with the protagonists' lively escapades, Jonson insisted that this harshness had a medicinal effect, and that *Volpone* should be taken as offering a moral lesson. The play's prologue declares its didactic purpose by way of a standard Horatian dictum: "In all his poems, still, has been this measure, | To mix profit with your pleasure" (Prologue, 4 and 7–8). In the dedicatory letter to Oxford and Cambridge with which he prefaced the play, Jonson famously justified the harshness of his ending by claiming that "my special aim being to put the snaffle in their mouths that cry out, we never punish vice in our interludes, &c., I took the more liberty" (Epistle, 113–15). Comedy, seen by many of his contemporaries as an essentially festive genre, was to him a vehicle for assailing audiences with the rigor of social imperatives, and thereby improving them morally, as noted in his comment, cited earlier, about using "sharp medicines or corrosives" in the cure of the mind.

With its ruthless wit and willingness to punish, *Volpone* embodies Jonson's idea of sharp verbal medicine. Yet if the play is a purgative cure, as Volpone's antics suggest, it is not clear which of the play's models for audiences might apply to the external audience who watch the play. Will the play purge the audience primarily of its money, as it does to its gulls, or its laughter, as it does to Volpone? For that matter, does the play present the forced expulsion of laughter, with its consequent loss of self-control, as necessarily desirable?[62] Jonson's critical writings suggest that the play's spectators should emerge improved by the experience, but the play's variable and ambiguous models for spectatorship leave it unclear exactly how and whether that improvement might come about.

If Jonson aspired to improve his audiences, he equally fervently wanted to improve the health of the public stage. His attacks on the theater were notorious, at times sharper than complaints brought by self-professed enemies of the stage. In his preface to *Volpone*, he complained "that now, especially in *dramatic*, or (as they term it) *stage poetry*, nothing but ribaldry, profanation, blasphemy, all licence of offence to God, and man, is practised" (Epistle, 35–8). The kinds of theatrical performance that he presented in *Sejanus* and *Volpone*, while very different from each other, both suggest troubling goals and effects. Framed in the conspiratorial politics of imperial Rome, Sejanus and Tiberius pursue manipulative and murderous plots in the service of insatiable appetite for power: "Is there not something more than to be Caesar?," Sejanus wonders; "Must we rest there?" (V.13–14). And although Volpone and Mosca direct their performances in the service of personal pleasures—in keeping with their lavish Venetian setting and comic genre—these pleasures, which consist of profit, seduction, and laughter at others' humiliations, are themselves mercenary and rapacious.

The plays do not stop at critique, however. Unlike most antitheatricalists, Jonson clearly delighted in the play-acting games he depicted, even as he also worried about them. On a broader scale, he wanted the theater not abolished, but reformed. Both plays, accordingly, turn to ambivalent drugs not only to frame their indictments of theatrical dissimulation, but to imagine ways in which theater could function as a beneficial, though often bitter, medicine. If the comforting and mind-numbing diversions of Sejanus's imagined juleps, opiates, apozems, and magistral syrups evoke Jonson's complaints about the cheap pleasures of the popular stage, the forcefully cathartic remedies which the play's trials offer—the poisons, or quasi-poisons, of Scoto's antimony and Tiberius's searing aconite—offer powerful, if painful, models for expelling impurities and beginning again. Webster, who clearly shared Jonson's impatience with contemporary plays and audiences, seems to have found this cathartic model compelling, even if more for the punitive damage it caused than for the new possibilities it offered. In *The White Devil*, his identification of Vittoria's seductive beauty with the grotesque but magical efficacy of mummia, as well as the subtle but piercing force of mercury, suggest a vision of theater as exerting a powerful, seductive, but ultimately hazardous impact on spectators. Although these two playwrights identify theater with different sorts of medical effects, both turn to powerful but dangerous drugs to portray plays as transforming both the minds and bodies of their spectators.

2

"A Thing Like Death": Shakespeare's Narcotic Theater

While the plays in the prior chapter explore a wide range of threatening medicines, two of Shakespeare's plays—*Romeo and Juliet* and *Antony and Cleopatra*—examine a specific category of risky substances: narcotic, or soporific, drugs. Unlike medicines intended solely to improve health, soporific drugs suggest a broader notion of remedy, directed simultaneously towards health, in the form of improved sleep, and pleasure, in the form of a languorous, quasi-erotic oblivion. Straying outside the boundaries of traditionally defined medical needs into the arena of luxury or indulgence, these drugs—typically based on opium or mandrake—generated both excitement and anxiety more intensely than standard medicines. In the plays explored in this chapter, Shakespeare, like contemporary medical writers, presents the effects of sleeping potions as hovering uneasily between remedial and harmful; in the process, he also portrays other desired remedies, such as erotic love, as similarly ambivalent. By linking these troubled remedies with metatheatrical reflections on the effects of spectacles on spectators, moreover, he casts the ambivalent escapist pleasures of narcotic drugs as a metaphor for the theater itself. Whereas Jonson and Webster portray plays as bitter medicines for social and moral ailments, Shakespeare presents them here as misleadingly soothing potions that lull spectators into dreamlike escapes, with uncertain consequences.

If the sleeping potions of *Romeo and Juliet* and *Antony and Cleopatra* reflect the form of the plays, they also underline the difficulty in classifying that form. As Shakespeare's only double tragedies and, along with *Othello*, his only ventures into the Italianate "tragedy of love," the plays represent a hybrid genre intrinsically divided between the domain of tragedy (death) and that of comedy (erotic desire).[1] The narcotic soporific drink, with its ambiguous position between medicine and poison, reflects this uncertain status: if the promise of ease, pleasure, and reawakening links sleeping potions with the realm of comedy, their implicit threat of death evokes the specter of tragedy as well. While the nature of these potions is uncertain for much of these plays, their final casting as poisons turns the plays' endings towards tragedy, and yet suggests that the poison of tragedy may be, in its own paradoxical way, medicinal.

Although *Romeo and Juliet* (1594–6) and *Antony and Cleopatra* (1606–7) mark very different points in Shakespeare's career, the two plays show striking parallels with each other, suggesting that the later play in many ways represents a revised version of the earlier. Shakespeare's return to ambiguous sleeping potions, years after exploring them the first time, demonstrates the development of his ideas about the effects of dramatic spectacles on spectators. As an actor, writer, and share-holder in London's commercial theaters, Shakespeare would certainly have been familiar with the debates surrounding plays, and the extensive metatheatrical reflections in his plays show that he actively grappled with questions about the nature and consequences of theatergoing. Through examining the treatment of drugs in the two plays, this chapter argues that both identify theatrical performances with ambivalent soporific remedies, but that *Antony and Cleopatra* builds on Shakespeare's intervening years of experience in the theater to make a more forceful claim about the theatrical self-awareness behind plays' powerful and dangerous effects on spectators.

ACCIDENTAL CONSUMERS: *ROMEO AND JULIET*

The device of the sleeping potion in *Romeo and Juliet* occupies a crucial intersection between the play's twin poles of desire and death and, similarly, between its warring genres of comedy and tragedy.[2] While many critics see Mercutio's death as the dividing point between the play's comic beginning and tragic ending, early foreshadowing and ongoing elements of farce show that the play's generic fortunes stay intertwined much longer. The sleeping potion and, by association, the imaginative realm of sleep and dreams temporarily suspend the play's identity, holding out the possibility of a return to comedy by offering the lovers the means to escape a tragic ending. The foreclosure of this possibility does not come about until the events catalyzed by the sleeping potion culminate in Romeo's fatal poison, which, even then, is described as a remedy returning the lovers to each other.

From the outset of the play, its primary problem—the misery caused by erotic love—is identified with the dangerous power of visual spectacles to destroy their onlookers. In his first scenes, Romeo is incapacitated with longing for Rosaline's unattainable beauty, but the proposed remedies mirror his troubles. When Benvolio advises him to "give liberty unto thine eye" (I.i.225), Romeo protests that gazing upon other women would only intensify his unhappiness by emphasizing Rosaline's incomparable perfection. Even Benvolio implicitly suggests that the solution may be at least as painful as the problem:

> Tut, man, one fire burns out another's burning;
> One pain is lessen'd by another's anguish;
> Turn giddy, and be holp by backward turning.
> One desperate grief cures with another's languish;
> Take thou some new infection to thy eye,
> And the rank poison of the old will die.
>
> (I.ii.45–50)

Even before Juliet has entered the play, her imminent appearance in Romeo's life is identified with the effect of a poison, albeit a curative one. Despite the comic ease and apparently pragmatic intentions of Benvolio's advice, the solution he offers has a distinctly dark undertone. His easy symmetries and correspondingly neat rhymes suggest that his cure will only replace one "anguish" and "desperate grief" with another: Juliet may be a remedy, but she will ultimately cause as much pain as does Rosaline, the infection that she is meant to treat.

After the sight of Juliet has jolted Romeo out of one crisis and into the next, Benvolio's vocabulary of poisonous cures echoes in Friar Lawrence's meditations on the powers and perils of medicinal herbs. Musing over the "baleful weeds and precious-juiced flowers" he collects (II.iii.4), the Friar considers the double-edged potential of his plants:

> Within the infant rind of this weak flower
> Poison hath residence, and medicine power:

> For this, being smelt, with that part cheers each part;
> Being tasted, stays all senses with the heart.
> Two such opposed kings encamp them still
> In man as well as herbs: grace and rude will;
> And where the worser is predominant
> Full soon the canker death eats up that plant.
>   (II.iii.19–26)

In explicating how herbal concoctions contain the potential for both poison and medicine, the Friar can be seen as unwittingly describing the erotic passion that the play dramatizes. The flower's "infant rind," with its evocation of newness, vulnerability, and yet the containment of powerful, if ambivalent, forces, suggests the lovers' passion, which has only just begun, but is already transforming Verona's social landscape.[3] The Friar's emphasis on the tension between the two "opposed kings," similarly, calls to mind the feud which lies at the core of the play. His reduction of the conflict, however, to an opposition between grace and "rude will," or lust, offers too simple an understanding of passion, one at odds with the portrait offered by the play itself. By differentiating between the scent, which cures, and the taste, which kills, the Friar suggests that the primary distinction between cordial and poison is one of degree: love may be broached, but not consumed. Although his identification of desire with the triumph of "the canker death" accurately foreshadows the play's ending, his moralistic condemnation of passion runs counter to the play, both in the playful celebrations of love endorsed by its comic moments, and in the solemnity ultimately bestowed on the lovers in the tragic ending.

Framed between Romeo's unseen entrance and his interruption to announce his love for Juliet and his request to be wed, the Friar's speech implicitly associates the lovers' fate with the equivocal effects of medicinal herbs. Romeo echoes this vocabulary in his plea for the Friar's support of his marriage: "Both our remedies," he tells the Friar, "Within thy help and holy physic lie" (II.iii.47–8). Unfortunately, as the Friar's musings have just shown, the "remedies" of his "holy physic" are distinctly risky. Not only are his professional judgment and authority shown to be questionable, casting doubt on his fitness to diagnose and cure the problems of the play, but his ingredients are in themselves profoundly ambivalent, as capable of killing as of curing.

The overlay of pharmacy, desire, and death in the Friar's speech is echoed in the following act, when he and his holy physic are called upon for another remedy: this time to the lovers' enforced separation after Romeo's banishment for Tybalt's death. In its presentation of one lover's apparent death and the other's readiness to die in response, this curious middle act provides an odd, almost farcical, foreshadowing of the play's ending. Because this crisis not only is resolved but leads to the consummation of the lovers' marriage, moreover, its events also offer a comic alternative to the ending, showing how easily the play's genre could be turned on its head.

After Romeo's duel with Tybalt, Juliet's query for news of her love elicits a characteristically confused and frantic exclamation from her nurse: "he's dead, he's dead, he's dead! | We are undone, lady, we are undone. | Alack the day, he's gone, he's kill'd, he's dead" (III.ii.37–9). The nurse's unwitting presentation of Romeo's apparent death has very different effects on her immediate audience, Juliet, and her broader audience, those watching the play. To the external audience, with their comfortable knowledge that Romeo is still alive, the nurse's breathless and repetitive hysteria, combined with the clarification that quickly follows, makes this scene a comic parody of a death-announcement.[4] Despite the conventional understanding that the play becomes a tragedy after Mercutio's death, the nurse's misinformation introduces anxiety, but fails to undermine the elated freedom of the lovers' comic world.

To the woefully underinformed Juliet, however, this hypothetical death is a figurative poison:

> Hath Romeo slain himself? Say thou but "Ay"
> And that bare vowel "I" shall poison more
> Than the death-darting eye of cockatrice.
>
> (III.ii.45–7)

As long as Romeo's death remains in the realm of language—and uncertain language at that—Juliet's poisons remain limited to language as well. The wounding power of the letter "I" goes deep, however, evoking the play's broader concerns, especially in its courtship scenes, with the vulnerability of the eye, or "I," to the darts of love.[5] The letter's poisons prove powerful; in response to the nurse's confirming chorus of "I"s,[6] Juliet immediately leaps to proclamations of suicide: "Vile earth to earth resign, end motion here, | And thou and Romeo press one heavy bier" (III.ii.59–60). Lacking the protective mediation of the audience's knowledge, Juliet experiences the nurse's words as near-fatal potions.

Even when it becomes clear that Romeo is still alive, news of his banishment and her wedding to Paris is enough to inspire doom, propelling Juliet's search for counter-potions. "I'll to the Friar to know his remedy," she announces; "If all else fail, myself have power to die" (III.v.241–2). As an alternative to death, the Friar's remedy is presented as its matched opposite. Once again, both the lovers' remedies lie within the Friar's help and holy physic; Juliet's figurative poisons hover uneasily between the threat of literalization and the promise of being replaced with medicinal cures.

Juliet echoes the juxtaposition of remedy and death when she confronts the Friar himself: "If in thy wisdom thou canst give no help, | Do thou but call my resolution wise, | And with this knife I'll help it presently" (IV.i.52–4). "I long to die," she repeats shortly, "If what thou speak'st speak not of remedy" (IV.i.66–7). In introducing the remedy of the sleeping potion, Friar Lawrence echoes Juliet in linking it with death, but to him the two are joined by similarity rather than opposition. If she has the strength of will to kill herself, he suggests,

> Then is it likely thou wilt undertake
> A thing like death to chide away this shame,
> That cop'st with death himself to scape from it.
> And, if thou dar'st, I'll give thee remedy.
> (IV.i.73–6)

As a "thing like death," the potion—or the comatose state it will induce—is intended to divert Juliet from "death himself," functioning as an apotropaic remedy.[7] But the likeness is so persuasive that the distinction becomes uncomfortably blurred. Even Juliet questions the drug's reliability, wondering "What if it be a poison, which the Friar | Subtly hath minister'd to have me dead . . .?" (IV.iii.24–5). This threat becomes a certainty to those who look upon her apparent corpse the following morning: unable to wake her, the nurse cries hysterically: "Lady! Lady! Lady! | Alas, alas! Help, help! My lady's dead!"; and, "She's dead, deceas'd! She's dead! Alack the day!" (IV.v.13–14, 23). Just as the perceived proclamation of Romeo's death affected Juliet as a poison, Juliet's own apparent corpse—the by-product of an intended remedy—proves devastating to its onstage audiences.

While the nurse's grief is sincere—and the play's audience, in fact, cannot be sure that she is mistaken in believing Juliet dead—the echoes of farce in her frenzied interjections remind us that the idea of the contrived false death as a plot device is typically a motif of comedy, or tragicomedy.[8] Typically, the eventual discovery that the death is not real provides renewed grounds for festive celebration; Juliet's temporary belief in Romeo's death, shortly followed by both the discovery that he was alive and the consummation of the lovers' marriage, partly fits this model. With the advent of the sleeping potion, however, the generic rules change: the nurse's wails are simultaneously wrong-headed and prophetic, and our laughter is uneasy. While false deaths in comedy tend to be constructed of rumor only, Juliet's is built of the more binding force of chemical intervention, a more dangerous realm for experimentation. The nurse's mistaken assumption will become true: Juliet's ambiguous potion ultimately, if indirectly, proves fatal.

Juliet's sleep has an uneasy dramatic status: as a likeness or imitation of death, it looks ahead to the tragedy of the play's ending, yet as an apotropaic substitute for actual death, it suggests the prototypically comic possibility of young lovers' triumph over adversity. In the first half of the play, sleep is associated with the carefree world of comedy. The Friar explicitly identifies it with the comforts of youth: "But where unbruised youth with unstuff'd brain | Doth couch his limbs, there golden sleep doth reign" (II.iii.33–4). Similarly, Romeo associates sleep with serenity and ease. "Sleep dwell upon thine eyes, peace in thy breast," he calls to the departing Juliet, "Would I were sleep and peace so sweet to rest" (II.ii.186–7). Like the potions that induce it, sleep promises a remedy to the problems brought on by erotic love, and yet at the same time threatens to intensify them.

Juliet's artificial sleep, the pivot of the play's action, becomes the occasion for her own private theater. "My dismal scene I needs must act alone," she comments before drinking the Friar's potion (IV.iii.19). Shakespeare emphasizes the dangers of her performance of death in his attention to its powerful effects on her audiences—the nurse, her parents, and ultimately Romeo—but even before she undertakes it, her anticipations of its potentially nightmarish consequences evoke the play's concerns with ambivalent remedies:

> Alack, alack! Is it not like that I
> So early waking, what with loathsome smells
> And shrieks like mandrakes torn out of the earth,
> That living mortals, hearing them, run mad . . .?
> (IV.iii.45–8)

Juliet's terror of the uncertain state that she will be entering leads her aptly to thoughts of mandrakes. A source of much fascination in the Renaissance, the mandrake, like Friar Lawrence's herbs, was understood to be both poisonous and medicinal.[9] As a medicine, it was believed to have soporific and aphrodisiac powers, linking it with Juliet's sleeping potion as well as with the love that necessitates it.[10] As the name suggests, mandrakes were also considered quasi-human: William Bullein wrote that "this hearbe is called also *Anthropomorphos* because it beareth the Image of a man."[11] Bullein also recorded the popular lore that "this herbe commeth of the seede of some conuicted dead men," and that when the root was dug up, bystanders would hear "the terreble shriek and cry of thys Mandrack. In which cry, it Doth not only dye it selfe, but the feare thereof kylleth the Dogge or Beast, whych pulled it out of the earth."[12] Webster's Duchess of Malfi, in a curious inversion of Juliet's quest, calls for death to be like mandrake: "Come, violent death, | Serve for mandragora to make me sleep" (IV.ii.231–2).[13] Simultaneously animate and inanimate, fertile and fatal, medicine and poison, the mandrake that haunts Juliet's imagination on the verge of her sleep suggests the suspended play of oppositions that her performance of sleep embodies.

Just as the accidental specter of Romeo's false death is succeeded by Juliet's actively engineered false death, Juliet's waking nightmares are followed by Romeo's dream of his own death. "If I may trust the flattering truth of sleep," Romeo rather inauspiciously opens the final act,

> My dreams presage some joyful news at hand.
> My bosom's lord sits lightly in his throne
> And all this day an unaccustom'd spirit
> Lifts me above the ground with cheerful thoughts.
> I dreamt my lady came and found me dead—
> Strange dream that gives a dead man leave to think!—
> And breath'd such life with kisses in my lips
> That I reviv'd and was an emperor.
> Ah me, how sweet is love itself possess'd
> When but love's shadows are so rich in joy.
>
> (V.i.1–11)

Romeo's naive faith in "the flattering truth of sleep" continues his belief, expressed earlier to Mercutio, in a dream as a negative omen.[14] This second dream marks a curious half-truth; as Marjorie

Garber points out, it is true that he will die and that Juliet will kiss him, although unfortunately he will not revive nor become an emperor.[15] Romeo's dream, like those Mercutio attributes to Queen Mab, represents a wish rather than a true prediction. Just as Juliet's sleep is arranged to evade the catastrophe of having to marry Paris, so Romeo's sleep offers an escape from the doom he has envisioned, promising to replace the tragic ending of death with the comic ending of an erotic consummation.

Both the lovers' sleeps, however, are only temporary; far from fulfilling the positive transformation they promise, they eventually bring about that which they sought to avert. Juliet's performance of death leads to its actuality. News of her death reaches Romeo through an unwittingly accurate euphemism: "Her body sleeps in Capels monument" (V.i.18). In response, Romeo vows to enter the same figurative sleep, cast in erotic terms: "Well, Juliet, I will lie with thee tonight. | Let's see for means" (V.i.34–5). While the false report of Romeo's death led to figurative and false poisons, and eventually to Juliet's false death, Juliet's more persuasive counterfeit of death leads to real poisons and Romeo's real death, which will itself be reflected back in her own actual death. Dangerous potions serve as the catalyst to a series of increasingly authentic performances: each one, by imitating the apparent death to which it responds, moves closer to the real thing.

Following the same trajectory, the play's drugs become both increasingly literal and increasingly dangerous. The figurative poisons that Juliet invokes on believing Romeo dead, as well as the ambivalent medicinal herbs mulled over by Friar Lawrence and the pseudo-poisons of her sleeping potion, become actual poisons when Romeo learns of her apparent death. Romeo's encounter with the apothecary parallels Juliet's visit to Friar Lawrence, but at an even higher pitch of desperation. Unlike the Friar, who volunteers his drugs, the apothecary sells his poisons under pressure and against his will, and whereas Juliet earlier sought temporary solutions for temporal problems—separation, exile, imposed marriage—Romeo seeks a final remedy for an apparently permanent ending:

> Let me have
> A dram of poison, such soon-speeding gear
> As will disperse itself through all the veins,
> That the life-weary taker may fall dead,
> And that the trunk may be discharg'd of breath

> As violently as hasty powder fir'd
> Doth hurry from the fatal cannon's womb.
>
> (V.i.59–65)

Romeo's odd assimilation of poison to gunpowder implicitly identifies death with rebirth, imagining the fatal shot as newly emerging
from a womb.[16] The figure also closely recalls the Friar's evocation of
gunpowder in expressing his early concern over the intensity of the
lovers' infatuation: "These violent delights have violent ends I And in
their triumph die, like fire and powder, I Which as they kiss consume" (II.vi.9–11). In evoking this earlier reference, Romeo's words
appropriate the scale and force of a cannon for his own humbler
means of death; they also serve to identify his suicidal frenzy with the
passion that led to it.

Romeo's actual death underlines the contradictions identified
with the play's potions and generic tensions. He explicitly identifies
his fatal drug as a remedy—"cordial, and not poison" (V.i.85)—and,
in his final words, casts death as a marriage, a reunion with Juliet.
"Here's to my love," he cries before drinking his poison; "O true
apothecary, I Thy drugs are quick. Thus with a kiss I die"
(V.iii.119–20). As M. M. Mahood notes, these final lines embody
their own paradox; the apothecary's drugs are "quick" in the sense
both of speedy and of life-giving, in that they return him to Juliet.[17]
Moments later a horrified Juliet echoes him both in action and in
words:

> What's here? A cup clos'd in my true love's hand?
> Poison, I see, hath been his timeless end.
> O churl. Drunk all, and left no friendly drop
> To help me after? I will kiss thy lips.
> Haply some poison yet doth hang on them
> To make me die with a restorative.[18]
>
> (V.iii.161–6)

Like Romeo's "quick" drugs, Juliet's hope to "die with a restorative" highlights the paradoxical status of the various potions that
haunt the play: each represents a remedy that ultimately fails. The
Friar's mock-poison is intended as a kind of love potion, a vehicle
returning Juliet to Romeo, yet it ultimately robs her of her love by
bringing about his suicide. Similarly, the apothecary's real poison
purports to offer Romeo a reunion with his wife in death, but prevents him from a nearly achieved reunion while still living. Despite

these bleak consequences, however, the lovers both die in a marital embrace, suggesting that at some level their potions have managed to bring them back together.

The lovers' marriage-in-death offers a darkly parodic version of the ending that would make the play a comedy. With it, however, the play's uneasy generic rivalry seems to end on the side of tragedy. After the audience's expectations have been disarmed by the play's affiliations with comedy, and especially by the elated consummation after Romeo's false death, this turn carries a sudden and even startling force, despite the familiarity of the story and the warning with which the chorus opened the play. Lulling its spectators into a soothing pleasure before revealing its more serious—if also pleasurable—dangers, the play itself mimics the ambivalent potions that it dramatizes.

NARCOTIC POTIONS, NARCOTIC PLAYS

Although *Romeo and Juliet* may offer the most famous dramatization of the confusion of narcotic with poison and of artificially-induced sleep with death, the device recurs throughout contemporary plays. Barabas, in Marlowe's *Jew of Malta*, recounts employing such a potion to escape notice, and punishment: "I drank poppy and cold mandrake juice; | And being asleep, belike they thought me dead" (V.i.81–2). Similarly, the queen in Shakespeare's *Cymbeline* is foiled in her attempt to poison Imogen when it turns out that her doctor substituted a sleeping potion for a poison. In Edward Sharpham's *The Fleire*, the Knight's attempt to poison Sparke and Ruffel is later revealed as unsuccessful when they awaken; in John Day's *Law Tricks*, the Counts Lurdo and Horatio are surprised when Lurdo's wife reappears to confront them after apparently having been poisoned by them; and Don John in Dekker's *Match Me in London* is similarly confronted with Don Valasco's survival of his poisoning.[19] Throughout these generically unstable plays, as in *Romeo and Juliet*, the sleeping potion becomes a pivot on which the play's ambiguity turns: it suspends the plot, holding out the simultaneous possibilities of death and rebirth. The recurrence of the motif suggests that narcotics held a special appeal to playwrights and audiences. The sleep that these potions induce onstage, moreover, parallels the suspension of time and identity produced in spectators by plays themselves, suggesting that these drugs offer not only a useful plot device, but a broader metatheatrical significance for the drama.

Playwrights' interest in the ambivalent pleasures of sleeping potions was informed by the radical shifts in early modern pharmacy discussed in the introduction. As noted, epidemics of plague and syphilis, combined with escalating interest in the chemical medicine of Paracelsus and other continental scientists, led to a surge in the use of the powerful, though often toxic, remedies. Medical accounts of the seductive overlay of pleasure and danger associated with soporific drugs, in particular, offered a compelling vocabulary for a theatrical establishment fascinated by this juxtaposition, especially in light of similar characterizations of the theater itself. Opium, newly popular as a treatment for plague, attracted both awe and trepidation. Thomas Bretnor's 1618 English translation of an Italian book on opium argued that the drug "doth merit to bee called the onely soueraigne salue for languishing people, seeing it ceaseth all their griefe, strengthneth their inward parts, maintaineth naturall heate, and produceth such miracles in nature, that none can imagine, but such as haue experience of the same."[20] Although many agreed with these rapturous claims for both health and comfort, others warned that these effects were deceptive, and temporary. Describing the increased use of opium during the plague, the physician Eleazer Dunk wrote in 1606 that the drug "was very acceptable to patients for a while, for it stayed the violent flowing of the humors, it procured present sleepe, and mitigated paine."[21] Ultimately, though, Dunk argued, its effects were fatal: "a great number had their lives cut off; some died sleeping, being stupied with that poisoned medicine."[22]

Although opium was the drug most commonly attacked for using the lure of pleasure and sleepy oblivion to seduce patients into unknown dangers, other new and controversial drugs incurred similar complaints. After the appearance of tobacco in England in the late sixteenth century, as noted in the introduction, celebrations of its miraculous medical properties were punctuated with complaints about a wide range of dangers, including narcotic effects. The physician Edmund Gardiner noted in 1610 that it brought about "an infirmitie like vnto drunkennes, & many times sleep, as after the taking of *Opium*";[23] Henry Buttes wrote in 1599 that it "Mortifieth and benummeth: causeth drowsinesse: troubleth & dulleth the sences: makes (as it were) drunke";[24] and Tobias Venner found in 1621 that "it ouerthroweth the spirites, perverteth the vnderstanding, and confoundeth the senses with a sodayne astonishment and stupidity of the whole body."[25] Although tobacco was more commonly seen as a stimulant than a soporific drug, its affinities with the pleasurable oblivion of drunkenness attracted attention and concern. Like opium, it occupied an uneasy position on the boundary between medicine and pleasure, and its remedial capacities were, accordingly, deeply suspect.

Complaints about the growing popularity of dangerous narcotic drugs echoed throughout the medical community, which drew on their dangers to emphasize a line of continuity between sleep and death. *Bulleins Bulwarke of Defence* (1579) claimed of poppy that "it causeth deepe deadly sleapes."[26] Similarly, in 1580 the physician Timothy Bright warned that opium must be taken in very small doses, "least it cast the patient into such a sleepe, as hee needeth the trumpet of the Archangell to awake him."[27] Philip Barrough echoed, in 1596, that with soporific drugs, "you may cause him to sleepe so, that you can awake him no more."[28] And lastly, in 1599 André Du Laurens wrote, "in the vse of all these stupefactiue medicines taken inwardly, wee must take heed to deale with very good aduise, for feare that in stead of desiring to procure rest vnto the sillie melancholie wretch, wee cast him into an endlesse sleepe."[29] The recurring medical pronouncements on this topic both testify to anxieties about the use (and overuse) of narcotic drugs, and emphasize the perceived fragility of the boundary between ordinary sleep and the endless sleep of death. Once the patient falls asleep, they suggest, the force of inertia, if given any assistance, will keep him that way. Shakespeare, whose son-in-law John Hall was a prominent physician, could hardly help but be aware of these concerns.[30] In the context of these portraits of sleeping drugs, Juliet's decline from slumber into death seems an inevitable response to Friar Lawrence's would-be remedy.

As the emphasis on the link between sleep and death suggests, fears about artificial sleeping drugs drew on concerns not only about pharmacy, but about sleep itself.[31] Sleep was widely seen as a remedy crucial to well-being: Sala's *Opiologica* refers to Paracelsus as claiming "that sleepe is such a great secret in Physicke, that being spoken without disgrace of other things hee would gladly haue any man tell him where he can *in all the world* find such a remedie, which can manifest such sodaine and actiue ease and reliefe, to the health of mans bodie as it doth."[32] At the same time, however, it was also seen as a near-relation to death. Medical accounts of sleep refer to its

capacity for enervation as well as restoration; Du Laurens describes
it as "the withdrawing of the spirits and naturall heate, from the outward parts, to the inward, and from all the circumference vnto the
center."[33] Paré expands on this definition, depicting sleep as

the rest of the whole body, and the cessation of the Animall facultie from
sense and motion. Sleepe is caused, when the substance of the braine is possessed, and after some sort overcome and dulled by a certaine vaporous,
sweete and delightsome humidity; or when the spirits almost exhaust by performance of some labour, cannot any longer sustaine the weight of the
body.[34]

Paré's description, like that of Du Laurens, portrays sleep as a temporary death, a cessation from sense and motion. The mind slips into
suspension—possessed, overcome, and dulled, losing any possibility
of control—while simultaneously the spirits lack the strength to
sustain the body. In fact, the medical disorder of excessive sleep is
explicitly linked with the idea of death; Barrough lists a lengthy catalog of sleep disorders that, somewhat monotonously, all come to be
equated with death.[35] Like soporific drugs, sleep is understood as
containing both medicinal and poisonous potential.

The representation of sleep in the theater shares these doctors' emphasis on the proximity of sleep and death, and the fragility of the
boundary between them. As David Bevington noted, both characters
and audiences have difficulties at times distinguishing between the
two states.[36] In *A Midsummer Night's Dream*, Helena wonders,
upon seeing Lysander spread out on the ground, "Dead, or asleep?"
(II.ii.101); later, in a mock-tragic mirror image of this scene, which
arguably parodies *Romeo and Juliet*, Thisbe interrogates Pyramus's
body, "Asleep, my love? | What, dead, my dove?" (V.i.324–5). This
confusion, which can be seen in countlesss other dramatic examples,
highlights a metatheatrical resonance: in the suspended reality of the
stage, all deaths are feigned, as are all sleeps, living out Lady
Macbeth's maxim that "The sleeping and the dead | Are but as pic-
tures" (II.ii.50–1).[37] Shakespeare's recurring trope of the play as a
dream, staged while the audience sleeps, suggests that images of
sleepers onstage can be understood to reflect the uncertain status of
the play's spectators as well. As noted in the introduction, for instance, Puck encourages the audience to think "That you have but
slumb'red here | While these visions did appear. | And this weak and
idle theme, | No more yielding but a dream" (*Midsummer Night's*

Dream, V.i.425–8). The framing device of Christopher Sly in *The Taming of the Shrew*, and Prospero's comments on sleep and theater at the end of *The Tempest*, suggest the same model.

In the light of medical accounts of sleep and sleeping drinks, the comparison is a dangerous one. In the theater as well, sleep is not only similar to death, but susceptible to it. Just as Juliet's deep sleep unwittingly catalyzes both her own death and Romeo's, sleeping in plays often proves fatal. Recounting his "foul murder" to his son, the ghost of King Hamlet repeatedly dwells on his oblivion to the murderer: "sleeping in my orchard, | A serpent stung me"; "Sleeping within my orchard, | My custom always of the afternoon, | Upon my secure hour thy uncle stole"; "Thus was I, sleeping, by a brother's hand | Of life, of crown, of queen at once dispatch'd" (I.v.35–6; 59–61; 74–5).[38] Lady Macbeth facilitates the murder of the sleeping Duncan by making the guards sleep soundly: "I have drugg'd their possets | That death and nature do contend about them, | Whether they live or die" (II.ii.6–8).[39] Even in the safer contexts of comedy or romance, sleeping is risky: in *The Taming of the Shrew*, Christopher Sly is tricked into a new identity after succumbing to drunken oblivion; the sleeping lovers in *A Midsummer Night's Dream* are medicined with trouble-making love potions; and Caliban schemes to murder Prospero while he sleeps. If sleep can be a figure for the world of the play, theatergoers are, by analogy, depicted as being at risk when they surrender themselves to it. The vulnerability associated with the passivity of sleep may be implicitly identified with the receptive position of the spectator.

Renaissance antitheatricalists drew precisely this comparison, identifying the suspended quality of theatrical performances with sleep and its concordant threatening associations of pleasure, sin, and death. "Stage-haunters are for the most part lulled asleepe in the *Dalilaes* lappe of these sinfull pleasures," William Prynne writes, "yea they are quite dead in sinnes and trespasses."[40] The biblical reference offers a resonant image of both the seductive temptation and the catastrophic results of surrender to sleep. Accordingly, just as medical writers insist on the necessity of moderating both sleep and intake of soporific drugs, Prynne suggests that exposure to the theater must be limited in order to avoid dangerous consequences:

the recreation must *not be overlong, not time-consuming*; it must be onely *as a baite to a traviler, a whetting to a Mower or Carpenter, or as an houres sleepe* in the day time to a wearied man; we must *not spend whole weekes, whole dayes, halfe dayes or nights on recreations* as now too many doe, *abundance of idlenesse in this kinde, being one of Sodomes hainous sinnes.*[41]

Prynne distinguishes between the potentially reviving capacity of a brief rest and the danger of excessively long leisure. For other moralizing critics, however, exposure to the theater operates on a continuum, defying safe containment in small quantities. Stephen Gosson invokes a model of incremental gradations to illustrate the contagious force of the theater, which, he writes, takes the audience "from pyping to playing, from play to pleasure, from pleasure to slouth, from slouth to sleepe, from sleepe to sinne, from sinne to death, from death to the Divel."[42]

If the stage lulls its spectators into the deathlike state of excessive sleep, the theater itself can be seen as a sleep-inducing drug. Prynne explicitly links theatrical idleness with toxic potions. "Such prevalency is there in these bewitching Stage-playes," he writes, "to draw men on to *sloth, to idlenesse, the very bane, the poyson, and destruction of mens peerelesse soules*" (506). Stage plays, according to his model, parallel the function of drugs in enticing spectators into sloth, a poisonous state. The transformation that plays bring about in spectators attains the potency of a permanent, and fatal, chemical reaction, and suggests that the ambiguous status of the sleeping potion onstage could ultimately reflect the impact, as well as the form, of the play that features it.

INTENTIONAL PERFORMANCE: *ANTONY AND CLEOPATRA*

In the context of his own demonstrated interest in sleep as a metaphor for both vulnerability and theatergoing, as well as the play's insistent attention to the consequences of dangerous spectacles, Shakespeare's ambivalent interweaving of sleep, potions, poisons, and plays in *Romeo and Juliet* can be seen to respond to the debates surrounding the theater at the time, identifying plays as pleasurable but risky narcotics. More than ten years after writing *Romeo and Juliet*, he developed and complicated this idea by returning to the same juxtaposition in a similarly hybrid love-tragedy. *Antony and Cleopatra* re-enacts essential aspects of *Romeo and Juliet*, with older and more seasoned protagonists: in both plays, lovers are divided by their allegiances to warring factions; in both, the female lover's staging of her death leads to her lover's suicide and ultimately her own; both plays oscillate between comedy and tragedy; and both are permeated with poisons and narcotic potions. Although the plays explore similar structures and themes, however, *Antony and Cleopatra* goes beyond the earlier play in forcefully identifying the effects of ambivalent drugs with the effects of the theater. In both plays, female protagonists are identified with visual spectacles that elate, intoxicate, seduce, and ultimately undo their male admirers, but whereas Juliet is unaware of her effects on spectators, Cleopatra not only recognizes but self-consciously orchestrates her theatrical power.[43] Through numerous echoes and revisions from the earlier play, Shakespeare emphatically links the play's pleasurable narcotics—both figurative and literal—with the impact of Cleopatra's dramatic performances, and, more broadly, with the effects of the play itself on audiences.

In the play's opening act, Cleopatra echoes Juliet by seeking refuge from her lover's absence in sleep-inducing potions. "Give me to drink mandragora," she orders Charmian, "That I might sleep out this great gap of time | My Antony is away" (I.v.4–6).[44] Cleopatra's choice of sleeping potion links her with Juliet, identifying Cleopatra's daydreams with Juliet's own nightmare vision of her mandrake-surrounded tomb. Yet mandragora, with its ambiguous conflation of sleeping potion, aphrodisiac, and poison, is here presented as a remedy to the unsettling emptiness created by Antony's departure, becoming a replacement or double for Antony himself. The sleep which it offers suggests both an erotically pleasurable idleness, and a death-like retreat which suspends time during Antony's absence.

Despite her call for mandragora, however, Cleopatra medicines herself at least as much with daydreams as with drugs. Distracting herself from her distress, she luxuriates in pleasurable fantasies:

> O Charmian,
> Where think'st thou he is now? Stands he, or sits he?
> Or does he walk? or is he on his horse?
> O happy horse to bear the weight of Antony!
> Do bravely, horse, for wot'st thou whom thou mov'st,
> The demi-Atlas of this earth, the arm
> And burgonet of men. He's speaking now,
> Or murmuring, "Where's my serpent of old Nile?"

> For so he calls me. Now I feed myself
> With most delicious poison.
>
> (I.v.18–27)

Cleopatra represents the absent Antony in her own internal theater, filling the empty horizon with a catalog of his imagined places, postures, and thoughts. Neatly inverting her own lack, she scripts him as looking for an absent Cleopatra. With its erotic charge and comforting reversal of roles, the private theater of her daydreams serves a pharmaceutical function, constructing the sleepy oblivion which she craves. Her remedy, though, has ambiguous effects: she describes her reveries as "most delicious poison," linking her escapist pleasures with corrosive perils. Cleopatra is simultaneously patient and pharmacist, consumer and producer of the drugs she craves. Her request for the sleepy aphrodisiac poison of the mandrake is answered in her erotic fantasies.

Although in this scene Cleopatra is drugged by her own sleepy reveries, throughout the play it is primarily Antony and his Roman soldiers who consume the pleasurable but dangerous soporifics associated with Egypt and its queen. Just as she herself conflates fantasy with narcotic drugs, so the Romans are seduced by a combination of Cleopatra's dramatic spectacles and her wine-steeped feasts, underlining the parallel between theatricality and sleepy potions. Alcohol, a drug with soporific consequences in its own right, features prominently in accounts of her hospitality, and Enobarbus's tales of Egyptian extravagance are laced with references to drunken somnolence. "We did sleep day out of countenance," he vaunts to Maecenas and Agrippa, just before describing Cleopatra's performance at Cydnus, "and made the night light with drinking" (II.ii.177–8). Scenes of drinking seem inevitably to conjure up Egypt, theatricality, and sleep: after negotiations with Pompey, Caesar, and Lepidus, Enobarbus asks Antony "Shall we dance now the Egyptian Bacchanals | And celebrate our drink?" (II.vii.101–2). The combined effect of music, dance, and wine intoxicates to the point of oblivion: "Come, let's all take hands," Antony responds, "Till that the conquering wine hath steeped our sense | In soft and delicate Lethe" (II.vii.104–6).

Although Enobarbus describes Egypt's alcoholic and theatrical revels in festive terms, Antony's allusion to Lethe, the river of forgetfulness, points to darker aspects of the surrender of consciousness that they represent. Somnolence, and the potions that produce it, threatens not only to suspend the self, but to dissolve it.[45] Antony's dependence on the sleepy calm brought on by drink becomes more desperate as the play progresses. Wine allays tensions with Cleopatra: amid their post-Actium reconciliation, Antony calls "Some wine within there, and our viands!" (III.xi.73). Later, after forgiving Cleopatra's conference with Caesar's deputy Thidias, he calls for "one other gaudy night . . . Fill our bowls once more" (III.xiii.183–4). Just as Juliet's sleeping potion held out the promise of reuniting her with Romeo, the sleepy draughts of wine offer to bring Antony back to Cleopatra and the comedic goal of marital bliss. While Juliet and Romeo each drink only a single dose of their respective potions, however, Antony's self-medication is ongoing and apparently insatiable. Rather than killing at once, his soporifics draw him into a self-perpetuating addiction that slowly and gradually destroys him.[46]

From a Roman perspective, Antony's constant consumption of sleep-inducing drink signals his broader surrender to the dangerously seductive charms of Egypt. "Let witchcraft join with beauty, lust with both," Pompey exults to Menocrates,

> Tie up the libertine, in a field of feasts,
> Keep his brain fuming; Epicurean cooks
> Sharpen with cloyless sauce his appetite,
> That sleep and feeding may prorogue his honour,
> Even till a Lethe'd dulness—
>
> (II.i.22–7)

Antony's surrender to sleep, according to Pompey, suggests he is victim to a form of witchcraft: he is lured into oblivion, a "Lethe'd dulness," by an inexorable assault on his appetites. Antony becomes an object rather than a subject, tied up, fumed, and prorogued.[47] Although others are also captivated by the intoxicating spectacles of Cleopatra's hospitality, Antony, as her primary audience, is the most forcefully ravaged by their subtly poisonous effects. If the effects of performances, like those of potions, vary according to the intensity of their concentration, Antony receives doses so powerful as to be near-fatal; those exposed to lesser amounts of Cleopatra, such as other Romans, Egyptians, and the play's external audiences, can be lulled and delighted without being undone.

Cleopatra and her performances are at the center of this luxurious but unsettling languor: in response to her faltering attempts to delay his departure for Rome, Antony chides, "But that your royalty | Holds idleness your subject, I should take you | For idleness itself" (I.iii.91–3). The paradoxical structure of his assertion captures an essential aspect of Cleopatra's nature: she seems simultaneously to embody somnolence and to control it, both to be implicated in an Egyptian passivity and to manipulate it, actively, for her own gains. The soporific drug for which she calls is both a potion at her disposal, and an emblem of her own effect on others.

As Antony's response to this scene of Cleopatra's suggests, his consumption of Egypt's soporific food and drink is paralleled with his spectatorship of Cleopatra's performances. Cleopatra's primary power lies in her ability to draw all eyes to her: describing her spectacular arrival at Cydnus, Enobarbus claims that the city's rush to view her on the barge left behind only air, "which, but for vacancy | Had gone to gaze on Cleopatra too, | And made a gap in nature" (II.ii.216–18). Antony is hardly immune to her magnetic pull: in a disconcerting reversal of roles, she turns down his dinner invitation to insist that he come to her, where he "for his ordinary, pays his heart, | For what his eyes eat only" (II.ii.225–6). Visual and oral consumption are conflated, and both prove dangerous.

Antony's pattern of gazing on Cleopatra and subsequently losing himself is repeated at Actium. Upon seeing Cleopatra withdraw from the battle, Antony "(like a doting mallard) | Leaving the fight in heighth, flies after her" (III.x.20–1). His will is no longer his own: "My heart was to thy rudder tied by the strings," he tells Cleopatra (III.xi.57). The scene depicts the culmination of a process that began at Cydnus, the dissolution of his autonomous self. "I never saw an action of such shame," Scarus tells Enobarbus; "Experience, manhood, honour, ne'er before | Did violate so itself" (III.x.22–4). Antony's surrender to Cleopatra's spectacles parallels, and extends, his surrender to the oblivion of drink and sleep, suggesting that spectators of the play (who also, of course, gaze on Cleopatra) share, at least temporarily, the loss of self the play dramatizes. The play's audience does not, however, actually witness these two particular spectacles; both of them, like so much of the play, are reported second-hand. Perhaps Cleopatra's most effective performances, like a basilisk or Gorgon, can only be withstood through an oblique view. As with actual potions, again, dosage is crucial.

As these ambivalent portrayals of Cleopatra's performances suggest, the play links her and her Egyptian world not only with the risky potions of narcotic drugs and wine, but also with literal, fatal poisons. Even Antony himself, despite his enchantment with Cleopatra, uses the vocabulary of poison to describe the effects of her Egyptian world. Early in the play, he worries that "Much is breeding, I Which like the courser's hair, hath yet but life I And not a serpent's poison" (I.ii.190–2). While he holds back from attributing poison to the magically animated hair, his choice of image and cautionary "yet" imply that it is only a matter of time. Shortly after this, he echoes Pompey's skeptical account of his Egyptian subjection by apologizing to Caesar that "poisoned hours had bound me up I From mine own knowledge" (II.ii.90). Even Cleopatra echoes the association, identifying herself as Antony's "serpent of old Nile" (I.v.25). These figurative versions of the poison that will later bring about the play's tragic end offer a physical vocabulary for the corrosion of Antony's will; they remind the audience from early on that the bawdy jests and playful banter of Cleopatra's court are not without troubling side effects.

The idea of Cleopatra's seductive appeal as a type of poison was explicitly encoded in Shakespeare's sources. North's translation of Plutarch's *Life of Marc Antonie* describes Antony's falling off from martial greatness as a kind of poisoning: Antony was "so rauished & enchaunted with the sweete poyson of her love, that he had no other thought but of her, & how he might quickly returne againe . . ."[48] Later he writes similarly that Caesar claimed "that *Antonius* was not Maister of him selfe, but that *Cleopatra* had brought him beside him selfe, by her charmes and amorous poysons."[49] North's "sweet poyson" and "amorous poysons" stem in both cases from Plutarch's "*pharmakoi*," evoking, like Cleopatra's mandrake, an ambiguous array of meanings: poison, remedy, drug, and aphrodisiac.[50] The embedded presence of North's language and its attendant ambiguities can be seen in the play's recurring imagery of poison, and particularly in its emphasis on the literal poison with which Cleopatra kills herself.

As in *Romeo and Juliet*, the play's close suggests that its near-poisons, or figurative poisons, metamorphose into literal and fatal poisons, that Lethe becomes lethal. The play's oscillations between farce and fear settle formally into a tragic ending as its ambiguous potions become defined as toxic. Shakespeare presents the long, slow drama of the lovers' deaths as beginning after the final lost battle, with Antony's rage at his perceived betrayal by Cleopatra. "The shirt of Nessus is upon me," he laments; "teach me, | Alcides, thou mine ancestor, thy rage" (IV.xii.43–4). Antony's reference to the shirt of Nessus is the last, and least heroic, of the allusions that throughout the play link him with Hercules.[51] Referring to the poisoned shirt with which Hercules' wife Deianeira brought about his death, the allusion suggests that Antony's death is already underway, brought about by Cleopatra's poisonous treachery.[52]

Antony's claim that he is dying of Cleopatra's poisons proves quickly, if indirectly, to be true. Alarmed by his accusations and threats, Cleopatra imitates Juliet in feigning death. Like Juliet, Cleopatra does not conceive of the idea independently; in response to her plea, "Help me, my women!" (IV.xiii.1), Charmian suggests that she lock herself in her monument and send word to Antony that she is dead. Unlike Juliet, however, Cleopatra seems to be aware that her ruse will hurt her lover, and even suspects that it may bring about his death.[53] Diomedes announces to the dying Antony that his mistress "had a prophesying fear | Of what hath come to pass," and that she has sent him, "fearing since how it [her ruse] might work" (IV.xiv.120–1, 125).[54] Cleopatra, in fact, seems more certain than fearful; when Diomedes returns from bearing the message, she immediately inquires, "How now? is he dead?" (IV.xv.6). Just as Juliet's imitation of death led directly to Romeo's actual death, here Cleopatra's carefully staged performance proves so devastating to Antony that it drives him immediately to suicide. In revisiting and revising this scene, however, Shakespeare significantly intensifies his message about the nature and consequences of play-acting: whereas Juliet's mock-death was undertaken with reassurances that Romeo would be warned, Cleopatra's relies for its efficacy precisely on Antony believing it true. Cleopatra's theatrical imagination, the metaphorical mandragora that she fed herself early in the play, ultimately acts as a poison that brings about Antony's death. Bolstered by more than ten years of further experience in the theater world since *Romeo and Juliet*, Shakespeare suggests not only that plays are capable of undoing their audiences, but that playwrights and actors are aware of that power; in fact, performances derive their emotional impact from their consciousness of it.

This destructive force, however, is not the play's final word on the effects of spectacles and the theatrical imagination. Fittingly, Cleopatra's performance of death leads Antony to a death envisioned as a long-awaited slumber: "Unarm, Eros," he responds, "the long day's task is done, | And we must sleep" (IV.xiv.35–6). Death offers Antony a purer version of the escapist oblivion he has courted in Egypt; like the drunken revels it imitates and intensifies, it also seems to promise a return to Cleopatra, and erotic union. "I will be | A bridegroom in my death," he pronounces, "and run into't | As to a lover's bed" (IV.xiv.99–101). What could be seen from a Roman perspective as the final dissolution of the self can equally be seen, from an Egyptian perspective, as the ultimate fusion of the self with another. Like Romeo, Antony merges together tragedy and comedy by identifying death with the triumph of marriage.

Just as Antony's temporary disappearance to Rome became the occasion for Cleopatra's dreamlike reveries and calls for mandragora, his permanent disappearance to death brings on a literal dream, leading her to call again for both sleep and poison. "I dreamt there was an Emperor Antony," Cleopatra tells Dolabella. "O such another sleep, that I might see | But such another man!" (V.ii.76–8). Cleopatra's resurrection of an "Emperor Antony" can be seen as the belated fulfillment of Romeo's dream "that I reviv'd, and was an emperor" (IV.i.9). Although the narcotic enchantment of her theatrical spectacles worked to undo the literal Antony, the same soporific imagination offers recompense by reconstituting his image in fantasy.[55] Theater, in this play, is both more destructive and more constructive than in *Romeo and Juliet*: its power is greater, for better and for worse.

Having brought about Antony's death and resurrection through the force of her theatrical imagination, Cleopatra sets about attending to her own. The play seems to begin anew, as she stages a reproduction of the spectacle that started her romance: "I am again for Cydnus," she tells her women, "To meet Mark Antony" (V.ii.227–8). In an ironic juxtaposition of genres, the asp that literalizes the play's figurative poisons is conveyed by an emblem of comedy: a clown. "What poor an instrument," Cleopatra comments, "May do a noble deed!" (V.ii.235–6). As the carrier of the poisons that will fulfill Cleopatra's tragic final scene, the clown's presence implicitly suggests that the play's earlier scenes, with their bawdiness and farce, were a necessary vehicle for what would follow: her playfully ambiguous mandragora has evolved into literal poisons with final and permanent effects.

Like Antony, and Romeo and Juliet before him, Cleopatra paradoxically looks to dying as revivification and reunion: "I have |

Immortal longings in me," she pronounces; "Husband, I come, |
Now to that name, my courage prove my title!" (V.ii.279–80,
286–7). Watching Iras die after a farewell kiss, Cleopatra identifies
poison as a remedy, linking it with a pain-alleviating, and even
seductive, oblivion:

> Have I the aspic in my lips? Dost fall?
> If thou and nature can so gently part,
> The stroke of death is as a lover's pinch,
> Which hurts, and is desir'd.
> (V.ii.292–5)

Cleopatra's attribution of erotic pleasure to death draws on the
play's frequent punning on dying as orgasm. In fact, the speed of
Iras's death evokes sexual jealousy: "If she first meet the curled
Antony," Cleopatra worries, "He'll make demand of her, and spend
that kiss | Which is my heaven to have" (V.ii.300–2). Death, as she
conceives it, will return her to Antony and erotic fulfillment. By staging her suicide as a marriage, Cleopatra confounds generic rules:
although the play ends as a tragedy, it also stages the traditionally
comic celebration of a wedding, and new life.

Shakespeare's detailed description of Cleopatra's death represents
an imaginative interpolation from his source. Plutarch refers to the
idea of the asp conveyed in a basket of figs as only one of a number
of possible manners of Cleopatra's death.[56] In contrast to Shakespeare's dramatization of the conveyance and biting of the asp,
Plutarch insists that we will never know exactly how she died. He
emphasizes, however, her ingenuity and preparations in researching
her means of death. In a particularly intriguing passage, Plutarch re-
lates that, since early in the troubles with Rome, Cleopatra had been
experimenting with the effects of various poisons on condemned
prisoners in order to find the most painless form of death:

So when she had dayly made diuers and sundrie proofes, she found none of
all them she had proued so fit, as the biting of an Aspicke, the which only
causeth a heauines of the head, without swounding or complaining, and
bringeth a great desire also to sleepe, with a little swet in the face, and so by
litle and litle taketh away the sences and vitall powers, no liuing creature per-
ceiuing that the pacients feele any paine. For they are so sorie when any
bodie waketh them, and taketh them up: as those that being taken out of a
sound sleepe, are very heauy and desirous to sleepe.[57]

Cleopatra's means of suicide, then, was chosen particularly for its resemblance to a sleeping potion; her death can be seen as a kind of remedy, a carefully choreographed extension of her earlier soporific pleasures.

Shakespeare essentially omits this striking anecdote from his play, limiting its mention to an afterthought by Caesar that "her physician tells me | She hath pursued conclusions infinite | Of easy ways to die" (V.ii.352–4). Its residual echoes, however, can be seen not only in the play's recurring references to narcotics, but in Shakespeare's association of Cleopatra's death with the peace and pleasure of sleep. "O for such another sleep," she muses after her dream of Mark Antony, "that I might see | But such another man!" (V.ii.77–8). And the play suggests that her desire for sleep is granted. "Peace, peace," she bids Charmian, as she hovers on the brink of dying, "Dost thou not see my baby at my breast, | That sucks the nurse asleep?" (V.ii.307–9). Poison, ultimately, is her sleeping potion: upon viewing her dead body, Caesar eulogizes that "she looks like sleep, | As she would catch another Antony | In her strong toil of grace" (V.ii.344–6). In her death, Cleopatra captures that aspect of sleep which differentiates it from death, and gives it the pleasure of comedy: its promise of waking. The images of renewal—the baby at her breast, another Cydnus, the catching of another Antony—suggest that her play is suspended, rather than over.

Antony and Cleopatra, like Romeo and Juliet before them, find a monument in death: "She shall be buried by her Antony," Caesar specifies; "No grave upon the earth shall clip in it | A pair so famous" (V.ii.356–8).[58] As their monuments suggest, both the plays' endings evoke a curious air of triumph, despite—or perhaps because of—the protagonists' deaths. The intermediate, uncertain generic mode of the sleeping potion may settle ultimately into the poison of tragedy, but even this poison turns out to be ambiguous in function. While it takes away the lovers' lives, it also returns them to their marriages, and bestows on them a new mythic status, leaving the ultimate nature of the ending uncertain.

The claims made for the nature of the theater in these plays are similarly ambivalent. In both plays, dramatic spectacles—especially of beautiful women—prove devastating, even fatal, to their onstage audiences, but at the same time provide powerful consolations, both to those same audiences and to the plays' external spectators themselves. The plays, however, differ in their representation of these effects: Juliet gains an unwitting power over her audiences when she is asleep, or apparently dead, whereas Cleopatra self-consciously manipulates this same power, both alive and in the act of dying. Where Juliet is an accidental actress, Cleopatra brings intentional force to her dreamlike imagination and dramatic performances, which Shakespeare explicitly identifies with the potions which pervade the play. She exerts an intoxicating, narcotic effect on all of her audiences. Antony, more acutely than Romeo, offers a model for the spectator as consumer of dangerous remedies: mesmerized, ensnared, undone, even annihilated, but—in the end—triumphantly reborn in the imagination. Yet he is not Cleopatra's only audience: she herself is drugged by her own reveries, as are—with more muted consequences—the spectators who consume her in smaller doses, both inside and outside the play.

By identifying the play's ambivalent potions with dramatic spectacles, Shakespeare suggests that the dangerous seduction of enchanting potions is akin to that of the theater itself; he presents a complex and sophisticated model of theatrical agency as seeping into audiences and transforming them with a chemical force. In portraying Cleopatra, the center of the play's potions and performances, as aware of her effects on audiences, moreover, he suggests that playwrights and actors understand and actively manipulate their effects on audiences. Going beyond a simple revisitation of the earlier play, *Antony and Cleopatra* exploits and advances the associations set up in *Romeo and Juliet,* transforming the earlier play's insights about the ambivalent effects of narcotic potions and spectacles into a more pointed claim about the theater's awareness of its power over audiences.

3

"Polluted with Counterfeit Colours": Cosmetic Theater

In the fourth act of *The Devil's Charter* (1606), Barnabe Barnes portrays Lucretia Borgia entering "richly attired with a Phyal in her hand." In the midst of painting her face, she suddenly cries out in dismay at a burning sensation. The cosmetics contained in her vial have proven treacherous: "rancke poyson | Is ministred to bring me to my death, | I feele the venime boyling in my veines."[1] Despite the immediate application of an antidote from her physician, Lucretia is dead before the end of the scene, destroyed by the paints that promised an artificial improvement of her beauty and, accordingly, power. Cosmetics, in this scene and elsewhere in early modern writings, prove not only morally, but physically dangerous. Disrupting material and immaterial boundaries alike, they give tangible form to the figurative threats of moral and epistemological contamination associated with falsifying one's face.[2] Spilling out of their rightful space to seep into consumers and spectators, infiltrating and tainting both body and soul, poisonous face-paints offer a disturbingly literal image of the vulnerability of the body to the invasive force of art.

A recurring threat in early modern plays, the idea that face-paints could poison offered a particularly vivid focal point for broader cultural fears that cosmetic remedies not only failed their claims to help and improve consumers, but actively caused harm.[3] Amid intensifying curiosity and concern about chemical technology, testimony from doctors as to the corrosive nature of cosmetic ingredients offered scientifically authorized support, as well as a distinctively material vocabulary, for moral diatribes against artificial beauty. A passage from the English translation of the art theorist Giovanni

Paolo Lomazzo's well-known *A Tracte Containing the Artes of Curious Paintinge Caruinge & Buildinge* warns women against face-painting by noting that mercury sublimate, the primary cosmetic foundation, is "very offensiue to mans flesh," and "is called *dead fier*; because of his malignant, and biting nature"; in *A Treatise Against Painting and Tincturing of Men and Women*, the moralist Thomas Tuke chides that "a vertuouis woman needs no borrowed, no bought complexion, none of these poysons."[4] Conflating immaterial and material threats, moral, medical, and theatrical writings alike represented the semiotic disorder and sexual impurity associated with cosmetics as "poysonous to the *body*, and pernicious to the *soul*."[5]

The representation of poisonous cosmetics in the theater of the early modern period is strikingly widespread. Beyond *The Devil's Charter*, plays featuring them include Thomas Kyd's *The Tragedye of Solyman and Perseda* (1592), *Jack Drum's Entertainment* (1600), *The History of the Tryall of Cheualry* (1601), George Chapman's *The Gentleman Usher* (1602), *The Revenger's Tragedy* (1607), *The Second Maiden's Tragedy* (1611), and Philip Massinger's *The Duke of Milan* (1622).[6] As the multiple stagings of this threat suggest, anxieties about the dangers of cosmetics became a particular concern of the theater; similarly, they reflect on early modern concerns about theatricality as well. In the light of pervasive and insistent identifications between face-paints and the theater, playwrights who depict cosmetics as hazardous can be seen as exploring concerns about the seductive and contaminating force of their own medium. Also routinely described as poisonous by its detractors, the theater, like face-paints, was routinely criticized as being not only erotically titillating, but also duplicitous and corrosive, unsettling the relationship between interior and exterior. The idea that deceptive spectacles could exert harmful effects on the body and soul points to early modern ideas about the dangerous efficacy of signs. In the case of cosmetic ingredients, an epistemological problem—the ease with which poisons can masquerade as benevolent substances—can translate directly into bodily vulnerability, and even death. Embodying and fusing together various levels of contamination, anxieties about cosmetics and painted bodies call attention to early modern convictions about the inseparability of external from internal, and material from immaterial, with implications for the powers and perils of the theater.

POISONS OF *THE DEVIL'S CHARTER*

Rarely attended to by readers or critics, *The Devil's Charter* offers an intriguing setting for a vivid depiction of murder by poisonous cosmetics.[7] Despite its relative obscurity and often bombastic rhetorical turns, the play is an exemplary representative of popular Jacobean revenge tragedy. In its relentless accumulation of vendettas and corpses, it verges on a parody of its genre, and presents a virtual catalog of some of the more spectacularly ingenious and morbid forms of murder on the Jacobean stage. Based on a mélange of contemporary rumors and stories from Guicciardini, *The Devil's Charter* dramatizes Roderigo Borgia allegedly making a bargain with the devil in order to become Pope Alexander VI; the plot involves, among multiple other murders, that of his daughter Lucretia. Corrupt in every possible way—Italian, Catholic, female, adulterous, murderous, from a bad family—Lucretia meets her fitting end through the corrosion of poisoned face-paints.

In the scene with which this chapter opened, Lucretia is in the midst of having her face made up when she interrupts with a sudden cry:

I feele a foule stincke in my nostrells,
Some stinke is vehement and hurts my braine,
My cheekes both burne and sting; give me my glasse.
Out out for shame I see the blood it selfe,
Dispersed and inflamed, give me some water.
  Motticilla rubbeth her cheekes with a cloth.
    Lucretia looketh in the glasse.
My braines intoxicate my face is scalded.
Hence with the glasse: coole coole my face, rancke poyson
Is ministred to bring me to my death,
I feele the venime boyling in my veines.

(IV.iii.2247–57)

Cosmetics, in this passage, create a crisis of permeability, penetration, and contagion. Lucretia's paints refuse to sit on the surface of her skin: they invade and pervade her body, entering her nostrils, seeping through her skin, coursing through her veins. Her description of the poisons calls attention to an invasive and corrosive heat: her cheeks "both burne and sting," her face is "scalded," her blood is "inflamed," and she feels "the venim boyling" in her veins. Just after this speech, she similarly cries "I burne I burne . . . | My braines are seard up with some fatall fire" (2265–6), and later reports that "a boyling heat I Suppes up the lively spirit in my lungs" (2276-7).[8] Starting at the surface, this pervasive fire works its way into progressively more interior sites, through her cheeks and face into her blood and veins, then her brain, and eventually her "lively spirit" itself. Faced with this corrosive heat, the skin loses its integrity as bodily boundary and barrier: the distinction between external surface and internal substance dissolves. Lucretia's death suggests that cosmetics go beyond the superficial—in fact, by erasing the line that separates the inner and outer, they call into question the category of the superficial, suggesting that artifice can never be only skin-deep.

Paints, in this model, are not only invasive, but uncontainable and irrevocable: their effects can be neither halted nor undone. Motticilla, Lucretia's maid, queries, "Ah me deere Lady; what strange leoprosie? I The more I wash the more spreads on your face" (2258-9). The physician, when called, confirms that "This poyson spreads and is incurable" (2278). His futile offer of "one precious antidote" (2279) has no hope of efficacy; from the first moment of application, the paint's force is irreversible. While other contemporary fears about the transformative effects of external trappings, such as clothing, suggest that changes can be undone by removing the threat, the chemical properties of face-paints evoke an uneasy sense of permanence.[9] Like original sin, or the mark of Cain, to which cosmetics were often compared, their taint was perceived as impossible to cleanse.[10]

MEDICAL POISONS, MORAL POISONS

As improbable as this scene from *The Devil's Charter* may seem, the traits it attributes to face-paints—burning heat, invasive force, and irreversible contagion—closely recall non-fictional depictions of cosmetics at the time. Although Barnes portrays Lucretia's face-paints as vehicles for externally imbued poisons, other Renaissance writers asserted that cosmetics themselves were innately poisonous. A glance at their chemical ingredients suggests that these claims were, for the most part, not unfounded. Most cosmetic foundations were made of mercury sublimate and ceruse, or white lead: a typical recipe for face-paint directs the reader to "Incorporate with a wooden pestle & in a wooden mortar with great labour foure ounces of sublimate, and one ounce of crude Mercurie," and Giambattista della

Porta, the Neapolitan philosopher of science and natural magic, speaks for many in his claim that there is "nothing better than quicksilver for womens paints, and to cleanse their faces, and make them shine."[11] Not only were these substances known to be toxic, but contemporary medical authorities classified them as hot and dry poisons that operated by burning, in contrast with poisons such as hemlock, nightshade, and henbane, which were understood to kill by coldness, through numbing and dulling of feeling.[12] Describing the effect of sublimate, for example, the French physician Ambroise Paré writes that victims will suffer from "the devouring and fierie furie of the poyson, rending or eating into the guts and stomacke, as if they were seared with an hot iron."[13] In context, the corrosive heat of Lucretia's paints in *The Devil's Charter* appears less a result of villainous adulteration of paints than an exaggerated confirmation of their inherent, and medically established, effects. Contemporary scientific accounts of the physiological effects of face-paints gave an authoritative material underpinning to fears about cosmetic corrosion and bodily vulnerability. The 1598 arrest of Barnabe Barnes, the play's author, for an attempted poisoning with mercury sublimate he had purchased at a grocer's, suggests that the link may not have been entirely coincidental.[14]

Medical interest in cosmetics, and debates about their chemical contents, point to an interesting anomaly in early modern perceptions of face-paints. Although at first glance cosmetics and medical remedies may seem unlikely bedfellows, the two areas were closely linked in early modern thought. Based on herbal and, increasingly, chemical-based recipes for self-improvement, cosmetics—or "face-physicks"—were widely understood as a form of medicine.[15] One book, in fact, described them as "the Beautifying Part of Physick."[16] "Since next to the Art of Physick, follows the Art of Adorning our selves," reasons the proem to one set of cosmetic recipes, "we shall set down the Art of Painting; and how to beautifie Women from Head to Foot, in many Experiments . . ."[17] Ladies' home cabinet books, freely mingling medical, cosmetic, and culinary recipes, enjoyed an explosive popularity during the early modern period. *The Secretes of the Reverende Maister Alexis of Piemount*, which juxtaposed recipes such as "To dye or colour heare," "To preserue and keepe Peches or other fructe," and "Agaynst the Plague" within a few pages of each other, went through fifteen full editions, and four separate editions of individual parts, between 1558 and 1614.[18]

Similarly, Sir Hugh Platt's *Delights for Ladies* went through sixteen editions between 1602 and 1656.[19] Other popular books of this genre included *A Closet for Ladies and Gentlewomen,* which was printed at least twelve times between 1608 and 1656, and *The Ladies Cabinet Opened,* printed five times between 1639 and 1667.

At the most mundane level, links between the cosmetic and the medicinal can be seen in recipes directed towards improving both health and appearance: soap, for instance, and toothpaste, are two of the ubiquitous items in these recipe books, as are ointments "To take spottes, lintelles, or redde piples, out of the face," or "To make wartes fall off."[20] Authors of these recipe-books apply the term "remedy" to medical and cosmetic substances interchangeably; della Porta refers to "Remedies to make the Eye brows black," as well as for changes of hair color, amending baldness, pimples, ring-worm, warts, etc.[21] Even the use of paints to whiten skin was linked to the medical effectiveness of chemical treatments for syphilis, such as mercury and arsenic, at concealing the facial pock-marks that branded the disease's victims with stigma. Yet cosmetics for the purposes purely of beautification also engage the idea of remedy, at a deeper level. Although the term "remedy" is derived from the same Latin root as medicine—*medeor,* to heal, restore, alleviate—the root itself, as well as uses of the term in Shakespeare's time, share an emphasis on the figurative rather than technical sense of healing that we might use now: a remedy can be a solution to a problem, an improvement, not merely a medical cure. "I write relieuing remedies of dearth," Hugh Platt explained in the opening epistle to his recipe book; "That Art might help where nature made a faile."[22] As recipe books emphasized, to their predominantly female readership, beauty—and the accompanying ability to charm or seduce—represented the optimal physical state. Just as medicines offered to bring ease and pleasure, and to improve one's physical well-being, so cosmetics issued a comparable promise of physical enhancement and happiness: effects, however, which critics argued that face-paints would not only fail to achieve, but would reverse.

Critics of cosmetics delighted in arguing that artificial beauty-aids could bring about the opposite of their intended effects, drawing on evidence about the chemical properties of paint to bolster their arguments. "The excellencie of this Mercurie Sublimate," the physician Andreas de Laguna writes, "is such that the women who often paint themselves with it, though they be very young, they presently turne

old with withered and wrinkeled faces like an Ape, and before age
can come upon them, they tremble (poore wretches) as if they were
sicke of the staggers, reeling, and full of quick-silver, for so are
they."[23] Extending this line of grotesque imagery, Lomazzo describes
in even more elaborate and morbid detail "the natures and qualities
of the ingredients"[24] of face-paints. On mercury sublimate, he writes:

This the Chirurgions call a *corrosiue*. Because if it bee put vpon mans flesh it
burneth it in a short space, mortifying the place, not without great paine to
the patient. Wherfore such women as vse it about their face, haue alwaies
black teeth, standing far out of their gums like a Spanish mule; an offensiue
breath, with a face halfe scorched, and an vncleane complexion. All which
proceede from the nature of *Sublimate*. So that simple women thinking to
grow more beautifull, become disfigured, hastening olde age before the time,
and giving occasion to their husbandes to seeke strangers insteede of their
wiues; with diuers other inconueniences.[25]

To Lomazzo, paint is a medium that not only fails, but actively
undermines, all of its own goals—it mortifies where it should en-
liven, blackens where it should whiten, and disfigures where it
should beautify—with diverse other inconveniences left to the
reader's imagination. Cosmetics, according to this model, carry in
them the seeds of their own destruction: like sirens, their seductive
promises of beauty mask an underlying ugliness and death.[26]
Lomazzo's portrait of sublimate emphasizes the same dangerous
bodily infiltration dramatized in *The Devil's Charter*. Beginning at
the skin and moving towards increasingly intimate arenas—teeth,
breath, marital relations—his catalog of consequences points to a
similarly progressive deepening of impact.

As Lomazzo's example suggests, accusations against cosmetics
drew on concerns about the permeability of the body to the contamination of a tainted world. Far from ignoring these concerns,
marketers of beauty products called explicit attention to them, arguing that cosmetics could respond to, and in fact cure, the problem of
the body's vulnerability. As the anonymous author of *Artificiall
Embellishments* wrote, "The Body, that weak and moving mansion
of mortality, is exposed to the treacherous underminings of so many
Sicknesses and Distempers, that its own frailty seems petitioner for
some artificial Enamel, which might be a fixation to Natures incon-
stancy, and a help to its variating infirmities."[27] Did the "Enamel" of
paints seal off the body from dangers, though, or did its chemical

properties serve to usher them in? Writers opposed to cosmetics argued that the corrosive effects of paints played upon, and intensified, the fragility of an already too-permeable body. In *Instruction of a Christen Woman*, Juan Luis Vives writes of face-painting, "The tender skynne wyl reuyll the more sone, and all the fauour of the face waxeth olde, and the breth stynketh, and the tethe rusten, and an yuell ayre all the bodye ouer, bothe by the reason of the ceruse, and quick siluer . . . Wherfore Ouyde called these doynges venomes, and not without a cause."[28] Sharing Lomazzo's emphasis on bodily corrosion, Vives dwells on the same triplicate blazon of skin, breath, and teeth, liminal zones where external surfaces bear the visible marks of their adjacent interior degeneration.[29] The signs of this erosion constitute visible proof of the idea of paints as "venomes" that literally, as well as figuratively, contaminate their wearer. Vives, like the physicians who wrote about the chemical properties of cosmetics, draws on material conditions in order to support his condemnation of face-painting.

The idea of cosmetics as invasive poisons, reinforced by the material properties of their chemical ingredients, offered moralists a forceful way to articulate links between face-paints and less tangible forms of transgression and contamination. Socially and politically, for example, the idea of cosmetic infiltration came to be aligned with concerns about the contamination of national and class identity.[30] More typically, cosmetics were associated with moral impurity. The most common complaint against cosmetics was that they sinned against truth: concealing true faces behind false, they undermined the trustworthiness of bodily signs, leading to a broader crisis of semiotic reliability.[31] Recurrent metaphors of forgery and counterfeiting emphasize the disparity between appealing surfaces and empty or corrupt substances. Tuke, for example, likens painted faces to "ill cloth of a good die; or to a *Letter* fairely written, and with good inke, but not without some false *English*, or ill contents."[32] Similarly, cosmetic deception was seen as "a tricke of a wanton";[33] motivated by the desire to seduce, it revealed a lascivious and impure soul. Tuke writes of the face-painting woman, "A good *Bed-friend* shee's commonly, delighting in sheetes more, then in shooes, making long nights, and short daies. All her *infections* are but to gaine affections, for she had rather *die*, then liue & not please. Her lips she laies with so fresh a *red*, as if she sang, *Iohn come kisse me now*."[34] The wayward sexuality of the face-painting woman was linked to the physical impurity of face-painting. The moralist Philip Stubbes cites patristic authority to argue that painting is a form of whoredom: "S. Ciprian amongst the rest, saith, a woman thorow painting and dying of her face, sheweth her selfe to be more then whorish. For (saith he) shee hath corrupted and defaced (like a filthie strumpet or brothel) the workmanship of God in her, what is this els but to turne truth into falshoode, with painting and slibbersawces?"[35] Stubbes's argument almost appears tautological—painting is whorish, because to paint is to be like a whore—but his explanation suggests a more complex association. The concealing and remaking of true faces with paint, he argues, suggests a disregard for purity, which, for a woman, translates directly into a lack of chastity.

The conjunction of sexual impropriety and cosmetic impurity was made most explicit in reference to the threat of adultery. John Downame, a puritan minister, cites Saint Augustine describing face-painting as "a fault which in some respects matcheth whoredome, for (saith he) *Ibi pudicitia, hic natura adulteratur*: In that chastity, in this nature it self is adulterated," drawing on the etymological identification between corrupting a substance and a marriage with a foreign and inferior supplement.[36] Commonly described as "adulterate beauty," or "adulterate and counterfeit Colours," cosmetic contamination was seen as inherently linked to marital infidelity.[37] Strikingly, face-painting was described as the more serious of the two sins. Vives warns the face-painter, "For though thou be nat an adulterar towarde man yet whan thou corruptest and marrest that whiche is goddis doyng thou art a worse adulterar."[38] The anticosmetic interlocutor in *A Discourse of Auxiliary Beauty* similarly charges that "all *painting* the face, or adding *to our handsomenesse*, in point of *Complexion*, is directly against *the 7th Commandment*; ... [not] to *commit adultery with others*," because "if all *Adultery* and *adulterating* arts ... are forbidden to us, how much more any such plots and practises, as tend to a *Self adulterating*."[39] As a dangerous external manifestation of the pollution associated with paints, adultery was understood as both a parallel and an inevitable accompaniment to poison, the most extreme and dangerous form of pollution. During the trial for the murder of Sir Thomas Overbury, Sir Edward Coke commented that adultery was responsible for the vast majority of poisoning cases.[40] In a self-perpetuating cycle, the figurative poison of adultery was seen as both cause and effect of the presence of literal poisons, cosmetic and otherwise.

The moral taint of face-paints was understood to undermine not only marital, but also religious fidelity: Tuke writes that "hee loues not God with all his heart, that would haue that affection or commendation, giuen to a picture, or a peece of art, which is due to the worke of God."[41] Lest his Protestant readers miss the implications of this statement, Tuke elsewhere asserts directly that "a painted face is not much vnlike an Idoll."[42] Face-painting women were depicted as actively proselytizing for amorous idolaters; Downame writes that "they inueagle others with carnall loue and fleshly lust, making them adore with their chiefe deuotions, a painted idoll, and a liuing image."[43] Pro-cosmetic books, intriguingly, confirmed his charges rather than refuting them, appropriating the same rhetoric in making their appeal to cosmetic consumers. The author of the anonymous *Artificiall Embellishments*, for example, embraced the vocabulary of idolatry:

Your Alabaster Armes and Hands Ladies, are the fleshie *altars* whereon your *superstitious* Inamorato's offer to you, as female Deities the *first fruits* of their devotion in zealous kisses. Your care should be to keep them in such a soul-inchanting symmetrie, that might confirm your Idolizing lovers in the opinion they have conceived, that you are more then mortal.[44]

Idolatry, from this perspective, is presented as a desirable power to have over men: a remedy to a lack of affection, rather than a distortion of that affection.

Not only were women who painted their faces seen by both supporters and detractors as seeking to be idolized, they were also seen as idolaters themselves. "A good face is her god," Tuke claims of the painted woman, "and her cheeke *well died*, is the *idoll* she doth so much adore."[45] In a curious act of self-division, the woman who paints is subjugated by the independent power of her own face; she is simultaneously altar and worshipper, object and subject.[46] The association between face-paints and idolatry both heightens the idea of paint as spiritually poisonous, and offers a link between idolatry and material poisons. Disillusioned to discover that "My glorious idoll, I did so adore, | Is but a vizard newly varnished ore," the Huguenot poet DuBartas describes Jezebel's face-paints as "poisons one would lothe to kisse"; similarly, he accuses her of bringing "Idol-Sin: | Painting, and Poysning" to the land of Samaria.[47] Borrowing from the vocabulary of paint's chemical properties, references to idolatry reinforce beliefs about the link between material and spiritual contamination.

The perceived correlation between outer impurity (painted faces) and inner impurity (tainted souls) was seen as working in two directions. While Tuke, DuBartas, and others suggest that cosmetics were primarily a symptom of an internal moral corruption, others more forcefully described paints as causing this corruption.[48] Philip Stubbes argues that bodily adornment sinks beyond the skin to contaminate the soul: he laments the use of "certaine oyles, liquors, *vnguentes*, and waters . . ., whereby they thinke their beautie is greatly decored; but who seeth not that their soules are thereby deformed?"[49] John Downame echoes this idea: "so doe they by this outward decking deforme and defile their owne soules, and bring vpon themselues sinne and condemnation."[50] Cosmetics, according to Stubbes and Downame, have an eerie ability to penetrate not only the borders of the body, but the boundary distinguishing body from soul. Material poisons applied to the skin reappear as internal, moral decay.

If the physical corrosion of cosmetics was understood as bringing about a spiritual pollution, that pollution, in turn, was represented as a kind of poison, simultaneously metaphorical and literal, which would spread its contagion to others. Citing Saint Jerome, Downame goes on to write, "If any wantonly deck themselues, to prouoke others in a wanton manner to gaze vpon them, though no hurt follow vpon it, yet they shall be liable to eternall iudgement, because they prepared a poyson, if there had beene any who would haue tasted of it."[51] Coming full circle, Jerome and Downame suggest that women who adorn themselves with the material poisons of paint not only suffer from spiritual contamination, but translate this taint back into material poisons which they transmit to other victims.

POISONOUS BODIES

As Downame's model of contamination suggests, the fatal powers so often ascribed to cosmetics are linked not only to the material nature of the paints themselves, but also to the bodies and objects associated with them. This certainly proves true in *The Devil's Charter*, where Lucretia's death is heralded by the uneasy identification between her own elaborately painted body and the array of objects related to her beautification. The fatal vial that contains her poisoned paints is linked to a catalogue of related props; a stage-direction reads "*Enter* two Pages with a Table, two looking glasses, a box with Combes and instruments, a rich bowle" (IV.iii.2186). The unusual specificity of these directions is echoed by Lucretia's explicit references to the role of these objects in her preparations: "Giue me some blanching water in this boule, | Wash my face *Motticilla* with this cloth" (2231–2). Another stage direction notes of Lucretia, "*She looketh into two glasses*" (2236), and she announces that she will "correct these arches with this mullet [tweezers]" (2244). The artificial beauty that will poison her is shown to be inseparable from the material objects that embody and facilitate it.

Associated with vanity and luxury, these objects—particularly the vial and "rich bowle"—evoke an image from the play's prologue. After a brief opening catalogue of the various sins to be dramatized, the prologue concludes with an image of the Whore of Babylon:

> Behold the Strumpet of proud Babylon,
> Her Cup with fornication foaming full
> Of Gods high wrath and vengeance for that evill,
> Which was imposd upon her by the Divill.
> (Prologue, 5–8)

Through direct iconographic links, Lucretia's face-painting scene is closely aligned with this moment: already proven a whore by the play, she enters the stage holding a cup filled with seductive poisons.[52] In the context of these close visual and thematic parallels, the fatal cosmetics in Lucretia's vial become a physical transmutation of the sexual and religious impurity associated with her Catholicism: the original image in Revelation describes a woman "arrayd in purple and scarlet colour, and decked with gold, and precious stone & pearls, hauing a golden cup in her hand, full of abominations and filthinesse of her fornication."[53] As the only boundary between these women and the poisons they carry, the cups themselves occupy a crucially liminal position in the transmission of these polluting materials.[54] Perennially open containers, they not only allow, but inevitably bring about, the transfer of their contents to any with whom they come into contact. Tainted by the dangerous materials they contain, these receptacles of poisons go on to spread their contamination further.

In their inability to keep their cosmetic contents within bounds, these vessels become uneasily interchangeable with the painted female bodies—or, in the case of the stage, male bodies painted as female—which become their new containers and display cases. One beauty marketer, in fact, explicitly identifies both painted and unpainted women with vessels of differing qualities, promising the purchaser of his merchandises that "Other Ladies in your company shall look like brown-bread sippets in a dish of snowie cream, or if you will, like blubberd juggs in a cupboard of Venice glasses, or earthen Chamberpots in a Goldsmiths shop."[55] Women, then, become not only inanimate objects, but open containers. With the corrosive addition of paint, this openness offers the troubling possibility of contagion. Just as cosmetic vials fail to safeguard their internal pollutions, women are depicted as leaky vessels containing poison.[56]

The idea of the female body as perilously open, both to absorption and to spillage, was rooted in the dominant Renaissance medical tradition, inherited from ancient Greece and associated primarily with Galen, that identified the body's uneasy permeability particularly with women. Through the tenuousness attributed to its boundaries, the female body was viewed as acutely vulnerable to the sort of bodily infiltration represented by cosmetic corrosion.[57] According to a Galenic understanding of the body, "a woman's flesh is more spongelike and softer than a man's," more easily absorbent, just as women's bodies and souls are more susceptible to overthrow in general: "The passive condition of womankind is subject unto more diseases and of other sortes and natures then men are."[58] Medical critiques of cosmetics similarly emphasized women's special fragility: "those paintings and embellishings which are made with minerals, and corrosiues, are very dangerous," Lomazzo writes, ". . . especially on the face of a woman, which is very tender & delicate by nature."[59] Because of this fragility, the female body was understood to be both more vulnerable to contamination than a man's and, when polluted, more contagious.[60]

Medical accounts of this two-way permeability lie behind and support literary depictions of women as dangerously open receptacles, whose unboundedness puts men at risk as well.[61] As the next chapter demonstrates, this idea is morbidly dramatized in a number of revenge tragedy scenes in which men die from kissing a painted female corpse. *The Devil's Charter* similarly, if less directly, illustrates the idea that women endanger men. Although Lucretia dies from exposure to her own paints, she is not their only victim: the duplicity and infidelity which her paints embody also lead her to kill her husband, Gismond. "Haild on with furie to revenge these wrongs

| And love impoison'd with thy jealousie," she soliloquizes, "I have devised such a curious snare, | As jealous *Vulcan* never yet devis'd" (I.v.594–8). It is precisely the threat that her scandalous reputation will contaminate those around her, in fact, that leads to Lucretia's own death: mulling over the multiple murders necessary for his plot, her Machiavellian brother Caesar mulls "Sister *Lucretia* thou must follow next: | My fathers shame and mine, endeth in thee" (III.v.1828–9). Although Lucretia is the play's most immediate victim of paint, then, the men whose lives touch her feel the effects of its taints in significant, if indirect, ways.

While women tend to be at the center of discussions of the dangers of face-paints, ample evidence indicates that men were significant consumers of cosmetic products as well. Tuke, for example, refers in his title to *Painting and Tincturing of Men and Women*, and Platt, among others, offers recipes on "How to colour the head or beard."[62] Bulwer similarly writes of

the like prodigious affectation in the Faces of effeminate Gallants, a bareheaded Sect of amorous Idolaters, who of late have begun to vye patches and beauty-spots, nay, painting, with the most tender and phantasticall Ladies, and to returne by Art their queasie paine upon women, to the great reproach of Nature, and high dishonour and abasement of the glory of man's perfection.[63]

"Painting is bad both in a foule and faire woman," he concludes, "but worst of all in a man."[64] These stated anxieties about male contact with paint, combined with dramatic scenes in which men die from kissing painted women, raise the possibility that what is at stake in anxieties about poisoned cosmetics may be not so much the problem of women's vulnerability as the corollary problem that it represents: the vulnerability of men. As the transvestite stage suggests, the permeable body that presents itself as female may, in actuality, be male beneath its paint and costumes. As a caricatured symbol for the precarious openness of the body, femininity may be more significant as metaphor than as fact.

STAGING POISONOUS SPECTACLES

Provocatively, for audiences, the painted women dramatized and demonized in plays are often closely affiliated with theatricality itself.

As a spectacle of monstrous femininity, Lucretia's demise in *The Devil's Charter* echoes and implicates other devious, duplicitous women of the revenge tragedy tradition. In preparing to murder her husband, she self-consciously and eagerly aligns herself with earlier dramatic "heroines": "If womanly thou melt then call to minde, | Impatient Medeas wrathfull furie, | And raging Clitemnestraes hideous fact" (I.v.586–8). Lucretia directly appeals to a theatrical tradition of women who carry out their revenge against their husbands by means of dissimulation and concealment: Medea and Clytemnestra famously lure their victims into the interior of their house under false pretenses in order to kill them. Her own Machiavellian schemes take on an explicitly theatrical vocabulary. She notes her husband's entrance with the announcement "Here comes the subject of my Tragedy" (I.v.609), and, having forced him to sign a will and statement clearing her name before she murders him, she muses "So now that part is playd, what followes now?" (I.v.684). Lucretia's skills at dissimulation unite her face-painting and her theatricality, suggesting an essential link between the two.

There is an incongruity, however, between Lucretia's actively duplicitous role in bringing about her husband's murder and her apparent passivity as a victim of the dissimulation inherent in poisonous paints, and it points to an intriguing anomaly in the play's metatheatrical resonances. Lucretia, who paints her face in front of her mirror, is simultaneously both actor and audience, spectacle and consumer. Although she prides herself on her mastery of the Machiavellian arts of deception and seduction, her own susceptibility to the pleasures of artificial beauty shows that she is ultimately no more in control of her dissembling allure than the men who submit to it. Just as Gismond's admiration of her "beauty," "amorous lookes," and "precious eyes" (I.v.631, 632, and 635) disarms him from anticipating and preventing Lucretia's murderous plans, similarly her delight at her new cosmetics, presented as a gift from a suitor, prevails over any possibility of suspicion:

> Kinde *Lodowike* hadst thou presented me,
> With *Persian* clothes of gold or Tinsilry,
> With rich *Arabian* Odors, pretious stones,
> Or what brave women hold in highest price,
> Could not have beene so gracious as this tincture,
> Which I more valew then my richest jewels . . .
>
> (IV.iii.2176–81)

Lucretia's elated elevation of paints over all other luxurious gifts, and her subsequent paean to her own vaunted beauty ("My beaming eyes yet full of Majesty, I . . . The Rosie Garden of these amourous cheekes, I My nose the gratious forte of conquering love, I . . . Sweet mouth the Ruby port to Paradice" (IV.iii.2212–15)) calls attention to her fundamental weakness: she has fallen prey to her own seductive power. As Thomas Tuke argued of painted women, she is her own idolater, simultaneously object and subject. Lucretia dies poisoned not only by her father, the actual source of her fatal paints, but by herself: like Guildenstern and Rosencrantz, who Hamlet describes as eagerly (if unwittingly) embracing their own destruction, she "did make love to this employment."[65]

Although Lucretia's death among her own paints is both distinctively feminine and strikingly self-orchestrated, in important ways it reflects the larger crisis that *The Devil's Charter* dramatizes: the self-destruction of the Borgia family, and in particular Roderigo Borgia, who becomes Pope Alexander VI.[66] In preparing to murder her husband, Lucretia exhorts herself to live up to the reputed wiliness of her family: "Let none of *Borgias* race in policies I Exceed thee *Lucrece*: now prove *Caesars* Sister, I So deepe in bloudy stratagems as hee" (I.v.582–4). At first glance, of course, Lucretia does not prove equal in cunning either to her brother, who kills their other brother, the Duke of Candy, and plots to kill her as well, or to her father, who successfully brings about multiple murders, including her own, over the course of the play. On deeper examination, however, the play shows her to be a very apt representative of her clan. Like her, her father and brother believe themselves to be sophisticated masters of theatrical dissimulation; her father, in fact, echoes some of her explicitly metatheatrical language, musing, upon preparing to poison his captive princes, Philippo and Astor, "Heere I must act a Tragecomoedie" (IV.v.2622). Yet also like her, both die from disguised poisons that they eagerly, and naively, consume. Belchar, one of the devils who helped Roderigo become Pope Alexander, switches bottles at a banquet: "That fatall wine which for his Cardinalls I He destined I tooke out of the place: I And plac'd his owne wine for those Cardinalls" (V.v.3263–5). Just as Lucretia dies from the poisons of a beauty that she used to destroy the men around her, Alexander dies, with Caesar, from wine that he had prepared and intended for others. As the manner of this death makes clear, the charter that seems to manipulate the devils into giving Alexander power actually surrenders his sovereignty to them: like Marlowe's Faustus, whom he at times closely echoes, he enjoys a temporary illusion of control rather than actual power. Like Lucretia, he dies consuming his own poisons, seduced by his own apparent power. Although both he and Lucretia are both actors in conniving plots against others, the image of treacherous face-paints suggests that not only audiences, but actors as well, can be both seduced and contaminated by dangerous spectacles.

As the metatheatrical implications of *The Devil's Charter* demonstrate, although complaints against cosmetics draw on an array of chemical and moral associations, the representation of cosmetic poisoning in the theater points to more complex and self-conscious reflections on the effects of spectacles on their consumers, both outside the play and within it. The significant role given to face-paints and scenes of painting within the play implicitly calls attention to the painting, costuming, and self-metamorphosing that constitute theatrical productions. Both metonymically and metaphorically, face-paints come to stand for the theater itself: as crucial theatrical props, they represent the mechanics of the stage, and as a means of deceiving and seducing spectators they embody the spirit of theatrical illusion. Consistently linked by both critics and supporters, plays and face-painting were seen as embodying the same seductive and contaminating effects. In the context of these shared associations, representations of death by cosmetic exposure take on a metatheatrical significance. If women such as the dissembling Lucretia, who die from direct contact with face-paint, may be likened to the painted players of stage-plays, the men who die from mediated poisons, through exposure to these painted women—such as Lucretia's husband, Gismond—seem to stand in for the audience, who absorb the contagious taint of the theater through the players. Due to its mimetic nature, the theater was understood as transmitting its contents into both actors and spectators; "Anglo-phile Eutheo," generally believed to be Anthony Munday, claims that "al other euils pollute the doers onlie, not the beholders, or the hearers . . . . Onlie the filthines of plaies, and spectacles is such, as maketh both the actors & beholders giltie alike."[67] Lucretia's death through her own application of paints points to the threat of women falling under the sway of their own seductive powers, but as passive spectators of painted faces and shows, men may occupy ultimately the most endangered place in the equation, becoming invaded, effeminized, and objectified by the poisons on which they gaze.

As standard stage props, face-paints were a deeply entrenched part of theatrical production: early theater company records include accounts such as "Payd to the paynter for payntyng the players facys, iiij d," and "Item, paid to the paynter ffor peyntyng of ther fasses Viij d."[68] Renaissance folk-etymologists played on the association: In his *An Apology for Actors*, Thomas Heywood offers a derivation of the word tragedy from "τρυξ, a kinde of painting, which the Tragedians of the old time vsed to stayne their faces with," suggesting that make-up was seen as the root of theater, both philologically and practically.[69] The two arts were understood as mutually reinforcing: Webster writes of the actor, "Hee is much affected to painting, and tis a question whether that make him an excellent Plaier, or his playing an exquisite painter."[70]

Critics of theater and face-painting—often the same in both cases—saw the two as linked in their shared epistemological and ontological confusion: both are associated with disguise, duplicity, and chameleon-like fluidity of identity.[71] Likening painted women to a standard figure for the theater, Stubbes writes that "Proteus, that monster, could neuer change himselfe into so many formes and shapes as these women doe."[72] John Earle asserts that "A Player" is "like our painting gentlewomen, seldom in his own face,"[73] and Thomas Draiton writes of the face-painting woman, "shee'le please men in all places: | For she's a Mimique, and can make good faces."[74] The false faces common to both cosmetics and the theater threaten semiotic stability: William Prynne condemns "this common *accursed hellish art of face-painting*" because it, like stage players, perverts God's works "*in putting a false glosse upon his creatures.*"[75]

Along with their shared associations with dangerous dissembling, the theater is also linked to face-painting by ideas of seduction through lascivious, excessive self-adornment and display. Bulwer says of face-painting that "in adorning and setting forth the Body [it] differs nothing from the ostentation of Stage-plaies, and is no lesse indecent then fiction in manners."[76] Prynne castigates face-painters who "adorne themselves like comicall women, as if they were entring into a Play-house to act a part."[77] William Cave writes that Christians should be "leaving *fucus's* and *paintings*, and *living pictures*, and fading beauty to those that belong to Playes and *Theatres.*"[78]

Concerns about ostentation and seduction in the theater, as well as cosmetics, merged with fears of infiltration and penetration. To moralist critics, theatergoing was inexorably associated with sexual vulnerability. Regardless of the play and its contents (although these were generally seen as intensifying, rather than alleviating, the problem), exposure to spectacles and spectators in a public space was seen as itself a threat to chastity, particularly for women. In an address "To the Gentlewomen Citizens of London" Stephen Gosson warns:

We walke in the Sun many times for pleasure, but our faces are taned before we returne: though you go to theaters to see sport, *Cupid* may catche you ere you departe. The litle God houereth aboute you, & fanneth you with his wings to kindle fire: when you are set as fixed whites, Desire draweth his arrow to the head, & sticketh it vppe to the fethers, and Fancy bestirreth him to shed his poyson through euery vaine. If you doe but listen to the voyce of the Fouler, or ioyne lookes with an amorous Gazer, you haue already made your selues assaultable, & yelded your Cities to be sacked.[79]

Gosson's vocabulary identifies the theater with a violently invasive sexuality, threatening the tenuous boundaries of the female body: women exposed to it become "assaultable," and yield their "Cities to be sacked," suggesting that the penetrating force of Cupid's arrow is in itself a sort of rape. His opening metaphor, of the effect of the sun on the faces of those who let themselves be publically exposed, links the dangerously invasive effects of the theater to both the "poyson" of desire and the perils of artificial color burnt into the faces.

As the metaphors of sunbeams, arrows, and poison suggest, attacks against the theater, like critiques of face-painting, understand its sexual and semiotic transgressions as an invasive contamination. Like the force of cosmetics, this pollution was envisioned, in a conflation of the material and immaterial, as seeping physically through the body in order to enter the soul. The theater, like cosmetics, problematizes the relationship between surface and substance. Not only are its external trappings misleading signs of what lies within, but its exterior show penetrates the boundaries of the audience's body through ears, eyes, and all senses, to take control of the mind and soul.

As we have seen earlier in this book, the theater's capacity for contamination was routinely understood in terms of poison by its detractors, just as its capacity for restoration was described as a medical treatment by its supporters. Although in the case of face-paints the associations with both helpful and harmful drugs were clearly catalyzed and reinforced by the fact of their chemical ingredients, the example of theater seems to yield to the same charges without the same directly material evidence. Plays do not observably alter the color or texture of their spectators' skin; nor do they erode the teeth or taint the breath. They can, however, seduce; as earlier chapters have shown, moreover, they can produce a wide range of powerful affective and physiological sensations in their audiences and actors. Just as critics of cosmetics identified face-paints with an indistinguishably spiritual and physical stain, plays suggest inseparably intertwined effects on body and soul. The perceived power of theater to invade, seduce, and corrupt the spectator lent itself naturally to the literalizing rhetoric of chemicals, even in the absence of literal drugs. Aligned with, and authorized by, fears about the invasive nature of paint's chemical properties, anticosmetic and antitheatrical rhetoric draws on concerns about the reliability of boundaries at large, pointing to corollaries in the distinct but overlapping discourses of medical, moral, and theatrical authors. As overdetermined symbols for this contaminating force, poisonous cosmetics and painted bodies point to vivid beliefs about the power of surfaces to seep into substances, of appearances to alter and endanger bodies and souls.

While antitheatricalists' complaints about poisonous cosmetics tend to be unsurprising, especially in the context of their similar condemnations of the contagious effects of the stage, Barnabe Barnes's portrayal of Lucretia's poisonous paints in *The Devil's Charter* is both more striking and more complex. By demonstrating the voluptuous pleasure with which Lucretia surrenders herself to the beautifying paints that bring about her death, and likening it to her father's own unwitting embrace of his own wine-steeped demise, Barnes suggests that actors are themselves acutely vulnerable to the contaminating effects of the medium they perpetrate on others. Further, and perhaps more strikingly, by blurring the line between actor and audience he implies that all consumers of spectacles are participants as well, actively seeking out, rather than passively submitting to, their own pleasurable poisons. Although critics of the theater often claimed that its effects were inexorable, necessarily tainting anyone exposed to its corrupt allure, Barnes suggests that perhaps the equation works the other way: we are transformed, drugged, even poisoned by the theater not because we cannot avoid it, but precisely because we crave the alluring seduction it offers.

4

Poisoned Kisses: Theater of Seduction

Near the end of *The Tragedye of Solyman and Perseda* (1592), the tyrant Soliman extracts a kiss from the dying Perseda, who, to escape his advances, has tricked him into killing her. "A kisse I graunt thee," she responds with unexpected alacrity, "though I hate thee deadly" (V.iv.67).[1] Very shortly, however, Soliman realizes that this concession may not have been the triumph it seemed at the time. "But stay," he wonders to himself; "let me see what paper is this?" (V.iv.116). His question is followed by a stage direction: "*Then he takes up a paper, and reedes in it as followeth: Tyrant, my lips were sawst with deadly poyson, to plague thy hart that is so full of poison.*" Soon enough, Soliman meets his rather gruesome end: "Ah, now I feele the peper tould me true; | The poison is disperst through euery vaine, | And boiles, like Etna, in my frying guts" (V.iv.142–4). Perseda's embrace, long imagined by Soliman as the fulfillment of all his desires, proves instead to be fatal.

While the play's engagingly heavy-handed rhetoric is its own, this peculiar dramatic device is surprisingly widespread. Towards the end of the sixteenth century and the beginning of the seventeenth, the idea of death by poisonous kiss emerges in a significant number of English tragedies: after *Solyman and Perseda*, it features in Shakespeare's *Romeo and Juliet* (1594–6), Anthony Munday's *The Death of Robert Earl of Huntington* (1601), *The Revenger's Tragedy* (1607), *The Second Maiden's Tragedy* (1611), Thomas Middleton's *Women Beware Women* (1623), John Webster's *The White Devil* (1612) and *The Duchess of Malfi* (1614), Elizabeth Cary's *The Tragedy of Mariam* (1613), and Philip Massinger's *The Duke of Milan* (1622), to name a few. In nearly all of these plays, moreover, the danger of the kiss stems from the painted female body

—usually, dead or dying—to which it is directed.[2] Whereas the previous chapter considered early modern anxieties about cosmetics in medical and theatrical depictions of the dangers they posed for women, this chapter examines related concerns about the dangers that the painted female body posed for men. In *The Second Maiden's Tragedy*, *The Duke of Milan*, and *The Revenger's Tragedy*, male characters turn to the artificial beauty of the female corpse as a remedy for loss, despair, and even death itself, but ultimately find it both spiritually and physically poisonous.

Painted corpses, like face-paints themselves, prove to be not only dangerous remedies, but explicitly theatrical ones. In each of the plays this chapter examines, the elaborate make-up, costuming, and display of the corpse mimics the theatrical medium in which it is presented; the men who embrace these lifeless forms, accordingly, represent spectators seduced by, and addicted to, alluring and idolatrous shows. The direct physical contact of the kiss, however, at the liminal boundary of the mouth, calls attention to the instability of the boundary between spectator and spectacle, and the idea of spectators as passive onlookers. More directly than in the plays examined by earlier chapters, male characters in these plays control, consume, and ultimately merge with the spectacles on which they gaze, blurring the lines between watching, directing, and participating in plays. The fact that the men who embrace painted corpses in each of these plays are tyrannical rulers, for whom death is a just punishment, adds political undertones to the erotic, religious, and theatrical crises the plays depict. Their insistent attempts to assert power over forces they cannot control, such as death, highlights the overlap between worldly and artistic forms of manipulation, and their dangerous consequences. The chapter begins by examining the association of the corpse with idolatry and spectatorship in *The Second Maiden's Tragedy*, moves next to Massinger's more explicitly metatheatrical revision of it in *The Duke of Milan*, and closes by examining these concerns in an earlier play, *The Revenger's Tragedy*, which takes the hazardous theatricality of the poisoned kiss to different levels by juxtaposing it not only with other threatening kisses, but with an actual theatrical performance that culminates in murder.[3] By examining the pervasiveness of the motif of the poisoned kiss, and studying its treatment in plays that have been critically neglected, this chapter demonstrates both how *The Revenger's Tragedy* fits into a broader set of plays meditating on the dangerous physical effects of theatrical seductions, and how distinctive it is in its treatment of those effects.

WOOING PAINTED IDOLS: *THE SECOND MAIDEN'S TRAGEDY*

The Second Maiden's Tragedy dramatizes a morbid narrative of unrequited desire turned pathological.[4] The play features an artificially typecast set of characters, evoking the allegorical world of a morality play; the Tyrant, who usurps the throne, is in love with the Lady, whose heart is given to her true lover (and the true king), Govianus. After the Lady chooses to kill herself rather than surrender to the Tyrant's desire, the Tyrant adorns and displays the Lady's dead body in a desperate attempt to deny her death, and eventually calls for a painter to restore her color with cosmetics. Govianus, in disguise, beautifies the body with poisoned paint, leading to the fatal kiss with which the play culminates.[5] The play depicts the appeal exerted by the Lady's corpse as idolatrous and, ultimately, addictive: an obsessive craving that intensifies the more it is indulged.[6]

Well before the corpse becomes a vehicle for poisons, it becomes the play's central focus and object of desire. This desire takes on an explicitly oral vocabulary; after the Lady's death, even Govianus, her upright and virtuous lover, describes her as a "delicious treasure of mankind" (III.i.244), and tells her corpse "I will kiss thee, | After death's marble lip" (III.i.248–51).[7] This implicit eroticization of the corpse becomes more insistent with the Tyrant's even bolder approach to the tomb. "Death nor the marble prison my love sleeps in | Shall keep her body locked up from mine arms," he proclaims; "I must not be so cozened" (IV.ii. 48).[8] In fact, far from cozening, death seems to facilitate the Tyrant's lust. In a figurative version of the rape that the Lady's willful chastity and subsequent suicide prevented him from accomplishing, he breaks into her tomb and robs it of her body.[9] Unlike the Lady, moreover, the stone can be interpreted as a willing, even desirous, recipient of the Tyrant's affections: "The monument woos me," he muses; "I must run and kiss it" (IV.iii.9).

The conflation of the Lady and her stone container suggests the figurative petrification of her body. Having instigated the play's crises by her disruptive power to incite desire, she is turned over to the shaping hands of the play's Pygmalions and transformed into a work of art.[10] Yet this process seems only to increase her desirability, escalating the problem of her effect on the play's men: the female body as object turns out to be at least as powerful as the female subject, if not more so.[11] Ironically, it also turns out to be at least as intransigent: whereas the monument seems to represent a more passive, and hence attainable, version of the Lady, it is also the "marble prison" standing as the Tyrant's rival for her possession: "No, wilt not yield? | Art thou so loath to part from her?" (IV.iii.43–4). The lifelessness of stone and body proves both facilitator and barrier to the Tyrant's idolatrous desire; the objectified corpse represents both a solution to and an intensification of the problem posed by the sexually alluring female body.

As the reactions of both Govianus and the Tyrant show, death intensifies rather than diminishes the erotic appeal of the Lady's body; emptied of spirit, the flesh exerts an unfettered pull. Lacking spirit of its own, moreover, the corpse becomes invested with the excess religious meaning of a mock-deity, or an idol. To the Tyrant, the Lady's objectified status seems to render her sacred: he refers to her as a "blessed object" (IV.iii.59), and an onlooking soldier describes the Tyrant's fixation as "mere idolatry" (V.ii.20). The fetishization the corpse inspires lays a foundation for the havoc it will later cause. Its allure, associated with erotic, necrophilic, and idolatrous desires, evokes larger concerns about the impact of lifeless images on their spectators and admirers.[12]

The Tyrant himself acknowledges the emptiness of the object of his affections: "Since thy life has left me," he tells the corpse, "I'll clasp the body for the spirit that dwelt in't,/And love the house still for the mistress' sake" (IV.iii.110–12). Recalling Herod, who, after the suicide of the virgin he loved, "preserved her body dead in honey, | And kept her long after her funeral," he vows to outdo him: "But I'll unlock the treasure house of art | With keys of gold, and bestow all on thee" (IV.iii.119–22). This evocative juxtaposition of art and honey points to the Tyrant's identification of the visual and the oral, seeing and consuming. Unlike Herod, however, the Tyrant not only hopes to maintain the Lady's beauty, but actually attempts to restore the corpse to life.[13] Bringing a full house to an empty one, the Tyrant vows to compensate for the hollowness of the Lady's dispirited body by heaping art upon it, literally refilling or reconstituting her from his treasury. He replaces spirit with art and wealth, suggesting confusion between spirit and matter, subject and object, and a dangerous over-investment in the latter. Substituting adornment for spiritual substance, this strategy mimics the idolatrous inclinations of which the Tyrant is accused.[14]

The Tyrant's treasure house draws explicitly on the theatrical arts of costuming and face-painting. As the Lady's ghost reports to Govianus, the Tyrant sends for "a hand of art | That may dissemble life upon [her] face" (IV.iv.74–5). The foundation for this particular dissembling art, though, begins prior to the painter's arrival, when the Tyrant arranges for the corpse "to be decked | In all the glorious riches of our palace" (V.ii.7–9). A stage direction specifies that attendants "*bring the body in a chair, dressed up in black velvet which sets out the palness of the hands and face, and a fair chain of pearl 'cross her breast, and the crucifix above it.*" The Lady is paraded as a spectacle; the theatricality of her costumed display implicitly identifies the project of animating the corpse with the art of the play. As such, spectatorship becomes a gluttonous form of consumption: the Tyrant announces, "I cannot keep from sight of her so long. | I starve mine eye too much," and goes on to claim that "Our mind has felt a famine for the time" (V.ii.6–7, 10).[15] His words recall the striking metaphor earlier in the play of a soldier who, looking on when the Tyrant exhumed the corpse from the grave, described the empty tomb as "a great city-pie brought to a table . . . The lid's shut close when all the meat's picked out. | Yet stands to make a show and cozen people" (IV.iii.131–4). The corpse itself, in these comments, becomes a material remedy to be consumed, calling to mind contemporary fascinations with mummia, the popular but controversial medicine made of powdered dead human flesh, as discussed in Chapter 1. In his figurative attempt to consume the remedy of the Lady's corpse, however, the Tyrant is an over-susceptible spectator: his desire for the performance to be real leads him to enter the spectacle itself, with toxic consequences.

The painted, costumed theatricality of the Lady's corpse seems to be as much a cause of her seductive power over the Tyrant as it is a symptom. Plays were routinely accused by their detractors of inciting dangerous lusts: William Prynne, for instance, argued that "Stage-playes pollute the eyes, the eares, the mindes, both of their Actors and Spectators, by ingendring unchaste, adulterous lewde affections in their hearts, by their obscene words, and lascivious gestures."[16] Complaining about idols, he declared that plays were, in fact, more erotically dangerous: "Certainely, if these livelesse pictures are so apt to ingenerate unchaste affections, or to pricke men on to whoredom and adultery: much more will these amorous actions, complements, kisses, and embracements; these lively pictures, these reall representations of adultery and uncleannesse in our Stage-playes, doe it."[17] Like idols, theatrical spectacles exploit their visual appeal to insinuate their way into viewers' eyes and desires. Built of actual bodies, however, they are even worse than idols: they are "lively pictures" and "reall representations."

This ambivalent spectacle, the Tyrant openly acknowledges, serves as compensation for the absence of the living Lady: "fate's my hindrance," he laments, "And I must only rest content with art, | And that I'll have in spite on't!" (V.ii.32–4). Yet the "it" towards which his spite is directed is ambiguous; it could point either to fate, for its ill usage of him, or to art, for its resistance to fulfilling his fantasy. As the play's references to idolatry suggest, art is attributed a capacity to recreate life itself. "It is no shame for thee, most silent mistress," the Tyrant cajoles the corpse, "to stand in need of art" (V.ii.41–2). As David Bergeron aptly comments, however, "she obviously needs life more than art. His hope is that art can imitate life."[18] Death, according to the Tyrant's desperation-driven conviction, can be conquered by appearance: "Let but thy art hide death upon her face,/That now looks fearfully on us, and but strive | To give our eye delight" (V.ii.81–3). "So shall we | By art," he goes on, "force beauty on yon lady's face | Though death sit frowning on't a storm of hail | To beat it off. Our pleasure shall prevail" (V.ii.109–12). The pleasure that will prevail, however, is a delight resting entirely on concealment of death through art: a precarious pedestal bound to collapse when leaned upon too heavily.[19]

The play's climactic final scene locates the kiss at a precarious boundary not only between two bodies, but between life and death, spirit and matter. Upon viewing the painted body, the Tyrant surrenders himself with pleasure to his newly reinforced illusion that the Lady lives. He explodes with joy, but only briefly:

> *Tyr.*   O, she lives again!
> She'll presently speak to me. Keep her up;
> I'll have her swoon no more; there's treachery in't.
> Does she not feel warm to thee?
> *Gov.*   Very little, sir.
> *Tyr.*   The heat wants cherishing, then. Our arms and lips
> Shall labour life into her. Wake, sweet mistress!

'Tis I that call thee at the door of life.
                    [*Kisses the body.*] Ha!
I talk so long to death, I'm sick myself.
Methinks an evil scent still follows me.
Gov.   Maybe 'tis nothing but the colour, sir,
       That I laid on.
Tyr.   Is that so strong?
Gov.   Yes, faith, sir.
       'Twas the best poison I could get for money.
                    [*Throws off his disguise.*]
                         (V.ii.114–25)

This scene, like the play at large, turns on a curious ambiguity as to the nature of the transformation brought about by paint and the kiss. According to the Tyrant, the combination of color and embrace should serve to bring the Lady back to life: the first inspires him to proclaim that "she lives again!," but for added measure he promises, "Our arms and lips | Shall labour life into her." In fact, however, not only does art fail to animate the Lady, but direct contact with it proves fatal to its consumer. By kissing the Lady's corpse, the Tyrant directly absorbs the poisonous nature of the lifeless painted idol he has created.

Kisses, like cosmetics, were a source of both fascination and anxiety in the Renaissance, in response to concerns about their corrosive effects on physiological, erotic, and spiritual boundaries. Renaissance medical writings worried about the mouth as a highly vulnerable site of bodily permeability. In *Sylua Syluarum* (1626), Francis Bacon comments that "It hath beene noted, that the *Tongue* receiueth, more easily, *Tokens* of *Diseases*, than the other *Parts* . . . The *Cause* is, (no doubt,) the *Tendernesse* of the Part; which thereby receiueth more easily all *Alterations*, than any other *Parts* of the *Flesh*."[20] The still-lingering impact of syphilis epidemics during this period offered evidence for this vulnerability; it was widely believed that syphilis could be transmitted through a kiss.[21] At a different level, the desire that the kiss inflamed was feared to be potentially toxic.[22] Complaining about the sexually inflammatory status of cross-dressed boy actors, John Rainolds likened the powerful effects of kisses to the sting of poisonous spiders, claiming "if they [spiders] do but touch men only with their mouth, they put them to wonderful pain and make them mad: so beautiful boys by kissing do sting and pour secretly in a kind of poison."[23] According to the popular

Neoplatonic conceit of the *mors osculi*, meanwhile, a kiss could facilitate a fatal loss of spirit. As the lover's soul passes through the gateway of the lips during the moment of the kiss, in a reciprocal passion two lovers exchange souls, but an unrequited lover loses his soul without gaining a compensatory one.[24] If the mouth is physiologically, erotically, and spiritually permeable, then, a kiss could facilitate disease, desire, and ultimately even the loss of one's soul.

The fatal kiss in *The Second Maiden's Tragedy* illustrates each of these areas for concern about kisses: the physiological, erotic, and spiritual. Not only does the scene call attention to the liminal position of the mouth as a gateway to the body and soul, moreover, but it also situates it on a boundary between the body and words. The Tyrant's triumphant cry, "O, she lives again!," identifies the Lady's recovery with the return of language: "She'll presently speak to me." When he proposes to "labour life into her" by means of his lips, he ostensibly refers to kisses, but his next words suggest that speech may play an equally important role: "Wake, sweet mistress! | 'Tis I that call thee at the door of life." Similarly, when he realizes that the corpse has contaminated him, he attributes its effect to his verbal interchange: "I talk so long to death, I'm sick myself." Despite Govianus's claim that " 'tis nothing but the colour" that poisons him through his kiss, the Tyrant's words suggest an uncanny double causation. The implicit association of the immaterial impact of words with the literal infusion of breath defines the kiss as a liminal zone in which not only separate bodies, but the separate realms of the bodily and the intellectual, fuse together.

Yet another boundary that the kiss collapses in this scene is the line between life and death.[25] As the kiss allows poison to travel into the body, or breath and spirit to travel out, it is both the imagined cause of bringing the Lady back to life, and the actual cause of the Tyrant's death. The Tyrant's belief in his ability to revive the Lady's corpse, moreover, signifies the escapist fantasy to which he surrenders most fully at the moment of the kiss. The kiss, then, points to the convergence of another tenuously separated dyad: that of spectacle and spectator, art and consumer. Already as much director and producer as audience, in the moment of the kiss the Tyrant becomes a co-actor as well: through the conduit it provides, he directly absorbs the illusion he has staged, and finds its effects fatal.

IDOLATRY, DEAD AND ALIVE: *THE DUKE OF MILAN*

While *The Second Maiden's Tragedy* is primarily preoccupied with the attraction of an inanimate corpse, Massinger's *The Duke of Milan*, written eleven years later in 1622, deepens the earlier play's emphasis on idolatry, and points to the roots of this necrophilic attachment in an idolatrous fixation prior to the woman's death. The Duke of Milan is Sforza, whose obsessive love for his wife, Marcelia, turns to jealous fears and eventually leads him to murder her. When Marcelia's innocence is belatedly proven, Sforza loses his sanity and refuses to believe that his wife is dead. While his doctors, terrified of his rage, humor his conviction that she is only pale because she is ill and sleeping, the play's revenger, Francisco, presents himself to them as a visiting doctor who can heighten the illusion of life by restoring her natural color with poison-laced paint. Borrowing extensively from *The Second Maiden's Tale*, Massinger revises its emphasis to show that the appeal of the corpse merely extends and intensifies a pre-existing fetishization of the female body. The play also eschews abstract archetypes (Lady, Tyrant) in favor of more fully developed characters and relationships, inviting the audience further into their minds and worlds. Where the earlier play hints at an association between the attractions of the painted corpse and the seductions of theatrical spectacles, moreover, Massinger offers a fuller and more complex reflection on the theatricality inherent in adorning and animating an inert form.

The play opens with insistent attention to the Duke's excessive and insidious infatuation. "It is the *Dutchesse* Birth-day," Tiberio announces:

> once a yeere
> Solemnized, with all pompe, and ceremony:
> In which, the Duke is not his owne, but hers:
> Nay, every day indeed, he is her creature,
> For never man so doted; but to tell
> The tenth part of his fondnesse, to a stranger,
> Would argue me of fiction.[26]

Tiberio's description of the Duke's dotage suggests that this love has edged past desire to signify a disconcerting loss of self: Sforza is "not his owne, but hers." Sforza's abdication of self-possession is a theatrical, ritualized act, "Solemnized, with all pompe, and ceremony":

he displays it as a pageant for the entire court. The occasion, moreover, intensifies rather than inverts the usual hierarchy of the house;
Tiberio hastens to specify that this subjection is by no means only a
factor of the festival, but takes place "every day indeed."[27]

Sforza's infatuation, like the Tyrant's in *The Second Maiden's
Tale*, is both emotionally and physically dangerous, but Massinger
goes further in identifying Sforza's infatuation explicitly and perva-
sively with idolatry. In his celebration of his wife, Sforza exacts from
Francisco the confirmation that Marcelia is "As a thing Sacred"
(I.iii.323). "It were a kind of Blasphemy," Francisco agrees, "to
dispute it" (I.iii.327). Sforza describes himself outright as "her
Idolator," a phrase echoed directly by his sister, Mariana, who refers
to "her Idolater, | My Brother" (I.iii.338 and II.i.107). His mother,
Isabella, similarly protests at having "to serve his idol" (I.ii.41). The
specter of idolatry is a matter of acknowledged anxiety to the play's
characters: "I might have falne into Idolatry," Sforza frets, "And
from the admiration of her worth, | Bin taught to think there is no
power above her" (IV.iii.50). Although Sforza expresses himself in a
past contrafactual conditional, however, his ritualized subjection to
his wife suggests that he has not been able to avoid this threat. "What
is idolatrie," the antitheatricalist Stephen Gosson asked, "but to giue
that which is proper to God, vnto them that are no gods?"[28] Sforza's
obsessive devotion to Marcelia is, from the outset, rooted in a category error: conflating mortal with divine, Sforza dehumanizes his
wife, transforming her into a lifeless symbol.

Despite Marcelia's apparently elevated status, the play's language
emphasizes that her influence is contingent on her status as an object,
rather than subject. Those around Sforza see his idealization of his
wife as displacing his sense of self ("not his owne, but hers"), but his
accolades describe her as property belonging to him: "my soules
comfort," "my happinesse," "mine owne" (I.iii.12, 17, and 18). Like
the Tyrant in *The Second Maiden's Tragedy*, his visual enjoyment
takes the form of consumption: "Let others feed | On those grosse
Cates," he proclaims at his dinner in her honor, "while *Sforza* ban-
quets with | Immortal Viands tane in at his Eyes" (I.iii.76–8). While
the Tyrant never possesses the Lady and worries about how to attain
her, however, Sforza has Marcelia's love but worries about losing it.
His possessive exclusion of "others" prefigures his ferocious jealousy: determined that no one else will ever enjoy her, he orders his
favorite, Francisco, to kill her if he should die in battle (I.iii.284–

381). His jealousy is so acute that when Francisco fabricates stories of her infidelity, Sforza, unlike Othello, does not even hesitate long enough to ask for proof: he immediately stabs her to death. Rather than reversing his infatuation, this murder takes it one step further, transforming Marcelia into a literal object.

The play's final scene, in which the dangers of Sforza's volatile and idolatrous passions culminate, echoes closely the ending of *The Second Maiden's Tragedy*. Overcome by the horror of realizing that he has wrongfully murdered his innocent wife, Sforza deludes himself into believing she is still alive. Stephano notes with wonder,

> But that melancholy,
> Though ending in distraction, should worke
> So farre upon a man as to compell him
> To court a thing that has nor sence, nor being,
> Is unto me a miracle.
>
> (V.ii.7–11)

Stephano attributes Sforza's passion for an inanimate body to grief-induced madness, an uneasy blend of melancholy and distraction, but in fact his idolatrous worship for an empty shell merely extends and intensifies his earlier fetishization of his wife. He has long worshipped her, not so much for her "sence, nor being," as for her beauty, which has yet to disappear.

Sforza's deluded fantasies of Marcelia's animation are fostered by the exiled Francisco, in his guise as a miracle-working doctor:

> I am no God sir,
> To give a new life to her, yet I'le hazard
> My head, I'le worke the sencelesse trunke t'appeare
> To him as it had got a second being,
> Or that the soule that's fled from't were call'd backe,
> To governe it againe; I will preserve it
> In the first sweetnesse, and by a strange vaper
> Which I'le infuse into her mouth, create
> A seeming breath; I'le make her vaines run high to
> As if they had true motion.
>
> (V.ii.140–9)

Fully aware of the artificial nature of the "new life" he offers Sforza, Francisco holds his own distance from the project he undertakes. He will fashion only a "seeming breath," veins which run "As if they had true motion": essentially, a simulacrum or theatrical representation of liveliness. His "strange vaper" becomes a pseudo-soul, an artificial animation that proleptically parodies Sforza's fatal kiss. Entering Marcelia's body through her lips, then travelling through them again to poison Sforza, this mysterious vapour will become a demonized and contagious version of the Neoplatonic *mors osculi*.

Francisco's opening rebuttal—"I am no God sir"—calls attention to the quasi-religious nature of the transgression he is asked to undertake, while evoking contemporary fears about both the arrogance, and the risks, of physicians' interfering with nature. In response to his query, "How do you like my workmanship?," his sister Eugenia says "I tremble | And thus to tirannize upon the dead | Is most inhumane" (V.ii.197–9). The desire Francisco fulfills, Sforza's urge to animate the "sencelesse trunke" of Marcelia's corpse, mirrors the Duke's earlier elevation of her body over her soul: still making her an idol, he projects an external spirit onto her objectified form.

In his project of animating an inert form to indulge his audience's imagination, Francisco, like Govianus before him, offers a demonized figure for the theater. The actor's body, which simulates death, life, and identities other than its own, epitomizes the category confusion identified with both the fetishized idol and the necrophilic kiss. Onstage, dead and living bodies are troublingly indistinguishable, even interchangeable; characters can move from one state to the other, and magically back again. Francisco's mock-resurrection presents the uncanny power of the theater at its most disturbingly transgressive.

Francisco's emphasis on his lack of godly powers, moreover, suggests a certain hubris in the stage's mimicry of the creation of life. In the effort to revive Marcelia, art competes with, and ultimately replaces, religion, as it does in the idolatrous attachment to the painted corpse both here and in *The Second Maiden's Tragedy*. As a triumph of image over spirit, idolatry was routinely identified with plays by antitheatricalist critics. Philip Stubbes wrote that stage plays were "sucked out of the deuil's teates, to nourish vs in idolatrie, heathenrie, and sinne"; William Prynne wrote that theatrical interludes were "invented, acted, fostered, frequented by Diuel-Idols, Pagans, Idolaters, lascivious dissolute graceless persons; and deuoted wholly to Idolatry, Idols, Diuels, and the lusts of carnall wicked worldly men"; and Stephen Gosson claimed that "euery play to the worldes end, if it be presented vp on the Stage, shall carry that brand on his backe to make him knowne, which the deuil clapt on, at the first beginning, that is, idolatrie."[29] The impurity associated with idolatry was seen as contagious, something a spectator could absorb by mere presence at a theatrical performance. With reference to the Eucharistic wafer, Stephen Gosson warned ominously, "yf we be carefull that no polution of idoles enter by the mouth into our bodies, how diligent, how circumspect, how wary ought we to be, that no corruption of idols, enter by the passage of our eyes & eares into the soule?"[30]

In their dramatizations of men kissing poisoned corpses, these two plays translate this pollution and corruption of idols into material, and fatal, form. The Tyrant and Sforza die from contact with the contaminating power of the lifeless idols they have created. The theatrical nature of their deaths, as well as the broader popular associations between the stage, cosmetics, and idolatry, suggests that the poisons which kill them are also those of the theater. Their fatal invasion by seductive spectacles holds out a threat for the play's audience as well, a threat even more explicitly dramatized in an earlier but more self-conscious treatment of this motif, *The Revenger's Tragedy*.

BARE BONES: *THE REVENGER'S TRAGEDY*

In *The Second Maiden's Tragedy* and *The Duke of Milan*, the erotic investment in a corpse that leads to the poisoned kiss is depicted as an extension of a prior obsession with the woman herself. While Marcelia, who lives for four acts, is given considerably more stage time than the Lady, who dies at the beginning of Act III, both plays trace a continuum between the living and the dead. In *The Revenger's Tragedy*, on the other hand, the focus is exclusively on the latter: the desired female is not only dead, but long decomposed, by the time the play opens, and the object of the poisoned kiss is not a corpse, but a skull. This hollowing out of the female body is mirrored in the hollowing out of the interior worlds of the play's other characters as well. As in *The Second Maiden's Tragedy*, the characters are abstractions—the Duke, Vindice (the revenger), Lussurioso (the lecherous), Castiza (the chaste), Younger Son—rather than individuals, evoking the artificial and allegorical world of a morality play.[31] The play dramatizes Vindice's attempt to take revenge on the Duke for the memory of his beloved Gloriana, whom the Duke murdered with poison when she refused to give in to his lust.[32]

Disguised as Piato, Vindice enters the Duke's employment, agreeing to procure women for his endless sexual appetites, while the Duke's wife conducts an incestuous affair with the Duke's bastard son. After Vindice succeeds in bringing the Duke into a poisonous embrace with Gloriana's painted and costumed skull, he kills the Duke's oldest son and other members of the court through acting in a masque that murders its own audience: a performance, strikingly neglected by critics, that presents a powerfully self-conscious image of the physically and spiritually corrosive effects of the theater.[33] Along with emptying both its corpse and its characters of interiority, then, the play multiplies its dangerous kisses and metatheatrical effects to present a witty, self-conscious parody of the genre it enacts. Although it depicts the theater as exerting a threatening power over audiences, the play simultaneously undermines that power by using farce and caricature to distance its own audiences from the dangerous spectacles it portrays.

Throughout its various plots, *The Revenger's Tragedy* is strangely crowded with images of both kisses and poisonings that dissolve, disintegrate, and undo.[34] From the outset, these effects are explicitly identified with the erotic power of Gloriana's body. In his opening soliloquy, Vindice's nostalgic meditations on Gloriana's former beauty foreshadow her role in his future revenge on the Duke: "Oh she was able to ha' made a usurer's son | Melt all his patrimony in a kiss" (I.i.26–9).[35] Even to an unsuccessful suitor, the corrosive force of Gloriana's attractions is apparently powerful enough to dissolve away everything, all property and inheritance. The contaminating power of kisses echoes dangerously elsewhere in the play. The bastard Spurio, seduced by his stepmother, the Duchess, declares prophetically "O, one incestuous kiss picks open hell" (I.ii.175). This intergenerational, intrafamilial kiss becomes both catalyst and symbol for the degeneration of order within the court.[36] As a bastard, Spurio already embodies the contamination of familial categories, undermining the integrity of his father's marriage; his incestuous embrace erodes these boundaries even further.[37]

Imagery of corrosive poisons extends and intensifies the dangerously polluted erotic permeability associated with mouths and kisses throughout the play. Vindice describes Spurio's incestuous liaison with the Duchess as "strong poison" that "eats | Into the duke . . .'s forehead" (II.ii.162–3). More literally, when Spurio reflects on the sin of his incestuous kiss, the Duchess chides him to stop thinking of

the Duke, "or I'll poison him" (III.v.214). Upon receiving the
grotesque command to go act as a bawd to his own sister, Vindice
cries "O! | Now let me burst; I've eaten noble poison" (I.iii.168–9).
Vindice contaminates his mother, Gratiana, with the poisonous sexuality of the court as well; when Gratiana lapses into the role of bawd,
Castiza berates her, "Mother, come from that poisonous woman
there!" (II.i.239); Vindice similarly accuses his corrupted mother of
turning "to quarled poison" (IV.iv.7). This figurative poison proves
not only contagious, but mimetic, returning to its source: when
Castiza, apparently persuaded to prostitute herself to Lussurioso,
echoes her mother's earlier words of encouragement, Gratiana
laments, "I spoke those words, and now they poison me" (IV.iv.136).

The play's pervasive poisons and kisses culminate in Act Three,
when Vindice paints, poisons, and costumes the skull of his former
love to set a fatal trap for the lecherous Duke. "This very skull," he
vaunts,

> Whose mistress the Duke poison'd, with this drug
> The mortal curse of the earth, shall be reveng'd
> In the like strain, and kiss his lips to death.
>
> (III.v.102–5)

With the dark symmetry characteristic of revenge tragedy, the remains of the poisoned Gloriana—and, symbolically, of all of the victims of the Duke's lust—become transformed into a weapon against
her poisoner. Her kiss reflects back to the Duke the figurative poisons
of his own "palsy-lust" (I.i.34), fused with the literal poisons with
which he killed Gloriana. As the pivot on which this mimetic act of
revenge turns, the skeleton's embrace comes to embody the seductive
but poisonous theatricality that pervades the play.

Gloriana's poisons lie at the heart of the corrosive contamination
the play dramatizes. Vindice opens the play by meditating on
Gloriana's poisoned beauty: "Thou sallow picture of my poison'd
love, | My study's ornament, thou shell of death" (I.i.14–15).[38]
Gloriana is defined by her status as murder-victim: she is first and
foremost the remnants of Vindice's "poisoned love." The contrast
between her former beauty and her current "shell of death" points
insistently and accusatorily to the evil that has intervened between
the two: Vindice addresses her,

> Thee when thou wert apparel'd in thy flesh,
> The old duke poison'd,

> Because thy purer part would not consent
> Unto his palsy-lust . . .

(I.i.31–4)

Gloriana's decay is not natural, but artificial; her deathliness has
been prematurely manufactured by the Duke. The poison of the
Duke's lust, both literal and figurative, has eaten away her insides
and left her hollow, a mere symbol of his degeneracy.

While Gloriana is apostrophized and praised as a co-conspirator,
even the primary actor, in Vindice's plot, the insistent presence of the
skull on stage reminds the audience that she is not a woman but the
decayed remains of one: a stage prop, not a player. In attempting to
punish, and hence correct, the Duke's objectifying lust, Vindice finds
himself mirroring the Duke himself: ultimately, both treat Gloriana
as an object, a vehicle through which to fulfill their own desires.[39]
Just as Vindice's ongoing preoccupation with Gloriana's skull ("Still
sighing o'er Death's vizard?" (I.i.50)) suggests an eroticized attachment paralleling the Duke's naive delight in "the bony lady"
(III.v.121), so his seduction scheme seems to furnish at least as much
erotic excitement for Vindice himself as for the duke. The cleverness
of his plan overwhelms him with pleasure: "O sweet, delectable,
rare, happy, ravishing!" (III.v.1). The expansive terms of his delight,
moreover, take on implicitly sexual overtones: "O, 'tis able | To
make a man spring up, and knock his forehead | Against yon silver
ceiling" (III.v.2–3).[40] In "the violence of [his] joy" (III.v.27), his
"throng of happy apprehensions" (III.v.30), Vindice can hardly even
express his plan to his confidant in all things, his brother.

Although he is ravished by the cleverness of his plot, however,
Vindice distances himself from the seductive force of Gloriana herself. When he finally presents her skull to his brother as the woman
he will offer the Duke, Vindice describes her, fittingly, in pieces:

> Here's an eye
> Able to tempt a great man—to serve God;
> A pretty hanging lip, that has forgot now to dissemble:
> Methinks this mouth should make a swearer tremble,
> A drunkard clasp his teeth, and not undo 'em
> To suffer wet damnation to run through 'em.
> Here's a cheek keeps her colour, let the wind
> Go whistle . . . .

(III.v.54–61)

Despite his own past susceptibility to Gloriana's beauty, Vindice now stands as a detached observer, contemptuously assessing the limited power of her morbid remains. The mocking blazon with which he imagines the impact of her features on other men offers a cruel but witty parody of a standard poetic form. In directing the Petrarchan catalogue of female body parts to a corpse rather than a living woman, he highlights the inherently objectifying effect of a poetics of piecemeal praise.[41] Eye, lip, mouth, and cheek, are each sardonically described in terms of their integrity; beyond life and sexual allure, they are beyond cosmetic dissembling and sexual tempting, beyond corruption and corruptibility. In its very emptiness, though, the skull possesses a curious power. Strangely, given his emphasis on minimizing its power, Vindice implicitly likens its effect to that of alcohol. Upon seeing her mouth, he claims, a drunkard would stop drinking, suggesting both that she would inspire a virtuous horror of death and, implicitly, that she would make drink unnecessary by replacing its effect. This curious aside recalls the identification of painted corpses with addictive consumption in the other plays this chapter has examined. The slightly incongruous combination of power and hollowness that Vindice ascribes to the skull make it a fit vehicle for the temptation and corrosion he has in mind; reduced to nothingness, a blank slate of sorts, Gloriana can now be whatever Vindice, and the Duke, care to imagine her.

Despite, or perhaps because of, Gloriana's dehumanized status as object or prop, the Duke is quickly and easily ensnared. Teasingly warned by Vindice with a series of puns—"after the first kiss my lord the worst is past" (III.v.133); "sh'has somewhat of a grave look with her" (III.v.135)—he falls ecstatically and unsuspectingly into his trap:

> How sweet can a duke breathe? Age has no fault.
> Pleasure should meet in a perfumed mist.
> Lady, sweetly encounter'd: I came from court,
> I must be bold with you. [*Kisses the skull.*] O, what's this? O!
> (III.v.143–6)

Although Vindice and the Duke are both spectators of Gloriana's poisonous skull, they represent very different kinds of spectatorship. While Vindice stands aside as a detached observer, the Duke—like the Tyrant and Sforza—enters the spectacle and, as a result, both consumes and is consumed by it. The Duke's erotic pleasure turns quickly into horror: "O, 't has poisoned me" (III.v.152). The contaminating power of the kiss is drawn out in an extended emphasis on oral imagery. "My teeth are eaten out," the Duke complains (III.v.161), to which Vindice jestingly notes "Then those that did eat are eaten" (III.v.163).[42] The Duke's lament "Oh my tongue!" meets with cruel jests: "Your tongue? 'Twill teach you to kiss closer, | Not like a slobbering Dutchman" (III.v.164–5). The kiss offers a grotesquely material version of the Neoplatonic exchange of souls: rather than consuming his spirit, Gloriana's skull consumes the Duke's lips, teeth, and tongue, gradually dissolving him out of existence.

The Duke's poisonous kiss is identified not only with contamination and the transgression of boundaries, but also—and perhaps even more explicitly—with spectatorship. Vindice underlines the theatrical nature of his punishment by forcing the Duke to gaze upon that which has undone him:

> Brother—
> Place the torch here that his affrighted eyeballs
> May start into those hollows. Duke, dost know
> Yon dreadful vizard? View it well; 'tis the skull
> Of Gloriana, whom thou poisonedst last.
>
> (III.v.147–51)

If the Duke's lechery stemmed from his greedy eye for feminine attractions, his punishment—being forced to stare at a grotesque parody of a painted woman—fits the crime. The Duke's "affrighted eyeballs" are forced to see his own misdeeds reflected back at him: "You have eyes still," Vindice continues; "Look, monster, what a lady thou hast made me | My once betrothed wife" (III.v.165–7).

The Duke's visual punishment continues with subjection to the horrid spectacle of another (figuratively) poisonous kiss, the incestuous liaison of his wife and his son: "Which most afflicting sight," Vindice has earlier planned, "will kill his eyes before we kill the rest of him" (III.v.23–4). "Nay, to afflict thee more," he now gloats, "Here in this lodge they meet for damned clips: | Those eyes shall see the incest of their lips" (III.v.183–5). This spectacle is in itself as fatal to the Duke as Gloriana's kiss: "O, kill me not with that sight!" (III.v.191).[43] Accordingly, the Duke's vision becomes all the more crucial for Vindice's purposes: "Thou shalt not lose that sight for all thy dukedom" (III.v.192). "Brother," he instructs Hippolito,

If he but wink, not brooking the foul object,
Let our two other hands tear up his lids,
And make his eyes, like comets, shine through blood;
When the bad bleeds, then is the tragedy good.
                                        (III.v.201–5)

In mulling over the explicitly visual nature of his revenge, Vindice delineates a theory not only of punishment, but of tragedy: the suffering of immoral characters constitutes theatrical success, justice attained by symmetry. His wittily self-conscious sense of staging a play both calls attention to the theatricality of the kiss and implicitly links it to the larger play in which he acts, raising troubling questions about the parallels and distinctions between the two performances. If the Duke represents the audience, are we, the play's external spectators, tortured like him with the fatal spectacle of Gloriana? Or are we, like Vindice, in a position to watch and gloat over the Duke's demise? Alternatively, are we, like the sightless Gloriana, the object of wooing, cajoling, and flattery in attempts at seduction? Ultimately, the play places us in each of these positions, but complicates these roles by taking care to distinguish its own effects from those that it represents.

After the Duke's death, the play continues to explore the question of the consequences of visual spectacles. Most forcefully, the final phase of Vindice's vindictive scheming, his performance of a masque in which he murders all the audience members, offers crucial parallels to the ingenious and aestheticizing violence of the staged kiss. This scene, which owes much to the similarly murderous performance of "Soliman and Perseda" in Kyd's *The Spanish Tragedy*, gestures towards an increasing ostentatiousness. The murderous masque not only reinforces the theatricality involved in the poisoned kiss, but fuses it emphatically with the form of the play itself, underlining both the play's preoccupation with its own effects, and its message that those effects may be palpably dangerous.

The murderous masque is closely allied with the poisonous kiss both in its elaborately costumed and staged impersonations and in the way it destroys through seducing; both devices appeal to privacy, intimacy, and pleasure in order to catch victims at their most unguarded. Vindice describes the masque in sensual, almost erotic terms: they will catch the nobles in "their pleasure sweet and good, | In midst of all their joys" (V.ii.21–2). The murder-scheme itself generates an excitement apparently similar to that of a play: the plan

"must glad us all" (V.ii.14). Like Gloriana's skull, which undoes the
Duke in "some fit place veil'd from the eyes o' th' court, | Some dark-
en'd, blushless angle" (III.v.13–14), and through the invasive inti-
macy of a kiss, the masquers make their attack from within
Lussurioso's revels, inside the privacy of a banquet room, as part of
the spectacle themselves. The parallelism between the Duke's lascivi-
ousness and that of Lussurioso underlines the similarities: when one
of his noblemen tells him "My gracious lord, please you prepare for
pleasure; | The masque is not far off," Lussurioso responds with
what could be seen as a concise summary of his character: "We are
for pleasure" (V.iii.12–13).

As his players exit the stage after successfully completing their
murders, Vindice takes the occasion for a metatheatrical joke: "No
power is angry when the lustful die: | When thunder claps, heaven
likes the tragedy" (V.iii.47–8). Echoing his earlier remarks about the
success of tragedy "when the bad bleed," Vindice suggests that the
clap of thunder that punctuates his performance serves as applause
from a celestial audience, pleased with the justice that his staging has
accomplished. In evoking this external sound effect, his comment
also reminds us that Vindice's dangerous theater is paralleled by the
larger play in which it is framed.

The elaborate staging of the poisonous kiss, combined with the
even more explicit theatricality of Vindice's murderous masque,
offers spectators a warning about the seductive, potentially harmful
powers of the stage. As the previous chapter demonstrated, the spectacle of the stage play was frequently imagined as a painted lady, an
alluring impersonation whose lively attractions concealed an underlying danger. In *The Revenger's Tragedy*, this idea is embodied in the
dead Gloriana, whose kisses contaminate the Duke with a literalized
reflection of his own poisonous lechery. Throughout the play, theatrical spectacle is depicted as a contagiously mimetic medium, con-
fronting spectators with reflections of both their worst fears and
their most dangerous desires. After his poisoning by lust, the Duke is
subjected to more poisonous kisses, in the spectacle of his wife's
liaison with Spurio. Lussurioso, similarly, is not only assaulted by
the festive masque for which he has called, but is forced to remain
alive, weakened and silenced, to watch the final murderous revels
and to listen to Vindice's triumphant revelation of what he has done.

The boundary separating spectators from their spectacles in this
play is tenuous at best, and dissolves at the slightest pressure: the

content of these performances both emerges from their audiences and seeps contagiously back into them upon exposure. Certain elements of reform and reconciliation suggest the possibility of a positive outcome from these poisonous performances, in accord with the morality play tradition in which *The Revenger's Tragedy* is rooted, but the larger impact of the play belies this optimistic model.[44] The final barrage of deaths offers its audiences, both inside and outside the play, a threatening vision of the consequences of spectatorship.

Like Gloriana, the play cloaks its corrosive threat with pleasure, suggesting that the play's external spectators, like the Duke, Lussurioso, and ultimately Vindice as well, may be seduced and transformed by the artificial spectacle to which they are exposed. If the play, however, represents spectacles as giving spectators what they deserve—or, perhaps more interestingly, what they want—then it is striking that it takes care to distinguish between forms of spectatorship, offering its audiences a range of positions to occupy. Both the Duke and Lussurioso are killed by performances, but the manners of their deaths differ sharply. Vindice, meanwhile, stands aside from the action, approaching it with a detachment that the play itself, with its black humor and cartoon-like parodies of characters, helps to foster. Within the play, of course, even Vindice ultimately succumbs to the pleasure of his theatrical creations, too ravished by his own cleverness to remain silent about his role. Constructing itself as a witty parody of the theatrical seductions it depicts, the play challenges its audiences to remain more detached than Vindice: to be drawn into the spectacle and yet simultaneously stay outside it.

In each of these plays—*The Second Maiden's Tragedy*, *The Duke of Milan*, and *The Revenger's Tragedy*—men drawn into an idolatrous fascination with the artificial painted beauty of the female corpse offer models for theatrical spectatorship. The poisonous kiss, with its power to dissolve boundaries between spectator and spectacle, epitomizes the vulnerability of the spectator trapped between these precarious positions. Even while warning their audiences against the threat of seduction by alluring spectacles, these plays simultaneously embody the theatrical contamination they depict and critique.

Within this shared framework, however, the three plays differ in their treatments of the poisoned kisses they depict. While *The Second Maiden's Tragedy* and *The Duke of Milan* vary in the realism and fullness of the characters they portray, both offer flesh and blood as well as corpses, dramatizing the progression from the idealization of a desired woman to the hungry fixation on her corpse after she dies. *The Revenger's Tragedy*, on the other hand, focuses emphatically on hollow remains—not even a corpse, but a skull—and parallels this hollowness with the hollow caricatures of the characters it portrays. With its murderous masque, *The Revenger's Tragedy* is the most explicitly and self-consciously metatheatrical of these plays, yet in its meditations on spectacle it offers its own antidote. By refusing to allow its audiences to identify too fully with its onstage figures, it implicitly instructs them in the cynical detachment embodied by Vindice, offering a model—albeit an imperfect one—for how to approach spectacles without either consuming or being consumed by their taint.

5

Vulnerable Ears:
Hamlet and
Poisonous Theater

For many modern readers and audiences, *Hamlet* represents the distilled essence of early modern theater. Fittingly, in the context of this book's argument, it also represents the period's most sustained and self-conscious investigation of both the theater's effect on audiences, and the effects of dangerous drugs on bodies. Shakespeare's emphatic attention to these themes represents self-conscious decisions; he departed notably from his known sources for the play both in having Hamlet stage a theatrical performance, and in transforming the murder of King Hamlet from a public stabbing to a private and unseen poisoning through the ears.[1] Both the poisoning and *The Mousetrap*, arguably the most striking features of the play, focus the audience's attention on the vulnerability not only of the body, but especially of the ear. Scholars who have written on the play's preoccupation with ears have tended to see their importance primarily on a figurative level, arguing that the play's interest in ears is predominantly about listening and comprehending.[2] The play's depictions of ears, however, demand an insistently literal reading: they function not only, nor even primarily, as a gateway to the mind, but as a troublingly unclosable entrance to the body.

With its extensive contemplation and introspection, *Hamlet* is a play almost universally associated with the intellect. Critics who have acknowledged the play's fascination with flesh and disease tend to read these concerns in opposition to the cerebral aspects of the text, and as sources of fear and loathing.[3] Yet the striking fixation on inwardness that critics such as Katharine Eisaman Maus have noted in the play, is, as David Hillman has argued, as physiological as it is philosophical: the play is obsessively interested in the interior of the body.[4] In particular, the play is insistently concerned with the question of how to reach this interior, how to penetrate from the external to the internal. Although the play's fascination with images of eating and digestion has captured critical attention, its attention to ears offers an even more powerful image of the intrusion of the outside world into the body: while we can choose whether or not to eat a given substance, ears remain open, and receptive, regardless of intent.[5] As an organ of both understanding and absorption, moreover, the ear fuses together Hamlet's epistemological and physiological interests, linking the theatrical realm of language firmly with the physical realm of the body.

The play's attention to the corporeal vulnerability of ears, and its translation of intellectual threats, such as duplicity, into the material form of poison, argue for a reading that acknowledges not only the centrality of the body, but the tenuousness of the boundary between the mental and the bodily.[6] Language, in the play, is imagined to take on a physical force.[7] *Hamlet*'s ears conjoin anxieties about the integrity of boundaries with fears and fascinations about the destabilizing effects of words—especially the artfully arranged words of theatrical performance—evoking the vulnerability of the interior self to the contaminating power of language. The capacity of words to act upon listeners is as exciting to Hamlet as it is terrifying; delighted by the theater, he turns to play-acting to diagnose and cure the problems of Denmark, but these intended remedies continually threaten to mimic the dangers they attempt to counteract. Simultaneously examining and embodying the theater's capacity to penetrate its listeners' minds and bodies, the play offers a brutal refutation of Hamlet's aspirations to a firmly enclosed private self.[8] In *Hamlet*, Shakespeare explores the permeability associated with poisons and ears in order to insist on the interpenetration both of the intellectual and the corporeal, and of spectacle and spectator.

VULNERABLE EARS

Well before any talk of literal poisonings, the ear is a strikingly fragile organ in *Hamlet*, prone to invasion by a host of contaminating dangers. While other plays, such as *A Midsummer Night's Dream*, privilege the eyes as the site of invasive forces, *Hamlet* presents the ear, with its perennial openness and sinuously winding interior chambers, as the body's most vulnerable orifice. With significantly more references than anywhere else in Shakespeare, the ear is a prominent object of attention. Like poison itself, it serves as a crucial nexus between the play's concerns with theatrical duplicity, and its attention to the body's interior. The play's abundant references to wounded, abused, and poisoned ears point to both a symbolic and literal fusion of these two domains.

From the start of the play, ears are recurringly evoked as a site of violent attack. In the play's opening scene, Barnardo prefaces his description of the ghost's appearance with a warning to Horatio: "let us once again assail your ears, | That are so fortified against our story" (I.i.33–4).[9] Explicitly identifying ears with the protective barriers of armor or fortification, the image attributes a violent invasiveness to the forthcoming speech, suggesting its effect on the play's audience as well: to listen to Barnardo's speech, either within the play or outside it, is to undergo a hostile siege.

Barnardo is only the first of many characters in the play who insist on breaking through the walls of unwilling or inattentive ears, even while calling attention to the violence of the act. In his meeting with Hamlet, the ghost obsessively reiterates his demands to be heard: "Mark me" (I.v.2), "lend thy serious hearing" (5), "thou shalt hear" (7), "List, list, O list!" (22), and "Now, Hamlet, hear" (34). But his emphatic commands to listen are interwoven with a detailed description of the perils of doing so.[10] The ghost describes the full force of his tale of death as disturbing enough to paralyze both soul and body:

> But that I am forbid
> To tell the secrets of my prison-house,
> I could a tale unfold whose lightest word
> Would harrow up thy soul, freeze thy young blood,
> Make thy two eyes like stars start from their spheres,
> Thy knotted and combined locks to part,
> And each particular hair to stand an end
> Like quills upon the fretful porpentine.
> But this eternal blazon must not be
> To ears of flesh and blood.
>
> (I.v.13–22)

Despite his apparently urgent desire to speak his story, the ghost begins by pausing with a disclaimer, a variation on the standard rhetorical trope of inexpressibility. Unusually, however, he claims that it is not his failing, but his audience's, that prevents him from conveying the full tale; the secrets of death cannot be withstood by mortal ears. Much more than a digression on the way to the ghost's story, this tantalizing retraction shows the material force attributed to language in the play. The ghost's elaborate description of the impact of "lightest words" on flesh and blood suggests a conception of language as a physically transformative agent. This direct, almost electric verbal impact freezes the body into a stiffened shell of itself, offering an uncanny parallel with the story the ghost is postponing, of the fatal vulnerability of his own "ears of flesh and blood."

Although he cannot portray the afterlife, the ghost conveys to Hamlet a detailed picture of his death. "Brief let me be," he begins:

> Sleeping within my orchard,
> My custom always of the afternoon,
> Upon my secure hour thy uncle stole
> With juice of cursed hebenon in a vial,
> And in the porches of my ears did pour
> The leperous distilment, whose effect
> Holds such an enmity with blood of man
> That swift as quicksilver it courses through
> The natural gates and alleys of the body,
> And with a sudden vigour it doth posset
> And curd, like eager droppings into milk,
> The thin and wholesome blood. So did it mine,
> And a most instant tetter bark'd about,
> Most lazar-like, with vile and loathsome crust
> All my smooth body.
>
> (I.v.59–73)

The ghost's account of his poisoning is striking for a number of reasons. Despite having been asleep at the time of his death, he speaks with an inexplicable omniscience about the details of the murder: who carried it out, the kind of poison used, the container in which it was carried, and the precise nature of its operations. Even more strangely, he is able to see inside his own body, meticulously tracing the poison's movements and effects.[11] Simultaneously asleep and alert, inside his own body and separate from it, the ghost derives his uncanny authority from his knowledge not only of a world beyond death, but of a world beneath the skin.

The ghost describes this interior world in a curiously architectural vocabulary, emphasizing the unsettling invasiveness of Claudius's poison. As the body's "porches," ears are strangely liminal structures, simultaneously external to the body and opening into it. Although porches imply entrance to private houses, however, the poison enters these too-open orifices to course through "the natural gates and alleys of the body," evoking entrances within entrances, passages within passages; we are not within a private self-contained house at all, but rather a crowded network of streets and further entryways. The body, it seems, is a liquid city, tenuously kept in order by fragile partitions, ever susceptible to rupture and rearrangement. The ghost's account of these insufficiently protective gates and structures identifies them with the external barriers that mirror them, and similarly fail to guard his person. Insulated by the oblivion of sleep, the "secure hour" of a customary time of rest, and the idyllic setting of an orchard—all within his kingdom—the king is enclosed within multiple layers of protective barriers. The penetration of his ears with poison represents the most intimate of a series of invasive violations.[12]

The disturbing effects of this poisonous infiltration offer telling parallels with the ghost's account of the effects of his story. In both passages, the ear becomes the gateway for a dangerous invasion which disorders the body's interior, freezing and curdling the blood. Also in both, this internal and invisible congealing is mirrored by an external bodily stiffening, jolting hair into quills and flesh into a "vile and loathsome crust."[13] The passage's explicit and grotesque description of the poison's consequences, especially when juxtaposed with the parallel effects in the prior passage, suggests fantasies of vividly material consequences for the violation of the ears. As the only speakable segment of an otherwise forbidden tale, this scene becomes a microcosm of the ghost's full story, coming to represent the terrible verbal power which would itself have created a similarly paralyzing effect.

Poison, in the ghost's account, functions like language; it offers a physical embodiment of the dangers that can invade through the ears, coursing through internal worlds and rearranging their tenuous geographies. As the identification between the two passages suggests, even to retell the scene is to reenact the violent penetration it represents: the ghost of King Hamlet poisons the ears of his son by recreating his murder. Just as the literal poison corrodes the king's insides and leaves him as a stiff, empty carcass, so he intends his toxic narrative to eat away at Hamlet's interior, taking over his thoughts and infecting him with the violence of the ghost's discontent and distrustfulness.[14] Hamlet's carefully cultivated sense of secluded interiority similarly begins to dissolve under the force of the ghost's words. By dramatizing the risks of open ears, Shakespeare reminds the audience of our own alignment with both the listening Hamlet and his sleeping father. We too, in hearing the play, will be infected, contaminated, corroded, even poisoned, by its paranoid and restless suspicions. By suggesting that we are invaded, and possessed, by what we hear, the ghost implicitly asserts his own ability to reshape the liquid cities of our own interior worlds.

ANATOMIZING THE EAR

Despite its apparent uniqueness as a literary device, Claudius's means of murder can be situated in a broader context of early modern concerns about the vulnerability of the ear. Although none of Shakespeare's known literary sources for *Hamlet* featured either poison or ears, Claudius's crime had several recent historical precedents.[15] Most conspicuously, it has been often noted that Hamlet's allusion to the murder of Gonzago shows that Shakespeare knew about the strange case of Francesco Maria I della Rovere, Duke of Urbino. After the Duke died in 1538, his barber-surgeon confessed under torture to having poisoned him by a lotion in the ears, at the instigation of Luigi Gonzaga, a kinsman of the Duchess.[16] Similarly, and more recently, the physician Ambroise Paré was accused in 1560 of having murdered Francois II of France by blowing a poisonous powder into his ear.[17] The method had already caught the imagination of Marlowe, whose Lightborn boasted the knowledge of poisoning by "tak[ing] a quill, | And blow[ing] a little powder in his ears."[18] While it could hardly be described as common, the idea of poisoning through the ear seems to have held some imaginative currency.

Early modern experiments in anatomy confirmed and intensified interest in the ear as a permeable orifice. In 1564 the anatomist Bartolomeo Eustachio identified the passage now known as the eustachian tube. As an open passage, the eustachian tube represents the ear's ability to transmit matter in or out of the body. As Eustachio commented, "Knowledge of this passage will be very useful to physicians for the correct use of medicaments, because now they will know that even thick material can be expelled or purged from the ears by a very ample pathway, either by nature or by the aid of those medicaments which are called *masticatoria*."[19] A passage that allowed matter to seep out could similarly be a site for absorption: the physicians A. R. Eden and J. Opland see Eustachio's treatise as "a clear indication that physicians of Shakespeare's time could know that fluid or pus in the middle ear could drain into the pharynx, and that a substance instilled into an ear with a tympanic-membrane perforation could find its way to the pharynx and be swallowed."[20] Through both its openness and its direct link to the throat, the ear comes to parallel the mouth as a direct gateway into the bodily interior, offering a striking physiological counterpart to the "greedy ear" with which Desdemona would "Devour up" Othello's stories.[21]

Eustachio's innovations spread quickly throughout Europe, and were well-known in England by Shakespeare's time.[22] Confronted with this disconcerting openness, anatomists hastened to call attention to the ears' natural defenses against the threat of invasion. Explaining the external structure of the ear in 1626, Thomas Vicary writes "that it should keep the hole that it standeth ouer, from things falling in that might hinder the hearing."[23] Ambroise Paré applies the same logic to the passages of the inner ear, which he says "were made thus into crooked windings, least . . . that little creeping things and other extraneous bodys as fleas & the like, should be staied in these windings and turnings of the waies."[24] If these insistent assertions of the difficulty of penetrating ears give the impression of protesting too much—conveying concerns that the system might not be foolproof —other moments in these anatomical writings confirm that the security of ears was not taken for granted. In a chapter titled "Of the stopping of the passage of the eares, and the falling of things thereinto," Paré recounts the dangers of the ears being blocked with "fragments of stones, gold, silver, iron and the like mettals, pearles, cherry-stones, or kernels, pease and other such like pulse."[25] Another anatomist, Christopher Wirtzung, has chapters with discomfiting titles such as "Of little wormes that grow in the Eares, and that do creepe into them outwardly, and such like," and "If any thing be gotten into the Eares from without."[26] Despite efforts to depict the ear as a reliable boundary keeping out contamination, these writers repeatedly betray a fear that it could more easily be a passageway allowing for direct entrance into the body.[27] With its ambiguous permeability, the ear can be seen as emblematic of a broader set of early modern concerns about the integrity of bodily boundaries.[28]

INVASIVE WORDS

Despite the play's detailed attention to the perils of liquids entering
through the ears, the most common invasive threat in *Hamlet* comes
not from matter, but from words. As shown by Barnardo's threat to
assail his hearer's ears, and the ghost's account of the chilling effects
of his tale, the violence that afflicts ears throughout the play is that of
language. Speech, in *Hamlet*, is portrayed as capable of both duplicity and disruption; fusing the play's concerns with hypocrisy, unset-
tled emotions, and the body's interior, it acquires a physical force
that allows it to penetrate to the body's core. Yet, despite popular
conceptions of *Hamlet*'s distinctiveness, the play's preoccupation
with the poisonous impact of language is strikingly representative,
both of the period's theater and of antitheatricalists' claims about the
effects of plays. For all its widely acclaimed singularity, *Hamlet* turns
out to differ from other early modern plays not in its attention to the
physically dangerous power of spoken language, but in the intensity,
frequency, and self-consciousness with which it explores this idea.

Most vividly, sharp words are described in the play as murderous
weapons: before visiting his mother in her bedroom, Hamlet muses "I
will speak daggers to her, but use none" (III.ii.387). Gertrude later
confirms his effect with an eerie echo of his image—"O speak to me
no more. | These words like daggers enter in mine ears" (III.iv.94–5)
—suggesting that his language has already figuratively penetrated her
imagination. Ultimately, the sharpness of Hamlet's accusations
proves supplemental to, rather than a substitute for, actual weapons;
in one of the play's more strikingly literalizing gestures, these two
references to Hamlet's verbal daggers frame his stabbing of Polonius
behind the arras (III.iv.20). Mistaking Polonius for Claudius, Hamlet
intends this attack as his revenge for his father's death, underlining
the symmetry between this transmutation of verbal into physical violence and the murder of the king. Penetrating both ears and eaves-
droppers with perilous material force, daggers become a crystallized
version of the poisons that rupture the inner workings of old Hamlet.

As Hamlet's opponent, and in many ways mirror image, throughout the play, Claudius also repeatedly identifies language with
dangerous bodily penetration. Evoking an unsettling image of aggressively invasive and disease-bearing insects, Claudius claims that
Laertes "wants not buzzers to infect his ear | With pestilent speeches
of his father's death" (IV.v.90–1). In the same scene, commenting on

one of the play's most disturbing verbal onslaughts, Claudius suggests that Ophelia's performance of mad songs exerts an impact
which is not only painful, but somehow fatal: "O my dear Gertrude,
this, | Like to a murd'ring-piece, in many places | Gives me super-
fluous death" (IV.v.94–6). Just as Hamlet's figurative daggers lead to
Polonius's literal death, Claudius's odd metaphor proves strangely
apt. A kind of cannon, a murdering-piece was so called because of its
ability to hit many men at once. Not only do Ophelia's songs undo
Claudius, Laertes, and Hamlet, but in the murderous duel to which
Claudius enjoins Laertes during this scene, a single weapon similarly
—if unexpectedly—brings about a number of deaths, including that
of Claudius himself.

The ghost of Hamlet's father, whose description of his murder sets
the events of the play in motion by poisoning Hamlet's ears, offers
another striking example of the threatening power of language to act
upon bodies. When Hamlet enjoins Horatio and Marcellus to swear
that they will never reveal what they have seen of the ghost, the
urgency of their pending speech act is underlined by an eerie and
invisible cry: "Swear" (I.v.157). Seeping through the floorboards
from a disconcerting location under the stage, the ghost's voice
seems to follow the listeners' bodies, physically propelling them
around the stage in their effort to escape the sound: "*Hic et
ubique?*," Hamlet queries in response to a second cry; "Then we'll
shift our ground. Come hither, gentlemen" (I.v.164–5). "Canst
work i'th'earth so fast?," he wonders, after another command; "A
worthy pioner!" (I.v.170–1). The uncanny power of the voice is
complicated by the comic overtones of Hamlet's apparently cavalier
response: "Ah ha, boy, say'st thou so?," he queries the first cry. "Art
thou there, truepenny? | Come on, You hear this fellow in the cellar-
age. | Consent to swear" (I.v.158–60). After the ghost's final com-
mand, he similarly banters, "Well said, old mole" (I.v.170). These
vestiges of comedy, however, strengthened by the odd spectacle of
three men shifting around onstage in an unsuccessful attempt to
evade an unseen voice, only serve to heighten the unsettling effect of
the scene, which dramatizes the physically coercive force of disem-
bodied words. The theatrical association of the cellarage space with
hell adds to the sinister power of the ghost's voice.[29]

While Hamlet's verbal daggers and Ophelia's painful mad songs
identify the physical force of language with the dangerous content
represented and conveyed by words, the unsettling impact of the

ghost's subterranean commands points to more abstract, and more haunting, anxieties about the contaminating power of language. Elsewhere in the play, concerns about language focus on the instability of words themselves, and the capacity for hypocrisy that they embody. As Maus has noted, Hamlet's distinction between external and internal realms, and his emphatic privileging of the internal, ultimately undercuts faith in the reliability of any external signs, including words.[30] While violent words are represented as forcefully and invasively penetrating the body, treacherously false words, incommensurate with what they claim to represent, threaten minds and bodies in different ways.

From the beginning of the play, lies, or misleading representations, are portrayed as a kind of physical assault: in response to Horatio's claim to "a truant disposition," Hamlet reproaches him, "Nor shall you do my ear that violence | To make it truster of your own report | Against yourself" (I.ii.169–73). Similarly, the ghost describes "the whole ear of Denmark" as "rankly abus'd" by false stories of his death (I.v.36–8), suggesting that his murder is mirrored, and magnified, by a subsequent poisoning of his realm with lies.

Direct references to the violent, abusive nature of false words and stories reflect the play's pervasive anxieties about lies, hypocrisy, and treachery. The play is filled with examples of deceptive resemblances, twinned doubles who are similar, but not quite identical.[31] Words, similarly, continually threaten false representation. Early in the play, for instance, Polonius warns Ophelia of the unreliability of Hamlet's words:

> Do not believe his vows, for they are brokers,
> Not of that dye which their investments show,
> But mere implorators of unholy suits,
> Breathing like sanctified and pious bonds,
> The better to beguile.
>
> (I.iii.127–31)

Words, Polonius suggests, are unreliable not accidentally, because of problems inherent in representation, but intentionally, because speakers lie in order to further their own desires. His eclectic and punning figures, however, seem to run away with themselves, suggesting that language may take on a force of its own, independent of the speaker. Evoking specific but overlapping registers of diction, Polonius associates the self-interested duplicity of language with "brokers"—agents, or bawds—wearing misleading clothing ("investments"). His reference to "implorators of unholy suits" plays on double meanings to evoke both courtship and clothing, echoing the "investments" they belie, while simultaneously introducing the metaphor of false religion, continued in "sanctified and pious bonds."[32] Although Polonius's range of referents is variable and often incongruous, all of his figures embody words in material, animate forms; his reference to breathing, accordingly, calls attention to the physicality of language itself.[33]

Polonius's account to Ophelia of the unreliability of Hamlet's vows, with its implications for the material nature of language, is echoed by Ophelia herself after being assaulted by Hamlet's words during the so-called "nunnery" scene. "And I," she laments,

> of ladies most deject and wretched,
> That suck'd the honey of his music vows
> Now see that noble and most sovereign reason
> Like sweet bells jangled out of tune and harsh,
> That unmatch'd form and feature of blown youth
> Blasted with ecstasy.
>
> (III.i.157–62)

Like Polonius, Ophelia mixes her metaphors to disconcerting effect; just as she is jarred by the transformation of the formerly "sweet bells," now "jangled out of tune and harsh," so her identification of vows simultaneously with music and with honey, as well as the curious elision between the music of Hamlet's vows and the bells of his reason, jars the audience's expectations. This linguistic disorientation is itself the theme of Ophelia's musing; her startlingly consumptive and erotic metaphor of sucking the honey of Hamlet's vows again casts language as a physical and liquid medium, absorbed into the listener's body with dangerous consequences.

The translation of the epistemological disruptions of signs, and especially language, into physical terms returns us to the play's most striking figure for the danger of misleading appearances, the image of poison. As the recurring juxtaposition of poison with ears suggests, poison becomes a crucial symbol for the link between the semiotic and the physical in this play. Shakespeare explicitly identifies language with poison in *Othello*, when Iago describes himself as poisoning Othello with his tales: "The Moor already changes with my poison: | Dangerous conceits are in their natures poisons."[34] Earlier,

Iago describes his plot by asserting "I'll pour this pestilence into his ear" (II.iii.347). Iago's corrosive fictions are portrayed as catalyzing an almost chemical reaction, shifting and unsettling the elements of Othello's mind until his jealous suspicions dissolve the vestiges of rationality and lead him to murder. In Iago's case, as with Claudius, the explicit association of this aural threat with falsehoods suggests that the link between language and poison rests not only on a perceived shared capacity for aggressively infiltrating body and soul, but also on parallel anxieties about reliable representation.

As we have seen, early modern complaints about poison also focused on its capacity for deception. Fluid, formless, and essentially invisible, poison was notorious for appearing as something other than what it was: food, drink, and medicine were only the most common of the many forms of disguise it was reputed to claim. "If these arts [of poison] should come in once amongst vs," writes Thomas Tuke,

who shal be secure? How can a man see who hurts him, & how shal a man preuent the blow, if he see not the arme that strikes him? Yea here a man shal be made away vnder the pretext of friendship, yea, hee shall perhaps thank a man for that, that is made to destroy him, which hath death lapt vp in it, which he thinks is sent or giuen him as a tokan of loue vnto him.[35]

Tuke's vehemence, shown by his repetitive bursts of parallel questions and clauses, suggests paranoia. His generalized rhetorical questions—"who shal be secure?"—suggest a sense of personal identification with the insecurity he depicts. The most striking threat of poison is the perpetual insecurity of not knowing when one might be under threat: an anxiety that, if taken seriously, entails a perception of continual threat.

If the openness of ears evokes concerns about invasion and contamination, the vulnerability they represent offers a close parallel with anxieties about the threat of poison, widely perceived as ubiquitous and impervious to boundaries. In *The Parable of Poyson*, for example, William Crashaw writes

There be poisons for our Meate, for Drinke, for Apparell, for Arrowes, Saddles, Seats, Stirrups, for Candles, Torches. Nothing that comes about a Man, nothing that he toucheth, or that toucheth him, but Mans wickednesse hath fitted, and prepared poison for it. . . . nothing a man takes into him or puts vpon him, nothing that toucheth him or comes neere him, that can be safe from bodily poison, if Gods prouidence preuent it not.[36]

Poison offers a nightmarish model of fatal bodily infiltration which can enter into the body anywhere—not only through the obvious openings of the mouth and ear, but through skin, and breath. If ears, those open porches, call attention to the impossibility of closing the body off from external dangers, poison represents the contaminating impurity which can, and will, invade at any opportunity.

The shared semiotic unreliability of language and poison makes poison an apt figure for the capacity of language to assume material powers, to act upon the body. The fantasy in *Hamlet* that words can exert a direct bodily impact, as well as the specific suggestion that they could operate as a kind of poison, evoke some of the more magically inflected lines of early modern thought. Beliefs about the physical efficacy of language held significant sway in popular folklore. A persistent line of medical thought held that words, or even letters, could have a talismanic effect on the body. John Aubrey, for example, wrote that to prevent ague, one should write out the letters ABRACADABRA in a triangle and wear it about the neck.[37] He also advocated the direct consumption of words: for "A spell to cure the Biting of a mad Dog," he offers "Rebus Rubus Epitepscum. Write these words in paper, and give it to the party, or beast bitten, to eate in bread: Mr. Dennys of Poole in Dorsetshire sayeth this Receipt never failes."[38]

The quasi-magical powers attributed to language were heatedly debated among sixteenth- and seventeenth-century thinkers. Although faith in the performative efficacy of words, as employed in magical spells and witchcraft, was still widespread, the skeptical discourses of science and Protestantism saw a significant revolt against such beliefs.[39] William Perkins insisted that "that which is onely a bare sound, in all reason can have no vertue in it to cause a reall worke"; words, according to him, cannot have "the power of touching a substance."[40] Reginald Scot, similarly, claimed that "By the sound of the words nothing commeth, nothing goeth."[41] The debate about verbal efficacy took place within the context of a broader developing conflict between magical and scientific belief systems. Particularly in the wake of the Reformation, the idea that words and signs held magical powers was heavily contested. While still widely clung to, it was nonetheless increasingly viewed with suspicion, as a remnant of dubious religious systems such as paganism and popery.

Hamlet's depiction of words as exerting a dangerously material impact on bodies resonates with other unsettling forms of bodily ingestion, and digestion, that the play explores. As Stephen Green-blatt has noted, Hamlet's morbid descriptions of Polonius's corpse at supper—"Not where he eats, but where a is eaten" (IV.iii.19)—followed by his reference to a "certain convocation of politic worms . . . your only emperor for diet" (IV.iii.19–20, 21), suggest anxieties about the Eucharist, the supper where the host does not eat but is eaten.[42] Greenblatt makes a powerful argument about the way that Eucharistic imagery, combined with a broader set of references to eating and being eaten, highlights the problem of the paternal body in the play; I would like to add that it also underlines the play's anxieties about the consequences of accepting powerful and trans-formative substances into the body. Like poison and spells, the con-troversies surrounding the Eucharist fused together concerns about representation with concerns about transformation and the body.[43] Did the wafer represent the body of Christ, or *was* it the body of Christ? And what would happen to the recipient who accepted it in one spirit, but was acted upon in another? If the mouth and the ear mirror each other, as argued earlier, this Eucharistic and cannibalis-tic imagery echoes not only the poisoning of Hamlet's father, but the play's own threat of entering its audiences, and transforming them in mysterious and ambivalent ways.

POISONOUS THEATER

Hamlet's preoccupations with the transformative powers of sub-stances taken into the body find their culmination in the theater. As an embodiment of imaginative fantasies in both words and images, the theater was seen by many moralizing critics as a particularly powerful, and hence dangerous, medium. In particular, antitheatri-cal critics emphasized its unique power to reach the soul through the ear. Comparing the flattering deceits of playwrights to those of cooks and painters, the moralist Stephen Gosson writes,

There set they abroche straunge consortes of melody, to tickle the eare; costly apparel, to flatter the sight; effeminate gesture, to rauish the sence; and wanton speache, to whet desire too inordinate lust. Therefore of both barrelles, I iudge Cookes and Painters the better hearing, for the one exten-deth his arte no farther then to the tongue, palate, and nose, the other to the eye; and both are ended in outwarde sense, which is common too vs with bruite beasts. But these by the priuie entries of the eare, slip downe into the hart, & with gunshotte of affection gaule the minde, where reason and vertue should rule the roste.[44]

Gosson attributes to the theatrical form a privileged access to both bodily and spiritual interiority, by way of its appeal to the ear. While cooks and painters appeal only to the apparently more "outwarde" or superficial senses, the poet, "by the priuie entries of the eare," is able to penetrate and capture both heart and mind. In his analysis of the physical and spiritual effects of various media, Gosson suggests both that theater is specifically directed to the ears, and that ears are the body's—and the soul's—most vulnerable point of entry.

Beliefs about the magical efficacy of words and, in particular, the theater, rest on an understanding of language as a performative, rather than merely descriptive, medium.[45] Beginning with the catalyzing effects of the ghost's words, *Hamlet* offers a striking illustration of the ambivalent possibilities of this linguistic power. As well as dramatizing a general concern with the danger of listening and the vulnerability of the ear, the play directs particular attention to the implications of these concerns for the theater. Both in meeting with the players and, crucially, in orchestrating the performance of *The Mousetrap*, Hamlet displays a deep fascination with the theater. Like other theatrical revengers—including Hieronimo, of *The Spanish Tragedy*, and Vindice, of *The Revenger's Tragedy*—he sees the lies and hypocrisy of the theater as paradoxically offering a remedy to the lies and hypocrisy of a corrupt court.

The arrival of the players—those that he was "wont to take such delight in, the tragedians of the city" (II.ii.326–7)—spurs Hamlet to an unusual burst of pleasure and curiosity. After barraging Rosencrantz and Guildenstern with questions, he receives the players with enthusiasm: "You are welcome, masters. Welcome, all.— I am glad to see thee well.—Welcome, good friends" (II.ii.417–18). If the players represent, synecdochically, the invasive force of theatrical performance, it is an invasive force that Hamlet accepts actively, knowingly, and with relish.

In his welcome to the players, Hamlet foregrounds the aural, and verbal, aspects of the theater: "Come, a passionate speech"; "I heard thee speak me a speech once"; "We'll hear a play tomorrow" (II.ii.428, 430, 530). The speech he has the first player recite, as Aeneas recounting the Trojan War to Dido, further reinforces this theme.[46] Describing the moving power of Hecuba's grief, Aeneas refers to its sound as poisonous: "the instant burst of clamour that she made," which "would have made milch the burning eyes of heaven | And passion in the gods," comes from her "tongue in venom steep'd" (II.ii.511, 513–14, 506). Hecuba's mournful cries, like Ophelia's mad songs—described as "the poison of deep grief" (IV.v.75)—are depicted as penetrating their hearers' ears, altering them both physically and emotionally. The player's performance not only represents this effect, furthermore; it also brings it about. Polonius stops the speech, asking "Look whe'er he has not turned his colour and has tears in's eyes. Prithee no more" (II.ii.515–16).

Hamlet's fascination with the player stems from his ability to transform himself, "in a fiction, in a dream of passion" (II.ii.546), into a state of mourning so forceful that it takes material form: "all his visage wann'd, | Tears in his eyes, distraction in his aspect, | A broken voice" (II.ii.548–50). Theater may be a fiction, a lie, but it is a lie so powerful that it changes both mind and body, giving its agent—the player himself—the power to alter his audiences as well. Hamlet, with his desire to reach the inmost core, to cut "to the quick of th' ulcer" (IV.vii.122), sees the theater as the most powerful instrument for penetrating through surfaces to something deeper. Troubled by his own inability to produce this forceful passion, he sees in the player a proxy through which he can act out the probing inquiry that will be both experiment and revenge.

If the theater's capacity to penetrate the body makes it an apt mirror for the poisonous murder it will revenge, its ability to elicit visible, material responses recommends it as a test to reveal Claudius's guilt. "I have heard," Hamlet famously pronounces, "That guilty creatures sitting at a play | Have, by the very cunning of the scene, | Been struck so to the soul that presently | They have proclaim'd their malefactions" (II.ii.584–7). The violence of dissembling, he believes, can serve to mirror, and hence bring to justice, his uncle's dissembling violence: "I'll have these players | Play something like the murder of my father" (II.ii.590–1).[47] Theater becomes, for Hamlet, a remedy. With its cathartic force, it will purge Denmark of the secrecy, lies, and moral decay that have pervaded it since his father's death, and usher in a return to just government. Specifically, its penetrating power promises medical efficacy. Hamlet proclaims of Claudius, "I'll tent him to the quick" (II.ii.592), referring to a medical instrument for examining or cleansing a wound.[48] Like other revengers examined in this book, Hamlet identifies poison—in this case, the poison of theatrical performance—with the purgative power of medicine.[49]

As we have seen, it is the sound of theatrical performance, its ability to invade the ear, that constitutes its most striking power for Hamlet. This emphasis suggests a solution to the long-debated problem of why Claudius reacts impassively to the dumb-show, but powerfully to the play itself, and, for that matter, of why the dumb-show is needed at all. In keeping with the play's preoccupation with doubleness, Hamlet instructs the players to recreate his father's murder not merely once, but twice, with and without words. The dumb show serves as a contrast to the effects of the play, showing that it is "the talk of the poisoning" (III.ii.300) that strikes Claudius. The performance shows Hamlet making the punishment fit the crime; he succeeds in pouring poison into Claudius's ears.[50] As the players "poison in jest" (III.ii.229), the play poisons in earnest.

Following this logic, *The Mousetrap* can be seen as the theatrical equivalent of a speech act: while dramatizing the act of a man pouring poison in another man's ears, it simultaneously does what it shows. Within the play, Lucianus speaks his poisons as he mixes them. "Thoughts black, hands apt, drugs fit, and time agreeing," he mutters,

> Confederate season, else no creature seeing,
> Thou mixture rank, of midnight weeds collected,
> With Hecate's ban thrice blasted, thrice infected,
> Thy natural magic and dire property
> On wholesome life usurps immediately.
> *Pours the poison in the sleeper's ears.*
> (III.ii.249–54)

Even apart from the actual poison they accompany, Lucianus's incantatory words seem to form a curse, embodying the poisonous power of performative language. His magical invocations and sing-song rhyme suggest a world of heightened linguistic efficacy; words are his "mixture rank," his "midnight weeds collected." His physical gesture of pouring poison into ears is a belated echo, almost subordinated to the verbal threat he enacts.

Strikingly, it is immediately following these words—and Hamlet's brief commentary on them—that Claudius rises to leave the play. Just as Lucianus's words imitate the poison he prepares, so the play seems to act as a poison carefully prepared by Hamlet, a model that also explains certain details of the play's title and plot. The play's original title, *The Murder of Gonzago*, represents a curious revision of its original source: in the actual Italian episode, Luigi Gonzaga was the murderer, whereas in Hamlet's version he becomes the victim. Similarly, it has been found odd that the murderer is identified as the nephew of the king, rather than his brother. Both of these details argue that what Hamlet is dramatizing in *The Mousetrap* has less to do with Claudius's murder of Hamlet Sr., than with Hamlet Jr.'s murder of the original murderer, his uncle.[51] This model confirms even more strongly the idea that the play becomes a performative act: it represents Hamlet pouring poison in Claudius's ear while simultaneously enacting the deed.

Just as Claudius's poisoning of the king is mirrored and punished by Hamlet's theatrical poisons, Hamlet's play is mirrored and punished by a show staged by Claudius. If Hamlet sees himself as a doctor of sorts, who will cure Denmark with this cathartic performance, it is striking that Claudius mirrors this imagery precisely with his own pervasive imagery of diseases and cures. Claudius describes himself as the "owner of a foul disease" (IV.i.21–3), and identifies Hamlet as the illness: "for like the hectic in my blood he rages" (IV.iii.69). Guildenstern describes him, after the performance of the play, as "marvelous distempered...with choler" (III.ii.293–5).[52] Yet just as Hamlet's idea of a cure involves purging Denmark of Claudius, Claudius intends to purge Denmark of Hamlet.

Claudius directs his own poisonous play of sorts, arranging Hamlet's duel with Laertes and the literally poisonous props—the rapier and chalice—which ensure that this performance of vengeance, unlike Hamlet's, will prove final.[53] Yet just as Hamlet's figurative poisons are deflected back to himself in literal form, so the revengers become the victims of their own poisons. When Laertes is wounded by the poisoned weapon, he announces the aptness of his own death: "Why, as a woodcock to mine own springe . . . I am justly kill'd with mine own treachery" (V.ii.312–13). Similarly, of Claudius's wounding at Hamlet's hands, Laertes again comments, "He is justly serv'd. It is a poison temper'd by himself" (332–3). Poison, it seems, offers the fullest proof of Hamlet's maxim that "'tis the sport to have the enginer | Hoist with his own petard" (III.iv.208–9). If the play identifies poison with language, these figures die poisoned not only by their own schemes, but by their own words.

Not only do the inhabitants of Elsinore ultimately consume their own poisons, but, more strikingly, they seem to embrace these fatal drugs with a strange eagerness. After Gertrude announces that she will carouse to Hamlet's fortune, Claudius tries to prevent her—"Gertrude, do not drink"—but she insists: "I will, my lord, I pray you pardon me" (V.ii.294–5). When Hamlet instructs him to report his story, similarly, Horatio at first refuses in order to partake of the poison: "I am more an antique Roman than a Dane. | Here's yet some liquor left" (V.ii.346–7). Hamlet has to insist that Horatio resist the apparently sweet allure of the drink: "As th'art a man | Give me the cup . . . Absent thee from felicity awhile" (V.ii.347–8, 352). Hamlet, of course, has long been craving the felicity of sleeplike death, which he has described as "a consummation | Devoutly to be wished" (III.i.63–4). The idea of death exerting an eroticized appeal echoes in Hamlet's description of Rosencrantz and Guildenstern bearing their own death-writ to the English king: "they did make love to this employment" (V.ii.57). Yet surrender to the "potent poison" (V.ii.358), in particular, suggests a distinctively sensual allure. Playing on the fact that Claudius has dissolved a "union" (V.ii.269), or pearl, in the cup, Hamlet identifies the drink with his illicit marriage: "Here, thou incestuous, murd'rous, damned Dane, | Drink off this potion. Is thy union here? | Follow my mother" (V.ii.330–2). With its powerful effects on bodily sensation, and its promise of the seductive oblivion of sleep, poison in *Hamlet* evokes medical writers' fears that patients would succumb to the "supposed pleasing ease" offered by drugs, and—whether actively or unwittingly—poison themselves.[54] If the play identifies poisons with language, and especially the theater, moreover, the apparent eagerness of everyone in Elsinore to drink themselves to their deaths suggests a claim about the seductive, addictive appeal of the theater.

As in other revenge tragedies this book has examined, *Hamlet*'s poisons have a medicinal function in the catharsis they bring about: purging Denmark of its impurities, they offer the possibility of beginning again.[55] Yet despite the neat symmetry with which the play's revengers are poisoned by their own schemes, the final scene of *Hamlet* suggests repetition rather than closure.[56] The play ends essentially where it began: another king of Denmark has just died of poisoning, and another usurper—Fortinbras—is stepping in to take over. This ominously cyclical note offers a parallel to the pervasive and inexorable threat of poison; there is no finite resolution, only an uneasy sense that the play's fears about the vulnerability of ears have been borne out. The verbal poisons that have been corroding Hamlet's insides since the ghost's tale finally achieve a literal, and fatal, culmination.

In an attempt to attain some sense of completion, and of justice, Hamlet's last words make an anxious plea for reliable representation. "Report me and my cause aright | To the unsatisfied" (V.ii.344–5), he tells Horatio; almost immediately after, he rephrases his stern and legalistic words with an increasingly poignant note of desperation: "in this harsh world draw thy breath in pain | To tell my story" (V.ii.353–4). Although he dies in a duel, Hamlet, like his father, meets his end through the invisible duplicity of poison; his dying anxiety about the accurate documentation of "his wounded name" recalls his father's complaints about "the whole ear of Denmark" being "rankly abus'd" by false stories of his death (I.v.36–8), suggesting a fear of further poisonous repetitions to come.

Throughout *Hamlet*, just as poisons are shown to share language's capacity for instability and deception, words can similarly be seen to function as poisons, infiltrating and corroding the body and mind. Shakespeare offers models of this performative power most strikingly in the effects of the ghost's speech on Hamlet, and the impact of *The Mousetrap* on Claudius, but each significant episode of listening, or spectatorship, within the play confirms it. Claudius, Gertrude, and Laertes are undone by listening to Ophelia's performance of mad songs; eavesdropping on Hamlet's conference with Gertrude leads to Polonius's death; and Claudius is killed as an onlooker at the duel he has staged. In each of these instances, as well as others throughout the play, the boundary between audiences and performances is seen to be precariously permeable; spectators unfailingly absorb, and are absorbed into, the spectacle they witness, with tragic consequences.

Strikingly, however, and in sharp contrast to prevailing critical thought on the play, each of these scenes also illustrates the limitations of words. Despite the urgency of the ghost's corrosive commands, his instructions dissipate from the table of Hamlet's memory. In his predilection for oblivion over action, in fact, Hamlet proves himself to be exactly what his father fears: "duller . . . than the fat weed | That roots itself in ease on Lethe wharf" (I.v.32–3). What spurs Hamlet to revenge, ultimately, is not language, but the pointed edge of Laertes's poisoned spear. Gertrude, similarly, declares her heart "cleft . . . in twain" by Hamlet's words (III.iv.158), but it seems to have knit itself back together by the next act, when she returns to Claudius and reports to him on their conversation. Claudius himself, although shaken by *The Mousetrap*, is neither penitent nor able to pray, and soon is plotting another poisonous murder. Even the most haunting verbally-induced transformations come undone all too quickly.

Words may be drugs, then—even dangerous, poisonous drugs— but they wear off. Their corrosive, chemical effects could be genuine, immediate, and physiological, but impermanent. As the body's im- mune system adjusts to the shock, it returns, ultimately, to a state of equilibrium. If the play's insistent dramatizations of the invasive, transformative effects of language, and epecially of the theater, reflect Shakespeare's thoughts on the power of his medium over its audiences, its stern warnings might also represent its own fantasy of the theatrical power to which it aspires. Hamlet's idea of the theater as a remedy for the disordered and dishonest world he inhabits will only work if the remedy is powerful enough to be dangerous. The play, then, explores two alternate hypotheses about the nature of theater: it may be dangerous because it is too powerful, or because it is not powerful enough. When the ghost—a role reportedly acted by Shakespeare himself—impresses upon Hamlet and the audience the risks of open ears, perhaps he is trying to persuade himself, as much as his listeners, of the terrifying, transformative, and unavoidable effects of hearing a passionate speech.[57] Perhaps he is instructing us on how to be audiences: how to be transformed, for better or for worse, by the plays that we hear.

Epilogue:
Theater's Antidotes

When Oberon, in *A Midsummer Night's Dream*, first tells Puck
about his plan to drug Titania with love-in-idleness, he refers also to
a second drug, an unnamed one, that many critics, readers, and spectators overlook. Later, he notes, he will "take this charm from off her
sight— | As I can take it with another herb" (II.i.183-4). When con-
fronted with the havoc of the lovers' confused desires, accordingly,
his thoughts move quickly to the antidote: literally, that which is
given against. Realizing that Lysander, at least, must be released
from the powerful influence of this drug, he tells Puck to distract the
lovers and drag them away from their quarrels:

> And from each other look thou lead them thus
> Till o'er their brows death-counterfeiting sleep
> With leaden legs and batty wings doth creep.
> Then crush this herb into Lysander's eye—
> Whose liquor hath this virtuous property,
> To take from thence all error with his might,
> And make his eyeballs roll with wonted sight.
> When they next wake, all this derision
> Shall seem a dream and fruitless vision . . .
>
> (III.ii.364-72)

The play begins again, in cyclical fashion, as the lovers go back to
sleep and receive a second drug in their eyes. As a substitute for the
real death that would be the endpoint for a tragedy, "death-counter-
feiting sleep" allows for a hiatus and another transformation: this
time towards the matched couplings conventional to comedy.
Whereas the erotically-charged potions of love-in-idleness led to
complicated and intoxicated frenzies, the power of this antidote is to
simplify and remove error: it will return Lysander's eyes to their
"wonted sight," him to Hermia, and the night's events to episodes in
a dream.

Puck carries out his tasks quickly and efficiently, narrating his activities and intents to the sleeping Lysander:

> On the ground sleep sound.
> I'll apply to your eye,
> Gentle lover, remedy.
> [*he drops the juice on Lysander's eyelids*]
> When thou wak'st thou tak'st
> True delight in the sight
> Of thy former lady's eye . . .
> (III.iii.36–41)

Puck's simple sing-song rhymes, both internal and end-stopped, as well as his key words, emphasize the reversal he is bringing about: his transformation of Lysander's vision, and the erotic pleasure it will provide. As a messenger of the fairies, he speaks in incantatory words that evoke a magical spell, blurring the line between the effects of the drug and those of his own theatrical language. The hypnotic rhythm of Puck's verse suggests its own medicating powers; perhaps, in fact, it undoes the force of the original drug, which was administered in similarly simple couplets ("Churl, upon thy eyes I throw | All the power this charm doth owe. | When thou wak'st, let love forbid | Sleep his seat on thy eyelid (II.ii.84–7)). The remedy to love-in-idleness, it seems, is both its opposite and more of the same.

While Puck carries out Oberon's bidding with Lysander, Oberon himself applies his antidote to Titania, echoing Puck's uncomplicated rhymes in his own incantatory fashion:

> Be as thou wast wont to be,
> See as thou was wont to see.
> Dian's bud o'er Cupid's flower
> Hath such force and blessed power.
> (IV.i.68–71)

In the play's most specific description of this drug, Oberon identifies it with Diana, the goddess of virginity, patron of Hippolyta's Amazons: an ironic figure, perhaps, to solve the dilemmas of a play dedicated to bringing about multiple marriages, but certainly an aptly cool antidote to the heat of Cupid's flower.[1] Although Diana's chastity directly opposes Cupid's amorous passion, though, Oberon's words also emphasize the parallelism between the two drugs. His first two lines are nearly identical, and the next two juxtapose them as one god's flower alongside another's. In echoing his earlier reference to making Lysander's eyes "roll with wonted sight," moreover, Oberon emphasizes the idea of return to the familiar, the customary, the habitual.

At the end of the play, all the lovers awake, and, as if living out Oberon's words that "all this derision | Shall seem a dream" (III.ii.371–2), begin to relegate the night's events to the status of sleeping visions.[2] Yet even in this new waking state, not all of the lovers have had their drugged states reversed. Lysander returns to his original love for Hermia, but although Titania is cured of her passion for Bottom, she finds herself newly enamored of Oberon, hardly the state in which she began the play. Demetrius, meanwhile, who receives no antidote, remains drugged into compliant desire for Helena. As noted at the start of this book, all of these lovers are firmly identified with the play's external audience: not only because of the shared act of watching a play, but especially because of Puck's description, in the epilogue, of the audience as sleepers who have dreamed the events of the play. But if audience members are the lovers, has the play drugged us, undrugged us, or both? Are we, like Lysander, recipients of an antidote that will return us to what we were? Alternatively, have we, like Demetrius, been permanently changed? Or perhaps have we, like Titania, been both returned and altered? The play leaves these questions in doubt. Puck suggests that if we have not yet received the antidote we need, we will: "Gentles, do not reprehend. | If you pardon, we will mend" (Epilogue, 7–8). But what is mending? Who needs an antidote? And who decides?

Of the many plays that this book examines, *A Midsummer Night's Dream* is the only one that explicitly offers an antidote for the theatrical drugs that it administers to its audiences. But if we might need an antidote for a drug that wreaks havoc with our vision and desires, might we also need antidotes for the purgative, corrosive, addictive, narcotic, contaminating, and poisonous drugs dramatized in the other plays this book has examined? What, if anything, can audiences take away from the theater to undo its effects on them? What remedy can it provide for its own dangerous remedies? Or, as the last chapter has argued of *Hamlet*, will these drugs inevitably wear off of their own accord? Might they contain within them their own antidotes? If playwrights assume that their plays' effects fade after a certain time, will we need renewed doses rather than counter-treatments?

As the passages with which Puck and Oberon accompany their

antidotes suggest, remedies for the theater's potions might lie both in their opposite, and in more of the same. If the purpose of antidotes is to return spectators to their "wonted sight," perhaps the end of the show, the return to everyday events, might be enough. But the parallelism between the administering of the first and second drugs suggests either that one potion counteracts another, or perhaps that the second drug is necessary to finish what the first drug failed to achieve. If the anxieties suggested in *Hamlet* are correct, and the powerful effects of words wear off all too quickly, perhaps the best remedy to a play's spell is putting oneself under another spell, of another play.[3] The remedies both displayed and embodied in the plays this book examines may be dangerous, but perhaps what they tell us is that it is more dangerous to ignore them than to consume them.

This book has argued that the theater of the early modern period is distinguished both by its intense interest in its own theatrical form, and by a fascination with the newly emerging world of ambivalent pharmacy, which offered a vocabulary for plays' simultaneously affective and physiological effects on their consumers. There is no one drug, though, that characterizes all playwrights', or all plays' models of the theater. *A Midsummer Night's Dream* identifies the theater with two drugs placed on sleeping eyes: one to incite new erotic desires, and one to return spectators to their original selves. *Sejanus* identifies theater with poisons that evacuate the body politic, clearing it for new developments. *The White Devil* presents it also as a poison, but as an ambivalent and seductive one, that both cures and contaminates as it lures and attracts. *Volpone* casts the theater as a purgative medicine, releasing—or robbing?—audiences of money, laughter, and other humors. In *Romeo and Juliet* and *Antony and Cleopatra*, with different degrees of self-consciousness, theatrical spectacles are narcotic drugs that lull their audiences into unguarded, erotically tinged oblivion, with dangerous consequences. *The Devil's Charter* presents theater as an alluring spectacle that sinks into the skin of its performers, undoing them with the very poisons they intended to present to others. *The Second Maiden's Tragedy*, *The Duke of Milan*, and *The Revenger's Tragedy*, in different ways, present the theater as an idol, an alluring but inanimate spectacle that fills its viewers with gluttonous desires, fostering addictive needs. *Hamlet*, finally, casts theater as both remedy and poison, penetrating its listeners through their vulnerable ears and consuming them, both more and less powerfully than its perpetrators imagine.

Like the antitheatrical debates that accompanied them, playwrights' identification of plays with ambivalent pharmacy flourished most in the Elizabethan and Jacobean periods, but continued until the 1642 closing of London's public theaters. In 1660, when the theaters reopened, the debates returned as well—1662 saw the publication of Richard Baker's *Theatrum Redivivum, or the Theatre Vindicated. In Answer to M. Pryns Histriomastix*, and in 1698, Jeremy Collier published a tract on *The Prophaneness and Immorality of the English Stage*—but the terms of the debates had changed in significant ways.[4] Actresses began to appear on the public stage, first alongside and then instead of boy actors, suggesting that direct exposure to the spectacle of desirable women was no longer considered intolerably dangerous.[5] More broadly, neither the commercial theaters, Protestantism, nor chemical pharmacy were as new and galvanizing as they had been half a century earlier. As the ideas of René Descartes circulated and grew in influence, moreover, belief in the mind's inseparability from the body, and in the possibility that words and images could simultaneously transform both, became increasingly antiquated and evanescent. The moral status of the theater would continue to be ambivalent, as would the medical status of powerfully transformative drugs, but conceptions of the nature and effects of the two realms would sharply, though gradually, diverge.

Today, for the most part, readers, critics, and audiences who turn to the plays examined in this book—many of which have become fundamental parts of what we understand as our cultural canon—do not think the way their authors and original audiences did. We tend either to brush over their powerfully physical terminology, or to understand it figuratively, as colorful turns of phrase, dead metaphors. Yet the plays themselves offer an antidote to this reading. The worlds they present, steeped in medicines, ointments, drugs, paints, and poisons, insist that words, plays, and selves are all material, tangible, embodied presences. If we look at them as they ask to be looked at, we can still find that they have this virtuous property: to make us see as we were wont to see.

Notes

INTRODUCTION: DANGEROUS REMEDIES

1. William Shakespeare, *A Midsummer Night's Dream*, in *The Norton Shakespeare*, ed. Stephen Greenblatt, Walter Cohen, Jean E. Howard, and Katharine Eisaman Maus (New York: Norton, 1997). Further references to this play and to other plays by Shakespeare, unless specified otherwise, will be to this edition.

2. For a brilliant discussion of eyes, vision, and their relationship with theatricality in the play, see David Marshall's "Exchanging Visions: Reading *A Midsummer Night's Dream*," *English Literary History*, 49:3 (1982), 543–75.

3. On pharmacy as a metaphor for language and literature, see esp. Jacques Derrida, "Plato's Pharmacy," in *Dissemination*, trans. Barbara Johnson (Chicago: University of Chicago Press, 1981), 63–171. This book follows Derrida's observations about the ambivalent nature of both pharmacy and literature, while situating that association in the specific historical, scientific, and literary context of early modern England.

4. Jonathan Gil Harris has shown how, in an age of increased international travel and commerce, drugs and poisons offered a vocabulary with which to articulate social anxieties about foreigners—particularly Italians, Jews, and witches—invading the English body politic. See *Foreign Bodies and the Body Politic: Discourses of Social Pathology in Early Modern England* (Cambridge: Cambridge University Press, 1998).

5. When, in *King Lear*, the poisoned Regan moans "Sick! O, sick!," Goneril responds with satisfaction, "If not, I'll ne'er trust medicine" (V.iii.96–7). I am indebted to Marie Borroff for calling my attention to the suggestive etymologies of poison and venom. Derrida explores these linguistic complexities throughout "Plato's Pharmacy," and Harris discusses them in *Foreign Bodies*, 51–2.

6. For a good overview of the changes in medical remedies during this period, see Andrew Wear, *Knowledge and Practice in English Medicine, 1550–1680* (Cambridge: Cambridge University Press, 2000), esp. 46–103.

7. See, for example, Andrew Wear, "Epistemology and learned medicine in early modern England," in *Knowledge and the Scholarly Medical Traditions*, ed. Don Bates (Cambridge: Cambridge University Press, 1995), 151–73.

8. In his 1548 commentary on Dioscurides, Pietro Mattioli worried that faulty transmission of classical medicinal knowledge had given rise to misidentifications of *materia medica*, leading physicians unwittingly to prescribe poisons as pharmaceutical remedies. See Pietro Mattioli, *Il Dioscoride dell' eccellente Dottor P. A. Matthioli* (Venice, 1548); and Richard Palmer, "Pharmacy in the republic of Venice in the Sixteenth Century," in *The*

Medical Renaissance of the Sixteenth Century, ed. A. Wear, R. K. French, and I. M. Lonie (Cambridge: Cambridge University Press, 1985), 100–17. On print and medical knowledge, see Paul Slack, "Mirrors of Health and Treasures of Poor Men: The Uses of the Vernacular Medical Literature of Tudor England," in *Health, Medicine, and Mortality*, ed. Charles Webster (Cambridge: Cambridge University Press, 1979), 237–73.

9. On Paracelsus, see esp. Walter Pagel, *Paracelsus: An Introduction to Philosophical Medicine in the Era of the Renaissance* (Basel: Karger, 1958); Charles Webster, *From Paracelsus to Newton: Magic and the Making of Modern Science* (Cambridge: Cambridge University Press, 1982); and Henry Pachter, *Paracelsus: Magic Into Science* (New York: Henry Schuman, 1951). On the impact of Paracelsus in England, see Allen Debus, *The English Paracelsians* (London: Oldbourne, 1965); and Paul Kocher, "Paracelsan Medicine in England," *Journal of the History of Medicine* 2 (1947), 451–80. On the relationship between Paracelsan conceptions of pharmacy and early modern political ideas about national identity and its boundaries, see Harris, *Foreign Bodies*.

10. Paracelsus, *Selected Writings*, ed. Jolande Jacobi, trans. Norbert Guterman (New York: Pantheon, 1958), 107.

11. Angelus Sala, *Opiologia: or, a Treatise Concerning the Nature, Properties, True Preparation and Safe Use and Administration of Opium*, trans. Thomas Bretnor (London, 1618), B5.

12. Sala, *Opiologia*, B4 and B4^v.

13. Francis Herring, *A Modest Defence of the Caueat Given to the Wearers of Impoisoned Amulets, as Preseruatiues from the Plague* (London, 1604), 23.

14. Giles Everard first described tobacco as the panacea, or cure-all, in *De Herba Panacea, quam alii Tabacum, alii Petum, aut Nicotianum Vocant, Breuis Commentariolus* (Antwerp, 1587; first English trans. published in 1659). Storms of complaints followed shortly thereafter. For an extended discussion of tobacco's ambivalent status as remedy, poison, and catalyst of recreational drug use in this period, see Tanya Pollard, "The Pleasures and Perils of Smoking in Early Modern England," in *Smoke: A Global History of Smoking*, ed. Sander Gilman and Zhou Xun (London: Reaktion Press, 2004), 38–45.

15. Narcotic drugs are discussed in more detail in Chapter 2.

16. Several decades later, William Walwyn decried what he saw as the poisonous effects of the purgatives and expulsives of Galenic medicine: "spiritfull, forcible, poysonous, fiery vapours, which like close-pent powder, rend and tear to force their passage through every crany, and fastness of the parts; sometimes settling and coroding one part, otherwhiles suffocating the vital and animal spirits." Walwyn, *Physick for Families: Or, The new, Safe, and Powerfull Way of Physick, upon Constant Proof Established* (London, 1674), 64.

17. John Cotta, *A Short Discoverie of the Vnobserued Dangers of Seuerall Sorts of Ignorant and Vnconsiderate Practicers of Physicke in England* (London, 1612), 7.

18. James I, "A Counterblaste to Tobacco" (1604), in *The Workes of the Most High and Mighty Prince Iames, By the Grace of God Kinge of Great Brittaine France & Ireland Defendor of the Faith &c.* (London, 1616), 220.

19. Cotta, *Short Discoverie*, 5.

20. On tobacco and the developing interest in the concept of addiction in early modern plays, see Dennis Kezar, "Shakespeare's Addictions," *Critical Inquiry* 30 (2003), 31–62.

21. The preamble of the Act—22 Henry 8, chapter 9—stated that poisoning had previously been a rare event in England, and must be severely punished lest it become more common. See Sir Thomas Smith, *The Commonwealth of England* (London, 1589), O2ᵛ, and Fredson Bowers, "The Audience and the Poisoners of Elizabethan Tragedy," *Journal of English and Germanic Philology* 36 (1937), 491–504, 496–7.

22. Lopez, as a Jew, Spaniard, and doctor, had all the characteristics of a classic poisoning suspect. On the details of the case, see Martin A. S. Hume, *Treason and Plot: Struggles for Catholic Supremacy in the Last Years of Queen Elizabeth's Reign* (London: James Nisbet & Co., 1901), esp. 143–4; on the association of Jews with poison in the period, see Harris, *Foreign Bodies*, and James Shapiro, *Shakespeare and the Jews* (New York: Columbia University Press, 1996). For further background on the Squire case, see *The Letters and the Life of Francis Bacon*, ed. James Spedding (London: Longmans, 1862), 2.108–20.

23. On the notoriety of these cases, as well as others, see Bowers, "Poisoners," esp. 498–501.

24. The literature on the Overbury poisoning is enormous. For records of contemporary accounts, for example, see Andrew Amos, *The Great Oyer of Poisoning: The Trial of the Earl of Somerset for the Poisoning of Sir Thomas Overbury, in the Tower of London* (London: Richard Bentley, 1846), and Francis Bacon, *A True and Historical Relation of the Poysoning of Sir Thomas Overbury* (London, 1651). For a recent scholarly analysis, see David Lindley, *The Trials of Frances Howard: Fact and Fiction in the Court of King James* (London: Routledge, 1993).

25. George Eglisham, *The Forerunner of Revenge. Vpon the Duke of Buckingham for the Poysoning of the Most Potent King Iames . . . and the Lord Marquis of Hamilton* (London, 1621), A3ᵛ.

26. Thomas Tuke, *A Treatise Against Painting and Tincturing of Men and Women. Wherein the Abombinable Sinnes of Murther and Poysoning, Pride and Ambition, Adultery and Witchcraft, are Set Foorth & Discouered* (London, 1616), 49.

27. Edward Coke, *The Third Part of the Institutes of the Laws of England* (London, 1602), 48. Other testimonies to contemporary anxieties about poison include Francis Bacon, "The Speech of Sir Francis Bacon at the Arraignment of the Earl of Somerset," in *The Connexion: Being Choice Collections of Some Principal Matters in King James his Reign* (London, 1681); and William Crashaw, *The Parable of Poyson. In Five Sermons of Spirituall Poyson. Wherein the Poysonfull Nature of Sinne, and the Spirituall Antidotes against it, are Plainely and Briefely Set Downe* (London, 1618).

28. On the identification of poison with suspect national, ethnic, and religious groups, see esp. Harris, *Foreign Bodies*.

29. Although I argue that playwrights' interests in drugs and poison goes beyond a straightforward reflection of a narrative already playing out on England's political and social stages, the link is worth noting in itself: Bowers writes that "While they gave a somewhat exotic fillip to the imagination, it cannot be

said that the poison scenes of the Elizabethan tragedy were entirely out-landish and did not present a certain surface realism to the audience" ("Poisoners," 504).

30. Plutarch, "How a Yoong Man Ought to Heare Poets, And How He May Take Profit By Reading Poemes," *The Philosophie, Commonlie Called, The Morals, Written by the Learned Philosopher Plutarch of Chaeronea*, trans. Philemon Holland (London, 1603), 19.

31. See esp. Andrew Gurr, *Playgoing in Shakespeare's London* (Cambridge: Cambridge University Press, 2nd edn. 1996), on the extent of the theater-going public. Gurr claims that "between the 1560s, when the first purpose-built playhouses were established, and 1642, when all playhouses were closed, well over fifty million visits were made to playhouses" (4).

32. The debates about the theater are collected in *Shakespeare's Theater: A Sourcebook*, ed. Tanya Pollard (Oxford: Blackwell, 2004). For a critical overview of these debates, see esp. Jonas Barish, *The Antitheatrical Prejudice* (Berkeley: University of California Press, 1981). On antitheatrical anxieties about images and idolatry, and the theater's response to them, see Huston Diehl, *Staging Reform, Reforming the Stage: Protestantism and Popular Theater in Early Modern England* (Ithaca, NY: Cornell University Press, 1997); and Michael O'Connell, *The Idolatrous Eye: Iconoclasm and Theater in Early Modern England* (Oxford: Oxford University Press, 2000). See Jean Howard, *The Stage and Social Struggle in Early Modern England* (London and New York: Routledge, 1995), on class and gender; and Laura Levine, *Men in Women's Clothing: Anti-theatricality and Effeminization 1579–1642* (Cambridge: Cambridge University Press, 1994) on gender and sexuality. On the protean notions of identity that characterize the development of both the commercial theater and capitalism, see Jean-Christophe Agnew, *Worlds Apart: The Market and the Theater in Anglo-American Thought, 1550–1750* (Cambridge: Cambridge University Press, 1986).

33. Anglo-phile Eutheo [Anthony Munday], *A Second and Third Blast of Retrait from Plaies and Theaters* (London, 1580), 101.

34. William Prynne, *Histriomastix: The Player's Scourge* (London, 1633), 467 and 38.

35. Stephen Gosson, *Schoole of Abuse* (London, 1579), A2.

36. Stephen Gosson, *Apologie of the Schoole of Abuse* (London, 1579), L8^v.

37. Eutheo, *Second and Third Blast*, 100–1.

38. John Downame, *Foure Treatises, Tending to Disswade all Christians from Foure no Lesse Hainous than Common Sinnes; Namely, the Abuses of Swearing, Drunkennesse, Whoredome, and Bribery* (London, 1613), 197.

39. William Rankins, *A Mirrour of Monsters* (London, 1587), 17.

40. I. G. [John Greene], *A Refutation of the Apology for Actors* (London, 1615), A3^v.

41. Prynne, *Histriomastix*, 467, 38, 140, 2, 38, and 7 ("Epistle Dedicatory").

42. Thomas Lodge, *A Defence of Poetry, Music, and Stage-Plays* (London, 1579), 5. Lodge was both a playwright and a physician himself, adding particular pertinence to his medical metaphors.

43. Lodge, *Defence*, 35.

44. Lodge's point is echoed, and further explicated, by a later defender of the theater: "Indeed, it is not so much the Player, that makes the Obscenity, as the Spectatour himself: as it is not so much the Juyce of the Herb, that makes

the *Honey*, or *Poyson*, as the *Bee*, or *Spider*, that sucks the Juyce. Let this man therefore bring a modest heart to a Play, and he shall never take hurt by immodest Speeches: but, if he come as a *Spider* to it, what marvel, if he suck Poyson, though the Herbs be never so sovereign." Richard Baker, *Theatrum Redivivum, or the Theatre Vindicated. In Answer to M. Pryns Histriomastix* (London, 1662), 30. Although Baker's tract was not published until 1662, it would have been written before his death in 1645, probably shortly after *Histriomastix*.

45. On contemporary views of theater as a potentially therapeutic medium— and medicine, likewise, as a kind of performance—see Natsu Hattori, "Performing Cures: Theater and Medicine in Early Modern England," D.Phil. thesis (Oxford University, 1995).

46. Melancholy, a complex fusion of emotional and physical symptoms, offers apt material for theatrical remedies to address. On early modern preoccupation with melancholy, see esp. Robert Burton's *Anatomy of Melancholy* (Oxford, 1621); recent critical accounts, including psychoanalytic, feminist, and physiological perspectives, include Lynn Enterline, *The Tears of Narcissus: Melancholia and Masculinity in Early Modern England* (Stanford, Calif.: Stanford University Press, 1995); Bridget Gellert Lyons, *Voices of Melancholy: Studies in Literary Treatment of Melancholy in Renaissance England* (London: Routledge, 1971); and Juliana Schiesari, *The Gendering of Melancholy* (Ithaca, NY: Cornell University Press, 1992).

47. John Webster, *The Duchess of Malfi*, in *English Renaissance Drama: A Norton Anthology*, ed. David Bevington, Lars Engle, Katharine Eisaman Maus, and Eric Rasmussen (New York and London: Norton, 2002).

48. Early in his scene, Sly is impatient—"What, would you make me mad? Am not I Christopher Sly, old Sly's son of Burton-Heath . . .?" (Ind., ii.15–16). As it progresses, however, he becomes both content and amorous: "Servants, leave me and her alone. Madam, undress you and come now to bed" (Ind., ii.116–17).

49. On the significance of this medical masque, see esp. William Kerwin, " 'Physicians are like Kings': Medical Politics and *The Duchess of Malfi*," *English Literary Renaissance* 28:1 (1998), 95–117. Middleton and Rowley depict a similar medicine of madmen in *The Changeling*.

50. See Derrida, "Plato's Pharmacy," 99. He goes on to note that "The pharmakon can never be simply beneficial."

51. Plato, *Republic*, esp. II. 382d and III. 389b. Derrida discusses this vocabulary in "Plato's Pharmacy."

52. Plato, *Republic*, III. 401bc.

53. Aristotle, *Poetics*, VI. 2–3.

54. Early modern beliefs in the magical efficacy of words are explored in further detail in Chapter 5. From a more general perspective, Geoffrey Hartman muses on the medicinal and poisonous capacities of words in "Words and Wounds," in *Medicine and Literature*, ed. Enid Rhodes Peschel (New York: Neale Watson Academic Publications, 1980), 178–88.

55. Paster, *The Body Embarrassed: Drama and the Disciplines of Shame in Early Modern England* (Ithaca, NY: Cornell University Press, 1993); and Schoenfeldt, *Bodies and Selves in Early Modern England: Physiology and Inwardness in Spenser, Shakespeare, Herbert, and Milton* (Cambridge: Cambridge University Press, 1999).

56. On the material powers attributed to the imagination in the Renaissance, see esp. the work of Lorraine Daston and Katharine Park, such as *Wonders and the Order of Nature, 1150–1750* (New York: Zone, 1998).

57. Thomas Fienus, *De Viribus Imaginationis* (Louvain, 1608), trans. in L. J. Rather, "Thomas Fienus' (1567–1631) Dialectical Investigation of the Imagination as Cause and Cure of Bodily Disease," *Bulletin of the History of Medicine* 4 (1967), 349–67; 356.

58. Philip Sidney, *Defense of Poesy* (London, 1595), 41.

59. George Puttenham, *The Arte of English Poesie* (London, 1589), 38.

60. In fact, Puttenham himself made precisely this point: "Therefore of death and burials, of th'aduersities by warres, and of true loue lost or ill bestowed, are th'onely sorrowes that the noble Poets sought by their arte to remoue or appease, not with any medicament of a contrary temper, as the *Galenistes* vse to cure [*contraria contrarijs*] but as the *Paracelsians*, who cure [*similia similibus*] making one dolour to expell another, and in this case, one short sorrowing the remedie of a long and grieuous sorrow" (*Arte*, 39).

61. For extensive discussion of the effect of plague on the theater of this period, see J. Leeds Barroll, *Politics, Plague, and Shakespeare's Theater* (Ithaca, NY, and London: Cornell University Press, 1991).

62. On sound, see Bruce Smith, *The Acoustic World of Early Modern England: Attending to the O-Factor* (Chicago: University of Chicago Press, 1999); Wes Folkerth, *The Sound of Shakespeare* (London and New York: Routledge, 2002); and Gina Bloom, "Choreographing Voice: Agency and the Staging of Gender in Early Modern England" (Ph.D. thesis, University of Michigan, 2001). On touch, see Carla Mazzio, "Acting with Tact: Touch and Theater in the Renaissance," in *Sensible Flesh: On Touch in Early Modern Culture*, ed. Elizabeth Harvey (Philadelphia: University of Pennsylvania Press, 2002), 159–86.

63. Robert Burton, *Anatomy of Melancholy*, vol. 2, ed. A. R. Shilleto (London: George Bell, 1893), 142.

64. Thomas Heywood, *An Apology for Actors* (London, 1612), F4^v.

65. On the effect of the succession on dramatic representations of mourning in two of these plays, see Steven Mullaney, "Mourning and Misogyny: *Hamlet, The Revenger's Tragedy* and the Final Progress of Elizabeth I, 1600–1607," *Shakespeare Quarterly* 45:2 (1994), 139–62. William Kerwin discusses the relationship between medicine and political struggles over sovereignty in " 'Physicians are like Kings'."

66. See James I, "A Counterblaste to Tobacco," and *Daemonologie in Forme of a Dialogue* (London, 1597). Harris notes that James not only presented himself as the nation's moral physician, but demonstrated a notable interest in Paracelsian medicine; see *Foreign Bodies*, 55–6. On James's interest in the theater, see, for instance, Alvin Kernan, *Shakespeare, the King's Playwright: Theater in the Stuart Court, 1603–1613* (New Haven: Yale University Press, 1995).

67. See, for instance, Steven Mullaney, *The Place of the Stage: License, Play, and Power in Renaissance England* (Ann Arbor: University of Michigan Press, repr., 1995); Louis Montrose, *The Purpose of Playing* (Chicago: University of Chicago Press, 1996); Howard, *Stage and Social Struggle*; Stephen Greenblatt, *Shakespearean Negotiations* (Berkeley: University of California Press, 1988), and Stephen Orgel, *The Illusion of Power: Political Theater in*

the English Renaissance (Berkeley: University of California Press, 1975).

68. Important recent work on the early modern body includes discussions of the humors and the relationship between body and mind, such as Paster, *Body Embarrassed*, and Schoenfeldt, *Bodies and Minds*. Harris has analyzed the ideological implications of the body as political allegory (*Foreign Bodies*); Jonathan Sawday has shown how fascinations with anatomy and dissection responded to Renaissance desires for knowledge in *The Body Emblazoned* (London: Routledge, 1995); and the contributors to *The Body in Parts*, ed. David Hillman and Carla Mazzio (New York and London: Routledge, 1997) have pointed to the complex social and cultural associations surrounding bodily limbs and organs.

69. Jonathan Crewe notes this ambivalence in "The Theatre of the Idols: Marlowe, Rankins, and Theatrical Images," *Theatre Journal* 36 (1984), 321–33, as does Peter Stallybrass in "Reading the Body: *The Revenger's Tragedy* and the Jacobean Theater of Consumption," *Renaissance Drama* 18 (1987), 121–48.

70. Levine, *Men in Women's Clothing*, 3.

71. Levine certainly notes these commonalities, calling attention both to the ways that playwrights explore hostile notions of theater and to the ways in which antitheatrical writings imitate the structures and titles of plays, but her argument ultimately emphasizes the idea that playwrights' "rehearsal" of these ideas offers "the possibility of a kind of 'working out'" (2–3).

72. Richard Helgerson describes poets' apprehensions about writing for the public theater in *Self-Crowned Laureates: Spenser, Jonson, Milton, and the Literary System* (Berkeley: University of California Press, 1983), 146.

73. Michel Foucault, *Discipline and Punish: The Birth of the Prison*, trans. Alan Sheridan (New York: Vintage Books 1995), 195–228.

74. Laura Mulvey, "Visual Pleasure and Narrative Cinema," *Screen* 16:3 (1975), 6–18; reprinted in *Visual and Other Pleasures* (Bloomington: Indiana University Press, 1989), 14–27.

75. Stephen Orgel, for example, calls attention to the powerful role of the monarchical audience to court masques in *The Jonsonian Masque* (Cambridge, Mass.: Harvard University Press, 1965).

76. Heather James explores the effects of male speech on female listeners in "Dido's Ear," *Shakespeare Quarterly* 52:3 (2001), 360–82.

77. *A Discourse of Auxiliary Beauty* (London, 1656), 150.

1. "UNNATURAL AND HORRID PHYSIC": PHARMACEUTICAL THEATER IN JONSON AND WEBSTER

1. Ben Jonson, *Volpone*, ed. Philip Brockbank, New Mermaids (New York: Norton, 1968), I.iv.11–22.

2. Ben Jonson, *Sejanus his Fall*, ed. Philip J. Ayres, The Revels Plays (Manchester: Manchester University Press, 1965). All citations to the text refer to this edition.

3. Medical treachery was a popular topic: beyond the plays explored in this chapter, doctors and apothecaries provide poisons in plays including Marlowe's *Massacre at Paris*, Shakespeare's *Romeo and Juliet*, Marlowe's

Jew of Malta, Dekker's *Match Me in London*, and Beaumont and Fletcher's *The Tragedy of Thierry and Theodoret*, and are alluded to as sources of poison in many more. The charges against doctors were even more pervasive outside of the theater, in both medical and political writings; two of the more famously publicized instances, mentioned in the Introduction, included Roderigo Lopez, Queen Elizabeth's personal physician, and the apothecary James Franklin, who was convicted of mixing poisons in the notorious murder of Sir Thomas Overbury. While the fixation in these plays on pharmacy and poison responds to specific contemporary issues, fears about doctors are of course hardly unique to the period. Throughout history doctors have been regarded with suspicion as well as awe, and have been routinely accused of murder. Archagathus, for example, purportedly the first Greek physician to practice in Rome, was popularly titled "carnifex" due to his alleged propensity for violently cutting and burning his patients. See Heinrich von Staden, "Liminal Perils: Early Roman Receptions of Greek Medicine," in *Tradition, Transmission, Transformation*, ed. F. Jamil Ragep and Sally P. Ragep with Steven Livesey (Leiden: Brill, 1996), 369–418.

4. John Cotta, *A Short Discoverie of the Vnobserved Dangers of Seuerall Sorts of Ignorant and Vnconsiderate Practicers of Physicke in England* (London, 1612), 1.

5. Intriguingly, doctors themselves were the most common sources of warning about medical dangers, using the threat of poison to demarcate the professional boundaries between true, learned physicians and unreliable impostors, including folk healers, quacks, empirics, and apothecaries. On the development of medicine as a profession, see Margaret Pelling, "Medical Practice in Early Modern England: Trade or Profession," in *The Professions in Early Modern England*, ed. Wilfred Prest (London: Croom Helm, 1987), 90–128. On the professional rivalry between physicians and apothecaries, which led to apothecaries attaining their own charter in 1617, see George Trease, *Pharmacy in History* (London: Baillière, Tindall & Cox, 1964); and F. N. L. Poynter, ed., *The Evolution of Pharmacy in Britain* (London: Pitman Medical Publishing, 1965).

6. Johannes Oberndoerffer, *The Anatomyes of the True Physition, and Counterfeit Mounte-banke: wherein both of them, are graphically described, and set out in their Right, and Orient Colours*, trans. F. H. [Francis Herring] (London, 1602), 18.

7. John Securis, *A Detection and Querimonie of the Daily Enormities and Abuses Committed in Physick* (London, 1566), Evi^v. In his otherwise clear and helpful study of pharmaceutical history, Trease misattributes this text to Robert Recorde, leading to erroneous statements both about Recorde and about the chronology of physician/apothecary conflicts. Trease bases his attribution on a reprinting of the section titled *A Detection of Some Ignorant Apothecaries* appended to the 1665 edition of Recorde's *The Urinal of Physick*, and attributed there simply to "a Doctor of Physick in Queen Elizabeths dayes." Robert Recorde's original 1548 edition has no such appendix, however, and the text is clearly attributed to Securis on the title page of its original 1566 edition. See Trease, *Pharmacy in History*, 91–2.

8. On the history of metaphors of the theater, see E. R. Curtius, *European Literature and the Latin Middle Ages*, trans. Willard Trask (Princeton: Princeton University Press, 1983), 138–44.

9. Cotta, *Short Discoverie*, 8.
10. James Primerose, *Popular Errours. Or The Errours of the People in matter of Physick*, trans. Robert Wittie (London, 1651), Bii[v].
11. Oberndoerffer, *Anatomyes*, 10.
12. Ibid. 32.
13. The relationship between face-paints, poison, and the theater is explored at greater length in Chapter 3.
14. On the idea of poison as remedy, see Jonathan Gil Harris, *Foreign Bodies and the Body Politic: Discourses of Social Pathology in Early Modern England* (Cambridge: Cambridge University Press, 1998).
15. Pliny the Elder, *The Historie of the World*, trans. Philemon Holland (London, 1634), 269, 270.
16. Ibid. 270. He continues, "for of this nature it is, that if it meet not with some poison or other in mens bodies for to kill, it presently sets vpon them and soon brings them to their end: but if it incounter any such, it wrestleth with it alone, as hauing found within, a fit match to deale with: neither entreth it into this fight, vnlesse it find this enemy possessed already of some noble and principall part of the body, and then beginneth the combat: a wonderfull thing to obserue, that two poisons, both of them deadly of themselues and their own nature, should die one vpon another within the body, and the man by that mean only escape with life" (270).
17. Ibid.
18. On the metaphor of the body politic and its health, see especially Harris, *Foreign Bodies*.
19. Numerous critics have commented on Jonson's hostility towards the theater. See, for instance, Jonas Barish, "Jonson and the Loathèd Stage," in *A Celebration of Ben Jonson*, ed. William Blissett, Juan Patrick, and R.W. Van Fossen (Toronto and Buffalo: University of Toronto Press, 1973), 27–53, repr. in *The Antitheatrical Prejudice* (Berkeley: University of California Press, 1981), 132–54; John Gordon Sweeney III, *Jonson and the Psychology of Public Theater* (Princeton: Princeton University Press, 1985), 82–3; Richard Helgerson, *Self-Crowned Laureates: Spenser, Jonson, Milton, and the Literary System* (Berkeley: University of California Press, 1983), 150.
20. Discussing Jonson's use of humoralism in his plays, in relation to the tradition of Roman moral philosophy with which he identifies himself, Katharine Maus notes that "bodily dysfunction provides the Romans—and Jonson—with a vocabulary for moral and intellectual defects," adding that "the analogy between body and soul can be extended further; philosophy, or responsible poetry, since it corrects errors and amends vices, becomes a kind of cure—'the physicke of the minde,' as Asper in *Every Man Out of His Humour* translates Cicero's 'animi medicina.'" See Maus, *Ben Jonson and the Roman Frame of Mind* (Princeton: Princeton University Press, 1984), 24.
21. Ben Jonson, "Explorata: or, Discoveries," in *Workes* (London, 1641), 125. Intriguingly, if speculatively, Katherine Duncan-Jones sees Jonson as the model for Jacques in Shakespeare's *As You Like It*: "Give me leave | To speak my mind, and I will through and through | Cleanse the foul body of th'infected world, | If they will patiently receive my medicine." *As You Like It*, in *The Norton Shakespeare*, ed. Stephen Greenblatt, Walter Cohen, Jean E. Howard, and Katharine Eisaman Maus (New York: Norton, 1997),

II.vii.58–61, and Duncan-Jones, *Ungentle Shakespeare* (London: Arden Shakespeare, 2001), 123–5.

22. Jonas Barish, "Jonson and the Loathèd Stage," 136.

23. Herbert Silvette finds that Webster's "stock of medical and surgical information was astonishingly large and well digested," and Robert Simpson notes that Webster is the only playwright of his time who rivals Shakespeare in the quantity and quality of medical references. See Herbert Silvette, *The Doctor on the Stage: Medicine and Medical Men in Seventeenth-Century England*, ed. Francelia Butler (Knoxville: University of Tennessee Press, 1967), 29; and Simpson, *Shakespeare and Medicine* (Edinburgh: E. & S. Livingston, 1959), 114. Studies of Webster's uses of medicine include Maurice Hunt, "Webster and Jacobean Medicine," *Essays in Literature* 16 (1989), 33–49; Caroline di Miceli, "Sickness and Physic in Some Plays by Middleton and Webster," *Cahiers Elisabethains* 26 (1984), 41–78; and William Kerwin, "'Physicians are like Kings': Medical Politics and *The Duchess of Malfi*," *English Literary Renaissance* 28:1 (1998), 95–117. On failed or dangerous remedies, Hereward T. Price notes that *The White Devil* alone contains thirty references to poison; see "The Function of Imagery in Webster," *PMLA* 70 (1955), 717–39. Other studies of Webster's interest in poison include Mariangela Tempera, "The Rhetoric of Poison in John Webster's Italianate Plays," in *Shakespeare's Italy: Functions of Italian Locations in Renaissance Drama*, ed. Michele Marrapodi, A. J. Hoenselaars, Marcello Cappuzzo, L. Falzon Stantucci (Manchester: Manchester University Press, 1993), 229–50; Louise T. Wright, "Webster's Lenative Poisons," *Journal of English Linguistics* 24 (1996), 182–5; and James T. Henke, "John Webster's Motif of 'Consuming'," *Neuphilologische Mitteilungen* 76 (1975), 625–41.

24. This distinction has not been noted by critics; Caroline di Miceli, in fact, conflates Galenic humoral theory with Paracelsan theory about the curative power of poisons in her description of the "common stock of knowledge and ideas" drawn upon by Renaissance dramatists ("Sickness and Physic," 43–4).

25. John Webster, *The White Devil*, ed. Christina Luckyj, New Mermaids (New York: Norton, 1966). All further citations refer to this edition.

26. Lynn Thorndike refers to it as an example of the "characteristically Paracelsan" use of medically employed poisonous arcana. See *A History of Magic and Experimental Science*, vol. 5, *The Sixteenth Century* (New York: Columbia University Press, 1941), 639. Variant spellings include mummy and mumia.

27. Alongside Mummia, the other three principles were Archeus, Iliaster, and Protoplastus. Neither matter nor spirit, mummia represented to Paracelsus the inner "balsam," or life power inherent in the flesh; the injunction "take mummia" became an incantational refrain throughout his recipes. See Henry Pachter, *Paracelsus: Magic Into Science* (New York: Henry Schuman, 1951), 213–15.

28. Criminals hanged at the gallows, or beheaded rebels, were also recommended; see Pachter, *Magic into Science*, 53; and Walter Pagel, *Paracelsus: An Introduction to Philosophical Medicine in the Era of the Renaissance* (Basel: Karger, 1958), 55. The Paracelsan enthusiast Oswald Croll is yet more specific: to be most effective, mummia should be prepared from the

corpse of a red-headed man 24 years old who has suffered a violent death. He further specifies that it should be cut into bits, sprinkled with powder of myrrh and aloes, soaked in alcohol, suspended in air and dried. See Oswald Croll, *Basilica Chymica* (Frankfurt, 1609), 75; and Thorndike, *Magic*, 5. 650.

29. See Pachter, *Magic into Science*, 38 and 53; this range of ingredients would stand in stark contrast to the largely herbal and non-toxic Galenic system.

30. Thomas Erastus, *Disputationum de Medicina Nova P. Paracelsi* (Basel, 1572), esp. III. 11, and IV. 140; See also Pagel, *Paracelsus*, 329; and Thorndike, 5. 659. Paracelsus vehemently denied that mummia's powers were magical in origin, insisting that its workings were entirely natural and explicable.

31. Vittoria adopts the metaphor to accuse the lawyers at her trial of deceptive wiles: "I discern poison I Under your gilded pills" (III.ii.190–1).

32. Gilders worked with a combination of gold and mercury, and would be exposed to fumes when drawing off the mercury with heat. The symptoms of mercury poisoning include general sluggishness or coldness as well as shaking and insanity.

33. The literature on the early history of syphilis is large, and currently growing; for a good overview on its social and medical impact in this period, see Johannes Fabricius, *Syphilis in Shakespeare's England* (London: Jessica Kingsley, 1994).

34. He was, however, vocal in condemning the dangerous methods by which mercury was typically administered at the time (such as directly applied ointments); see Pachter, *Magic into Science*, 178–85, and Pagel, *Paracelsus*, esp. 24 and 76.

35. See esp. Pachter, *Magic into Science*, 337–8. Interestingly for the terms of this play, Paracelsus associated mummia with mercury.

36. William Bullein, *Bulleins Bulwarke of Defence against All Sicknesse, Soarenesse, and Woundes that Doe Dayly Assaulte Mankinde* (London, 1579), 70 and 69ᵛ.

37. To assert, as Mariangela Tempera does, that unicorn's horn "was already so thoroughly disqualified at the time" as to render its citation here obviously ironic, is misjudged ("The rhetoric of poison in John Webster's Italianate plays," 237): Paracelsus, along with many others, believed very strongly in the power of unicorn's horn. It is true, however, that its status as antidote was at the time controversial; Ambroise Paré, for example, notes that "There are very many at this day who thinke themselves excellently well armed against poyson and all contagion, if they be provided with some powder of Unicornes horne, or some infusion made therewith," but he reports the conclusion of his own examination to be that such powers, if they exist at all, are strictly accidental. See *The Workes of that Famous Chirurgion Ambroise Parey*, trans. Thomas Johnson (London, 1634), 813.

38. The doctor's association with lechery offers another link between the "black lust" (III.ii.7) attributed to Vittoria and the poisonous medicines which permeate the play.

39. The symbolic force of the poisonous kiss is considered at greater length in Chapter 4.

40. On the rarity of direct references to plague in the literature of this plague-ridden period, see, for example, Katherine Duncan-Jones, "Playing Fields or

Killing Fields: Shakespeare's Poems and *Sonnets*," *Shakespeare Quarterly* 54:2 (2003), 127–41.

41. Dieter Mehl comments on Brachiano's association with theatricality in *The Elizabethan Dumb Show: The History of a Dramatic Convention* (Cambridge, Mass.: Harvard University Press, 1966), 140–1, but does not explicitly identify theater with poison in the play.

42. Lynn Enterline makes a similar argument about Webster's imagery of poisonous and infectious spectacles in *The Duchess of Malfi*; see " 'Hairy on the In-side': *The Duchess of Malfi* and the Body of Lycanthropy," *Yale Journal of Criticism* 7:2 (1994), 85–129, and later version in *The Tears of Narcissus: Melancholia and Masculinity in Early Modern Writing* (Stanford, Calif.: Stanford University Press, 1995).

43. Peter Murray writes that Vittoria "is ever the consummate actress, and Webster manages things so that instead of condemning her as a liar and hypocrite, we admire her lies and hypocrisies as part of her great performance. We naturally forget that as a great actress creating illusions she is the white devil still." See *A Study of John Webster* (Paris and The Hague: Mouton, 1969), 66.

44. Lee Bliss makes the similar observation that "Webster further distances the whole interview by introducing a third perspective, Cornelia's. The seduction scene becomes a series of receding groups, and this arrangement emphasizes our own position as critical spectators." See Bliss, *The World's Perspective: John Webster and the Jacobean Drama* (Brighton: Harvester Press, 1983), 104.

45. The white devil refers to evil disguised in a beautiful exterior; on the play's preoccupation with duplicity, and its link with poisons, see especially Murray, *A Study of John Webster*, 32–40.

46. On the trial as an example of misogyny engrained in the legal system, see Kathryn Finin-Farber, "Framing (the) Woman: *The White Devil* and the Deployment of Law," *Renaissance Drama*, NS 25 (1994), 219–45.

47. Don D. Moore writes that "There is little doubt that Webster would prefer to be read by the 'light' of the first two learned playwrights [Chapman and Jonson], and with Jonson's defensive Preface to *Sejanus* before him, no doubt saw himself as above the popular theatre." See Moore, "Introduction," *John Webster: The Critical Heritage*, (London and New York: Routledge, 1981, repr. 1995), 3. Elizabeth M. Brennan describes *The White Devil* as paralleling Jonson's tragedies, especially *Sejanus*, in its interest in historical events, its dark satiric tone, its failure on the popular stage, and the author's impatience with its audience. See Brennan, "An Understanding Auditory: An Audience for John Webster," in *John Webster*, ed. Brian Morris (London: Ernest Benn, 1970), 3–19.

48. Philip J. Ayres, in his introduction to the Revels Plays edition of *Sejanus*, notes a series of parallels between *Sejanus* and *Volpone*: their darkness of tone, their protagonists' fascination with intrigue and plotting, and their unsettling trial scenes. See "Introduction," *Sejanus his Fall*.

49. Critics have commented extensively on the play's fascination with the world of the theater. Ian Donaldson noted that the play's central seductive pleasure is "the art of impersonation and deception: an art which for Volpone and Mosca is more thrilling than sex itself." See "Unknown Ends: *Volpone*," in Donaldson, *Jonson's Magic Houses: Essays in Interpretation* (Oxford:

Clarendon Press, 1997), 121. Helgerson claims, "As *Hamlet* is the English Renaissance's greatest tribute to theatrical man, so *Volpone* is the finest attack" (*Self-Crowned Laureates*, 159). Other insightful commentaries on the play's preoccupation with theatricality include Barish, "Jonson and the Loathèd Stage"; Stephen Greenblatt, "The False Ending in *Volpone*," *Journal of English and Germanic Philology* 75 (1976), 90–104; Robert Watson, "*Volpone*: Surprised by Morality," in *Ben Jonson's Parodic Strategy* (Cambridge, Mass.: Harvard University Press, 1987), 80–97; and Alvin Kernan, "Introduction," *Volpone*, ed. Kernan (New Haven: Yale University Press, 1962).

50. Harriet Hawkins links medicine with the theatrical in "Folly, Incurable Disease, and *Volpone*," *Studies in English Literature* 8 (1968), 335–48. Jonathan Gil Harris discusses the play's treatment of drugs and medicines in relation to anxieties about foreign trade; see "'I am sailing to my port, uh! uh! uh! uh!': The Pathologies of Transmigration in *Volpone*," *Literature and Medicine* 20:2 (2001), 109–32.

51. A stage direction in the play notes "Volpone *mounts stage*" (II.ii.32). Silvette discusses the relationship between this scene, actual mountebanks, and Jonson's theatrical art, in *The Doctor on the Stage*, esp. 68–9.

52. John Webster, *The Devil's Law Case*, in *John Webster: Three Plays*, ed. David Gumby (New York: Penguin, 1972), III.ii.43–4.

53. On the centrality of purgative treatments to Galenic medicine, and their privileged place in comedy, see Gail Kern Paster, "Covering His Ass: The Scatological Imperatives of Comedy," in *The Body Embarrassed: Drama and the Disciplines of Shame in Early Modern England* (Ithaca, NY: Cornell University Press, 1993), 113–62.

54. Francis Bacon, *Sylua Syluarum: Or A Naturall Historie* (London, 1626), 12. Others who wrote about the effects of antimony include Gervase Markham, who noted "*Antimonium*, or *Stibium*, is cold and dry, it bindeth, mundifieth and purgeth" (*Markhams Maister-Peece* (London, 1610), 483), and Pliny, who, interestingly in the context of Volpone's emphasis on selling beautifying medicines, also described it as "a principal and peculiar medicine to be imployed about the eies; for therupon it was that most men called it Platyophthalmon, for that being put into those ointments that are to beautifie the eies of women . . . it seemes to extend the compasse of the eies, and make them appeare open, faire, and large withall" (*Historie of the World*, 473). Jonson, intriguingly, also referred to the substance in *The Alchemist*: when Subtle asks "What's your *ultimum supplicium auri*?" [ultimate punishment for gold], Face responds "Antimonium," which was meant to make gold less malleable. See *The Alchemist*, II.v.30, in *English Renaissance Drama: A Norton Anthology*, ed. David Bevington, Lars Engle, Katharine Eisaman Maus, and Eric Rasmussen (New York and London: Norton, 2002).

55. Bacon, *Sylua Syluarum*, 12–13.

56. Ibid. 13.

57. Philip Brockbank notes the parallels between Volpone's performance here and Jonson's move to the larger popular audience of the Globe theater after being formerly accustomed to the more fashionable and elite arena of Blackfriars; he comments "It is quite probable that Jonson glances archly and sardonically at his own art as public entertainer" (*Volpone*, ed. Brockbank, 48).

58. As noted earlier, Jonson disliked the public stage; he preferred the private theater to it, and preferred masques for aristocratic patrons to either. On his complaints about the theater, see especially Barish, "Jonson and the Loathèd Stage."

59. Watson writes that "what is new in *Volpone* is the degree to which the satiric manipulators delude and injure themselves in the process of deluding and injuring their gulls" ("Surprised by Morality", 82).

60. For other epilogues inviting audience votes, see, for instance, Prospero at the end of *The Tempest*, or Rosalind at the end of *As You Like It*.

61. Alexander Leggatt writes that "If the audience applauds—and it will—it is registering its approval of a character who has broken rule after rule in a serious moral scheme that lies beneath the entire Jonson canon. That Jonson allows this shows he is willing to identify Volpone with his own delight in artistic creation, a delight that supplements and at times overrides his critical judgement of the character." See *Ben Jonson: His Vision and His Art* (London and New York: Methuen, 1981), 29.

62. Jonson himself, in fact, explicitly argued in his critical writings that moving audiences to laughter was morally suspect: "Nor, is the moving of laughter alwaies the end of *Comedy*, that is rather a fowling for the peoples delight, or their fooling. For, as *Aristotle* saies rightly, the moving of laughter is a fault in Comedie, a kind of turpitude, that depraves some part of a mans nature without a disease" ("Explorata," 129–30).

2. "A THING LIKE DEATH": SHAKESPEARE'S NARCOTIC THEATER

1. I use the term "double tragedy" to refer to tragedies with two protagonists of equal stature, both named in the title, both of whom die. The term could also, however, describe the many other forms of generic and thematic doubleness encompassed in these particular plays. On the rise of love tragedy in this period, and its intrinsic generic complications, see especially Martha Tuck Rozett, "The Comic Structures of Tragic Endings: The Suicide Scenes in *Romeo and Juliet* and *Antony and Cleopatra*," *Shakespeare Quarterly* 36:1 (1985), 152–64; and Charles Forker, "The Love-Death Nexus in English Renaissance Tragedy," in *Skull Beneath the Skin: The Achievement of John Webster* (Carbondale and Edwardsville: Southern Illinois University Press, 1986), 235–53. As Rozett observes, the genre was new in the 1590s, and *Romeo and Juliet* seems to have been the first English play in which love was the subject of tragedy (152). On the mixing of genres in *Romeo and Juliet*, see esp. Susan Snyder, *The Comic Matrix of Shakespeare's Tragedies* (Princeton: Princeton University Press, 1979), 56–70. On *Antony and Cleopatra*, see Janet Adelman, *The Common Liar: An Essay on* Antony and Cleopatra (New Haven: Yale University Press, 1973), esp. 1–52; J. L. Simmons, "The Comic Pattern and Vision in *Antony and Cleopatra*," *English Literary History* 36 (1969), 493–510; and Barbara C. Vincent, "Shakespeare's *Antony and Cleopatra* and the Rise of Comedy," *English Literary Renaissance* 12:1 (1982), 53–86.

2. On genre, see Snyder, *Comic Matrix*. Much has been written on the play's yoking of love and death; see, for example, Marilyn Williamson, "Romeo

and Death," *Shakespeare Studies* 14 (1981); 129–37; and Lloyd Davis, "'Death-marked love': Desire and Presence in *Romeo and Juliet*," *Shakespeare Survey* 49 (1996), 57–67.

3. Less directly, it could be seen as evoking the extreme youth of the lovers themselves, which Shakespeare altered his source to emphasize; see Susan Snyder, "Ideology and the Feud in *Romeo and Juliet*," *Shakespeare Survey* 46 (1998), 87–8.

4. The ambivalent comedy of the nurse's response is echoed by the musicians' banter after Juliet's apparent death; both scenes are replayed, more darkly, with Balthasar's false report of Juliet's death to Romeo at the beginning of Act V.

5. Strikingly, whereas Romeo is powerfully affected by the sight of his love, Juliet is particularly susceptible to the spoken word. In the orchard scene she identifies Romeo not by sight but by sound: "My ears have yet not drunk a hundred words | Of thy tongue's uttering, yet I know the sound" (II.ii.58–9). The effect of the Nurse's "I" in the passage discussed above lingers in Juliet's subsequent worry that "Some word there was, worser than Tybalt's death" (III.ii.108), and Romeo later imagines him reacting to his name "As if that name, | Shot from the deadly level of a gun, | Did murder her" (III.iii.102–4). Romeo, on the other hand, is undone by Juliet's beauty, and appears to be almost oblivious to speech: in frustration with his inability to listen, the Friar exclaims "O, then I see that madmen have no ears" (III.iii.61).

6. "I saw the wound, I saw it with mine eyes . . . I swounded at the sight" (III.ii.52–6).

7. The friar similarly tells the families, at the end of the play, that his sleeping potion achieved his intended aim in giving her "the form of death" (V.iii.246).

8. Snyder points out that the reputed deaths of Hero in *Much Ado About Nothing*, Helena in *All's Well That Ends Well*, Claudio in *Measure for Measure*, and Hermione in *A Winter's Tale* all succeed in their goal to avert or resolve a conflict by effecting a transformation in other characters (Snyder, *Comic Matrix*, 67). The generic ambivalence in each of these plays could be seen to identify them with tragicomedy, where the same motif is prevalent; see, for example, Beaumont and Fletcher's *Philaster* and *A King and No King*, and Dekker's *Match Me in London*. On characteristics and motifs of tragicomedy, see, for example, Gordon McMullan and Jonathan Hope, *The Politics of Tragicomedy: Shakespeare and After* (London and New York: Routledge, 1992); and Marvin T. Herrick, *Tragicomedy: Its Origins and Development in Italy, France, and England* (Urbana: University of Illinois Press, 1955).

9. On the range of associations with mandragora, see C. J. S. Thompson, *The Mystic Mandrake* (London: Rider, 1934). Other noted literary references to mandrake in the period appear in John Donne's poems "Song" ("Go, and catch a falling star") and "Twicknam Gardens," as well as Webster's *The White Devil* and *The Duchess of Malfi*.

10. The French physician Ambroise Paré, for instance, noted that "Mandrage taken in great quantity, either the root or fruit causeth great sleepinesse, sadnesse, resolution, and languishing of the body, so that . . . the patient falls asleep in the same posture as hee was in, just as if hee were in a Lethargie" (*The Works of that famous Chirurgion Ambroise Parey*, trans. Thomas

Johnson (London, 1634), 806). William Bullein remarked that it is "properly geuen to helpe conception, some say, as it appeereth by the Wyues of the holy Patryarche *Iacob*, The one was fruictful, the other did desire help, by the meanes of Mandracke, brought out of the fyeldes, by the handes of *Ruben Leas* sonne" (*Bulleins Bulwarke of Defence against All Sicknesse, Soarenesse, and Woundes that doe dayly assuaulte mankinde* (London, 1579), 41ᵛ–42).

11. Ibid. 41ᵛ.

12. Ibid.

13. Cited from John Webster, *The Duchess of Malfi*, in *English Renaissance Drama: A Norton Anthology*, ed. David Bevington, Lars Engle, Katharine Eisaman Maus, and Eric Rasmussen (New York and London: Norton, 2002).

14. In response to Mercutio's claim "That dreamers often lie," he rebuts, "In bed asleep, where they do dream things true" (I.iv.51–2).

15. See Marjorie Garber, "Dream Language: *Romeo and Juliet*," in *Dream in Shakespeare: From Metaphor to Metamorphosis* (New Haven and London: Yale University Press, 1974), 44–7. Garber suggests, however, that Romeo's dream is not false, as the resurrection it envisions is metaphorically borne out in the monuments that enshrine the lovers' memory.

16. He repeats this imagery upon approaching the Capulet's tomb, which he describes as "detestable maw, thou womb of death" (V.iii.45).

17. M. M. Mahood, *Shakespeare's Wordplay* (London: Methuen, 1957), 72.

18. This line must have hung in the mind of Anthony Munday when he was composing the ending of *The Death of Robert Earl of Huntington* (London, 1601): "See how he seekes to suck, if he could drawe, | Poyson from dead Matildaes ashie lips" (3005–6). The idea of the poisoned kiss is discussed in detail in Chapter 4.

19. Although this brief catalogue emphasizes examples from drama, there are numerous non-dramatic instances of this motif as well; see, for instance Basilius, who wakes up after an apparent poisoning in Sidney's *Arcadia*.

20. Angelus Sala, *Opiologia: or, a Treatise Concerning the Nature, Properties, True Preparation and Safe Use and Administration of Opium*, trans. Thomas Bretnor (London, 1618), 65.

21. Eleazer Dunk, *The Copy of a Letter written by E.D. [Eleazer Dunk] Doctour of Physicke to a Gentleman* (London, 1606), 31.

22. Ibid.

23. Edmund Gardiner, *The Triall of Tabacco. Wherein, his Worth is most Worthily Expressed: as, in the Name, Nature, and Qualitie of the Sayd Hearb; his Speciall Vse in all Physicke, with the True and Right Vse of Taking it, aswell for the Seasons, and Times* (London, 1610), 9ᵛ.

24. Henry Buttes, *Dyets Dry Dinner* (London, 1599), P5ᵛ.

25. Tobias Venner, *A Briefe and Accurate Treatise, Concerning The Taking of the Fume of Tobacco* (London, 1621), B3. King James I predicted, colorfully, that if a man uses tobacco, "all his members shall become feeble, his spirits dull, and in the end, as a drowsie lazie belly-god, he shall euanish in a Lethargie." James I, "A Counterblaste to Tobacco" (1604), in *The Workes of the most High and Mighty Prince Iames, by the Grace of God Kinge of Great Brittaine France & Ireland Defendor of the Faith &c.* (London, 1616), 220.

26. Bullein, *Bulleins Bulwarke*, 25ᵛ.
27. Timothy Bright, *A Treatise: Wherein is Declared the Sufficiencie of English Medicines, for Cure of all Diseases, Cured with Medicine* (London, 1580), 15–16.
28. Philip Barrough, *The Method of Phisick, Containing the Causes, Signes, and Cures of Inward Diseases in Mans Body from the Head to the Foote* (London, 1596), 24.
29. André Du Laurens, *A Discourse of the Preservation of the Sight: of Melancholike diseases; of Rheumes, and of Old age*, trans. Richard Surphlet (London, 1599), 115.
30. John Hall married Susannah Shakespeare in 1607, but Shakespeare seems to have known him for some time before this. The fact that Shakespeare included Hall in his business dealings and made the couple the executors of his will suggests that he approved of the match. Although Shakespeare's writings are not as saturated with medical imagery and references as some contemporary plays, such as those of Jonson and Webster, doctors and apothecaries appear in a number of his plays, including *Cymbeline*, *King Lear*, *Macbeth*, and *All's Well That Ends Well*. Interestingly, in contrast to most contemporary literary portrayals of doctors as sinister and malicious, Shakespeare's doctors tend to be competent and kindly, and his observations about current medical treatments are for the most part very accurate. For more background on Shakespeare's medical knowledge and representations of doctors, see Robert Simpson, *Shakespeare and Medicine* (Edinburgh: E. & S. Livingston, 1959); and Herbert Silvette, *The Doctor on the Stage: Medicine and Medical Men in Seventeeth-Century England*, ed. Francelia Butler (Knoxville: University of Tennessee Press, 1967).
31. For an overview of medical perspectives on sleep in this period, see Karl H. Dannenfeldt, "Sleep: Theory and Practice in the Late Renaissance," *Journal of the History of Medicine and Allied Sciences* 41 (1986), 415–41.
32. *Opiologica*, 28–9.
33. Du Laurens, *Discourse*, 95.
34. Paré, *Workes*, 35.
35. He describes, for example, "*the Lethargie*," "*Carus or Subeth*," "*Congelation or taking*," and "*dead sleepe*" or "*Coma*" (Barrough, *The Method of Phisick*, 24, 29, 30).
36. See Bevington, "Asleep Onstage," in John A. Alford, ed., *From Page to Performance: Essays in Early English Drama* (East Lansing: Michigan State University Press, 1995), 51–83.
37. To point to merely a few other instances in Shakespeare, in *The Taming of the Shrew* a Lord asks of Christopher Sly, "What's here? One dead, or drunk?" (Ind. I.30); in *2 Henry IV*, Hal mistakes his sleeping father for dead (IV.v.21–47); and in *Cymbeline*, Lucius, like many others, wonders of Imogen, "Or dead or sleeping . . .?" (IV.ii.356).
38. George Walton Williams comments on the play's uneasiness towards sleep in "Sleep in *Hamlet*," *Renaissance Papers 1964*, ed. S. K. Heninger, Peter G. Phialas, and George Walton Williams (Durham, NC: Southeastern Renaissance Conference, 1965), 17–20.
39. Other examples abound; in *Richard III*, the young princes are killed while sleeping in the tower (IV.iii.1–22).
40. William Prynne, *Histriomastix* (London, 1933), 956.

41. Prynne, *Histriomastix*, 946–7.
42. Stephen Gosson, *The Schoole of Abuse* (London, 1579), 6ᵛ–7.
43. Cleopatra's theatricality has been discussed by a number of critics. For a sampling of arguments about its uses and effects, see Adelman, *Common Liar*; Jonathan Dollimore, "Shakespeare, Cultural Materialism, Feminism, and Marxist Humanism," *New Literary History* 21 (1990), 471–93; Heather James, "The Politics of Display and the Anamorphic Subjects of *Antony and Cleopatra*," in Susanne Wofford, ed., *Shakespeare's Late Tragedies* (Upper Saddle River, NJ: Simon & Schuster, 1996), 208–34; Phyllis Rackin, "Shakespeare's Boy Cleopatra, the Decorum of Nature and the Golden World of Poetry," *PMLA* 87 (1972), 201–12; and Jyotsna Singh, "Renaissance Anti-theatricality, Anti-Feminism, and Shakespeare's *Antony and Cleopatra*," *Renaissance Drama* NS 20 (1989), 99–119.
44. All references to *Antony and Cleopatra* are to the Arden edition, ed. M. R. Ridley (London: Methuen, 1954).
45. On imagery of dissolution and deliquescence, see esp. Adelman, *Common Liar*.
46. The escalation, rather than satiation, of Antony's need evokes Enobarbus's description of Cleopatra's shape-changing, or "infinite variety," as addictive: "Other women cloy | The appetites they feed, but she makes hungry | Where most she satisfies" (II.iii.236–8).
47. The unusual verb "prorogue" offers an interesting link with *Romeo and Juliet*, where it is used twice, both times in connection with the lovers' trials; at II.ii.78 Juliet declares dying preferable to postponing death for a life without Romeo, and at IV.i.48 the Friar refers to the apparent impossibility of postponing Juliet's marriage to Paris. Shakespeare's only other use of the word comes after *Antony and Cleopatra*, in *Pericles*.
48. Plutarch, "The Life of Marcus Antonius," *The Lives of the Noble Grecians and Romanes*, trans., Thomas North (London, 1579), 987.
49. Ibid. 998.
50. Plutarch, "Antony," *Plutarch's Lives,* ed. Bernadotte Perrin (London: William Heinemann, 1920), 37:4, 60:1.
51. On Antony's explicit links to Hercules throughout the play, see esp. Eugene M. Waith, *The Herculean Hero in Marlowe, Chapman, Shakespeare, and Dryden* (New York: Columbia University Press, 1962).
52. According to myth, the shirt was given to Deianeira by the centaur Nessus, who was shot by Hercules with a poisoned arrow. Believing the shirt to be a love charm, Deianeira gave it to Hercules, unwittingly causing his death. The allusion represents the tragic culmination of Antony's Herculean unmanning, comically depicted earlier in the scene in which Cleopatra trades clothing with Antony ("I drunk him to his bed; | Then put my tires and mantles on him, whilst | I wore his sword Philippan" (II.v.21–3)), which alludes to Hercules' bondage to Omphale.
53. The play anticipates this strategy by showing Antony's remorseful response to the death of his first wife, Fulvia, earlier in the play: "She's good, being gone, | The hand could pluck her back that shov'd her on" (I.ii.123–4). Although Cleopatra is not onstage to hear these actual words, she certainly notes—with displeasure—the alacrity with which Antony returned to his Roman obligations after hearing the news.
54. Arguing that Cleopatra's theatrical feigning is malicious, Laura Levine cites

this scene as the basis for broader claims about the theater's dramatization of its own dangers: "Such a moment seems to cast theatre itself as something so potent and so dangerous it has the capacity to make its spectator go home and kill himself. It casts theatre, in other words, in terms much more bleak than the terms of the attacks." See *Men in Women's Clothing: Anti-theatricality and Effeminization 1579–1642* (Cambridge: Cambridge University Press, 1994), 2.

55. On the literary self-consciousness associated with dreams and the imagination, see Jennifer Lewin, "'Your Actions are my Dreams': Sleepy Minds in Shakespeare's Last Plays," *Shakespeare Studies* 31 (2003), 184–204.

56. "Others say againe, she kept it in a boxe, and that she did pricke and thrust it with a spindell of golde, so that the Aspicke being angerd withall, lept out with great furie, and bitte her in the arme. Howbeit fewe can tell the troth. For they report also, that she had hidden poyson in a hollow raser which she caried in the heare of her head: and yet was there no marke seene of her bodie, or any signe discerned that she was poysoned, neither also did they finde this serpent in her tombe" (Plutarch, "Marcus Antonius," *Noble Grecians and Romanes*, 1010).

57. Ibid. 1004. Interestingly, Cleopatra's experiments with poisons make an implicit reappearance in *Cymbeline*, when the physician Cornelius describes how the Queen (probably played by the same boy actor who played Cleopatra) had practiced poisoning animals in preparing her attempted murder of Imogen (V.vi.249–58).

58. The Montagues, similarly, promise to raise a "statue in pure gold" for Juliet, and the Capulets claim "As rich shall Romeo's by his lady's lie" (V.iii.298, 302).

3. "POLLUTED WITH COUNTERFEIT COLOURS": COSMETIC THEATER

1. Barnabe Barnes, *The Devil's Charter*, ed. Jim C. Pogue (New York and London: Garland, 1980), IV.iii.2255–7. Further citations to the play will be to this edition.

2. Attention to anxieties about contamination and the transgression of boundaries is necessarily indebted to Mary Douglas; see *Purity and Danger: An Analysis of Concepts of Pollution and Taboo* (London: Routledge & Kegan Paul, 1966). Much intelligent work on contamination has taken ancient Greece as its model; see Louis Moulinier, *Le Pur et l'impur dans la pensée et la sensibilité des Grecs* (Paris: Université de Paris, 1950); Robert Parker, *Miasma: Pollution and Purification in Early Greek Religion* (Oxford: Clarendon Press, 1983); and Jean-Pierre Vernant, "The Pure and the Impure," in *Myth and Society in Ancient Greece* (New York: Zone, 1988).

3. The fullest discussion of early modern discomfort with face-paint is Annette Drew-Bear, *Painted Faces on the Renaissance Stage: The Moral Significance of Face-Painting Conventions* (Lewisburg, Pa.: Bucknell University Press, 1994). Other thoughtful studies include Frances Dolan, "Taking the Pencil Out of God's Hand: Art, Nature, and the Face-Painting Debate in Early Modern England," *PMLA* 108 (1993), 224–39; Laurie Finke, "Painting

Women: Images of Femininity in Jacobean Tragedy," *Theatre Journal* 36 (1984), 357–70; Shirley Nelson Garner, "'Let Her Paint an Inch Thick': Painted Ladies in Renaissance Drama and Society," *Renaissance Drama* NS 20 (1989), 123–39; and Jacqueline Lichtenstein, "Making Up Representation: The Risks of Femininity," *Representations* 20 (1987), 77–87. Jean E. Howard discusses early modern opposition to cosmetics in relation to antitheatricality, with an emphasis on misogyny and fear of self-fashioning, in *The Stage and Social Struggle in Early Modern England* (London and New York: Routledge, 1994), esp. 37–9. For useful accounts of similar concerns in neighboring periods, see R. Howard Bloch, "Medieval Misogyny," *Representations* 20 (1987), 1–24; and Tassie Gwilliam, "Cosmetic Poetics: Coloring Faces in the Eighteenth Century," in *Body and Text in the Eighteenth Century*, ed. Veronica Kelly and Dorothea Von Mucke (Stanford, Calif.: Stanford University Press, 1994), 144–59. Taking a transhistorical perspective, Katherine Stern sees hostility to cosmetics as a manifestation of discomfort towards femininity; see "What is Femme? The Phenomenology of the Powder Room," *Women: A Cultural Review* 8:2 (1997), 183–96. While building on arguments from these essays regarding the identification between cosmetics, femininity, and art, this essay departs from prior scholarship in identifying anticosmetic attitudes specifically with fears about the physical effects of theater, rooted in a shared vocabulary of failed remedies drawing on contemporary chemical technology.

4. Giovanni Paolo Lomazzo, *A Tracte Containing the Artes of Curious Paintinge Caruinge & Buildinge*, trans. Richard Haydocke (London, 1598), 130; and Thomas Tuke, *A Treatise Against Painting and Tincturing of Men and Women: Against Murther and Poysoning: Pride and Ambition: Adulterie and Witchcraft. And the Roote of all These, Disobedience to the Ministery of the Word* (London, 1616), 21. Lomazzo, a Milanese painter and critic of art, did not include this discussion of cosmetics in his original treatise; Haydocke, an Oxford scholar and practicing physician, added it in his translation (his only publication). Tuke, a minister and committed royalist, wrote and translated a number of other treatises on moral topics, including sin, death, heaven, and Catholicism.

5. John Downame, cited in *A Discourse of Auxiliary Beauty* (London, 1656), 106. On the conflation of signs with things characteristic of magical thinking, see Keith Thomas, *Religion and the Decline of Magic* (London: Weidenfeld & Nicolson, 1971); Thomas Greene, "Language, Signs and Magic," in *Envisioning Magic*, ed. Peter Schäfer and Hans. G. Kippenberg (Leiden: Brill, 1997), 255–72; and Brian Vickers, "Analogy vs. Identity: The Rejection of Occult Symbolism, 1580–1680," in Brian Vickers, ed., *Occult and Scientific Mentalities in the Renaissance* (Cambridge: Cambridge University Press, 1984), 95–163.

6. *The Revenger's Tragedy*, *The Second Maiden's*, and *The Duke of Milan* are examined in more detail in Chapter 4. As discussed in Chapter 1, cosmetics are also closely juxtaposed with poisons in Jonson's *Sejanus* (1603); numerous other plays feature similar variations on this theme.

7. The recent appearance of an inexpensive paperback modern-spelling edition of *The Devil's Charter* in the Globe Quartos series, ed. Nick Somagyi (London: Nick Hern Books, 1999) may both indicate and facilitate a growth of interest in the play.

8. Lucretia's self-conscious description of the poison's effect on her brains evokes, and perhaps echoes, the old queen of Navarre in Marlowe's *Massacre at Paris*, narrating her own death by poisoning: "The fatal poison | Works within my head; my brain-pan breaks; | My heart doth faint; I die!" (I.iii.19–21). See Christopher Marlowe, *The Complete Plays*, ed. J. B. Steane (New York: Penguin, 1969). On the phenomenon of characters describing their own deaths, see Matthew Greenfield, "Christopher Marlowe's Wound Knowledge," *PMLA* 119:2 (2004), 233–46.

9. On fears about the power of garments to alter the body's gender, see Laura Levine, *Men in Women's Clothing: Anti-theatricality and Effeminization* (Cambridge: Cambridge University Press, 1994).

10. The physician Andreas de Laguna, for example, writes that "this infamy is like to original sinne, and goes from generation to generation, when as the child borne of them, before it be able to goe, doth shed his teeth one after another, as being corrupted and rotten, not through his fault, but by reason of the vitiousnesse and taint of the mother that painted her selfe" (*The Invective of Doctor Andreas de Laguna, a Spaniard and Physition to Pope Iulius the third, against the Painting of Women*, trans. Elizabeth Arnold, printed in Tuke, *Treatise*, B4).

11. See Sir Hugh Platt, *Delights for Ladies, to Adorne their Persons, Tables, Closets, and Distillatories: with Beauties, Banquets, Perfumes, and Waters* (London, 1617), 92; and Giambattista della Porta, *Natural Magick by John Baptista Porta, a Neapolitane* (London, 1658), 242. For discussions of toxic ingredients in cosmetics, see, for example, Maggie Angeloglou, *A History of Make-up* (London: Macmillan, 1970), 48; Elizabeth Burton, *The Pageant of Stuart England* (New York: Charles Scribner's Sons, 1962), 335–7; and Drew-Bear, *Painted Faces*, 22–3.

12. See, for example, Petrus Abbonus, *De Venenis*, trans. Horace M. Brown, *Annals of Medical History* 6 (1924), 25–37; also Ambroise Paré, "Of Poysons," *The Workes of that famous Chirurgion Ambroise Parey*, trans. Thomas Johnson (London, 1634), 775–815. Although it was a medieval text, *De Venenis* was regularly reprinted throughout the Renaissance and remained the primary toxicological authority.

13. Paré, "Of Poysons," 810.

14. See Mark Eccles, "Barnabe Barnes," in *Thomas Lodge and other Elizabethans*, ed. Charles J. Sisson (Cambridge, Mass.: Harvard University Press, 1933), esp. 175–92.

15. *A Discourse of Auxiliary Beauty* (London, 1656), 150.

16. John Jeans Wecker, *Cosmeticks Or, The Beautifying Part of Physick*, trans. Nicholas Culpepper (London, 1660).

17. Della Porta, *Natural Magick*, 233.

18. *The Second Part of the Secretes of Maister Alexis of Piemount*, trans. William Ward (London, 1563), 5, 7, and 19. Drew-Bear cites these figures from the *Short Title Catalogue* in *Painted Faces*, 28.

19. Drew-Bear refers to finding sixteen in the *STC* (*Painted Faces*, 28); a current search of the *STC* shows discrepancies between the printed and CD-rom versions—each of which lists ten versions, but not the same ten, adding up to a total of fifteen—and neither acknowledges the British Library's 1617 edition, so the number may be even higher.

20. *The Secretes of the Reverende Maister Alexis of Piemount* (First Part), trans.

William Warde (London, 1558), 72, and *A Verye Excellent and Profitable Booke . . . of the Expert and Reuerend Mayster Alexis, which he Termeth the Fourth and Finall Booke of his Secretes,* trans. Richard Androse (London, 1569), 44.

21. Della Porta, *Natural Magick,* 238, 235, 247, and 248.

22. Platt, *Delights,* A2.

23. de Laguna, *Invective,* B3.

24. Lomazzo, *Tracte,* 129.

25. Ibid. 130.

26. Like many feminist critics, Finke echoes these arguments, identifying the "life-denying tendencies" of cosmetics with patriarchal poetic ideals of female beauty: "by attempting to kill herself into art, to realize in her own flesh the idealizations of the lyricists, [the] painted woman literally kills herself" ("Painting Women," 358 and 364). While acknowledging the literal dangers of early modern chemical make-up, I align myself with Stern's argument that feminist support for attacks on cosmetics suggests complicity with an entrenched antagonism towards the seductive adornment and proteanism often associated with both art and "femininity" ("What is Femme?").

27. *Artificiall Embellishments* (Oxford, 1665), 5.

28. Juan Luis Vives, *Instruction of a Christen Woman,* trans. Richard Hyrde (London, 1541), G3^v.

29. Teeth were widely identified as a protective barrier to the body's interior; an anonymous beauty-writer notes, "Least the Microcosme might be supprized by any treacherous *invader,* the teeth are set as ivory *Portcullis's* to guard its entrance" (*Artificiall Embellishments,* 142). These guards, however, were notoriously vulnerable to the effects of mercury: Della Porta complains of women's "rugged, rusty, and spotted Teeth," noting that "they all almost, by using Mercury sublimate, have their Teeth black or yellow" (*Natural Magick,* 250).

30. The relationship between cosmetics, expanded trade, and English attitudes towards foreign nations, is a large and separate topic that cannot be adequately developed in the context of this chapter. It is worth noting, however, that fears of paint's corrosive power to penetrate the skin were paralleled by the threat of exotic and morally suspect foreign imports infiltrating English markets and identity: John Bulwer complained that "Our English Ladies . . . seeme to have borrowed some of their Cosmeticall conceits from Barbarous Nations," and E. Westfield writes of painted women, "Complexion speaks you Mungrels, and your Blood | Part *Europe,* part *America,* mixtbrood; | From *Britains* and from *Negroes* sprung, your cheeks | Display both colours, each their own there seeks" (Bulwer, *Anthropometamorphosis: Man Transform'd: or, The Artificiall Changling* (London, 1653), 260–1; and E. Westfield, printed in Misospilus, *A Wonder of Words: or, A Metamorphosis of Fair Faces Voluntarily Transformed into Foul Visages* (London, 1662), A2iii). On the impact of foreign trade on cosmetic practices, see Neville Williams, *Powder and Paint: A History of the Englishwoman's Toilet, Elizabeth I–Elizabeth II* (London: Longmans, 1957), 17–18; and Angeloglou, *History of Make-up,* 42–4. On the representation of foreigners as poisonous threats to the English body, see Jonathan Gil Harris, *Foreign Bodies and the Body Politic* (Cambridge: Cambridge University Press, 1998).

31. To early modern thinkers, the skin was understood as the sign through which one could read the body; see, for example, Margaret Pelling, "Medicine and Sanitation," in *William Shakespeare: His World, His Work, His Influence*, vol. 1, ed. John F. Andrews (New York: Charles Scribner's Sons, 1985), 79, and Carroll Camden, "The Mind's Construction in the Face," in *Renaissance Studies in Honor of Hardin Craig*, ed. Baldwin Maxwell, W. D. Briggs, Francis R. Johnson, E. N. S. Thompson (Stanford, Calif.: Stanford University Press, 1941). On epistemology and the desire to find proof in the body, see esp. Stanley Cavell, *Disowning Knowledge in Six Plays of Shakespeare* (Cambridge: Cambridge University Press, 1979); and David Hillman, "Visceral Knowledge: Shakespeare, Skepticism, and the Interior of the Early Modern Body," in *The Body in Parts: Fantasies of Corporeality in Early Modern Europe*, ed. David Hillman and Carla Mazzio (London: Routledge, 1997), 81–105.

32. Tuke, *Treatise*, 14.

33. Ibid. 12.

34. Ibid. 58.

35. Philip Stubbes, *Anatomie of Abuses* (London, 1583), Fi.

36. John Downame, *Foure Treatises, Tending to Disswade all Christians from Foure no Lesse Hainous than Common Sinnes; Namely, the Abuses of Swearing, Drunkennesse, Whoredome, and Bribery* (London, 1613), 203.

37. Ibid. 165, and Misopsilus, *Wonder of Words*, 1. Painted women were routinely described as "*polluted with counterfeit colours*" (Tuke, *Treatise*, 5).

38. Vives, *Instruction*, I, 2ᵛ–3.

39. *Discourse*, 33 and 34.

40. Francis Bacon wrote "He therein observed how adultery is most often the begetter of that sin [poisoning]"; see *A True and Historical Relation of the Poysoning of Sir Thomas Overbury* (London, 1651), 15.

41. Tuke, *Treatise*, 41.

42. Ibid. 2. Early modern anxiety about idolatry is a complex and wide-ranging topic, which I treat at greater length in the following chapter. Important critical writings on literary preoccupations with idolatry in this period include Michael O'Connell, *The Idolatrous Eye: Iconoclasm and Theater in Early Modern England* (Oxford: Oxford University Press, 2000); Huston Diehl, *Staging Reform, Reforming the Stage: Protestantism and Popular Theater in Early Modern England* (Ithaca, NY: Cornell University Press, 1997); Kenneth Gross, *The Dream of the Moving Statue* (Ithaca, NY: Cornell University Press, 1992); Ernest Gilman, *Iconoclasm and Poetry in the English Reformation* (Chicago: University of Chicago Press, 1986); and James Siemon, *Shakespearean Iconoclasm* (Berkeley: University of California Press, 1985).

43. Downame, *Foure Treatises*, 203.

44. *Artificiall Embellishments*, 160.

45. Tuke, *Treatise*, 57. Tuke similarly queries an imagined self-painter, "dost thou loue thy selfe artificiall, and like an Idoll . . .?" (8).

46. On idolatry and the precarious boundaries between subjects and their potential objectification, see "Introduction," *Subject and Object in Renaissance Culture*, ed. Margareta de Grazia, Maureen Quilligan, and Peter Stallybrass (Cambridge: Cambridge University Press, 1996), 3. On early modern beliefs about the autonomy of body parts, see David Hillman

and Carla Mazzio, "Introduction: Individual Parts," in *The Body in Parts*, xi–xxix.

47. Guillaume DuBartas, *Divine Weeks and Works*, trans. Josuah Sylvester (London, 1608); "The Decay," 4th book of 4th day of 2nd week, ll. 153–4 and 173–5.

48. Intriguingly, some cosmetics recipes similarly assume spiritual effects from physical interventions, albeit in a more positive direction: a recipe from 1660 offers "*A Lye to make the hair yellow, bright, and long; and to help the Memory*" (Wecker, *Cosmeticks*, 45).

49. Stubbes, *Anatomie of Abuses*, Eviii.

50. Downame, *Foure Treatises*, 203.

51. Ibid. Downame similarly describes harlots as "sweet, but poysonous potions, which delight in the taste, but kill in the digestion" (166–7).

52. Anonymous libels warn of Lucretia's whoredom: "For neuer was the shameless *Fuluia*, | Nor *Lais* noted for so many wooers, | Nor that vncast profuse *Sempronia*, | A common dealer with so many doers, | So proud, so faithlesse, and so voyd of shame, | As is new brodel bride *Lucretia*" (I.iii.296–301). Noting the link between these scenes, Drew-Bear comments that the whore of Babylon's "branded forehead provides the biblical source for using a marked face to symbolize lust and other sins" (*Painted Faces*, 51).

53. See Revelation, 17:4. The image became a popular one for the sensual and spiritual temptations of Catholicism: John Downame writes with alarm of "that cup of carnall fornications, wherewith the great whore of Babylon allureth the Kings and inhabitants of the earth to drinke also of the cup of her spirituall whoredome, and as it were the great drag-net, whereby she catcheth and captiueth more in her idolatries and superstitions, then by almost any other meanes whatsoeuer" (*Foure Treatises*, 134).

54. The image of the polluting cup evokes Protestant invectives against the Eucharistic chalice.

55. *Artificiall Embellishments*, A5.

56. On women as model of the troublingly unbounded body in the Renaissance, see Gail Kern Paster, "Leaky Vessels: The Incontinent Women of City Comedy," in *The Body Embarrassed: Drama and the Disciplines of Shame in Early Modern England* (Ithaca, NY: Cornell University Press, 1993), 23–63, first printed in *Renaissance Drama*, NS 18 (1987), 43–65; also, Peter Stallybrass, "Patriarchal Territories: The Body Enclosed," in *Rewriting the Renaissance: The Discourse of Sexual Difference in Early Modern Europe*, ed. Margaret Ferguson, Maureen Quilligan, and Nancy Vickers (Chicago: University of Chicago Press, 1986), 123–42.

57. Ruth Padel explicates classical Greek beliefs about women's greater physical and spiritual susceptibility to invasion in "Women: Model for Possession by Greek Daemons," *Images of Women in Antiquity*, ed. Averil Cameron and Amélie Kuhrt (London: Croom Helm, 1983), 3–19.

58. Hippocrates, "Diseases of Women 1," trans. Anne Hanson, *Signs* 1 (1975), 572; and Edward Jorden, *A Briefe Discourse of a Disease Called the Suffocation of the Mother* (London, 1603), B1. On general medical beliefs about the female body in the early modern period, see Ian Maclean, *The Renaissance Notion of Woman* (Cambridge: Cambridge University Press, 1980).

59. Lomazzo, *Tracte*, 132–3.

60. Heinrich von Staden notes in early Greek culture "a recurrent, well-known tradition according to which women are exceptionally susceptible to impurity and dirt" ("Women and Dirt," *Helios* 19 (1992), 13); see also Parker, *Miasma*, 101–3.
61. Padel similarly finds in Greek medicine and literature a "general notion that women endanger men by being enterable" ("Women: Model for Possession", 11).
62. Platt, *Delights for Ladies*, 102.
63. Bulwer, *Anthropometamorphosis*, 263. For further examples and analysis, see Drew-Bear, *Painted Faces*, 28–31, 73–8, and 82–4. Scenes satirizing male face-painting occur in comedies such as Marston's *Antonio and Mellida*, Glapthorne's *The Lady Mother*, Massinger's *The Bashful Lover*, and Ford's *The Fancies Chaste and Noble*.
64. Bulwer, *Anthropometamorphosis*, 263.
65. Shakespeare, *Hamlet*, ed. Harold Jenkins, Arden edn. (London and New York: Methuen, 1982), V.ii.57.
66. Alexander is the play's clear center: the play's full name, from its title page, is *The Divils Charter: A Tragaedie Conteining the Life and Death of Pope Alexander the Sixt*, and it is often referred to simply as *The Tragedy of Pope Alexander the Sixth*.
67. Anglo-phile Eutheo, *A Second and Third Blast of Retrait from Plaies and Theaters* (London, 1580), 2.
68. From 1548 and 1499; see *Coventry*, in *Records of Early English Drama*, ed. R. W. Ingram (Toronto: University of Toronto Press, 1981), 181 and 93. For other references and discussion, see Drew-Bear, *Painted Faces*, 32–3. On the use of blackface in productions of *Othello*, see Dympna Callaghan, "Othello Was a White Man," in *Alternative Shakespeares II*, ed. John Drakakis (London: Routledge, 1996), 192–215.
69. See Thomas Heywood, *An Apology for Actors* (London, 1612), D1ᵛ. Curiously, Heywood's adversary, I. G., offers the same theory about "the *Wine leese* with which they besmeared their faces, (before that *Aeschilus* deuised vizors for them) called in Greek τρυγας" (I. G. [John Greene], *A Refvtation of the Apology for Actors* (London, 1615), C3).
70. John Webster, "An excellent Actor," in *New and Choise Characters, of Seuerall Authors* (London, 1615), reprinted in *The Complete Works of John Webster*, Vol. 4, ed. J. H. Lucas (London: Chatto & Windus, 1966), 43.
71. Moralists who attacked both face-painting and the stage include Philip Stubbes, William Prynne, and Stephen Gosson. See also Howard on the links between antitheatrical and anticosmetic writings, with an emphasis on their misogyny and fear of self-fashioning (*Stage and Social Struggle*, esp. 37–9).
72. Stubbes, *Anatomie of Abuses*, 67.
73. John Earle, *Microcosmography* (London, 1628), 57.
74. Thomas Draiton, "Of tincturing the face," printed in Tuke, *Treatise*, B2.
75. William Prynne, *Histriomastix* (London, 1633), 159–60.
76. Bulwer, *Anthropometamorphosis*, B2ᵛ.
77. "Cut therefore from thee all this counterfeiting," he continues; "circumcise from thee all this demeanour of the Stage and Players: for God is not mocked. These things are to be left to Players and Dancers, and to those who are conversant in the Play-house: no such thing is suitable to a chaste and sober woman" (*Histriomastix*, 219–20).

78. William Cave, *Primitive Christianity* (London, 1673), II.66.
79. Stephen Gosson, *The Schoole of Abuse* (London, 1579), F2ᵛ.

4. POISONED KISSES: THEATER OF SEDUCTION

1. Thomas Kyd, *The Tragedye of Solyman and Perseda*, ed. John J. Murray (New York and London: Garland, 1991).
2. The use of the painted female body—or, more particularly, the corpse—as a poisonous prop in fact becomes something of a revenge tragedy convention. This rather striking topos can be seen as a gendered subset of a broader generic fascination with using bodies and body parts as props; Robert Watson comments on this macabre revenge tragedy motif in "Tragedy," in *The Cambridge Companion to Renaissance Drama*, ed. A. R. Braunmuller and Michael Hattaway (Cambridge: Cambridge University Press, 1990), 319.
3. It is worth noting that the authorship of two of these plays—*The Revenger's Tragedy* and *The Second Maiden's Tragedy*—is uncertain, and they may both be by Middleton (in part or in full). The edition of *The Revenger's Tragedy* cited here, by R. A. Foakes, joins many in attributing the play to Tourneur, but recent arguments have been put forth for Middleton; see, for example, R. V. Holdsworth, "Introduction" and "*The Revenger's Tragedy* as a Middleton Play," in *Three Revenge Tragedies*, ed. R. V. Holdsworth (Basingstoke: Macmillan, 1990), 11–25 and 79–105. The play will appear, edited by Macdonald P. Jackson, in *The Collected Works of Thomas Middleton*, gen. ed. Gary Taylor (Oxford: Oxford University Press, forthcoming). Similarly, while the authorship of *The Second Maiden's Tragedy* is uncertain, current critical consensus leans towards Middleton; see Anne Lancashire's introduction to her edition of the play (The Revels Plays; Manchester: Manchester University Press, 1978). This play will also appear, under the title of *The Lady's Tragedy*, edited by Julia Briggs, in *The Collected Works of Thomas Middleton*. If the two plays are in fact both by Middleton, the trilogy examined here includes his revision of his own treatment of this particular theme. If either or both of the plays are collaboratively written, as has also been argued, this fact could shed an interesting light on their concerns with art and contamination.
4. On the play's authorship, see n. 3, above.
5. The play also has a subplot of similarly problematic and triangulated desire, involving a husband who persuades his best friend to seduce his wife; while this narrative is not irrelevant to the play's anxieties about seduction, this chapter bypasses it in order to focus on the literal poisoned kiss.
6. As discussed in Chapter 3, painting the face would convey recognizable connotations of idolatry, even if the Lady were still alive. On idolatry in this play, see Susan Zimmerman, "Animating Matter: The Corpse as Idol in *The Second Maiden's Tragedy*," *Renaissance Drama* NS 31 (2002), 215–43.
7. All citations refer to Lancashire's edition of the play.
8. The idea of kissing a lifeless object echoes an image from the Tyrant's plaint of unrequited love earlier in the play. Upon seeing the Lady with Govianus, he frets "There's the kingdom I Within yon valley fixed, while I stand here I

Kissing false hopes upon a frozen mountain, | Without the confines"
(I.i.142–5).

9. Anne Lancashire notes that this "secret exhumation of a corpse would also
have been associated by Jacobeans with witchcraft and thus in this way too
with the devil" (see "Introduction," *The Second Maiden's Tragedy*, 28). A
1604 statute made it a felony to take up a dead body for magical purposes
(ibid. 76, n. 190; see also Keith Thomas, *Religion and the Decline of Magic*
(London: Weidenfeld & Nicolson, 1971), 443).

10. Valerie Traub discusses monumentalizing women as a "strategy of contain-
ment" taming the disconcerting sexual power of the female body; see Traub,
Desire and Anxiety: Circulations of Sexuality in Shakespearean Drama
(London and New York: Routledge, 1992), 25–49. See also Abbe Blum,
" 'Strike all that look upon with mar[b]le': Monumentalizing Women in
Shakespeare's Plays," *The Renaissance Englishwoman in Print: Counter-
balancing the Canon*, ed. Anne M. Haselkhorn and Betty S. Travitsky
(Amherst: University of Massachusetts Press, 1990), 99–118.

11. On the complex status of these categories in the Renaissance, see *Subject and
Object in Renaissance Culture*, ed. Margareta de Grazia, Maureen
Quilligan, and Peter Stallybrass (Cambridge: Cambridge University Press,
1996), especially the introduction. In its fascination with the woman as
statue, this scene recalls *The Winter's Tale*, which preceded it by a year or
two.

12. Discussing *The Revenger's Tragedy* and *The Spanish Tragedy*, Huston Diehl
discusses over-attachment to a corpse as a form of idolatry, a problem
identified both with "provocative questions about how the living should remember the dead," and with concerns about the idolatrous nature of the
stage. See Diehl, *Staging Reform, Reforming the Stage: Protestantism and
Popular Theater in Early Modern England* (Ithaca, NY: Cornell University
Press, 1997), 122.

13. On the fantasy of animating a lifeless female form, see Lynn Enterline,
" 'You speak a language that I understand not': The Rhetoric of Animation
in *The Winter's Tale*," *Shakespeare Quarterly* 48:1 (1997), 17–44, and revised version in Enterline, *The Rhetoric of the Body from Ovid to
Shakespeare* (Cambridge: Cambridge University Press, 2000), 198–226.

14. The Tyrant's ornamental strategy also closely echoes early modern warnings
about the decking out of idols. As the "Homilie Against Peril of Idolatrie"
warned, "Nowe concerning outragious decking of Images and Idolles, with
paynting, gilding, adourning, with pretious vestures, pearle, and stone, what
is it else, but for the further prouocation and intisement to spirituall fornication, to decke spirituall harlottes most costly and wantonly, which the idolatrous Church vnderstandeth well ynough." See "An Homilie Against Peril
of Idolatrie, and Superfluous Decking of Churches," in *Certaine Sermons or
Homilies Appointed to be Read in Churches* (London, 1582), Ff7ᵛ.

15. The Tyrant's hunger calls to mind Antony's desire for Cleopatra, whom
Enobarbus describes (as mentioned in Chapter 2) as an addictive substance:
"Other women cloy | The appetites they feed, but she makes hungry | Where
most she satisfies." Shakespeare, *Antony and Cleopatra*, Arden edn., ed.
M. R. Ridley (London: Methuen, 1954), II.iii.236–8.

16. William Prynne, *Histriomastix* (London, 1633), 353.

17. Ibid. 387.

18. David Bergeron, "Art Within *The Second Maiden's Tragedy*," *Medieval and Renaissance Drama in England* 1 (1984), 183.

19. Elisabeth Bronfen discusses artistic representations of female corpses as strategies for the aestheticization, and hence denial, of death in *Over Her Dead Body: Death, Femininity, and the Aesthetic* (Manchester: Manchester University Press, 1992).

20. Francis Bacon, *Sylua Syluarum: or A Naturall Historie* (London, 1626), 172.

21. In Erasmus's colloquy, *A Marriage in Name Only* (1523), for example, Gabriel informs Petronius that "the disease is transmitted not only by one means alone but spreads to other persons by a kiss" (*The Colloquies of Erasmus*, trans. C. R. Thompson (Chicago and London: University of Chicago Press, 1965), 410). Current studies suggest that because of the intensity of the disease, kisses could in fact have proven contagious; see Johannes Fabricius, *Syphilis in Shakespeare's England* (London: Jessica Kingsley, 1994).

22. On the poetic tradition of describing desire as a sweet poison, see Robert Gaston, "Love's Sweet Poison: A New Reading of Bronzino's London *Allegory*," *I Tatti Studies* 4 (1991), 249–90. Interestingly, other interpretations of the painting that inspires Gaston's commentary have seen it as depicting a personification of syphilis, suggesting the historical link between syphilis and ideas of sexual poison at this time; see J. F. Conway, "Syphilis and Bronzino's London *Allegory*," *Journal of the Warburg and Courtauld Institutes* 49 (1986), 250–5.

23. See Rainolds, *Th'Overthrow of Stage-Playes* (London, 1583), 18. Rainolds borrows the comparison from Xenophon's *Memorabilia*, in which Socrates criticizes Critobulus for kissing the son of Alcibiades.

24. Described by Ficino, Pico della Mirandola, and Castiglione, this Neoplatonic idea has roots in Hebrew Kabbalistic writings and Christian mysticism, as well as in an epigram (very tenuously) attributed to Plato. See esp. Nicolas Perella, *The Kiss Sacred and Profane: An Interpretative History of Kiss Symbolism and Related Religio-Erotic Themes* (Berkeley: University of California Press, 1969). While early modern English playwrights are unlikely to have been directly influenced by philosophers such as Ficino and Pico, the poetic legacy of the *mors osculi* trope was immense, entering the English poetic vocabulary through vernacular Italian and French erotic poetry, which in turn often derived from Renaissance Neo-Latin poets such as Johannes Secundus. Marlowe offers a striking dramatization of the conceit in Faustus's courtship of the illusory Helen of Troy: "Sweet Helen, make me immortal with a kiss. | Her lips suck forth my soul: see where it flies! | Come, Helen, come, give me my soul again" (Christopher Marlowe, *Doctor Faustus*, ed. John D. Jump, The Revels Plays (Manchester, 1962), xviii.101–3). That the Helen whom Faustus loves is actually a guise assumed by one of Mephistophilis's devils adds undertones of irony to these lines: as a succubus, she literally sucks forth Faustus's soul with her kiss.

25. The idea that kissing a dead body could prove fatal has an intriguing literary precedent in the world of folklore. In a series of old English and Scottish ballads, a visit from the ghost of a departed lover prompts the still-living lover to plead for a final kiss, and is warned that such a kiss would prove fatal: "My lips they are so bitter, | My breath it is so strong, | If you get one kiss of my ruby lips, | Your days will not be long" (See Frances James Child, *The*

English and Scottish Popular Ballads, ed. Robert Graves (New York: Macmillan, 1957), 231). The ballad suggests that the dead lover's lips are dangerous not because they lack breath, but because their breath is too strong: they contain a tangible deathliness that will penetrate through the kiss, rather than merely an emptiness that will drain the other of life. While *mors osculi* poems posit that a kiss can be fatal in and of itself, these ballads suggest that it is necrophilia, rather than simply the kiss, that kills: death, like a disease, can be transmitted magically through oral contact.

26. Massinger, *The Duke of Milan*, in *The Plays and Poems of Philip Massinger*, vol. 1, ed. Philip Edwards and Colin Gibson (Oxford: Clarendon Press, 1976), I.i.99–105; further citations will be in the text.

27. Amidst a more or less consistent consensus that Massinger borrows very little from Shakespeare, critics have made the exception of noting the influence of *Othello* on *The Duke of Milan*, as a narrative of a passionate husband induced by jealousy to murder his wife. See, for example, M. J. Thorssen, "Massinger's Use of *Othello* in *The Duke of Milan*," *Studies in English Literature* 19 (1979), 313–26, and David Frost, *The School of Shakespeare: The Influence of Shakespeare on English Drama 1600–1642* (Cambridge: Cambridge University Press, 1968), 111–15. While the echoes from *Othello* are certainly significant, it is worth noting the powerful presence here of *Antony and Cleopatra*: Tiberio's report of Sforza's immeasurable dotage closely echoes Philo's opening comments on Antony: "Nay, but this dotage of our general's | O'erflows the measure . . ." (Shakespeare, *Antony and Cleopatra*, I.i.1–2); Marcelia is directly likened to "the Aegyptian Queene" (II.i.38), and Sforza protests "I can be my selfe, and thus shake off | The fetters of fond dotage" (III.iii.148–9), echoing Antony's similar insistence that "These strong Egyptian fetters I must break, | Or lose myself in dotage" (I.ii.113–14).

28. Stephen Gosson, *Playes Confuted in Five Actions* (London: 1582), D7ᵛ.

29. Philip Stubbes, *The Anatomie of Abuses* (London, 1583), L6; Prynne, *Histriomastix*, 545; and Gosson, *Playes Confuted*, E7. For discussions of the perceived relationship between the theater and idolatry, see Diehl, *Staging Reform*; and Michael O'Connell, *The Idolatrous Eye: Iconoclasm and Theater in Early-Modern England* (Oxford: Oxford University Press, 2000).

30. Gosson, *Playes Confuted*, B8ᵛ. Although the Church of England continued to hold communion, Protestant and Catholic theological understandings of the Eucharist differ sharply on the question of whether the wafer *is*, or merely *symbolizes*, the body of Christ. The Puritan writer William Perkins wrote of "the Popish Masse, in which the priest imagines that he holds and carries Christ bodily in his handes," that "this, no doubt, is horrible and detestable idolatrie: and it were better to endure many deaths, then so much as once to be a doer in it." See William Perkins, *A Warning Against the Idolatrie of the Last Time* (Cambridge, 1601), 9–10.

31. This hollowness stands in sharp contrast to *Hamlet*, a play with which *The Revenger's Tragedy* has much in common and is often compared. Preoccupations with interiority in *Hamlet* are explored in the following chapter.

32. Naming a female skull Gloriana, in a play written only a handful of years after the death of Elizabeth I, inevitably raises the specter of the politically and emotionally charged transition England was undergoing at this time; on

this topic, see Steven Mullaney, "Mourning and Misogyny: *Hamlet, The Revenger's Tragedy* and the Final Progress of Elizabeth I, 1600–1607," *Shakespeare Quarterly* 45:2 (1994), 139–62. Although my emphasis is on the play's depiction of the effects of the theater, rather than its relationship to contemporary political events, it is striking—as noted earlier in this book—that the period's most densely metatheatrical and drug-steeped plays occur during this time of ambivalent transformation in England itself.

33. Remarkably, even criticism that directly engages with the play's meta-theatricality has ignored the murderous masque that completes Vindice's revenge. See, for instance, Jonathan Dollimore, "Two Concepts of Mimesis: Renaissance Literary Theory and *The Revenger's Tragedy*," in *Drama and Mimesis*, ed. James Redmond (Cambridge: Cambridge University Press, 1980), 25–50; Peter Stallybrass, "Reading the Body: *The Revenger's Tragedy* and the Jacobean Theater of Consumption," *Renaissance Drama* 18 (1987), 121–48; and Karin Coddon, " 'For Show or Useless Property': Necrophilia and *The Revenger's Tragedy*," *English Literary History* 61 (1994), 71–88. Coddon, in fact, goes so far as to claim that the two acts following the Duke's murder are "radically superfluous" (85), ignoring the fact that they include the play's fullest representation of the fatal power of the-atrical spectacle.

34. Stallybrass suggests that the kiss is "imagined as the grossest of bodily con-tacts" in the play; it "is emblematic of every contaminating touch" ("Reading the Body," 133). This chapter concurs with these and others of his points, although I second Karin Coddon's critique of his claim that death resolves the problem of Gloriana's sexual, and hence contaminating, body (" 'For Show or Useless Property'," 71). Not only does her body seem to me to continue to be very much a problem in the play, but in fact its contamin-ating power is the source of Vindice's murderous plot.

35. *The Revenger's Tragedy*, ed. R. A. Foakes, Revels Plays Edition (Man-chester: Manchester University Press, 1966). All following citations refer to this edition. On the question of the play's authorship, see n. 3, above.

36. Scott McMillin suggests that the play's references to incest "signify the the-atrical doubling of identities and meanings that occurs in all aspects of the play"; he points out that both "incest and acting . . . depend upon the ambi-guity of two identities or roles in one person—the actor and character blend-ing in the person of the stage performer, the son and husband blending in the person of the incestuous lover." See McMillin, "Acting and Violence: *The Revenger's Tragedy* and Its Departures from *Hamlet*," *Studies in English Literature* 24:2 (1984), 286. On the play's troubled family relations, see also Jonas Barish, "The True and False Families of *The Revenger's Tragedy*," in *English Renaissance Drama: Essays in Honor of Madeleine Doran and Mark Eccles*, ed. Standish Henning et al. (Carbondale: Southern Illinois University Press, 1976), 142–54.

37. The incestuous kiss between Spurio and the Duchess is echoed, albeit with less explicitly sordid overtones, by another mother–son embrace in the play. After Gratiana's confession and recantation of her avarice-inspired willing-ness to prostitute her daughter, Vindice and Hippolito celebrate by reclaim-ing her as their mother: "Nay, I'll kiss you now," says Vindice; "kiss her, brother, | Let's marry her to our souls, wherein's no lust, | And honourably love her" (IV.iv.56–8). His passionate evocation of marriage and merging

is recalled later in the same scene, when Castiza similarly reconciles with her mother: "O mother, let me twine about your neck, I And kiss you till my soul melt on your lips" (IV.iv.146–7). Despite Vindice's idealization of this joining of souls "wherein's no lust," the shadow of the incestuous kisses of the court lingers uncomfortably behind these images of melted and fused identities.

38. As an eroticized *memento mori*, Gloriana's skull, both here and in its return in Act III, occasions musings on mortality, variations on Hamlet's lamentations for poor Yorick; unlike Yorick, however, who died a natural death at an old age, Gloriana is defined by her status as murder victim. On links between the two plays, see esp. Andrew Sofer, "The Skull on the Renaissance Stage: Imagination and the Erotic Life of Props," *English Literary Renaissance* 28:1 (1998), 47–74, and its revised version, "Dropping the Subject: The Skull on the Jacobean Stage," in his *The Stage Life of Props* (Ann Arbor: University of Michigan Press, 2003), 89–115; also, Richard T. Brucher, "Fantasies of Violence: *Hamlet* and *The Revenger's Tragedy*," *Studies in English Literature* 21:2 (1981), 260–1; and McMillin, "Acting and Violence," 278–80.

39. Coddon identifies him not only with the Duke but with Gloriana herself, suggesting that "The wholesale instability of Vindice's identity accounts for the play's somewhat solipsistic quality; on a symbolic level, he is both Gloriana and her ravisher, for on a semiotic and hence epistemological level the play makes it impossible to distinguish him, whose 'life's unnatural,' from the 'hollow bones' and 'bony lady'" (Coddon, "'For Show or Useless Property'," 81).

40. Coddon comments on "the slippage between lust and the ecstasy of violence" in this interchange ("'For Show or Useless Property,'" 83). The self-satisfied erotic charge of successful plotting here evokes Mosca's gleeful soliloquy in Jonson's *Volpone*: "I fear, I shall begin to grow in love I With my dear self, and my most prosperous parts, I They do so spring and burgeon; I can feel I A whimsy in my blood: I know not how, I Success hath made me wanton" (III.i.1–5).

41. On the dismemberment and objectification associated with the Petrarchan blazon, see, for instance, Nancy Vickers, "Diana Described: Scattered Woman and Scattered Rhyme," in *Writing and Sexual Difference*, ed. Elizabeth Abel (Chicago: University of Chicago Press, 1982), 95–109.

42. As noted in the prior chapter, decayed teeth were a common symptom of mercury poisoning.

43. The idea of killing by sight evokes the Renaissance fascination with the basilisk, a mythical beast that kills the eyes of the spectator. References to the basilisk and related myths, such as Medusa, permeate Petrarchan love poetry, in which the sight of the beautiful mistress brings the lover pain. Sergei Lobanov-Rostovsky analyzes links between the basilisk and Renaissance theories of vision and anatomy in "Taming the Basilisk," in *The Body in Parts*, ed. David Hillman and Carla Mazzio (New York and London: Routledge, 1997), 195–217.

44. The remnants of the morality tradition can be seen in the play's style as well as its structure; with their comically allegorical names, the cast reads like cartoon icons of good and evil, evoking the type-names of the morality play. On the relation of the morality tradition to the play, see esp. Leo Salingar,

"*The Revenger's Tragedy* and the Morality Tradition," *Scrutiny* 6 (1938), 402–44, reprinted in Salingar, *Dramatic Form in Shakespeare and the Jacobeans* (Cambridge: Cambridge University Press, 1986), 206–21; Alvin Kernan also discusses the relationship in *The Cankered Muse* (New Haven: Yale University Press, 1959), 223–32.

5. VULNERABLE EARS: *HAMLET* AND POISONOUS THEATER

1. See Saxo's *Historiae Danicae* and Belleforest's *The Hystorie of Hamblet*, in Israel Gollancz, *The Sources of Hamlet* (New York: Octagon, 1967), 100–1 and 186–7. Nothing is known of the treatment of these details in the so-called *Ur-Hamlet* often attributed to Kyd.

2. Critical examinations of ears and hearing in the play include Lee Sheridan Cox, *Figurative Design in* Hamlet: *The Significance of the Dumb Show* (Ohio: Ohio State University Press, 1973), 35–52; Peter Cummings, "Hearing in *Hamlet*: Poisoned Ears and the Psychopathology of Flawed Audition," *Shakespeare Yearbook* 1 (1990), 81–92; Kenneth Gross, "The Rumor of *Hamlet*," *Raritan* 14:2 (1994), 43–67, and revised version in Gross, *Shakespeare's Noise* (Chicago: University of Chicago Press, 2001), 10–32; Norman Holland, "The Dumb-Show Revisited," *Notes and Queries* 203 (1958), 191; and Leonard Mustazza, "Language as Poison, Plague, and Weapon in Shakespeare's *Hamlet* and *Othello*," *Pennsylvania English* 2 (1985), 5–14. Gross's essay, which examines the play's preoccupation with hearing in the context of Elizabethan attitudes towards slander, has been the most rich for my purposes. I have also made substantial use of Holland's comment, although, while intelligent and suggestive, it is extremely brief. Mustazza's, while having close thematic parallels to this essay, argues for "a movement from the literal to the purely figurative, the transformation of the objective into the symbolic" (5), which is precisely the opposite of the function I want to suggest for poison: that it facilitates a translation from semiotic concerns into literal bodily harm. In an Aristotelian reading, Cummings takes the play's preoccupation with ears as a sign that Hamlet's "fatal flaw" is that he "is figuratively hard of hearing, a sensitive, brilliant, and volatile man whose hearing is paradoxically corrupted, blocked, or distracted by his own very fertile and noisy mind" (86): a conclusion with which I do not agree. Cox's chapter offers a useful study of imagery of ears in the play, but his concern is less with the workings of language per se than with noise at large.

3. John Hunt, for instance, explores the play's corporeal imagery in the context of arguing that Hamlet has a "despairing contempt for the body"; see "A Thing of Nothing: The Catastrophic Body in *Hamlet*," *Shakespeare Quarterly* 39:1 (1988), 27–44, 27.

4. See Katharine Eisaman Maus, *Inwardness and Theater in the English Renaissance* (Chicago: University of Chicago Press, 1995); and David Hillman, "Hamlet, Nietzsche, and Visceral Knowledge," in *The Incorporated Self: Interdisciplinary Perspectives on Embodiment*, ed. Michael O'Donovan-Anderson (Lanham, Md., and London: Rowman & Littlefield, 1996), 93–110; different versions of this essay appear as "Hamlet's Entrails," in *Strands Afar Remote: Israeli Perspectives on Shakespeare*, ed.

Avraham Oz (Newark and London: University of Delaware Press, 1998), 176–202, and "The Inside Story," in *Historicism, Psychoanalysis, and Early Modern Culture*, ed. Carla Mazzio and Doug Trevor (New York and London: Routledge, 2000), 299–324.

5. On imagery of eating and digestion, see esp. Stephen Greenblatt, "The Mousetrap," *Shakespeare Studies* 35 (1997), 1–32, and revised version in Stephen Greenblatt and Catherine Gallagher, *Practicing New Historicism* (Chicago: University of Chicago Press, 2000), 136–62, as well as Hillman, "Hamlet, Nietzsche, and Visceral Knowledge".

6. Ramie Targoff suggests a correlation between physical and mental worlds by calling attention to the curious contrast between Hamlet's declared separation of inner and outer, and his actual willingness to believe that external form—such as Claudius's prayer—might both reflect and shape the inward self. See "The Performance of Prayer: Sincerity and Theatricality in Early Modern England," *Representations* 60 (Fall 1997), 49–69, and revised version in *Common Prayer* (Chicago: University of Chicago Press, 2001), 1–13.

7. Bruce Smith describes the material status attributed to sound and language in his innovative study of early modern sound, *The Acoustic World of Early Modern England: Attending to the O-Factor* (Chicago: University of Chicago Press, 1999); Wes Folkerth explores the impact of sound in Shakespeare's plays in *The Sound of Shakespeare* (London and New York: Routledge, 2002). On *Hamlet* in particular, Margaret Ferguson analyzes Hamlet's "rhetorical tactics," and particularly puns, as demonstrating the play's "curious effect of materializing the word"; see "Hamlet: Letters and Spirits," *Shakespeare and the Question of Theory*, ed. Patricia Parker and Geoffrey Hartman (London: Routledge, 1986), 292. While I find her argument suggestive, I would like to go further in showing that words exert a physical impact on actual bodies in the play.

8. On Hamlet's anxieties about autonomous identity, see esp. Stanley Cavell, "Hamlet's Burden of Proof," in *Disowning Knowledge in Six Plays of Shakespeare* (Cambridge: Cambridge University Press, 1987), 179–91, and Janet Adelman, "'Man and Wife is One Flesh': *Hamlet* and the Confrontation with the Maternal Body," in *Suffocating Mothers: Fantasies of Maternal Origin in Shakespeare's Plays, Hamlet to The Tempest* (New York and London: Routledge, 1992), 11–37.

9. William Shakespeare, *Hamlet*, Arden edn., ed. Harold Jenkins (London and New York: Methuen, 1982). All citations to the play refer to this edition.

10. In a play peopled with doubles, the ghost's demand for filial attention to his story is foreshadowed by Polonius's lectures to both Laertes and Ophelia, as well as Laertes' advice to Ophelia. Ironically, while demanding her uncritical and obedient attention, both men chide Ophelia for having listened too well (to Hamlet): Laertes warns against the consequences "if with too credent ear you list his songs" (I.iii.30), and Polonius reproaches that "you yourself | Have of your audience been most free and bounteous" (I.iii.92–3).

11. Analyzing a similar phenomenon in Marlowe's plays, Matthew Greenfield finds that characters' detailed accounts of their own fatal wounds create both a distinctly literal version of interiority and a special metatheatrical claim to audiences' attention; see "Christopher Marlowe's Wound Knowledge," *PMLA* 119:2 (2004), 233–46.

12. Kenneth Gross sees an "ambiguously sexual character" to the scene, reading

the murderous intrusion on the passive, sleeping person as "a kind of aural rape or castration" ("Rumor," 61).

13. Maurice Charney identifies the play's many references to skin disease with this passage, noting that these images "create a feeling of ulceration, leprosy, and cancer, all of which must be artfully concealed beneath smiling public appearances." See "The Imagery of Skin Disease and Sealing," in his *Hamlet's Fictions* (New York and London: Routledge, 1988), 120–30; 123–4.

14. Invaded by another's taint, Hamlet evokes the terrifying loss of integrity and self-containment experienced by Euripides' Hippolytus, who, upon being told of his stepmother's desire for him, wants to "go to a running stream and pour its waters into [his] ear to purge away the filth;" he "cannot even hear such impurity, and feel [him]self untouched." Euripides, *Hippolytus*, trans. David Grene, in *Euripides: Four Tragedies*, ed. David Grene and Richmond Lattimore (Chicago: University of Chicago Press, 1955), ll. 652–5. The intensity of Hippolytus's physical revulsion towards even the narration of desire suggests that verbal penetration here becomes identified with the sexual impurity of a rape.

15. See n. 1, on sources.

16. See Jenkins, "Introduction," *Hamlet*, 102; Geoffrey Bullough, *Narrative and Dramatic Sources of Shakespeare* (New York: Columbia University Press, 1957–1975) 7.28–34; and Bullough, "The Murder of Gonzaga," *Modern Language Review* 30 (1935), 433–44.

17. See, for example, Wallace B. Hamby, *Ambroise Paré: Surgeon of the Renaissance* (St Louis, Mo.: Warren H. Green, 1967), 96.

18. Christopher Marlowe, *Edward II*, in *The Complete Plays*, ed. J. B. Steane (New York: Penguin, 1969), V.iv.33–4.

19. Bartolomeo Eustachio, *De Auditus Organis*, in *Opuscula Anatomica* (Rome, 1564), 163; trans. C. D. O'Malley, "Bartolomeo Eustachi: An Epistle on the Organs of Hearing. An Annotated Translation," *Clio Medica* 6 (1971), 59.

20. A. R. Eden and J. Opland, "Bartolommeo Eustachio's *De Auditus Organis* and the Unique Murder Plot in Shakespeare's *Hamlet*," *New England Journal of Medicine*, 307:4 (1982), 259–61. Pointing to further contemporary confirmation of this process, they add that "the likelihood that a substance will reach the pharynx from the middle ear through a tympanic-membrane perforation is well known today; patients often report a bitter taste in the mouth when using ear drops for chronic otitis media" (261).

21. Shakespeare, *Othello*, ed. M. R. Ridley, Arden edn. (London and New York: Routledge, 1958, repr. 1993), I.iii.149–50.

22. At the opening of his discussion of ears, the anatomist Helkiah Crooke directly acknowledges his indebtedness to Eustachio: "wee will endeuour our selues for your satisfaction to acquaint you what we haue learned, as well by dissections as out of the writings of learned men, especially *Fallopius, Eustachius, Volcherus, Arantius, Aquapendens* and *Placentinus*." See Helkiah Crooke, *Mikrokosmographia: A Description of the Body of Man* (London, 1631), 573.

23. Thomas Vicary, *The Englishmans Treasure: With the True Anatomie of Man's Body* (London, 1626), 19.

24. Ambroise Paré, *The Workes of that Famous Chirurgion Ambroise Parey*, trans. Thomas Johnson (London, 1634), 189–90.

25. Ibid. 655.

26. Wirtzung, *The General Practise of Physicke: Conteyning All Inward and Outward Parts of the Body*, trans. Iacob Mosan (London, 1617), 112, 113. The latter chapter parallels that of Paré; Wirtzung writes, "These things are of two sorts, as it also happeneth, that the one child doth put peason [*sic*], small stones, or cherry stones into the eare of another: the other be soft things, as water, fleas, Earewigs, and such like. If this happen, then is not the same to be slept upon or delayed, for those things require helpe and aduice with all speede, for there is great danger imminent, especially if that which is growen therein be of any bad nature, for of that commeth great paine, and consequently great sicknesse" (*General Practise*, 113).

27. Like many medical writers of the time, Paré gives explicit instructions on how to respond to this problem: "If any creeping things or little creatures, as fleas, ticks, pismires, gnats and the like, which sometimes happeneth, shall get therein, you may kill them by dropping in a little oyle and vineger. There is a certaine little creeping thing, which for piercing and getting into the eares, the French call *Perse-oreille* (wee an Eare-wigge). This, if it chance to get into the eare, may be killed by the aforesaid meanes, you may also catch it, or draw it forth by laying halfe an apple to your eare, as a bait for it" (*Workes*, 655).

28. On concerns about bodily enclosure in the Renaissance, see Peter Stallybrass, "Patriarchal Territories: The Body Enclosed," in *Rewriting the Renaissance: The Discourse of Sexual Difference in Early Modern Europe*, ed. Margaret Ferguson, Maureen Quilligan, and Nancy Vickers (Chicago: University of Chicago Press, 1986), 123–42; also, Gail Kern Paster, "Leaky Vessels: The Incontinent Women of City Comedy," *Renaissance Drama*, NS 18, ed. Mary Beth Rose (1987), 43–65, and revised version in Paster, *The Body Embarrassed: Drama and the Disciplines of Shame in Early Modern England* (Ithaca, NY: Cornell University Press, 1993).

29. See Jenkins's notes in the Arden edn., 225 and 457–9, on the links between the cellarage and hell, and more broadly on the scene's ambivalent tone.

30. Maus, *Inwardness and Theater*, 1.

31. See, for example, Frank Kermode, "Cornelius and Voltemand: Doubles in *Hamlet*," in *Forms of Attention* (Chicago: University of Chicago Press, 1985), 33–63; on a rhetorical embodiment of this preoccupation, see George T. Wright, "Hendiadys and *Hamlet*," *PMLA* 96 (1981), 168–93.

32. In the Arden edn., Jenkins replaces the "bonds" of the Quarto and Folio with a conjectural "bawds"; although he supports this substitution by claiming that bawds can be more logically described as "breathing" than bonds, I would argue that the entire passage is constructed of discordant personifications, and that the slightly jarring sense does not justify altering the printed texts here.

33. Elsewhere, Shakespeare has Falstaff similarly remind us of the physicality of words: "What is honor? A word. What is in that word, honor? What is that honor? Air—a trim reckoning!" (Shakespeare, *1 Henry IV*, V.i.134–5).

34. Shakespeare, *Othello*, ed. M. R. Ridley (London: Routledge, 1958), III.iii.330–1.

35. Thomas Tuke, *A Treatise Against Painting and Tincturing of Men and Women: Against Murther and Poysoning: Pride and Ambition: Adulterie and Witchcraft. And the Roote of all These, Disobedience to the Ministery of the Word* (London, 1616), 49–50.

36. William Crashaw, *The Parable of Poyson* (London, 1618), 14.
37. John Aubrey, *Remaines of Gentilisme and Judaisme* (1686–7); ed. James
    Britten (London, 1881), 124, and Aubrey, *Miscellanies* (London, 1696),
    106; he notes by way of explanation that "Dr Bathurst saith, that this spell
    is corrupt Hebrew, sc. dabar is verbu, and abraca is benedixit (i.) verburum
    benedixit" (*Gentilisme*, 124). Although Aubrey translates "dabar" as
    "verbu," it is worth noting that the term refers specifically to the spoken,
    rather than the written, word, emphasizing an implicit appeal to the ear even
    in what is presented as a written spell. For more background on these and re-
    lated verbal medicines, see also Keith Thomas, *Religion and the Decline of
    Magic* (London: Weidenfeld & Nicolson, 1971), 177–211; and Roy Porter,
    "Medicine and the Decline of Magic," *Cheiron Newsletter: European
    Society for the History of the Behavioral and Social Sciences* (Spring, 1988),
    40–6.
38. Aubrey, *Gentilisme*, 125. Although he cannot offer a direct explanation in
    this instance, he suggests "Perhaps this spell may be the anagramme of some
    sence or recipe: as Dr Bathurst hath discovered in Abracadabra, which I
    thought had been nonsense." The same recipe appears, with less annotation,
    in *Miscellanies*, 107.
39. See Thomas M. Greene, "Language, Signs, and Magic," in *Envisioning
    Magic*, ed. Peter Schäfer and Hans G. Kippenberg (Leiden: Brill, 1997),
    255–72; and Brian Vickers, "Analogy vs. identity: the rejection of occult
    symbolism, 1580–1680," in Brian Vickers, ed., *Occult and Scientific
    Mentalities in the Renaissance* (Cambridge: Cambridge University Press,
    1984), 95–163.
40. William Perkins, *A Discourse of the Damned Art of Witchcraft* (Cambridge,
    1608), 631.
41. Reginald Scot, *The Discoverie of Witchcraft* (Arundel: Centaur Press,
    1964), 189.
42. See Greenblatt, "The Mousetrap." As editions typically note, the 1521 Diet
    (council) of Worms, presided over by the Holy Roman Emperor, was the site
    of the church's condemnation of Luther and his doctrines; see Jenkins, 340.
43. On concerns about the Eucharist, pollution, and idolatry, see the brief dis-
    cussion in the previous chapter, p. 113 and note 30.
44. Stephen Gosson, *The Schoole of Abuse* (London, 1579), 14ᵛ.
45. On language as performative, see J. L. Austin, *How to Do Things with
    Words*, ed. J. O. Urmson and Marina Sbisà (Cambridge, Mass.: Harvard
    University Press, 1962). Recent work on the effects of words includes Judith
    Butler, *Excitable Speech: A Politics of the Performative* (New York and
    London: Routledge, 1997).
46. Noting Shakespeare's ongoing interest in the figure of Dido, Heather James
    discusses this passage in the context of examining tragedy's ability to evoke
    powerful sympathetic, and potentially politically transgressive, responses
    from its listeners; see "Dido's Ear," *Shakespeare Quarterly* 52:3 (2001),
    360–82.
47. As Jenkins points out in the notes to these lines, his pronouncement here that
    he will have the players perform a play like the murder of his father is of
    course somewhat belated; Hamlet has already, sixty lines earlier, ordered
    the players to prepare *The Murder of Gonzago*. On the vicissitudes and
    significances of mirroring or imitation in the play, see David Scott Kastan,

"'His semblable is his mirror': *Hamlet* and the Imitation of Revenge," *Shakespeare Studies* 19 (1988), 111–24.

48. See Jenkins, 273. Jenkins cites Sidney's claim that tragedy "openeth the greatest wounds, and showeth forth the ulcers that are covered with tissue." Hamlet, strikingly, refers to disease and illness, especially ulcers, throughout the play; he tells Gertrude, for instance, that applying an "unction" to her soul "will but skin and film the ulcerous place, | Whiles rank corruption, mining all within, | Infects unseen" (III.iv.149–51), and refers to Claudius as "this canker of our nature" (V.ii.69).

49. See, for instance, Tiberius in *Sejanus*, and Flamineo in *The White Devil*, as discussed in Chapter 1.

50. See Holland, "Dumb-Show," 191.

51. See Jenkins, 507–8; he also mentions the significance of Pyrrhus as a figure for yoking together the roles of murderer and avenger (507).

52. Hamlet responds, on a more physiological note than Guildenstern seems to have intended, "Your wisdom should show itself more richer to signify this to the doctor, for for me to put him to his purgation would perhaps plunge him into more choler" (III.ii.296–9).

53. The language of this scene emphasizes the link with playing: the lord who announces the duel tells Hamlet "The Queen desires you to use some gentle entertainment to Laertes before you fall to play" (V.ii.222–3). Hamlet similarly tells Laertes that he "will this brothers' wager frankly play" (V.ii.249).

54. John Cotta, *A Short Discoverie of the Vnobserved Dangers of Seuerall Sorts of Ignorant and Vnconsiderate Practicers of Physicke in England* (London, 1612), 5.

55. As noted above, other examples of revenge tragedies in which poisons become medicinal by dint of their purgative effect include especially *Sejanus* and *The White Devil*, discussed in Chapter 1.

56. On the cyclical reprisals inevitably associated with revenge, see René Girard, *Violence and the Sacred*, trans. Patrick Gregory (Baltimore and London: Johns Hopkins University Press, 1972).

57. On the claim "that the top of [Shakespeare's] Performance was the Ghost in his own *Hamlet*," see Nicholas Rowe, "Account," in William Shakespeare, *Works*, ed. Rowe (London, 1709), I. xii–xiii, quoted in Samuel Schoenbaum, *William Shakespeare: A Compact Documentary Life* (Oxford: Oxford University Press, 1977), 201.

EPILOGUE: THEATER'S ANTIDOTES

1. Perhaps this drug, which goes unnamed, should be dubbed chastity-in-idleness?

2. In response to Oberon's order, "Now, my Titania, wake you my queen," Titania bursts forth, "My Oberon, what visions have I seen!" (IV.i.72–3). Lysander answers Egeus "amazedly, | Half sleep, half waking" (IV.i.143–4). Demetrius ponders, in some perplexity, over the melting of his love to Hermia, and decides that "It seems to me | That yet we sleep, we dream" (IV.i.184–91), and Bottom marvels "I have had a most rare vision. I have had a dream past the wit of man to say what dream it was" (IV.i. 199–201).

3. On the idea of the pharmakon as its own antidote, see Jacques Derrida, "Plato's Pharmacy," in *Dissemination*, trans. Barbara Johnson (Chicago: Chicago University Press, 1981), 63–171.
4. Richard Baker, who had died in 1645, would have actually written *Theatrum Redivivum* shortly after Prynne's *Histriomastix* (to which it responds); the belatedness of its publication may be due to the intervening political upheaval.
5. On the issue of boy actors playing female roles, see especially Stephen Orgel, *Impersonations* (Cambridge: Cambridge University Press, 1996).

Bibliography

Abbonus, Petrus. "*De Venenis* of Petrus Abbonus." Translated by Horace M. Brown. *Annals of Medical History* 6 (1924), 25–37.

Adelman, Janet. *The Common Liar: An Essay on* Antony and Cleopatra. New Haven: Yale University Press, 1973.

——. *Suffocating Mothers: Fantasies of Maternal Origin in Shakespeare's Plays,* Hamlet *to* The Tempest. New York and London: Routledge, 1992.

Agnew, Jean-Christophe. *Worlds Apart: The Market and the Theater in Anglo-American Thought, 1550–1750.* Cambridge: Cambridge University Press, 1986.

Alexis of Piemount. *The Second Part of the Secretes of Maister Alexis of Piemount.* Translated by William Ward. London, 1563.

——. *The Secretes of the Reverende Maister Alexis of Piemount.* Translated by William Ward. London, 1558.

——. *A Verye Excellent and Profitable Booke . . . of the Expert and Reuerend Mayster Alexis, which he Termeth the Fourth and Finall Booke of his Secretes.* Translated by Richard Androse. London, 1569.

Amos, Andrew. *The Great Oyer of Poisoning: The Trial of the Earl of Somerset for the Poisoning of Sir Thomas Overbury, in the Tower of London.* London: Richard Bentley, 1846.

Angeloglou, Maggie. *A History of Make-up.* London: Macmillan, 1970.

Aristotle. *Poetics.* Edited and translated by W. Hamilton Fyfe. Loeb Classical Library. London: William Heinemann, 1973.

Artificiall Embellishments, or Arts Best Directions How to Preserve Beauty or Procure It. Oxford, 1665.

Aubrey, John. *Miscellanies.* London, 1696.

——. *Remaines of Gentilisme and Judaisme.* Edited by James Britten. London, 1881.

Austin, J. L. *How to Do Things with Words.* Edited by J. O. Urmson and Marina Sbisà. Cambridge, Mass.: Harvard University Press, 1962.

Bacon, Francis. "The Speech of Sir Francis Bacon at the Arraignment of the Earl of Somerset." In *The Connexion: Being Choice Collections of Some Principal Matters in King James his Reign,* 93–120. London, 1681.

——. *Sylua Syluarum: or A Naturall Historie.* London, 1626.

——. *A True and Historical Relation of the Poysoning of Sir Thomas Overbury.* London, 1651.

The Letters and the Life of Francis Bacon. Edited by James Spedding. Vol. 2. London: Longmans, 1862.

Baker, Richard. *Theatrum Redivivum, or the Theatre Vindicated. In Answer to M. Pryns Histriomastix*. London, 1662.

Barish, Jonas. *The Antitheatrical Prejudice*. Berkeley: University of California Press, 1981.

——. "The True and False Families of *The Revenger's Tragedy*." In *English Renaissance Drama: Essays in Honor of Madeleine Doran and Mark Eccles*. Edited by Standish Henning et al., 142–54. Carbondale: Southern Illinois University Press, 1976.

Barnes, Barnabe. *The Devil's Charter*. Edited by Jim C. Pogue. New York and London: Garland, 1980.

——. *The Devil's Charter*. Edited by Nick Somagyi. Globe Quartos series. London: Nick Hern Books, 1999.

Barroll, J. Leeds. *Politics, Plague, and Shakespeare's Theater*. Ithaca, NY, and London: Cornell University Press, 1991.

Barrough, Philip. *The Method of Phisick, Containing the Causes, Signes, and Cures of Inward Diseases in Mans Body from the Head to the Foote*. London, 1596.

Beaumont, Francis, and Fletcher, John. *A King and No King*. In *The Dramatic Works in the Beaumont and Fletcher Canon*. Vol. 2. Edited by George Walton Williams; general editor Fredson Bowers. Cambridge: Cambridge University Press, 1970.

——. *Philaster*. In *The Dramatic Works in the Beaumont and Fletcher Canon*. Vol. 1. Edited by Robert K. Turner; general editor, Fredson Bowers. Cambridge: Cambridge University Press, 1966.

——. *The Tragedy of Thierry and Theodoret*. In *The Dramatic Works in the Beaumont and Fletcher Canon*. Vol. 3. Edited by Robert K. Turner; general editor, Fredson Bowers. Cambridge: Cambridge University Press, 1966.

Belleforest, Francois. *The Hystorie of Hamblet*. In *The Sources of Hamlet*. Edited by Israel Gollancz, 166–311. New York: Octagon, 1967.

Bergeron, David. "Art Within *The Second Maiden's Tragedy*." *Medieval and Renaissance Drama in England* 1 (1984), 173–86.

Bevington, David. "Asleep Onstage." In *From Page to Performance: Essays in Early English Drama*. Edited by John A. Alford. 51–83. East Lansing: Michigan State University Press, 1995.

——, Lars Engle, Katharine Eisaman Maus, and Eric Rasmussen, eds. *English Renaissance Drama: A Norton Anthology*. New York and London: Norton, 2002.

Bliss, Lee. *The World's Perspective: John Webster and the Jacobean Drama*. Brighton: Harvester Press, 1983.

Bloch, R. Howard. "Medieval Misogyny." *Representations* 20 (1987), 1–24.

Bloom, Gina. "Choreographing Voice: Agency and the Staging of Gender in Early Modern England." Ph.D Thesis, University of Michigan, 2001.

Blum, Abbe. " 'Strike all that look upon with mar[b]le': Monumentalizing Women in Shakespeare's Plays." In *The Renaissance Englishwoman in Print: Counterbalancing the Canon*. Edited by Anne M. Haselkhorn and Betty S. Travitsky, 99–118. Amherst: University of Massachusetts Press, 1990.

Bowers, Fredson. "The Audience and the Poisoners of Elizabethan Tragedy." *Journal of English and Germanic Philology* 36 (1937), 491–504.

Brennan, Elizabeth. "An Understanding Auditory: an Audience for John Webster." In *John Webster*. Edited by Brian Morris, 3–19. London: Ernest Benn, 1970.

Bright, Timothy. *A Treatise: Wherein is Declared the Sufficiencie of English Medicines, for Cure of all Diseases, Cured with Medicine*. London, 1580.

Bronfen, Elisabeth. *Over her Dead Body: Death, Femininity, and the Aesthetic*. Manchester: Manchester University Press, 1992.

Brucher, Richard T. "Fantasies of Violence: *Hamlet* and *The Revenger's Tragedy*." *Studies in English Literature* 21:2 (1981), 257–70.

Bullein, William. *Bulleins Bulwarke of Defence against All Sicknesse, Soarenesse, and Woundes that Doe Dayly Assaulte Mankinde*. London, 1579.

Bullough, Geoffrey. "The Murder of Gonzaga." *Modern Language Review* 30 (1935), 433–44.

——. *Narrative and Dramatic Sources of Shakespeare*, Vol. 7. London: Routledge & Kegan Paul, 1964.

Bulwer, John. *Anthropometamorphosis: Man Transform'd: or, The Artificiall Changling*. London, 1653.

Burton, Elizabeth. *The Pageant of Stuart England*. New York: Charles Scribner's Sons, 1962.

Burton, Robert. *Anatomy of Melancholy*. Oxford, 1621.

——. *Anatomy of Melancholy*. Edited by A. R. Shilleto. London: George Bell, 1893.

Butler, Judith. *Excitable Speech: A Politics of the Performative*. New York and London: Routledge, 1997.

Buttes, Henry. *Dyets Dry Dinner*. London, 1599.

Callaghan, Dympna. "Othello was a White Man." In *Alternative Shakespeares II*. Edited by John Drakakis, 192–215. London: Routledge, 1996.

Camden, Caroll. "The Mind's Construction in the Face." In *Renaissance Studies in Honor of Hardin Craig*, ed. Baldwin Maxwell, W. D. Briggs, Francis R. Johnson, E. N. S. Thompson. Stanford, Calif.: Stanford University Press, 1941.

Cary, Elizabeth. *The Tragedy of Mariam*. London, 1613.

Cave, William. *Primitive Christianity*. London, 1673.

Cavell, Stanley. *Disowning Knowledge In Six Plays of Shakespeare*. Cambridge: Cambridge University Press, 1987.

Chapman, George. *The Gentleman Usher.* Edited by John Hazel Smith. Lincoln: University of Nebraska Press, 1970.

Charney, Maurice. "The Imagery of Skin Disease and Sealing." In *Hamlet's Fictions*, 120–30. New York and London: Routledge, 1988.

Child, Frances James. *The English and Scottish Popular Ballads.* Edited by Robert Graves. New York: Macmillan, 1957.

Coddon, Karin. "'For Show or Useless Property': Necrophilia and *The Revenger's Tragedy.*" *English Literary History* 61 (1994), 71–88.

Coke, Edward. *The Third Part of the Institutes of the Laws of England.* London, 1602.

Collier, Jeremy. *The Prophaneness and Immorality of the English Stage.* London, 1698.

Conway, J. F. "Syphilis and Bronzino's London *Allegory.*" *Journal of the Warburg and Courtauld Institutes* 49 (1986), 250–5.

Cotta, John. *A Short Discoverie of the Vnobserved Dangers of Seuerall Sorts of Ignorant and Vnconsiderate Practicers of Physicke in England.* London, 1612.

Cox, Lee Sheridan. *Figurative Design in* Hamlet: *The Significance of the Dumb Show.* Ohio: Ohio State University Press, 1973.

Crashaw, William. *The Parable of Poyson. In Five Sermons of Spirituall Poyson. Wherein the Poysonfull Nature of Sinne, and the Spirituall Antidotes Against It, are Plainely and Briefely Set Downe.* London, 1618.

Crewe, Jonathan. "The Theatre of the Idols: Marlowe, Rankins, and Theatrical Images." *Theatre Journal* 36 (1984), 321–33.

Croll, Oswald. *Basilica Chymica.* Frankfurt, 1609.

Crooke, Helkiah. *Mikrokosmographia: A Description of the Body of Man.* London, 1631.

Cummings, Peter. "Hearing in *Hamlet*: Poisoned Ears and the Psychopathology of Flawed Audition." *Shakespeare Yearbook* 1 (1990), 81–92.

Curtius, E. R. *European Literature and the Latin Middle Ages.* Translated by Willard Trask. Princeton: Princeton University Press, 1983.

Dannenfeldt, Karl H. "Sleep: Theory and Practice in the Late Renaissance." *Journal of the History of Medicine and Allied Sciences* 41 (1986), 415–41.

Daston, Lorraine, and Park, Katharine. *Wonders and the Order of Nature, 1150–1750.* New York: Zone, 1998.

Davis, Lloyd. "'Death-marked love': Desire and Presence in *Romeo and Juliet.*" *Shakespeare Survey* 49 (1996), 57–67.

Day, John. *Law Tricks.* Edited by John Crow. Malone Society Reprints. Oxford: Oxford University Press, 1949.

Debus, Allen. *The English Paracelsians.* London: Oldbourne, 1965.

de Grazia, Margareta, Quilligan, Maureen, and Stallybrass, Peter, eds. *Subject and Object in Renaissance Culture.* Cambridge: Cambridge University Press, 1996.

Dekker, Thomas. *Match Me in London.* In *The Dramatic Works of Thomas*

Dekker. Vol. 2. Edited by Fredson Bowers. Cambridge: Cambridge University Press, 1958.

de Laguna, Andreas. "The Invective of Doctor Andreas de Laguna, a Spaniard and Physition to Pope Iulius the third, against the Painting of Women." Translated by Elizabeth Arnold. In Thomas Tuke, *A Treatise Against Painting and Tincturing of Men and Women. Against Murther and Poysoning: Pride and Ambition: Adulterie and Witchcraft. And the Roote of all These, Disobedience to the Ministery of the Word.* London, 1616.

Della Porta, Giambattista. *Natural Magick by John Baptista Porta, a Neapolitane.* London, 1658.

Derrida, Jacques. "Plato's Pharmacy." In *Dissemination.* Translated by Barbara Johnson. 63–171. Chicago: University of Chicago Press, 1981.

Diehl, Huston. *Staging Reform, Reforming the Stage: Protestantism and Popular Theater in Early Modern England.* Ithaca, NY, and London: Cornell University Press, 1997.

di Miceli, Caroline. "Sickness and Physic in Some Plays by Middleton and Webster." *Cahiers Elisabethains* 26 (1984), 41–78.

A Discourse of Auxiliary Beauty. London, 1656.

Dolan, Frances. "Taking the Pencil Out of God's Hand: Art, Nature, and the Face-Painting Debate in Early Modern England." *PMLA* 108 (1993), 224–39.

Dollimore, Jonathan. "Shakespeare, Cultural Materialism, Feminism, and Marxist Humanism." *New Literary History* 21 (1990), 471–93.

——. "Two Concepts of Mimesis: Renaissance Literary Theory and *The Revenger's Tragedy.* In *Drama and Mimesis.* Edited by James Redmond, 25–50. Cambridge: Cambridge University Press, 1980.

Donaldson, Ian. *Jonson's Magic Houses: Essays in Interpretation.* Oxford: Clarendon Press, 1997.

Donne, John. *The Complete English Poems.* Edited by A. J. Smith. Harmondsworth: Penguin, 1971.

Douglas, Mary. *Purity and Danger: An Analysis of Concepts of Pollution and Taboo.* London: Routledge, 1966.

Downame, John. *Foure Treatises, Tending to Disswade all Christians from Foure no Lesse Hainous than Common Sinnes; Namely, the Abuses of Swearing, Drunkennesse, Whoredome, and Bribery.* London, 1613.

Drew-Bear, Annette. *Painted Faces on the Renaissance Stage: The Moral Significance of Face Painting Conventions.* Lewisburg, Pa.: Bucknell University Press, 1994.

DuBartas, Guillaume. *Divine Weeks and Works.* Translated by Josuah Sylvester. London, 1608.

Du Laurens, André. *A Discourse of the Preservation of the Sight: of Melancholike diseases; of Rheumes, and of Old age.* Translated by Richard Surphlet. London, 1599.

Duncan-Jones, Katherine. "Playing Fields or Killing Fields: Shakespeare's Poems and *Sonnets*." *Shakespeare Quarterly* 54:2 (2003), 127–41.

———. *Ungentle Shakespeare*. London: Arden Shakespeare, 2001.

Dunk, Eleazer. *The Copy of a Letter written by E. D. [Eleazer Dunk] Doctour of Physicke to a Gentleman*. London, 1606.

Earle, John. *Microcosmography*. London, 1628.

Eccles, Mark. "Barnabe Barnes." In *Thomas Lodge and other Elizabethans*. Edited by Charles J. Sisson, 175–192. Cambridge, Mass.: Harvard University Press, 1933.

Eden, A. R., and Opland, J. "Bartolommeo Eustachio's *De Auditus Organis* and the Unique Murder Plot in Shakespeare's *Hamlet*." *New England Journal of Medicine*, 307:4 (1982), 259–61.

Eglisham, George. *The Forerunner of Revenge. Vpon the Duke of Buckingham for the Poysoning of the Most Potent King Iames . . . and the Lord Marquis of Hamilton*. London, 1621.

Enterline, Lynn. "'Hairy on the In-side': *The Duchess of Malfi* and the Body of Lycanthropy." *Yale Journal of Criticism* 7:2 (1994), 85–129.

———. *The Rhetoric of the Body from Ovid to Shakespeare*. Cambridge: Cambridge University Press, 2000.

———. *The Tears of Narcissus: Melancholia and Masculinity in Early Modern Writing*. Stanford, Calif.: Stanford University Press, 1995.

———. "'You speak a language that I understand not': The Rhetoric of Animation in *The Winter's Tale*." *Shakespeare Quarterly* 48:1 (1997), 17–44.

Erasmus, Desiderius. "A Marriage in Name Only." In *The Colloquies of Erasmus*. Translated by C. R. Thompson, 401–12. Chicago and London: University of Chicago Press, 1965.

Erastus, Thomas. *Disputationum de Medicina Nova P. Paracelsi*. Basel, 1572.

Euripides. *Hippolytus*. Translated by David Grene. In *Euripides: Four Tragedies*. Edited by David Grene and Richmond Lattimore. Chicago: University of Chicago Press, 1955.

Eustachio, Bartolomeo. *De Auditus Organis*. In *Opuscula Anatomica*, 148–64. Rome, 1564.

———. "Bartolomeo Eustachi: An Epistle on the Organs of Hearing. An Annotated Translation." Translated by C. D. O'Malley. *Clio Medica* 6 (1971), 49–62.

Eutheo, Anglo-phile. [Anthony Munday]. *A Second and Third Blast of Retrait from Plaies and Theaters*. London, 1580.

Everard, Giles. *De Herba Panacea, quam alii Tabacum, alii Petum, aut Nicotianum Vocant, Breuis Commentariolus*. Antwerp, 1587.

Fabricius, Johannes. *Syphilis in Shakespeare's England*. London: Jessica Kingsley, 1994.

Ferguson, Margaret. "*Hamlet*: Letters and Spirits." In *Shakespeare and the*

Question of Theory. Edited by Patricia Parker and Geoffrey Hartman, 292–309. London: Routledge, 1986.

Fienus, Thomas. *De Viribus Imaginationis.* Louvain, 1608. Translated by L. J. Rather, in "Thomas Fienus' (1567–1631) Dialectical Investigation of the Imagination as Cause and Cure of Bodily Disease." *Bulletin of the History of Medicine* 4 (1967), 349–67.

Finin-Farber, Kathryn. "Framing (the) Woman: *The White Devil* and the Deployment of Law." *Renaissance Drama*, NS 25 (1994), 219–45.

Finke, Laurie. "Painting Women: Images of Femininity in Jacobean Tragedy." *Theatre Journal* 36 (1984), 357–70.

Folkerth, Wes. *The Sound of Shakespeare.* London and New York: Routledge, 2002.

Ford, John. *The Fancies Chaste and Noble.* Edited by Dominick J. Hart. New York: Garland, 1984.

Forker, Charles. *Skull Beneath the Skin: The Achievement of John Webster.* Carbondale and Edwardsville: Southern Illinois University Press, 1986.

Foucault, Michel. *Discipline and Punish: The Birth of the Prison.* Translated by Alan Sheridan. New York: Vintage Books 1995.

Frost, David. *The School of Shakespeare: The Influence of Shakespeare on English Drama 1600–1642.* Cambridge: Cambridge University Press, 1968.

Garber, Marjorie. "Dream and Language: *Romeo and Juliet.*" In *Dream in Shakespeare: From Metaphor to Metamorphosis*, 35–47. New Haven and London: Yale University Press, 1974.

Gardiner, Edmund. *The Triall of Tabacco. Wherein, his Worth is Most Worthily Expressed: as, in the Name, Nature, and Qualitie of the Sayd Hearb; his Speciall Vse in all Physicke, with the True and Right Vse of Taking it, aswell for the Seasons, and Times.* London, 1610.

Garner, Shirley Nelson. " 'Let Her Paint an Inch Thick': Painted Ladies in Renaissance Drama and Society." *Renaissance Drama* NS 20 (1989), 123–39.

Gaston, Robert. "Love's Sweet Poison: A New Reading of Bronzino's London *Allegory.*" *I Tatti Studies* 4 (1991), 249–90.

Gilman, Ernest. *Iconoclasm and Poetry in the English Reformation.* Chicago: University of Chicago Press, 1986.

Girard, René. *Violence and the Sacred.* Translated by Patrick Gregory. Baltimore and London: Johns Hopkins University Press, 1972.

Glapthorne, Henry. *The Lady Mother.* London, 1635.

Gollancz, Israel. *The Sources of Hamlet.* New York: Octagon, 1967.

Gosson, Stephen. *Apologie for the Schoole of Abuse.* London, 1579.

———. *Playes Confuted in Five Actions.* London, 1582.

———. *The Schoole of Abuse.* London, 1579.

Greenblatt, Stephen. "The False Ending in *Volpone.*" *Journal of English and Germanic Philology* 75 (1976), 90–104.

Greenblatt, Stephen. "The Mousetrap." *Shakespeare Studies* 35 (1997), 1–32.

——. *Shakespearean Negotiations*. Berkeley: University of California Press, 1988.

——, and Gallagher, Catherine. *Practicing New Historicism*. Chicago: University of Chicago Press, 2000, 136–62.

G., I. [Greene, John]. *A Refutation of the Apology for Actors*. London, 1615.

Greene, Thomas. "Language, Signs and Magic." In *Envisioning Magic*. Edited by Peter Schäfer and Hans G. Kippenberg, 255–72. Leiden: Brill, 1997.

——. "Poetry and Permeability." New Literary History 30:1 (1999), 75–91.

Greenfield, Matthew. "Christopher Marlowe's Wound Knowledge." *PMLA* 119:2 (2004), 233–46.

Gross, Kenneth. *The Dream of the Moving Statue*. Ithaca, NY: Cornell University Press, 1992.

——. "The Rumor of *Hamlet*." *Raritan* 14:2 (1994), 43–67.

——. *Shakespeare's Noise*. Chicago: University of Chicago Press, 2001.

Gurr, Andrew. *Playgoing in Shakespeare's London*. Cambridge: Cambridge University Press, 2nd edn., 1996.

Gwilliam, Tassie. "Cosmetic Poetics: Coloring Faces in the Eighteenth Century." In *Body and Text in the Eighteenth Century*. Edited by Veronica Kelly and Dorothea Von Mucke, 144–59. Stanford, Calif.: Stanford University Press, 1994.

Hamby, Wallace B. *Ambroise Paré: Surgeon of the Renaissance*. St Louis, Mo.: Warren H. Green, 1967.

Harris, Jonathan Gil. *Foreign Bodies and the Body Politic: Discourses of Social Pathology in Early Modern England*. Cambridge: Cambridge University Press, 1998.

——. "'I am sailing to my port, uh! uh! uh! uh!': The Pathologies of Transmigration in *Volpone*." *Literature and Medicine* 20:2 (2001), 109–32.

——. "'Narcissus in thy face': Roman Desire and the Difference it Fakes in *Antony and Cleopatra*." *Shakespeare Quarterly* 45:4 (1994), 408–25.

Hartman, Geoffrey. "Words and Wounds." In *Medicine and Literature*. Edited by Enid Rhodes Peschel, 178–88. New York: Neale Watson Academic Publications, 1980.

Hattori, Natsu. "Performing Cures: Theater and Medicine in Early Modern England." D.Phil. thesis. Oxford University, 1995.

Hawkins, Harriet. "Folly, Incurable Disease, and Volpone." *Studies in English Literature* 8 (1968), 335–48.

Helgerson, Richard. *Self-Crowned Laureates: Spenser, Jonson, Milton, and the Literary System*. Berkeley: University of California Press, 1983.

Henke, James T. "John Webster's Motif of 'Consuming'." *Neuphilologische Mitteilungen* 76 (1975), 625–41.

Herrick, Marvin T. *Tragicomedy: Its Origin and Development in Italy, France, and England*. Urbana: University of Illinois Press, 1955.

Herring, Francis. *A Modest Defence of the Caueat Given to the Wearers of Impoisoned Amulets, as Preseruatiues from the Plague*. London, 1604.

Heywood, Thomas. *An Apology for Actors*. London, 1612.

Hillman, David. "Hamlet's Entrails." In *Strands Afar Remote: Israeli Perspectives on Shakespeare*. Edited by Avraham Oz, 176–202. Newark and London: University of Delaware Press, 1998.

——. "Hamlet, Nietzsche, and Visceral Knowledge." In *The Incorporated Self: Interdisciplinary Perspectives on Embodiment*. Edited by Michael O'Donovan-Anderson, 93–110. Lanham, Md., and London: Rowman & Littlefield, 1996.

——. "The Inside Story." In *Historicism, Psychoanalysis, and Early Modern Culture*. Edited by Carla Mazzio and Doug Trevor, 299–324. New York and London: Routledge, 2000.

——. "Visceral Knowledge: Shakespeare, Skepticism, and the Interior of the Early Modern Body." In *The Body in Parts: Fantasies of Corporeality in Early Modern Europe*. Edited by David Hillman and Carla Mazzio, 81–105. London: Routledge, 1997.

——, and Mazzio, Carla, eds. *The Body in Parts: Fantasies of Corporeality in Early Modern Europe*. London: Routledge, 1997.

Hippocrates. "Diseases of Women 1." Translated by Anne Hanson. *Signs* 1 (1975), 567–84.

The History of the Tryall of Cheualry. In *A Collection of Old English Plays*, vol 3. Edited by A. H. Bullen. New York: Benjamin Blom, 1882–5; repr. 1964.

Holdsworth, R. V. "*The Revenger's Tragedy* as a Middleton Play." In *Three Revenge Tragedies*. Ed. R. V. Holdsworth, 79–105. Basingstoke, Macmillan, 1990.

Holland, Norman. "The Dumb-Show Revisited." *Notes and Queries* 203 (1958), 191.

"An Homilie Against Peril of Idolatrie, and Superfluous Decking of Churches." In *Certaine Sermons or Homilies Appointed to be Read in Churches*. London, 1582.

Howard, Jean. *The Stage and Social Struggle in Early Modern England*. London and New York: Routledge, 1994.

Hume, Martin A. S. *Treason and Plot: Struggles for Catholic Supremacy in the Last Years of Queen Elizabeth's Reign*. London: James Nisbet & Co., 1901.

Hunt, John. "A Thing of Nothing: The Catastrophic Body in *Hamlet*." *Shakespeare Quarterly* 39:1 (1988), 27–44.

Hunt, Maurice. "Webster and Jacobean Medicine: The Case of *The Duchess of Malfi*." *Essays in Literature* 16 (1989), 33–49.

Ingram, R. W., ed. *Records of Early English Drama*. Toronto: University of Toronto Press, 1981.

Jack Drum's Entertainment. Edited by John S. Farmer. Tudor Facsimile Texts. New York: AMS Press, 1912: repr. 1970.

James I, King of England. "A Counterblaste to Tobacco." 1604. In *The Workes of the Most High and Mighty Prince Iames, By the Grace of God Kinge of Great Brittaine France & Ireland Defendor of the Faith &c.* London, 1616.

——. *Daemonologie in Forme of a Dialogue*. London, 1597.

James, Heather. "Dido's Ear." *Shakespeare Quarterly* 52:3 (2001), 360–82.

——. "The Politics of Display and the Anamorphic Subjects of *Antony and Cleopatra*." In *Shakespeare's Late Tragedies*. Edited by Susanne Wofford, 208–34. Upper Saddle River, NJ: Simon & Schuster, 1996.

Jonson, Ben. *The Alchemist*. In *English Renaissance Drama: A Norton Anthology*. Edited by David Bevington, Lars Engle, Katharine Eisaman Maus, and Eric Rasmussen. New York and London: Norton, 2002.

——. "Explorata: or, Discoveries." In *Workes*. London, 1641.

——. *Sejanus his Fall*. Edited by Philip J. Ayres. The Revels Plays. Manchester: Manchester University Press, 1965.

——. *Volpone*. Edited by Philip Brockbank. New Mermaids. New York: Norton, 1968.

——. *Volpone*. Edited by Alvin Kernan. New Haven: Yale University Press, 1962.

Jorden, Edward. *A Briefe Discourse of a Disease Called the Suffocation of the Mother*. London, 1603.

Kastan, David Scott. "'His semblable is his mirror': *Hamlet* and the Imitation of Revenge." *Shakespeare Studies* 19 (1988), 111–24.

Kermode, Frank. "Cornelius and Voltemand: Doubles in *Hamlet*." In *Forms of Attention*, 33–63. Chicago: University of Chicago Press, 1985.

Kernan, Alvin. *The Cankered Muse*. New Haven: Yale University Press, 1959.

——. *Shakespeare, the King's Playwright: Theater in the Stuart Court, 1603–1613*. New Haven: Yale University Press, 1995.

Kerwin, William. "'Physicians are like Kings': Medical Politics and *The Duchess of Malfi*." *English Literary Renaissance* 28:1 (1998), 95–117.

Kezar, Dennis. "Shakespeare's Addictions." *Critical Inquiry* 30 (2003), 31–62.

Kocher, Paul. "Paracelsan Medicine in England." *Journal of the History of Medicine* 2 (1947), 451–80.

Kyd, Thomas. *The Spanish Tragedy*. Edited by Philip Edwards. The Revels Plays. Manchester: Manchester University Press, 1977.

——. *The Tragedye of Solyman and Perseda*. Edited by John J. Murray. New York and London: Garland, 1991.

Leggatt, Alexander. *Ben Jonson: His Vision and His Art*. London and New York: Methuen, 1981.

Levine, Laura. *Men in Women's Clothing: Anti-theatricality and Effeminization 1579–1642*. Cambridge: Cambridge University Press, 1994.

Lewin, Jennifer. "'Your Actions are my Dreams': Sleepy Minds in Shakespeare's Last Plays." Shakespeare Studies 31 (2003), 184–204.

Lichtenstein, Jacqueline. "Making Up Representation: The Risks of Femininity." *Representations* 20 (1987), 77–87.

Lindley, David. *The Trials of Frances Howard: Fact and Fiction in the Court of King James*. London: Routledge, 1993.

Lobanov-Rostovsky, Sergei. "Taming the Basilisk." In *The Body in Parts: Fantasies of Corporeality in Early Modern Europe*. Edited by David Hillman and Carla Mazzio, 195–217. New York and London: Routledge, 1997.

Lodge, Thomas. *A Defence of Poetry, Music, and Stage-Plays*. London, 1579.

Lomazzo, Giovanni Paolo. *A Tracte Containing the Artes of Curious Paintinge Caruinge & Buildinge*. Translated by Richard Haydocke. Oxford, 1598.

Lyons, Bridget Gellert. *Voices of Melancholy: Studies in Literary Treatment of Melancholy in Renaissance England*. London: Routledge, 1971.

Maclean, Ian. *The Renaissance Notion of Woman*. Cambridge: Cambridge University Press, 1980.

McMillin, Scott. "Acting and Violence: *The Revenger's Tragedy* and Its Departures from *Hamlet*." *Studies in English Literature* 24:2 (1984), 275–91.

McMullan, Gordon, and Hope, Jonathan. *The Politics of Tragicomedy: Shakespeare and After*. London and New York: Routledge, 1992.

Mahood, M. M. *Shakespeare's Wordplay*. London: Methuen, 1957.

Markham, Gervase. *Markhams Maister-Peece*. London, 1610.

Marlowe, Christopher. *Doctor Faustus*. Edited by John D. Jump. The Revels Plays. Manchester: Manchester University Press, 1962.

——. *Edward II*. In *Christopher Marlowe: The Complete Plays*. Edited by J. B. Steane. New York: Penguin, 1969.

——. *The Jew of Malta*. In *Christopher Marlowe: The Complete Plays*. Edited by J. B. Steane. London: Penguin, 1969.

——. *Massacre at Paris*. In *Christopher Marlowe: The Complete Plays*. Edited by J. B. Steane. Harmondsworth: Penguin, 1969.

Marshall, David. "Exchanging Visions: Reading *A Midsummer Night's Dream*." *English Literary History*, 49:3 (1982), 543–75.

Marston, John. *Antonio and Mellida*. Edited by W. Reavley Gair. The Revels Plays. Manchester: Manchester University Press, 1991.

Massinger, Philip. *The Bashful Lover*. In *The Plays and Poems of Philip*

Massinger, vol. 4. Edited by Philip Edwards and Colin Gibson. Oxford: Clarendon Press, 1976.

——. *The Duke of Milan*. In *The Plays and Poems of Philip Massinger*, vol. 1. Edited by Philip Edwards and Colin Gibson. Oxford: Clarendon Press, 1976.

Mattioli, Pietro. *Il Dioscoride dell'eccellente Dottor P. A. Matthioli*. Venice, 1548.

Maus, Katharine. *Ben Jonson and the Roman Frame of Mind*. Princeton: Princeton University Press, 1984.

——. *Inwardness and Theater in the English Renaissance*. Chicago: University of Chicago Press, 1995.

Mazzio, Carla. "Acting with Tact: Touch and Theater in the Renaissance." In *Sensible Flesh: On Touch in Early Modern Culture*. Ed. Elizabeth Harvey, 159–86. Philadelphia: University of Pennsylvania Press, 2002.

Mehl, Dieter. *The Elizabethan Dumb Show: The History of a Dramatic Convention*. Cambridge, Mass.: Harvard University Press, 1966.

Middleton, Thomas. *The Lady's Tragedy*. Edited by Julia Briggs. In *The Collected Works of Thomas Middleton*, general editor Gary Taylor. Oxford: Oxford University Press, forthcoming.

——. *The Revenger's Tragedy*. Edited by Macdonald P. Jackson. In *The Collected Works of Thomas Middleton*, general editor Gary Taylor. Oxford: Oxford University Press, forthcoming.

——. *Women Beware Women*. Edited by Roma Gill. New Mermaids. New York: Norton, 1968.

——. [attrib. Tourneur.]. *The Revenger's Tragedy*. Edited by R. A. Foakes. The Revels Plays. Cambridge, Mass.: Harvard University Press, 1966.

——. [attrib.]. *The Second Maiden's Tragedy*. Edited by Anne Lancashire. The Revels Plays. Manchester: Manchester University Press, 1978.

Middleton, Thomas, and Rowley, William. *The Changeling*. In *English Renaissance Drama: A Norton Anthology*. Edited by David Bevington, Lars Engle, Katharine Eisaman Maus, and Eric Rasmussen. New York and London: Norton, 2002.

Misospilus. *A Wonder of Words: or, A Metamorphosis of Fair Faces Voluntarily Transformed into Foul Visages*. London, 1662.

Montrose, Louis. *The Purpose of Playing*. Chicago: University of Chicago Press, 1996.

Moore, Don D., ed. *John Webster: The Critical Heritage*. London and New York: Routledge, 1981, repr. 1995.

Moulinier, Louis. *Le Pur et l'impur dans la pensée et la sensibilité des Grecs*. Paris: Université de Paris, 1950.

Mullaney, Steven. "Mourning and Misogyny: *Hamlet*, *The Revenger's Tragedy*, and the Final Progress of Elizabeth I, 1600–1607." *Shakespeare Quarterly* 45:2 (1994), 139–62.

——. *The Place of the Stage: License, Play, and Power in Renaissance*

England. Ann Arbor: University of Michigan Press, repr. 1995.

Mulvey, Laura. "Visual Pleasure and Narrative Cinema." *Screen* 16:3 (1975), 6–18. Reprinted in *Visual and Other Pleasures*, 14–27. Bloomington: Indiana University Press, 1989.

Munday, Anthony. *The Death of Robert Earl of Huntington*. London, 1601.

Murray, Peter. *A Study of John Webster*. Paris and The Hague: Mouton, 1969.

Mustazza, Leonard. "Language as Poison, Plague, and Weapon in Shakespeare's *Hamlet* and *Othello*." *Pennsylvania English* 2 (1985), 5–14.

Oberndoerffer, Johann. *The Anatomyes of the True Physition, and Counterfeit Mounte-banke: Wherein Both of Them, are Graphically Described, and Set out in their Right, and Orient Colours*. Translated by F.H. [Francis Herring]. London, 1602.

O'Connell, Michael. *The Idolatrous Eye: Iconoclasm and Theater in Early Modern England*. Oxford: Oxford University Press, 2000.

Orgel, Stephen. *The Illusion of Power: Political Theater in the English Renaissance*. Berkeley: University of California Press, 1975.

———. *Impersonations*. Cambridge: Cambridge University Press, 1996.

———. *The Jonsonian Masque*. Cambridge, Mass.: Harvard University Press, 1965.

Pachter, Henry. *Paracelsus: Magic into Science*. New York: Henry Schuman, 1951.

Padel, Ruth. "Women: Model for Possession by Greek Daemons." In *Images of Women in Antiquity*. Edited by Averil Cameron and Amélie Kuhrt, 3–19. London: Croom Helm, 1983.

Pagel, Walter. *Paracelsus: An Introduction to Philosophical Medicine in the Era of the Renaissance*. Basel: Karger, 1958.

Palmer, Richard. "Pharmacy in the Republic of Venice in the Sixteenth Century." In *The Medical Renaissance of the Sixteenth Century*. Edited by A. Wear, R. K. French, and I. M. Lonie, 100–17. Cambridge: Cambridge University Press, 1985.

Paracelsus. *Selected Writings*. Edited by Jolande Jacobi and translated by Norbert Guterman. New York: Pantheon, 1958.

Paré, Ambroise. *The Workes of that Famous Chirurgion Ambroise Parey*. Translated by Thomas Johnson. London, 1634.

Parker, Robert. *Miasma: Pollution and Purification in Early Greek Religion*. Oxford: Clarendon Press, 1983.

Paster, Gail Kern. *The Body Embarrassed: Drama and the Disciplines of Shame in Early Modern England*. Ithaca, NY: Cornell University Press, 1993.

———. "Leaky Vessels: The Incontinent Women of City Comedy." *Renaissance Drama* NS 18 (1987), 43–65.

Pelling, Margaret. "Medical Practice in Early Modern England: Trade or

Profession." In *The Professions in Early Modern England*. Edited by Wilfred Prest, 90–128. London: Croom Helm, 1987.

——. "Medicine and Sanitation." In *William Shakespeare: His World, His Work, His Influence*, vol. 1. Edited by John F. Andrews, 153–72. New York: Charles Scribner's Sons, 1985.

Perella, Nicolas. *The Kiss Sacred and Profane: An Interpretative History of Kiss Symbolism and Related Religio-Erotic Themes*. Berkeley: University of California Press, 1969.

Perkins, William. *A Discourse of the Damned Art of Witchcraft*. Cambridge, 1608.

——. *A Warning Against the Idolatrie of the Last Time*. Cambridge, 1601.

Plato. *The Republic*. Translated by Paul Shorey. 2 vols. Loeb Classical Library. London: William Heinemann, 1930.

Platt, Hugh. *Delights for Ladies, to Adorne their Persons, Tables, Closets, and Distillatories: with Beauties, Banquets, Perfumes, and Waters*. London, 1617.

Pliny the Elder. *The Historie of the World*. Translated by Philemon Holland. London, 1634.

Plutarch. "How a Yoong Man Ought to Heare Poets, And How He May Take Profit By Reading Poemes." In *The Philosophie, Commonlie Called, The Morals, Written by the Learned Philosopher Plutarch of Chaeronea*. Translated by Philemon Holland. 17–50. London, 1603.

——. *The Lives of the Noble Grecians and Romanes*. Translated by Thomas North. London, 1579.

——. *Plutarch's Lives*. Translated and edited by Bernadotte Perrin. Loeb Classical Library. London: William Heinemann, 1920.

Pollard, Tanya, ed. *Shakespeare's Theater: A Sourcebook*. Oxford: Blackwell, 2004.

——. "The Pleasures and Perils of Smoking in Early Modern England." In *Smoke: A Global History of Smoking*. Edited by Sander Gilman and Zhou Xun, 38–45. London: Reaktion Press, 2004.

Porter, Roy. "Medicine and the Decline of Magic." *Cheiron Newsletter: European Society for the History of the Behavioral and Social Sciences* (Spring, 1988), 40–6.

Poynter, F. N. L., ed. *The Evolution of Pharmacy in Britain*. London: Pitman Medical Publishing, 1965.

Price, Hereward T. "The Function of Imagery in Webster." *PMLA* 70 (1955), 717–39.

Primerose, James. *Popular Errours. Or The Errours of the People in matter of Physick*. Translated by Robert Wittie. London, 1651.

Prynne, William. *Histriomastix*. London, 1633.

Puttenham, George. *The Arte of Englishe Poesie*. London, 1589.

Rackin, Phyllis. "Shakespeare's Boy Cleopatra, the Decorum of Nature and the Golden World of Poetry." *PMLA* 87 (1972), 201–12.

Rainolds, John. *Th'Overthrow of Stage-Playes*. London, 1583.

Rankins, William. *A Mirrour of Monsters*. London, 1587.

Rozett, Martha Tuck. "The Comic Structures of Tragic Endings: The Suicide Scenes in *Romeo and Juliet* and *Antony and Cleopatra*." *Shakespeare Quarterly* 36:1 (1985), 152–64.

Sala, Angelus. *Opiologia: or, a Treatise Concerning the Nature, Properties, True Preparation and Safe Use and Administration of Opium*. Translated by Thomas Bretnor. London, 1618.

Salingar, Leo. "*The Revenger's Tragedy* and the Morality Tradition." *Scrutiny* 6 (1938), 402–44. Reprinted in Salingar, *Dramatic Form in Shakespeare and the Jacobeans*, 206–21. Cambridge: Cambridge University Press, 1986.

Sawday, Jonathan. *The Body Emblazoned*. London: Routledge, 1995.

Saxo. *Historiae Danicae*. In *The Sources of Hamlet*. Edited by Israel Gollancz, 94–163. New York: Octagon, 1967.

Schiesari, Juliana. *The Gendering of Melancholy*. Ithaca, NY: Cornell University Press, 1992.

Schoenbaum, Samuel. *William Shakespeare: A Compact Documentary Life*. Oxford: Oxford University Press, 1977.

Schoenfeldt, Michael. *Bodies and Selves in Early Modern England: Physiology and Inwardness in Spenser, Shakespeare, Herbert, and Milton*. Cambridge: Cambridge University Press, 1999.

Scot, Reginald. *The Discoverie of Witchcraft*. Arundel: Centaur Press, 1964.

Secundus, Johannes. *Basia*. Translated by George Ogle and edited by Wallace Rice. Boston: Colonian, 1901.

Securis, John. *A Detection and Querimonie of the Daily Enormities and Abuses Committed in Physick*. London, 1566.

Shakespeare, William. *Antony and Cleopatra*. Edited by M. R. Ridley. Arden edition. London: Methuen, 1954.

——. *Hamlet*. Edited by Harold Jenkins. Arden edition. London: Methuen, 1982.

——. *The Norton Shakespeare*. Edited by Stephen Greenblatt, Walter Cohen, Jean E. Howard, and Katharine Eisaman Maus. New York: Norton, 1997.

——. *Othello*. Edited by M. R. Ridley. Arden edition. London: Routledge, 1958.

——. *Romeo and Juliet*. Edited by Brian Gibbons. Arden edition. London: Methuen, 1980.

——. *Works*. Edited by Nicholas Rowe. London, 1709.

Shapiro, James. *Shakespeare and the Jews*. New York: Columbia University Press, 1996.

Sharpham, Edward. *The Fleer*. Edited by Lucy Munro. London: Nick Hern Books, 2004.

Sidney, Philip. *A Defense of Poetry*. London, 1595.

Sidney, Philip. *The Old Arcadia*. Edited by Katherine Duncan-Jones. Oxford: Oxford University Press, 1985.

Siemon, James. *Shakespearean Iconoclasm*. Berkeley: University of California Press, 1985.

Silvette, Herbert. *The Doctor on the Stage: Medicine and Medical Men in Seventeenth-Century England*. Edited by Francelia Butler. Knoxville: The University of Tennessee Press, 1967.

Simmons, J. L. "The Comic Pattern and Vision in *Antony and Cleopatra*." *English Literary History* 36 (1969), 493–510.

——. "The Tongue and its Office in The Revenger's Tragedy." *PMLA* 92 (1977), 56–68.

Simpson, Robert. *Shakespeare and Medicine*. Edinburgh: E. & S. Livingston, 1959.

Singh, Jyotsna. "Renaissance Anti-theatricality, Anti-feminism, and Shakespeare's *Antony and Cleopatra*." *Renaissance Drama* NS 20 (1989), 99–119.

Slack, Paul. "Mirrors of Health and Treasures of Poor Men: The Uses of the Vernacular Medical Literature of Tudor England." In *Health, Medicine and Mortality in the Sixteenth Century*. Edited by Charles Webster, 237–73. Cambridge: Cambridge University Press, 1979.

Smith, Bruce. *The Acoustic World of Early Modern England: Attending to the O-Factor*. Chicago: University of Chicago Press, 1999.

Smith, Thomas. *The Commonwealth of England*. London, 1589.

Snyder, Susan. "Ideology and the Feud in *Romeo and Juliet*." *Shakespeare Survey* 46 (1998), 87–96.

——. *The Comic Matrix of Shakespeare's Tragedies*. Princeton: Princeton University Press, 1979.

Sofer, Andrew. "Dropping the Subject: The Skull on the Jacobean Stage." In *The Stage Life of Props*. Ann Arbor: University of Michigan Press, 2003, 89–115.

——. "The Skull on the Renaissance Stage: Imagination and the Erotic Life of Props." *English Literary Renaissance* 28:1 (1998), 47–74.

Stallybrass, Peter. "Patriarchal Territories: The Body Enclosed." In *Rewriting the Renaissance*. Edited by Margaret Ferguson, Maureen Quilligan, and Nancy Vickers, 123–44. Chicago: University of Chicago Press, 1986.

——. "Reading the Body: *The Revenger's Tragedy* and the Jacobean Theater of Consumption." *Renaissance Drama* NS 18 (1987), 121–48.

Stern, Katherine. "What is Femme? The Phenomonology of the Powder Room." *Women: A Cultural Review* 8:2 (1997), 183–96.

Stubbes, Phillip. *The Anatomie of Abuses*. London, 1583.

Sweeney, John Gordon III. *Jonson and the Psychology of Public Theater*. Princeton: Princeton University Press, 1985.

Targoff, Ramie. *Common Prayer*. Chicago: University of Chicago Press, 2001.

——. "The Performance of Prayer: Sincerity and Theatricality in Early Modern England." *Representations* 60 (Fall 1997), 49–69.

Tempera, Mariangela. "The Rhetoric of Poison in John Webster's Italianate Plays." In *Shakespeare's Italy: Functions of Italian Locations in Renaissance Drama*. Edited by Michele Marrapodi, A. J. Hoenselaars, Marcello Cappuzzo, and L. Falzon Stantucci, 229–50. Manchester: Manchester University Press, 1993.

Thomas, Keith. *Religion and the Decline of Magic*. London: Weidenfeld & Nicolson, 1971.

Thompson, C. J. S. *The Mystic Mandrake*. London: Rider, 1934.

Thorndike, Lynn. *A History of Magic and Experimental Science*. Vol. 5, *The Sixteenth Century*. New York: Columbia University Press, 1941.

Thorssen, M. J. "Massinger's Use of *Othello* in *The Duke of Milan*." *Studies in English Literature* 19 (1979), 313–26.

Traub, Valerie. *Desire and Anxiety: Circulations of Sexuality in Shakespearean Drama*. London and New York: Routledge, 1992.

Trease, George. *Pharmacy in History*. London: Baillière, Tindall & Cox, 1964.

Tuke, Thomas. *A Treatise Against Painting and Tincturing of Men and Women. Against Murther and Poysoning: Pride and Ambition: Adulterie and Witchcraft. And the Roote of all These, Disobedience to the Ministery of The Word*. London, 1616.

Venner, Tobias. *A Briefe and Accurate Treatise, Concerning The taking of the Fume of Tobacco*. London, 1621.

Vernant, Jean-Pierre. "The Pure and the Impure." In *Myth and Society in Ancient Greece*. New York, Zone, 1988.

Vicary, Thomas. *The Englishmans Treasure: With the True Anatomie of Man's Body*. London, 1626.

Vickers, Brian. "Analogy vs. Identity: The Rejection of Occult Symbolism, 1580–1680." In *Occult and Scientific Mentalities in the Renaissance*. Edited by Brian Vickers, 95–163. Cambridge: Cambridge University Press, 1984.

Vickers, Nancy. "Diana Described: Scattered Woman and Scattered Rhyme." In *Writing and Sexual Difference*. Edited by Elizabeth Abel, 95–109. Chicago: University of Chicago Press, 1982.

Vincent, Barbara C. "Shakespeare's *Antony and Cleopatra* and the Rise of Comedy." *English Literary Renaissance* 12:1 (1982), 53–86.

Vives, Juan Luis. *Instruction of a Christen Woman*. Translated by Richard Hyrde. London, 1541.

von Staden, Heinrich. "Liminal Perils: Early Roman Receptions of Greek Medicine." In *Tradition, Transmission, Transformation*. Edited by F. Jamil Ragep and Sally P. Ragep with Steven Livesey. 369–418. Leiden: Brill, 1996.

——. "Women and Dirt." *Helios* 19 (1992), 7–30.

Waith, Eugene M. *The Herculean Hero in Marlowe, Chapman, Shakespeare, and Dryden.* New York: Columbia University Press, 1962.

Walwyn, William. *Physick for Families: Or, The new, Safe, and Powerfull Way of Physick, upon Constant Proof Established.* London, 1674.

Watson, Robert. *Ben Jonson's Parodic Strategy.* Cambridge, Mass.: Harvard University Press, 1987.

———. "Tragedy." In *The Cambridge Companion to Renaissance Drama.* Edited by A. R. Braunmuller and Michael Hattaway, 301–51. Cambridge: Cambridge University Press, 1990.

Wear, Andrew. "Epistemology and Learned Medicine in Early Modern England." In *Knowledge and the Scholarly Medical Traditions.* Edited by Don Bates. 151–73. Cambridge: Cambridge University Press, 1995.

———. *Knowledge and Practice in English Medicine, 1550–1680.* Cambridge: Cambridge University Press, 2000.

Webster, Charles. *From Paracelsus to Newton: Magic and the Making of Modern Science.* Cambridge: Cambridge University Press, 1982.

Webster, John. *The Devil's Law Case.* In *John Webster: Three Plays.* Edited by David Gumby. New York: Penguin, 1972.

———. *The Duchess of Malfi.* In *English Renaissance Drama: A Norton Anthology.* Edited by David Bevington, Lars Engle, Katharine Eisaman Maus, and Eric Rasmussen. New York and London: Norton, 2002.

———. "New and Choise Characters, of Seuerall Authors." In *The Complete Works of John Webster,* vol. 4. Edited by J. H. Lucas, 42–3. London: Chatto & Windus, 1966.

———. *The White Devil.* Edited by Christina Luckyj. New Mermaids. New York: Norton, 1966.

Wecker, John Jeans. *Cosmeticks Or, The Beautifying Part of Physick.* Translated by Nicholas Culpeper. London, 1660.

Williams, George Walton. "Sleep in *Hamlet.*" In *Renaissance Papers 1964.* Edited by S. K. Heninger, Peter G. Phialas, and George Walton Williams, 17–20. Durham, NC: Southeastern Renaissance Conference, 1965.

Williams, Neville. *Powder and Paint: A History of the Englishwoman's Toilet, Elizabeth I–Elizabeth II.* London: Longmans, 1957.

Williamson, Marilyn. "Romeo and Death." *Shakespeare Studies* 14 (1981), 129–37.

Wirtzung, Christopher. *The General Practise of Physicke: Conteyning All Inward and Outward Parts of the Body.* Translated by Iacob Mosan. London, 1617.

Wright, George T. "Hendiadys and *Hamlet.*" *PMLA* 96 (1981), 168–93.

Wright, Louise T. "Webster's Lenative Poisons." *Journal of English Linguistics* 24 (1996), 182–5.

Zimmerman, Susan. "Animating Matter: The Corpse as Idol in *The Second Maiden's Tragedy.*" *Renaissance Drama* NS 31 (2002), 215–43.

Index

Abbonus, Petrus 169 n. 12
aconite 20, 29–31, 33, 54
addiction 7, 19, 51, 73, 103, 117,
  146–7, 151 n. 20
Adelman, Janet 162 n. 1, 166 n. 43,
  n. 45, 181 n. 8
adultery 7–8, 35–8, 41, 83, 87, 89, 111;
  see also cuckoldry
Aeneas 137
Agnew, Jean-Christophe 152 n. 32
alchemy 5
Alexis of Piemount 85, 169 n. 18, n. 20
Amos, Andrew 151 n. 24
Angeloglou, Maggie 169 n. 11, 170
  n. 30
antidote 21–22, 38, 50, 144–8
antimony 20, 46–7, 49, 54
antitheatricalists 9–11, 13, 16, 20–21,
  53, 69, 100, 110, 112, 130, 136,
  148, 152 n. 32; see also Anglo-phile
  Eutheo, Stephen Gosson, I[ohn]
  G[reene], William Prynne, William
  Rankins
aphrodisiacs 1, 10–11, 19, 41, 64, 71–2,
  75, 144
apothecaries 63–4
Aristotle 13–15, 153 n. 53, 162 n. 62
arsenic 5–6, 8, 86
Artificiall Embellishments 87, 170
  n. 27, n. 29, 171 n. 44, 172 n. 55
asps 77–8, 167 n. 56
Aubrey, John 135, 184 n. 37, n. 38
Augustine 89
Austin, J. L. 184 n. 45
Ayres, Philip J. 160 n. 48

Bacon, Francis 47, 107, 151 n. 22,
  n. 24, n. 27, 161 n. 54, n. 55, n. 56,
  171 n. 40, 176 n. 20
Baker, Richard 148, 153 n. 44, 186
  n. 4
Barish, Jonas 10, 33, 152 n. 32, 157
  n. 19, 158 n. 22, 161 n. 49, 162
  n. 58, 178 n. 36

Barnes, Barnabe
  The Devil's Charter 21, 81, 83–5, 87,
    91–97, 100, 147, 167 n. 1, 168 n.
    7, 173 n. 66
Barroll, J. Leeds 154 n. 61
Barrough, Philip 67–8, 165 n. 28, n. 35
basilisk 179 n. 43
Beaumont, Francis 156 n. 3, 163 n. 8
beauty, female 19–21, 35, 40, 49–50,
  54, 57, 73, 81, 85–7, 89, 92, 95–6,
  98, 102, 104, 106, 111, 114–5,
  117, 121, 163 n. 5
Belleforest, Francois 180 n. 1
Bentham, Jeremy 19
Bergeron, David 106, 176 n. 18
Bevington, David 68, 165 n. 36
Blackfriars Theater 161 n. 57
Bliss, Lee 160 n. 44
Bloch, Howard 168 n. 3
Bloom, Gina 154 n. 62
Blum, Abbe 175 n. 10
Borroff, Marie 149 n. 5
Bowers, Fredson 151 n. 21, n. 23, n. 29
Brennan, Elizabeth M. 160 n. 47
Bretnor, Thomas 66, 164 n. 20
Bright, Thomas 67, 165 n. 27
Brockbank, Philip 161 n. 57
Bronfen, Elisabeth 176 n. 19
Brucher, Richard T. 179 n. 38
Buckingham, Duke of 7
Bullein, William 37, 62, 67, 159 n. 36,
  164 n. 10, n. 11, n. 12, 165 n. 26
Bullough, Geoffrey 182 n. 16
Bulwer, John 98, 170 n. 30, 173 n. 64,
  n. 76
Burton, Elizabeth 169 n. 11
Burton, Robert 15, 153 n. 46, 154
  n. 63
Butler, Judith 184 n. 45
Buttes, Henry 66, 164 n. 24

Cain 84
Callaghan, Dympna 173 n. 68
Camden, Carroll 171 n. 31

Cary, Elizabeth
  The Tragedy of Mariam 101
cassia 6
Castiglione , Baldassare 176 n. 24
catharsis 14, 15, 54, 141; see also
  purgation, purgatives
Catholicism, Catholics 9, 34, 83, 92,
  135, 177 n. 30
Cave, William 98, 174 n. 78
Cavell, Stanley 171 n. 31, 181 n. 8
ceruse; see lead
Chapman, George
  The Gentleman Usher 82
Charney, Maurice 182 n. 13
chemical 5–6, 16, 20–21, 37, 61, 66, 70,
  81, 84–7, 90, 134, 143, 148
Child, Frances James 176 n. 25
A Closet for Ladies and Gentlemen 86
Clytemnestra 95
Coddon, Karin 178 n. 33, n. 34, 179
  n. 39, n. 40
Coke, Edward 8, 89, 151 n. 27
Collier, Jeremy 148
comedy 11–12, 43–44, 52–3, 56–7, 59,
  61, 63, 65, 71, 77–9, 144
Conway, J. F. 176 n. 22
corpses 21, 34, 60, 102–109, 112–14,
  121–2, 136; see also skull
cosmetics: see face-paints
Cotta, John 6–7, 26–7, 150 n. 17, n. 19,
  156 n. 4, 157 n. 9, 185 n. 54
Cox, Lee Sheridan 180 n. 2
Crashaw, William 134, 151 n. 27, 184
  n. 36
Crewe, Jonathan 155 n. 69
Croll, Oswald 158–9 n. 28
Crooke, Helkiah 182 n. 22
cuckoldry 37, 41; see also adultery
Cummings, Peter 180 n. 2
Cupid 1, 50, 99, 145; see also desire and
  seduction
Curtius, E. R. 156 n.8
Cyprian 89

Dannenfeldt, Karl H. 165 n. 31
Daston, Lorraine 154 n. 56
Davis, Lloyd 163 n. 2
Day, John
  Law Tricks 65
Debus, Allen 150 n. 9
de Grazia, Margareta 171 n. 46, 175
  n. 11
Deianeira 76, 166 n. 52

Dekker, Thomas
  Match Me in London 65, 156 n. 3,
  163 n. 8
de Laguna, Andreas 86, 169 n. 10, 170
  n. 23
Delilah 69
della Porta, Giambattista 84–6, 169
  n. 11, n. 17, 170 n. 21, n. 29
Derrida, Jacques 13, 149 n. 3, n. 5, 153
  n. 50, n. 51, 186 n. 3
Descartes, René 148
desire, erotic 1–4, 10–11, 19–21, 39,
  55–8, 61–2, 71–2, 88, 99,
  101–122, 146–7; see also seduction
Dido 137, 184 n. 46
Diehl, Huston 152 n. 32, 171 n. 42, 175
  n. 12
di Miceli, Caroline 158 n. 23, n. 24
Dioscurides 149 n.8
A Discourse of Auxiliary Beauty 89,
  155 n. 77, 169 n. 15, 171 n. 39
doctors 10–15, 23–54, 79, 81, 84, 88,
  109, 111, 128–9, 140, 156 n. 3,
  n. 5, 165 n. 30, 185 n. 52; see also
  apothecaries, mountebanks
Dolan, Frances 167 n. 3
Dollimore, Jonathan 166 n. 43, 178
  n. 33
Donaldson, Ian 160 n. 49
Donne, John 163 n. 9
Douglas, Mary 167 n. 2
Downame, John 11, 89, 91, 152 n. 38,
  168 n. 5, 171 n. 36, n. 37, n. 43,
  172 n. 50, n. 51, n. 53
Draiton, Thomas 98, 173 n. 74
dreams 55–6, 62–3, 68, 71–2, 77, 79,
  144, 146, 164 n. 14, n. 15, 185 n. 2
Drew-Bear, Annette 167, n. 3, 169
  n. 11, n. 19, 172 n. 52, 173 n. 68
drunkenness 51, 66, 72–3, 77, 117; see
  also wine
DuBartas, Guillaume 90–91, 172 n. 47
Du Laurens, André 67–8, 165 n. 29,
  n. 33
Duncan-Jones, Katherine 157 n. 21, 159
  n. 40
Dunk, Eleazer 66, 164 n. 21, n. 22

Earle, John 98, 173 n. 73
ears 21, 25, 113, 123–43, 147, 163 n. 5
eating 8, 52, 72–4, 105, 110, 118, 124,
  133, 136, 166 n. 46, 172 n. 51, 175
  n. 15, 180 n. 2, 181 n. 5, 182–3

Eccles, Mark 169 n. 14
Eden, A. R. 182 n. 20
Eglisham, George 8, 151 n. 25
Egypt, Egyptian 72–5, 77
Elizabeth I 7, 156 n. 3, 177 n. 32
Enterline, Lynn 153 n. 46, 160 n. 42,
    175 n. 13
Erasmus, Desiderius 176 n. 21
Erastus, Thomas 35, 159 n. 30
Essex, Earl of 7
Eucharist 113, 136, 172 n. 54, 177
    n. 30, 184 n. 43
Euripides 182 n. 14
Eustachio, Bartolomeo 128–9, 182
    n. 19, n. 20, n. 22
Eutheo, Anglo-phile 11, 97, 152 n. 33,
    n. 37, 173 n. 67
Everard, Giles 150 n. 14
eyes 1–3, 19, 50–51, 57, 59, 61, 96,
    110, 113, 116–19, 124, 136, 138,
    144–7, 163 n. 5

Fabricius, Johannes 159 n. 33, 176 n. 21
face-paints 20–21, 28, 81–121, 148
farce 44, 56, 59, 61, 114
Ferguson, Margaret 181 n. 7
Ficino, Marsilio 176 n. 24
Fienus, Thomas 14, 154 n. 57
Finin-Farber, Kathryn 160 n. 46
Finke, Laurie 167 n. 3, 170 n. 26
Fletcher, John 156 n. 3, 163 n. 8
Folkerth, Wes 154 n. 62, 181 n. 7
Forker, Charles 162 n. 1
Foucault, Michel 19, 155 n. 73
Franklin, James 156 n. 3
Frost, David 177 n. 27
fucus; see face-paints

Galen, Galenic medicine 4–5, 6, 14, 35,
    37, 46, 93
Garber, Marjorie 164 n. 15
Gardiner, Edmund 66, 164 n. 23
Garner, Shirley Nelson 168 n. 3
Gaston, Robert 176 n. 22
Gilman, Ernest 171 n. 42
Girard, René 185 n. 56
Globe Theater 161 n. 57
Gollancz, Israel 180 n. 1
Gonzaga, Luigi 128, 140
Gosson, Stephen 10–11, 70, 99, 110,
    112–13, 136–7, 152 n. 35, n. 36,
    166 n. 42, 173 n. 71, 174 n. 79,
    177 n. 28, n. 29, n. 30, 184 n. 44

Greenblatt, Stephen 136, 154 n. 67, 161
    n. 49, 181 n. 5, 184 n. 42
G[reene], I[ohn] 11, 152 n. 40, 173
    n. 69
Greene, Thomas 168 n. 5, 184 n. 39
Greenfield, Matthew 169 n. 8, 181 n. 11
Gross, Kenneth 171 n. 42, 180 n. 2, 181
    n. 12
guiacum 4
Guicciardini, Francesco 83
Gurr, Andrew 152 n. 31
Gwilliam, Tassie 168 n. 3

Hall, John 67, 165 n. 30
Hamby, Wallace 182 n. 17
Harris, Jonathan Gil 149 n.4, n.5, 150
    n.9, 151 n. 22, n. 28, 154 n. 66,
    155 n. 68, 157 n. 14, n. 18, 161
    n. 50, 170 n. 30
Hartman, Geoffrey 153 n. 54
Hattori, Natsu 153 n. 45
Hawkins, Harriet 161 n. 50
Haydocke, Richard 168 n. 4
hebenon 126
Hecuba 137–8
Helen of Troy 9–10, 176 n. 24
Helgerson, Richard 155 n. 72, 161 n. 49
hellebore 5
hemlock 29, 39, 85
henbane 85
Henry, Prince 7
herbs, herbal medicine 4, 6, 37, 57–8,
    62–3, 144
Hercules 76, 166 n. 52
Herod 104
Herrick, Marvin T. 163 n. 8
Herring, Thomas 5–6, 26, 150 n. 13
Heywood, Thomas 15–16, 98, 154
    n. 64, 173 n. 69
Hillman, David 123, 155 n. 68, 171
    n. 31, 171 n. 46, 180 n. 4, 181 n. 5
Hippocrates 27, 172 n. 58
History of the Trial of Chivalry 82
Holdsworth, R. V. 174 n. 3
Holland, Norman 180 n. 2, 185 n. 50
Homer
    The Odyssey 9–10
"An Homilie Against Peril of Idolatrie"
    175 n. 14
honey 10, 11, 104, 133
Hope, Jonathan 163 n. 8
Howard, Jean 152 n. 32, 154 n. 67, 168
    n. 3, 173 n. 71

Hume, Martin A. S. 151 n. 22
Hunt, John 180 n. 3
Hunt, Maurice 158 n. 23
humors 5, 12, 14, 45, 47, 66

iatrochemical medicine: see chemicals, Paracelsus
idolatry 15, 21, 90, 94, 102–7, 109–113, 147, 171 n. 42, n. 45, n. 46, 174 n. 6, 177 n. 29, 184 n. 43
imagination 2, 8, 14, 16–18, 22, 62, 76–7, 80
Ingram, R. W. 173 n. 68
Italy, Italians 8–9, 34, 83; see also Rome, Venice

Jack Drum's Entertainment 82
James I 6–8, 17, 150 n. 18, 154 n. 66, 164 n. 25
James, Heather 155 n. 76, 166 n. 43, 184 n. 46
Jenkins, Harold 182 n. 16, 183 n. 29, n. 32, 184 n. 42, n. 47, 185 n. 48, n. 51
Jerome 91
Jews 7, 9, 151 n. 22
Jezebel 90
Jonson, Ben
    The Alchemist 161 n. 54
    Explorata: or Discoveries 32–33, 157 n. 21, 162 n. 62
    Sejanus 19–20, 24–6, 28–33, 40–43, 48, 50, 53–4, 147, 155 n. 2, 160 n. 47, n. 48, 168 n. 6, 185 n. 49, n. 55
    Volpone 3, 17, 19–20, 23–4, 43–54, 147, 155 n. 1, 160 n. 48, 179 n. 40
Jorden, Edward 172 n. 58

Kastan, David Scott 184 n. 47
Kermode, Frank 183 n. 31
Kernan, Alvin 154 n. 66, 161 n. 49, 180 n. 44
Kerwin, William 153 n. 49, 154 n. 65, 158 n. 23
Kezar, Dennis 151 n. 20
kisses 20–21, 39–40, 45, 62, 64, 78, 101–3, 106–8, 112–15, 117–21, 164 n. 18, 176 n. 21, n. 24, n. 25, 178 n. 34, n. 37
Kocher, Paul 150 n.9
Kyd, Thomas
    Soliman and Perseda 82, 101, 174 n. 1

The Spanish Tragedy 119, 137, 175 n. 12
The Ladies Home Cabinet Opened 86
Lancashire, Anne 175 n. 9
laughter 45, 47–8, 50, 53, 147, 162 n. 62
lead 84
Leggatt, Alexander 162 n. 61
Leicester, Earl of 7
Lethe 72–3, 75, 142
Levine, Laura 18, 152 n. 32, 155 n. 70, n. 71, 166–7, n. 54, 169 n. 8
Lewin, Jennifer 167 n. 55
Lichtenstein, Jacqueline 168 n. 3
Lindley, David 151 n. 24
Lobanov-Rostovsky, Sergei 179 n. 43
Lodge, Thomas 11, 152 n. 42, n. 43, n. 44
Lomazzo, Giovanni Paolo 82, 87–8, 93, 168 n. 4, 170 n. 24, n. 25, 172 n. 59
London 7–8, 15–17, 56, 99
Lopez, Roderigo 7, 151 n. 22, 156 n. 3
love-potion; see aphrodisiac
love-tragedy 56, 70, 162 n. 1
Lyons, Bridget Gellert 153 n. 46

Machiavelli, Machiavellian 35, 94–5
Maclean, Ian 172 n. 58
Mahood, M. M. 164 n. 17
make-up: see face-paints
mandragora, mandrake 6, 20, 29, 55, 61–2, 65, 71–2, 75–7, 163 n. 9, n. 10
Markham, Gervase 161 n. 54
Marlowe 49
    Doctor Faustus 97, 176 n. 24
    Edward II 128, 182 n. 18
    The Jew of Malta 65, 156 n. 3
    Massacre at Paris 155 n. 3, 169 n. 8
marriage 58–9, 61, 64–65, 73, 77–9
Marshall, David 149 n.2
Massinger, Philip
    The Duke of Milan 21, 82, 101–2, 109–113, 121, 147, 168 n. 6, 177 n. 26, n. 27
Mattioli, Pietro 149 n.8
Maus, Katharine Eisaman 123, 132, 157 n. 20, 180 n. 4, 183 n. 30
Mazzio, Carla 154 n. 62, 155 n. 68, 172 n. 46
McMillin, Scott 178 n. 36, 179 n. 38
McMullan, Gordon 163 n. 8

Medea 95
medicine; see chemicals, doctors, Galen, herbs, Paracelsus, pharmacy
Medusa 179 n. 43
Mehl, Dieter 160 n. 41
melancholy 12–15, 111, 153 n. 46
mercury 5, 20, 36–7, 41, 54, 84–7, 159 n. 32, 179 n. 42
Middleton, Thomas
  The Revenger's Tragedy 3, 17, 19, 21, 82, 101–2, 113–122, 137, 147, 168 n. 6, 174 n. 3, 175 n. 12, 177 n. 31, 178 n. 35
  The Second Maiden's Tragedy 21, 82, 101–13, 121, 147, 168 n. 6, 174 n. 3, n. 4, n. 5, n. 7, 175 n. 9
  Women Beware Women 101
Misospilus, 170 n. 30, 171 n. 37
money 43–7, 53
Montrose, Louis 154 n. 67
Moore, Don D. 160 n. 47
mors osculi 108, 112, 176 n. 24; see also kisses
Moulinier, Louis 167 n. 2
mountebanks 45–6, 48–9
mouth 30, 39, 52, 96, 102, 107–8, 111–14, 116–18
Mullaney, Steven 154 n. 65, n. 67, 178 n. 32
Mulvey, Laura 19, 155 n. 74
mummia 20, 34–7, 54, 105, 158 n. 27, n. 28
Munday, Anthony 101, 164 n. 18; see also Anglo-phile Eutheo
Murray, Peter 160 n. 43, n. 45
Mustazza, Leonard 180 n. 2

narcotics 6, 19–20, 26, 30, 32, 55–6, 65–7, 70–72, 75, 77, 79–80, 146–7; see also sleeping potions
necrophilia 21, 101–22, 177 n. 25
Nessus 76, 166 n. 52
nightshade 85
North, Thomas 75

Oberndoerffer, Johann 26–7, 156 n. 6, 157 n. 11, n. 12
O'Connell, Michael 152 n. 32, 171 n. 42, 177 n. 29
Omphale 166 n. 52
opium, opiates 4, 6, 20, 23, 25–6, 29, 43, 54–5, 65–7
Opland, J. 182 n. 20

Orgel, Stephen 154 n. 67, 155 n. 75, 186 n. 5
Overbury, Thomas 7–8, 89, 151 n. 24, 156 n. 3
Ovid 88

Pachter, Henry 150 n.9, 158 n. 28, 159 n. 29, n. 34, n. 35
Padel, Ruth 172 n. 57, 173 n. 61
Pagel, Walter 150 n.9, 158 n. 28, 159 n. 30, n. 34
Palmer, Richard 149 n.8
Panopticon 19
Paracelsus, Paracelsian medicine 4–5, 15, 30, 33–5, 37–8, 66–7, 150 n.9, n. 10
Paré, Ambroise 68, 128–9, 159 n. 37, 163 n. 10, 165 n. 34, 169 n. 12, n. 13, 182 n. 17, n. 24, n. 25, 183 n. 26, n. 27
Park, Katharine 154 n. 56
Parker, Robert 167 n. 2, 173 n. 60
Paster, Gail Kern 14, 153 n. 55, 155 n. 68, 161 n. 53, 172 n. 56, 183 n. 28
Pelling, Margaret 156 n. 5, 171 n. 31
Perella, Nicholas 176 n. 24
Perkins, William 135, 177 n. 30, 184 n. 40
Petrarch 50, 117, 179 n. 41, n. 43
pharmacy, pharmaceutical 3–7, 24, 26, 29–30, 32, 35, 38, 58, 66–7, 72, 147–8, 149 n. 8
pharmakon 4, 9, 13, 75
physicians; see doctors
Pico della Mirandola, Gianfrancesco 176 n. 24
plague 15, 39, 66
Plato 13–14, 153 n. 51, n. 52, 176 n. 24
Platt, Hugh 86, 94, 169 n. 11, 170 n. 22, 173 n. 62
Pliny 30, 157 n. 15, n. 16, n. 17, 161 n. 54
Plutarch
  Lives 75, 78, 166 n. 48, n. 49, n. 50, 167 n. 56, n. 57
  Moralia 9–10, 152 n. 30
Pollard, Tanya 150 n. 14, 152 n. 32
poppy; see opium, opiates
Porter, Roy 184 n. 37
Poynter, F. N. L. 156 n. 5
Price, Hereward T. 158 n. 23
Primerose, James 27, 157 n. 10

Protestant, Protestantism 90, 135, 148, 172 n. 54, 177 n. 30; see also Reformation
Proteus, protean 6, 8, 26–8, 98
Prynne, William 11, 69–70, 98, 105, 112, 148, 152 n. 34, n. 41, 153 n. 44, 165 n. 40, 166 n. 41, 173 n. 71, n. 75, n. 77, 175 n. 16, n. 17, 177 n. 29, 186 n. 4
purgation, purgatives 20, 31–3, 45–8, 51, 53, 139–41, 146–7, 161 n. 53, 185 n. 55; see also catharsis
Puttenham, George 15, 154 n. 59, n. 60

quicksilver; see mercury
Quilligan, Maureen 171 n. 46, 175 n. 11

Rackin, Phyllis 166 n. 43
Rainolds, John 107, 176 n. 23
Rankins, William 11, 152 n. 39
Red Bull Theater 42
Recorde, Robert 156 n. 7
Reformation 135; see also Protestantism
religion; see Catholicism, Eucharist, Protestantism, Reformation
revenge 20, 33, 43, 83, 109, 113–15, 119, 137, 138, 140, 142
The Revenger's Tragedy; see Middleton, *Revenger's Tragedy*
rhubarb 6
Rome, Romans 25, 31–2, 34, 41, 43, 53, 72–4, 77–8
Rowe, Nicholas 185 n. 57
Rozett, Martha Tuck 162 n. 1

Sala, Angelus 5, 67, 150 n. 11, n. 12, 164 n. 20, 165 n. 32
Salingar, Leo 179–80 n. 44
Sawday, Jonathan 155 n. 68
Saxo 180 n. 1
Schiesari, Julia 153 n. 46
Schoenbaum, Samuel 185 n. 57
Schoenfeldt, Michael 14, 153 n. 55, 155 n. 68
scorpions 30–1
Scot, Reginald 135, 184 n. 41
Secundus, Johannes 176 n. 24
Securis, John 27, 156 n. 7
seduction 3, 6–7, 10–11, 20–21, 28, 34, 49–50, 69, 71–2, 75, 78, 80, 82, 86, 88, 90, 95–7, 100–122, 147; see also desire, erotic

serpents 71, 75
Shakespeare, William
   All's Well That Ends Well 163 n. 8, 165 n. 30
   Antony and Cleopatra 3, 17, 19–20, 55–56, 70–80, 147, 166 n. 43, n. 44, 175 n. 15, 177 n. 27
   As You Like It 157 n. 21, 162 n. 60
   Cymbeline 65, 165 n. 30, n. 37, 167 n. 57
   Hamlet 3, 17, 19, 21, 69, 96, 123–43, 146–7, 173 n. 65, 177 n. 31, 179 n. 38, 181 n. 9
   Henry IV Part One 183 n. 33
   Henry IV Part Two 165 n. 37
   King Lear 149 n. 5, 165 n. 30
   Macbeth 68–9, 165 n. 30
   Measure for Measure 163 n. 8
   A Midsummer Night's Dream 1–3, 21–22, 68–9, 124, 144–7, 149 n.1, n.2
   Othello 55, 111, 129, 133–4, 177 n. 27, 182 n. 21, 183 n. 34
   Pericles 166 n. 47
   Richard III 165 n. 39
   Romeo and Juliet, 19–20, 55–65, 67–71, 73, 75–7, 79–80, 101, 147, 155 n. 3, 166 n. 47, 167 n. 58
   The Taming of the Shrew 12–14, 69, 153 n. 48, 165 n. 37
   The Tempest 69, 162 n. 60
   A Winter's Tale 163 n. 8, 175 n. 11
Shapiro, James 151 n. 22
Sharpham, Edward
   The Fleire 65
Sheffield, Lord 7
Sidney, Philip 15, 154 n. 58, 164 n. 19, 185 n. 48
Siemon, James 171 n. 42
Silvette, Herbert 158 n. 23, 161 n. 51, 165 n. 30
Simpson, Robert 158 n. 23, 165 n. 30
Singh, Jyotsna 166 n. 43
skull 113–17, 120, 122, 179 n. 38
Slack, Paul 150 n. 8
sleep 1–2, 29, 44, 55–6, 61–3, 65–74, 76–80, 126–7, 141, 144–6, 165 n. 31, 185 n. 2
sleeping potions 19–20, 29, 55–7, 60–63, 65–73, 79; see also narcotics, opium, opiates
Smith, Bruce 154 n. 62, 181 n. 7
Smith, Thomas 151 n. 21

snakes: see asps, serpents, vipers
Snyder, Susan 162 n. 1, n. 2, 163 n. 3,
    n. 8
Sofer, Andrew 179 n. 38
Spain, Spaniards 39, 87
spells 135–6, 145, 147, 184 n. 37, n. 38
spiders 11, 38, 107
Squire, Edward 7, 151 n. 22
Stallybrass, Peter 155 n. 69, 171 n. 46,
    172 n. 56, 175 n. 11, 178 n. 33,
    n. 34, 183 n. 28
Stern, Katherine 168 n. 3, 170 n. 26
Stubbes, Philip 89, 91, 98, 112, 171
    n. 35, 172 n. 49, 173 n. 71, n. 72,
    177 n. 29
Sweeney, John Gordon III 157 n. 19
syphilis 4, 37, 66, 86, 107, 159 n. 33,
    176 n. 21, n. 22

Targoff, Ramie 181 n. 6
Tempera, Mariangela 158 n. 23, 159
    n. 37
Thomas, Keith 168 n. 5, 175 n. 9, 184
    n. 37
Thompson, C. J. S. 163 n. 9
Thorndike, Lynn 158 n. 26
Thorssen, M. J. 177 n. 27
tobacco 4, 6, 17, 66–7, 150 n. 14
tragedy 11, 27, 43–4, 55–9, 63, 65, 71,
    75, 77–9, 144
tragicomedy 61, 96, 163 n. 8
transvestism 94, 107, 166 n. 52, 186
    n. 5
Traub, Valerie 175 n. 10
Trease, George 156 n. 5, n. 7
trial 30–1, 41–2, 50–52
Tuke, Thomas 8, 82, 88, 90–91, 94, 96,
    134, 151 n. 26, 168 n. 4, 169 n. 10,
    171 n. 32, n. 33, n. 34, n. 37, n. 41,
    n. 42, n. 45, 183 n. 35

unicorn's horn 35, 38, 159 n. 37

Venice 43–4, 50–51, 53, 93
Venner, Tobias 66, 164 n. 25

Vernant, Jean-Pierre 167 n. 2
Vicary, Thomas 129, 182 n. 23
Vickers, Brian 168 n. 5, 184 n. 39
Vickers, Nancy 179 n. 41
Vincent, Barbara C. 162 n. 1
vipers 11, 31, 35
Vives, Juan Luis 88, 89, 170 n. 28, 171
    n. 38
von Staden, Heinrich 156 n. 3, 173
    n. 60

Waith, Eugene M. 166 n. 51
Walwyn, William 150 n. 16
Watson, Robert 161 n. 49, 162 n. 59,
    174 n. 1
Wear, Andrew 149 n. 6
Webster, Charles 150 n. 9
Webster, John
    The Devil's Law Case 46, 161 n. 52
    The Duchess of Malfi 12–14, 62, 101,
        153 n. 47, n. 49, 160 n. 42, 163
        n. 9, 164 n. 13
    New and Choise Characters 98, 173
        n. 70
    The White Devil 19–20, 24, 33–43,
        54, 101, 147, 158 n. 25, 163 n. 9,
        185 n. 49, n. 55
Wecker, John Jeans 169 n. 16, 172 n. 48
Westfield, E. 170 n. 30
Whore of Babylon 92, 172 n. 52, n. 53
Williams, George Walton 165 n. 38
Williams, Neville 170 n. 30
Williamson, Marilyn 162 n. 2
wine 51, 72–3, 75, 96; see also
    drunkenness
Wirtzung, Christopher 129, 183 n. 26
witchcraft 7, 11, 17, 35, 73, 135, 175
    n. 9
Wright, George T. 183 n. 31
Wright, Louise T. 158 n. 23

Xenophon 176 n. 23

Zimmerman, Susan 174 n. 6